The Delicate Force

by

Chris Thomason

The Delicate Force

Chris Thomason

Disclaimer

The events, names and activities referenced primarily in the lectures in the story are all real, and wherever possible, search terms have been provided at the end of the book to enable the reader to research these for themselves. All the other characters appearing in this work are fictitious excepting for three — Annalie, Jennifer and Margaret, who appear with their kind permission. Any other resemblance to real persons, living or dead, is purely coincidental.

To James and Stephanie

And for the unsung hero

Prologue

Brain cells don't have individual names for there are so many of them. However, if Reece Tassicker had wanted to name his brain cells, he might have named them after gods. Because each one performed a miracle, hundreds of times every second.

A perpetual storm raged inside Reece Tassicker's skull as billions of his brain cells each fired off tiny, electrical-impulses to its neighbours. Like most people, he had close to a hundred-billion brain cells, and each was linked to around ten-thousand other brain cells by thin connectors called axons. Each axon had a tiny gap in the middle called a synapse, that the electrical-impulses needed to cross. If the impulse had enough energy to spark across this gap, it continued on its way to the next brain cell, where it was amplified and sent on to other brain cells. If the impulse wasn't powerful enough to cross the synapse, then it would fade into oblivion.

As each brain cell received an incoming electrical-impulse, it instantly decided which of its connections should have that specific impulse forwarded on to them. Sometimes the brain cell would deem just a few-hundred other cells to be worthy recipients. At other times it acted differently, and sent the impulse forward to thousands of neighbouring cells. The moment these next cells received it, they would in turn go through their own instantaneous decision process on how the impulse should be managed.

What caused the cells to decide which of their myriad of neighbours to communicate with, was unknown to science. It was a mysterious force of nature that we all accessed. But it enabled every single thought, for every single person, in every single moment of every single day to occur. It was god-like in its magnificence.

Often, the pattern of brain cells that fired in response to any situation was similar to what had happened previously. As a result, Reece like most others, ended up thinking similar thoughts and doing similar things to what he had always done before in that situation. There were trillions of synapses inside Reece's brain, and many of these tiny gaps had never before been leapt by a spark. They were unused. This meant the two brain cells on either side of the synapse had never communicated with each other. This particular day, at one specific synapse, in a tiny fraction of a second from now, something different was going to happen in Reece Tassicker's brain.

For the previous thirty-seven years of his life, every time an impulse reached this specific synapse, it hadn't enough energy to spark and make the leap across the gap. For some unknown reason, today was a different day. As the impulse, in the form of a simple electrical-charge reached the synapse, the axon released a small spray of electrically-conductive chemicals into the gap, just as it usually did. Today, the impulse had a fraction more charge than ever before, and it was able to spark across the gap and reach the other side of the synapse. It then continued on its way and reached its destination brain cell for the first time.

If this brain cell was capable of individual emotion, it may have displayed an element of surprise, as it had never before received an incoming impulse along this particular axon. It knew exactly what it was supposed to do though, and without any hesitation, it amplified the impulse and sent it out along a different pattern of its own axons. Within this pattern that it selected, there were some other synapses that had never been crossed before, and as the impulse kept being amplified and forwarded by brain cells along the chain, many more previously unused synapses were being crossed for the first time. Within this tiny fraction of a second, the number of Reece's brain cells operating differently reached a critical threshold. And within the storm raging in his brain, a new flash of inspiration occurred.

At that precise moment, Reece Tassicker was in his car driving along the M25 motorway. Reece enjoyed times of solitude — though he didn't admit it to anyone for fear of sounding like a walking personality disorder. It was a good feeling to be alone with your own thoughts, especially with some interesting music in the background.

Right now the radio was playing the song *2-4-6-8 Motorway,* and he'd just passed the blue, exit sign that indicated he was approaching junction eight for Reigate, when he felt a peculiar sensation in his head. It was as if two hands in prayer, suddenly appeared in the middle of his skull and parted, pushing the left and right halves of his brain aside to create a void in the middle. This caused a pulse in his head and he felt momentarily disconnected from his body. It was as if the hands had paused his thinking, to make a silent announcement. That he *Reece Tassicker* should pay attention to something new that was about to arrive unexpectedly. It was a peculiar feeling that he'd had many times before.

Then, without any forewarning of subject-matter or purpose, an idea filled the void in his head, seemingly coming from nowhere. The idea rapidly rendered itself into a fully-formed concept, and it was a brilliant concept too. It brought a faint smile of satisfaction to his lips. Reece loved the sensation when an idea seemed to miraculously appear in his head like that. But he could never understand how it actually happened.

However, in just a few days' time, he would understand how it happened.

And he'd be the first person in the history of mankind to have this understanding.

Chapter 1 Four weeks ago

Reece is staring at an enormous archway made of bricks. Their rich, red colour flecked with inclusions of black, blue and grey. The perfectly-formed semicircle of the arch extends vertically down each side, in the form of two long, straight columns.

The archway recedes slowly into the distance and the vertical sides appear to get longer and longer. Then another identical archway appears both on the left- and right-sides of the first arch. They are joined together to form a triple-archway. Then two more arches join these, one on either side. All now have long, vertical extensions reaching down to the ground.

Reece now sees what the structure is. A brick viaduct spanning a deep valley. It's been built to carry the world's first railway line along the top of it. There is no visual indication of this; it is simply a known and unquestionable fact. This dates the scene to sometime in the early nineteenth century.

The pairs of tall columns that each support an arch, create a panel of exquisitely-slender windows of the type Reece has usually seen in cathedrals. At that moment, through one of the viaduct window-arches, there appears a cathedral. It's London's St Paul's cathedral — and it's sitting on the floor of the valley. The outline of its magnificent central-dome perfectly concentric to the curvature of the viaduct arches.

The perspective of the view changes as the viaduct moves rapidly closer to Reece, then passes overhead. The view of St Paul's is much clearer now, and it's surrounded by huge, cube-like buildings made from the same red-brick as the viaduct. These are Lancashire cotton mills with large, arch-shaped windows along the sides of every floor of the building. Adjacent to each cube is a towering, red-brick chimney stack.

The juxtaposition of the huge dome of St Paul's, the mill-building cubes and their associated chimneys, resembles an enormous mosque. This is a strange coincidence, for at that moment, a minaret and balcony appear on top of each chimney. Standing on one of the balconies is a chanting muezzin, calling the Muslim faithful to prayer.

His incantations change from their initial, melodious tones to a staccato, monotone stream. Not a song. Not words. Just repetitive bursts of noise. Like a chirping electronic-bird that can only produce one highly-irritating tone. Beep-beep-beep-beep-beep...

Reece stretched out a hand and switched off his alarm clock. He immediately recognised that he'd been dreaming as the alarm sounded, and so he reached for the open notepad and pen that he kept on the bedside table. Trying to recall as much of the dream as possible, he wrote key-words and phrases that captured the content. It was a race against time as the dream rushed away from him. He hung on to its tail for as long as he could, but after a short while it was gone. He finished his sketch of a viaduct with a cathedral dome visible through one of the arches to close out his recollection. He'd review his notes over breakfast to see if the dream became meaningful in any way.

Reece knew that you could always find a better answer, given time to think about the issue. This stemmed from his childhood where he'd frequently been referred to as a dreamer, for he would often be lost in his own thoughts. He found there was always so much to imagine or think about, and even though he spent much of his childhood alone, he was never lonely. Not with the thoughts that went through his mind. From considering strange questions such as why does wind gust rather than flow evenly, to imagining if it would ever be possible to share a thought with another person without using words.

Through his twenties and early-thirties, he still liked to make plenty of time to think about things. Well, truthfully, it was more that his lifestyle *allowed* him plenty of time to think about things. When all his school and university friends seemed to be marrying and starting families, he'd remained single.

Reece had always had a feeling that there was something more to life, and to the world we live in, than meets the eye. That there were some things we, as a race, were for some reason *unaware of.* He had the sense that we all have an individual purpose to achieve something significant, but that nobody really knows what that purpose is. He believed that many people gave up on their purpose because they couldn't define it. However, they retained a nagging feeling that some of the things that occurred in their lives acted as personal reminders to them that this tantalisingly-hidden purpose still existed.

Life also seemed to have determined it wasn't time for Reece Tassicker to have that mystical *relationship with someone special* just yet; but he had a moderately-active social life which he enjoyed. As the British would say, *he had nothing to complain about.*

He'd moved companies and changed roles several times, until he eventually found himself where he was now, as a partner in a consultancy. He worked with large organisations finding innovative ways to grow their business. His specific role was in helping the client to ask bold questions – questions that their competition would consider too difficult to achieve – and then answering them in ingenious ways. Effectively, he was helping his clients to *out-think* their competition.

There was plenty of thinking involved, which he loved. He'd been told that he was good at what he did, and he accepted the compliments with the quiet modesty that defined him as a person. He knew that his success was entirely due to his ability to think differently from anybody else. While others preferred to respond immediately with supposed best courses of action, he tended to listen and consider the issues more deeply before suggesting alternate options for consideration.

Even though Reece was introspective in nature, he knew that finding a quiet place to kick-back for a while and to wait for a great idea to come along in a serendipitous moment, never worked. Fresh thinking required unusual techniques that stimulated creative thought. One unusual technique that Reece used was to sleep on things. *Literally.*

The difficult issue he was working on currently was for a bank who wanted to identify a new range of products for their customers. The previous night as he'd started to fall asleep, he'd put a simple question in his mind.

What could be a new banking product that would be meaningful for people?

He'd focused on this as he fell asleep, knowing that it would influence his dreams. He repeated the question over and over in his mind, which caused him to fall asleep quickly. He tended to dream a lot, and if his mind was going to be busy dreaming, it may as well be busy doing something useful for him.

"You are what you eat," he muttered to himself, staring into his breakfast muesli. It seemed to have an exceptional number of nuts in today. *Quite appropriate considering the dream I had* he thought. He studied the sentence fragments and rough sketches he'd made on his notepad. This stimulated the voices in his head to start their dialogue.

What do a railway viaduct, St Paul's cathedral, a cotton mill, a chimney stack and a mosque have in common?

Well, they're big, noticeable buildings.

All made of brick and stone.

All built a long time ago.

St Paul's and the mosque represent religions.

Which have also been around a long time.

Agreed. But what's the human element involved here?

They are designed to be used by people in different ways.

Skilled individuals designed them.

They were all built using many human hands.

And all those people are now dead.

Whoa! Where did that thought come from?

It's true isn't it? Nobody involved in the design or construction of those structures is alive anymore.

Good point.

But what have dead people got to do with this bank project?

What if you could sell a product to dead people?

You'd have a huge market.

Why?

Well, there are many more dead people than living ones.

Ha! That's an unusual thought.

The discussion inside his head sometimes took strange directions, but it usually led him somewhere interesting. He waited, but for now the dialogue seemed to have stopped. Reece let the dead-people thought hang around for a while in his mind. It would be a dynamite concept if he could make it work in some way — but nothing immediately came to him, so he parked it away in the back of his mind. It was something he'd come back to later when he had more time.

He chuckled aloud to himself as he imagined telling the client's marketing team that they needed to advertise a service that got the attention of dead people. *That would keep them busy for a while!*

Later that morning, Reece was alone in his car driving along the M25 motorway, when the song *2-4-6-8 Motorway* by the Tom Robinson Band came on the radio. The chorus *2-4-6-8. Ain't never too late* repeated throughout the song, and he subconsciously started to sing along.

2-4-6-8. Ain't never too late.

He noticed he was just approaching the junction eight off-ramp for Reigate, which he thought coincidental. The first part of the chorus began to cycle repeatedly in his mind.

2-4-6-8.

2-4-6-8.

To-4-6-8.

To-4-6-8.

To-for-6-8.

To-for-6-8.

To-for-sicks-8.

To-for-sicks-8.

To-for-sicks-late.

To-for-sicks-late...

He felt an abrupt pulse. As if a single, massive heartbeat occurred in the middle of his head. His mind felt like a crowded dance-floor where the music had unexpectedly stopped. As the dancers retreated to their seats, a single, bright spotlight pierced the dark, creating a circle of rapt attention in the middle of the floor. All the other thoughts active in his head stilled themselves, in anticipation of a new star, about to make an appearance. Reece recognised this sensation in his head as portend of a powerful and beneficial moment. He knew something interesting was about to happen.

The dream came back to him. Viaducts and cathedrals. Mills and mosques. All built by dead people. Then, the concept appeared in the dance-floor spotlight and the voices took over.

To-for-sicks-late.

Sick? Late?

People get old and sick — and then they die and become late.

As in the late John Smith?

Yes.

To? For?

It isn't about selling a banking product to *dead people, but selling it* for *dead people.*

Sell a product for people who are going to die?

I like that because there's one thing we know for certain.

That everyone will die sometime?

Yes!

But why would people want to buy a product for when they die?

Because all those big structures in the dream were built in the past by people who are long dead.

Yes. And their structures still remain, long after their death.

Acting as resilient, practical and valued monuments to their efforts.

So, what if people could get a product from a bank that would act as a resilient, practical and valued monument for when they eventually died — even if they were in full health now?

A wave of elation flowed through Reece's body as he recognised this was the insight he'd been looking for. Part of the elation was due to the idea itself, but the remainder was his amazement at how his subconscious mind had been working on the banking-product question in the background — and how it had suddenly pushed a solution out. It was as if his brain had a secret compartment where it could work on issues without him interfering. Whichever way it worked he was grateful — and he gave himself a mental pat on the back.

Why was his brain giving his back a pat when the back had nothing to do with it?

Oh, forget it! Sometimes you ask yourself questions that are too weird.

Chapter 2 Friday 04h55

I'm standing as upright as I can. Rigid like a plank. Back straight, chest out, stomach pulled in. Feet so tightly together that my big toes, heels and ankles touch each other. Hands by my side, palms pressed firmly against my thighs. Fingers pointing straight down, straining to reach the ground. I'm facing forward. Eyes wide and unblinking, staring straight ahead into the distance.

The sergeant major's face appears from my right-side, filling my field of view. I try not to look into his eyes, but to remain focussed on an imaginary object, a half-mile behind his head. His mouth is open wider than a mouth is supposed to open. He's shouting at me so violently, his voice makes my head vibrate.

'What's your number soldier?' barks the open mouth, which is now taking up half of the sergeant major's face.

'Three. One. Four. One. Five. Zero. Three. One,' I answer, adding an explosive 'Sir!' at the end.

'And just how will you make sure you remember that soldier?' yells back the mouth so loudly, it makes his lips ripple and form two bright-red snakes. Each of which is now swallowing the other's tail.

'I'll remember it as thirty-one, forty-one, fifty, thirty-one. Sir!'

'What did you say?' roars the mouth which is so big it has taken up the whole of the sergeant major's head.

'I said I'll remember it as thirty-one, forty-one, fifty, thirty-one. Sir!'

'You'd better remember that for as long as you are in the army soldier because that is your number for life. And don't you ever forget it!' screams the mouth as the two red snakes form the outline of a giant head with a pink mattress as a huge tongue.

'Yes sir!' I shriek in reply as the sergeant major's snake-mattress-head moves on to the soldier on my left. I must remember this number, so I silently start repeating the mantra in my mind.

'Thirty-one. Forty-one. Fifty. Thirty-one.'

'Thirty-one. Forty-one. Fifty. Thirty-one.'

The silent shouting in my head seems unusual but it's helping me to remember the number sequence.

'Thirty-one. Forty-one. Fifty. Thirty-one.'

'Thirty-one. Forty-one. Fifty. Beep.'

'Thirty-one. Forty-one. Beep. Beep.'

'Thirty-one. Beep. Beep. Beep.'

Beep. Beep. Beep. Beep...

Reece put out a hand, pressing the button on top of the alarm clock. It was five o'clock, his usual wake up time. The alarm had stopped, but why did he still have a beep, beep, beep noise running through his mind?

Your number. Don't forget your number!

A moment of blankness before the image of the sergeant major's snake-mattress-head returned to him.

Thirty-one. Forty-one. Fifty. Thirty-one, silently shouted in his mind.

He quickly captured the number on his bedside pad. Remembering a dream so clearly was always a good start to the day for Reece. Today's dream was a little mystifying though. This wasn't the usual kind of dream containing a rambling selection of distorted realities. This time there was the number, which was obviously meant to be extracted from the dream and retained. *But why*? He looked again. The number 31415031 meant nothing to him. At least he'd managed to capture it — which was important.

There was, however, something more perplexing on his mind. This was the third-time in the last few months he'd had a dream where he knew he was supposed to remember something specific from it.

Chapter 3 Friday 05h10

Reece changed and set off for his morning run. Everyone has a time of day when they feel at their best, and for Reece, the early morning was his. Even more so when it involved a good run. His lungs worked hard drawing in the clean, crisp morning-air and transferring the oxygen it contained into his bloodstream. His elevated heart-rate pumped the oxygen-enriched blood around his body and flooded his brain with it. Reece's brain was much like everybody else's. It only accounted for two per cent of his body-weight, but it consumed around twenty per cent of his oxygen intake. Reece found that running helped with him to focus on things, which made for some very interesting thinking. And this morning he was thinking about his dreams.

The first dream he was supposed to remember occurred back in February. It was about a young girl with a name that sounded like *Gara.* She kept repeating her name to him and telling him that she had something important that he must listen to. Throughout the dream he'd kept asking her what it was, but she replied that she couldn't tell him until he found her. And it was important that he did find her.

At the time he'd recognised this wasn't one of his usual kinds of dream. It wasn't normal to have to remember something specific from a dream. He'd spent time searching the internet for the meaning of dreams but found it to be a highly-imprecise subject. The way you categorised your dream gave it different meanings, and the websites he checked weren't even consistent in their interpretations of the same dream-topic.

During his browsing, Reece found a website about the number of different dreams there were. Seven-billion people live on Earth, all of whom would sleep at some point in every twenty-four hour period. Most of these people would dream, even if they didn't remember their dreams, and most would have several dreams each time they slept. As there were tens of billions of dreams happening in every rotation of the planet, he imagined that there had to be some dream duplication. There were discussions on a wide range of dream-related topics — even one called dream sharing, where people had the same dream at the same time, but there was nothing of relevance to Reece's dream.

His second dream had been about a stone-building with a shiny, black door. The name *Derby* was carved in stone above the door. He was staring at the name and from behind him a huge crowd of people kept chanting the word *Derby* incessantly throughout the dream. He knew he was also supposed to remember this word. After this dream, he'd gone back to the discussion forum he'd visited earlier, and posted a question on the subject of remembering specific words from dreams. He'd got into a discussion with two people who also seemed to have dreams with elements they were supposed to remember. Their usernames were Bonita1974 and SweetDreamer, which Reece assumed were female names. They had discussed the subject quite intensely with Reece for a few days, but nothing came out of the conversation that helped him understand the real meaning of his own dream. Then, the two women had abruptly stopped posting comments. That had been in early June.

He had an idea to create a website that allowed people to log their memorable dreams to see if there was any commonality between them. A web-designer friend, who owed Reece a favour for putting a big job his way, said it would be quick to set up, as long as it didn't get too much usage. Reece said this was fine and gave him the outline of how it should work. He wrote a comment on the discussion forum that he was setting up a dream-sharing website, and several of the members indicated that they'd like to use it to see if anyone was having the same dreams as them. Someone calling themselves Mentat12 was the exception and was the only person critical of his idea, replying how it would be a complete waste of people's time.

He'd eventually seen the preview of the website and it was basic, but suitable for the purpose. Users posted a brief outline of the dream they were meant to remember, and the date they had it. Then, if others had a similar dream, they could put their details next to the user's dream. It wasn't perfect, but if he did find someone else having the same dream as him, then… well, if that happened he didn't know what he'd do. But he was sure it would start an interesting discussion.

When he posted the outline of it on the forum, he again received some positive feedback. Excepting for the lone comments of Mentat12, who again railed against dream-sharing and how being associated with a dream website for weirdo's would seriously damage Reece's professional reputation.

Reece thought this peculiar. Why would someone on a discussion forum for dreams be so critical of a website for helping people share their dreams? *And how did Mentat12 know he had a professional reputation to maintain?*

But that was last week. As he approached the end of his run, his mind was made up. He was definitely going ahead with the dream-sharing website, especially after this morning's strange dream.

While he cooled down from his run and ate some cereal, he told the forum that he'd been invited to speak at *The Potential of the Human Mind* conference next week in London, and that he'd announce the website launch there. Reece picked up his cereal bowl to get the last few spoonfuls out, and was staring blankly at the screen when a response to his post appeared from Mentat12.

YOU ARE GOING TO FIND THIS HARMFUL IF YOU PROCEED.

Mentat12 had just threatened him.

Chapter 4 Friday 11h00

Canary Wharf is part of the East End of London where the high-street banks have their mine's-bigger-than-yours competition for the height of their head-office tower blocks. Reece was gazing out of a floor-to-ceiling window on the thirty-second floor of his client's building, the snaking-route of the Thames leading his eye towards the heart of the city.

His mind wasn't on the view though. He was preparing to present the findings of the new-products project to the executive team of the bank. The presentation needed to be done elegantly, setting up a storyline to prepare their minds for what he would show them. He ran the first-three sentences he would say over in his mind — but they didn't sound right. He changed a few words around. He always felt nervous before an important presentation, but he'd learnt a trick that getting the first-three sentences to flow well was the key to setting up the tone for the rest of the presentation.

As he mentally rehearsed the sentences, they finally firmed themselves up. They sounded good. His energy levels were high. *This is going to be a great presentation* he told himself. He allowed his eyes to follow the course of the river again, until he lost it among the buildings in the centre of the city. He started thinking about how this project had started.

In January he'd had an article printed in the Harvard Business Review called *Popcorn and the Art of Fine Thinking.* In the article he'd explained the innovative model he applied for thinking about business issues, and he'd used the analogy of making popcorn. He'd described how all the assets a company used in the normal course of its business, were like popcorn kernels in a large pan. Big programs that tried to coordinate all the kernels so they popped at the same time never worked. You had to let each piece pop when it was ready. Turning up the heat by applying powerful, creative thinking was how you got individual kernels — or business assets — to pop precisely when, and how, you needed them to. He'd explained how businesses could successfully pop any, and every, asset with a toolkit he'd provided.

The article had caught the attention of company executives and had brought in some great new business — including the bank he was now about to present to.

A smartly-attired young man came up to Reece and guided him into the boardroom, where he found the bank's senior executives waiting to hear his presentation. Reece introduced himself briefly, paused, looked around the room to get their attention, and then started with his three, rehearsed opening sentences. He saw the nods of agreement and knew he was addressing their important issues. Over the next hour, he presented a number of concepts to them, saving the best for last.

"The final opportunity I'd like to present is unusual. It's a product intended for dead people." He let that point hang to heighten the level of expectation.

"Our research shows that when aged people make out their wills, they have deep concerns that when they die, the inheritances they leave behind will be used wisely. Indeed, when you die, what *do* you leave behind?"

Reece paused to let them consider his rhetorical question.

"Your whole life converts into the memories people have of you, some artefacts, a pile of money, and hopefully some positive behaviours that you have passed on." He let this most generic of eulogies settle gently on the shoulders of those present. Especially the more aged ones.

"We've designed a new product that allows people to leave behind a legacy for individual family members that encourages good financial practice. The product is taken out during the life of the customer and it activates on their death. They can leave as little as £5,000 for each recipient, which is paid in the form of five £1,000 amounts, spread over the years following the individual's death. The recipient can put these amounts in any product the bank offers, and they are encouraged to use a range of investments to understand where they make the best returns at the lowest risk."

"Each year, a voucher for the amount is delivered to the recipient, together with a pre-written personal message from the sender — ideally around the subject of making sound investments for the future. This gives the bank a five-year investment portfolio that is a natural lead-in for future re-investment by the recipients. It also gives you probate over the will of the deceased."

Reece saw their heads nodding in approval. Some were also making notes — which was always a good sign.

"This new product has a high public-relations potential as it's a socially responsible product. It's also interesting and unusual in the way it allows the deceased to provide some guidance towards sound financial management for a period beyond their death."

He paused before he made his final point.

"It's also a meaningful, emotional and wise memorial of the individual. A service you can offer that reflects the standing any good bank would want in society." *And believe me, that's what you need* he added to himself.

The presentation concluded with the CEO thanking Reece for his time and also for his willingness to fly to Johannesburg the next day to give the presentation to their southern-hemisphere management team. It had been one of this team who had initially commissioned the project.

They had then taken a lunch-break and invited Reece to join them. Several of the executives had complimented him on the product for dead people, and asked if there could be other similar opportunities like it. He'd explained how most companies tended to look to the far horizons for new things, rather than looking at the simple and obvious opportunities hidden away inside their business. One of the directors had then spoken to him about the possibility of Reece's company helping them to identify more growth areas on a systematic basis. Reece smiled inwardly. *Another success!* Things seemed to be going really well for him at the moment.

Unfortunately for Reece, things were about to go wrong — and in a most peculiar way.

Chapter 5 Friday 15h14

Gareth Jones was not a patient man. However, he was now watching the clock on his computer closely. At fourteen minutes and fifteen seconds past three, the new webpage he'd created went live — just as he'd scheduled it to. He refreshed the website page-list he was watching on the screen, and the new webpage he'd just created appeared at the top of the list.

DATE: 11-JUL-2014
TIME: 15:14:15
WEBPAGE: HTTP://WWW.PECKHAMINSTITUTE.ORG.UK/SFFDF-UBTTJDLFS-1

This was the second time in two days he'd posted a new webpage on this subject. Within an hour, the first of the many search-engine spiders that roamed incessantly across the internet looking for new content, found the page. The spider scanned it for content and returned its findings back to its host computer server to index in the master search catalogue. However, at the host server, nothing was indexed.

The page was completely blank.

Chapter 6 Friday 17h35

Reece tapped his Oyster card on the yellow contact-pad of the ticket barriers. They dutifully opened, and he exited the tube station out onto the main concourse of Paddington railway station. He checked the departure board which indicated the next shuttle to Heathrow airport would leave in fifteen-minutes. Enough time to buy the essential items; a train ticket, a book for the flight and a coffee.

He headed towards the station's large WH Smith bookshop and went straight to the management books at the back of the store. A life-size, cardboard cut-out of a stern-looking man wearing a Union Jack waistcoat caught his attention. It was Professor Sir Simon Bartlett. Reece knew that he was scheduled to give the opening address at the conference he was attending next week, and his new book, *Mind the Future*, was being promoted.

He read the back cover, flicked through a few pages and decided to buy it. The book he was holding had a torn dust-cover, and some page-corners were bent over, so he swapped it for the one good copy remaining on the shelf. Reece paid for it with his credit card, and put it in the side-pocket of his carry-on bag. He then walked over to the Heathrow Express ticket machine and bought his ticket. There was still ample time before the train left, so he headed toward the nearby coffee bar.

It wasn't busy, and the young barista making his Grande Latte engaged him in casual conversation. She seemed charming and chatty and his intuition kicked-in. He impulsively handed a ten-pound note and a business card to her.

"Caroline," he said, glancing at her name badge. "Would you do me a favour? If someone wearing a suit orders a coffee, take the cost out of this money. Tell them it's courtesy of me and then give them that card. Whatever money is left over, you can keep."

"Oooh, this sounds unusual. What sort of person do you mean?"

"Preferably a business-looking person — which is why I mentioned the suit. Not too stuck-up. And someone who's a bit chatty like you."

She looked at the business card he'd given her. "Reece Tassicker. Business Designer," she read aloud. "I've never met one of those before. What usually happens?"

"Sometimes people call or send me an email. All my details are on there so they can check me out online to make sure I'm not a crazy."

"Sounds a bit crazy to me — if you don't mind me saying so." She blushed slightly. "But crazy in a nice way."

"I suppose it does. I've written a little message on the back."

She turned the card over to see that Reece had written:

If you'd like to hear about an ingenious way to grow your business, then I'd love to talk to you. Enjoy the drink! Reece T

He carried a few business cards with this written on the back for whenever he intuitively felt the opportunity was right to leave one behind.

"Got to dash," said Reece. "Enjoy your day."

"You too." Caroline turned his business card over in her hands. *At least one interesting thing has happened to me today,* she thought.

Reece had done this before and occasionally it had generated new business introductions. Some recipients of a card found it an innovative approach and wanted to know more. It wasn't something he ever planned to do — it was more of an impulsive act. Reece found it stimulating when a stranger phoned him up as a result of getting a free coffee — for he had to think quickly about what to say, based on the opening comment from the caller.

As he walked to his train, he looked up at the magnificent, soaring arches of the roof of Paddington station. Built by Isambard Kingdom Brunel in the mid-1800s, he realised it was a similar memorial to those he'd had in the dream that started his thinking on products for dead people.

Reece boarded the train and took his seat just as the train accelerated away from the platform. He pulled the new book out of his carry-on and, sipping on his coffee, turned to read the contents page. After seeing the book's structure, he let the pages quickly flick through his fingers to get a feel for how it was written. Text, text, more text, a few tables, text, more text, a diagram, more text, a flash of green, then more text. He stopped. *What was the green thing he'd seen?* The rest of the book seemed to be in black and white. Flicking slowly back through the book, one page flopped open. Stuck to the page was a square, lime-green Post-it note, and hand-written on it were the words

DON'T GO AHEAD WITH YOUR DREAM SHARING WEBSITE

Chapter 7 Saturday 08h20

"Come. Come. Come. Come. Come." Beulah Aronga was worried. Very worried. She was late sending in her dream. They'd told her that she had to send it in by eight o'clock each morning, but it was now almost twenty-past, and she still had a bit left to type. *But there was so much to type today.* "They should give me extra time for these long dreams. Please, please, please don't let them be angry with me," she muttered to herself.

As a little girl growing up in Nigeria, she'd always had lots of dreams that seemed so much livelier and real than her friend's dreams. She was able to remember incredible details about the adventures she had when she slept, while her friends didn't remember much at all about their dreams. She would dream of many things, and every morning she would tell her old Nana all the wonderful things she'd done. Her Nana used to say that having dreams was a good thing, because that was one way in which her ancestors spoke to her. Nana was wise in the ways of the ancestors. She often told Beulah stories about how the ancestor spirits helped us, and that she should respect what they showed her. This was why she'd always paid good attention to her dreams.

Beulah had come to the UK when her parents moved here over twenty years ago. Many lowly-paid jobs, numerous council-subsidised accommodations, and several cheap-bastard boyfriends later, she'd found herself working as a cashier at a small supermarket. She had a nine-year old daughter who'd grown up to be a lovely child. Especially once cheap-bastard boyfriend number six had upped-and-left one night after an argument.

One evening, she'd been using her mobile phone to add her latest dream to a Facebook dream discussion page, when she saw an advert. It was looking for people who were good dreamers, and who wanted to earn some extra cash as part of a research project. Extra cash really appealed to Beulah, so she submitted her details.

It was almost eighteen-months since the people first got in touch with her. They called her on her mobile and asked questions about her life. What she did during the day, and how well she slept at night. They asked her about some of her most recent dreams, how many she had each night, and how much detail she was able to recall from them. They said she should be honest in what she told them as they had some equipment that was checking the stress levels in her voice, so they'd know if she was lying. She thought this a bit rude. In fact she thought it very rude. But the fact that they were going to pay her fifty pounds if they decided to use her — well, fifty pounds was a lot of money. So she made sure she told them the truth, which they seemed happy with, as they said they wanted to go ahead with the test.

The man called Gareth, with the funny Welsh accent, then told her that in two-days' time they would be very interested in the dreams that she'd had the previous night. She was to write down all she could remember as soon as she woke up. They would call her later that morning, and she was to read back her notes to them. Gareth told her not to drink alcohol the night before, and not to eat any abnormally-rich food, and that she should go to bed at whatever time she usually did — to get a good night's sleep.

She'd made her notes the next morning and she remembered telling Gareth about a small boy wearing a blue T-shirt with a picture of a zebra on. He was in the basket of a bright-orange, hot-air balloon and the basket had eight ropes tying it to the balloon. There was a kitten-shaped, pink birthday cake with white icing, where the eleven candles on it started burning so fiercely that smoke was billowing into the sky, and the fire brigade came to put the candles out. There were animals flying to the moon on a rocket that looked like Noah's Ark, and many other strange things too.

She'd felt sure that wasn't what she was supposed to have dreamed of, but she hoped she'd get her fifty pounds at least. Gareth said she'd done very well and that he wanted to meet her to pay the fifty pounds, — and to offer her even more money if she'd like to keep telling them about her dreams.

Her flat was very small, but she always tried to keep it clean and tidy. The tidy bit was easy, as she didn't have much of anything to her name. Some second-hand furniture, a modest wardrobe of clothes for her and her daughter, much of which were bought at charity shops. Such was life as an unqualified, black-woman earning £260 a week. The fifty pounds from Gareth would make a big difference to Beulah. However, it wasn't the money that Gareth brought with him that made a difference for her. It was what else he said.

He told her that his organisation was really impressed with the quality of her dream recall, and that he wanted to invite her to be part of a longer-term programme. He explained how they were a research institute studying the types of dreams that people had, and they were especially interested in the little details that some people could remember. Lots of people could remember the bigger picture — but not the detail. Gareth told Beulah how she had shown herself to be very good at recalling the detail, which was why he was giving her this special invitation.

He asked what sort of work she did and what she liked and didn't like about it. She told him all the details of her work, and how she would love to be able to spend more time with her daughter — as they didn't have much in life except for each other. Gareth listened closely to what she said, and made plenty of notes. Finally he told her that because she was such a good dream-recaller, he was going to offer her £350 a week for at least the next year — and quite possibly a lot longer. There were some conditions, she heard him say, just before she burst into tears of joy.

It took quite a while for her sobbing to subside, and Gareth just sat there and waited for her to stop. Beulah thought he seemed a very patient man. He told her they would set up a computer for her to use and they would pay to have an internet connection installed in her flat. Someone would come round to show her how to use the computer, and she would need to send her dreams to Gareth by email every morning. This was to be done no later than eight o'clock at the absolute latest. He also told her that they would call every few days to ask her some questions about her dreams. When they did, they would be using the stress-detector to make sure she was telling them the truth.

He also asked if he could rub a cotton-bud inside her cheek as part of a standard health check they did on their research subjects. She agreed straight away. For the money he was paying, he could put the cotton-bud anywhere he damn-well wanted to.

It was a week after that when the computer was installed, and she was shown how to use it to email her dreams each day. With her two-finger typing it took a long time to do, so she adjusted her sleeping pattern to wake up at six o'clock, to have plenty of time to type up her dreams. It was a small change to make for the extra money she was making. Gareth had asked her not to speak to people about what she was doing and how much she was getting paid. He said that if anyone found out, they may get jealous, and that wouldn't help Beulah at all. For practically the first time in her life since she stopped being a little girl in Nigeria, she felt that she wasn't struggling to survive any more. Life was just a little better than it had been at any time in her recent past.

This morning wasn't one of the better mornings though. A neighbour that she was friendly with, had banged on her front door earlier asking for help with her mother, who had collapsed. The ambulance eventually arrived, and had taken the mother to hospital.

This meant Beulah had lost over an hour this morning — which was why she'd only now pressed the SEND button, at just after eight-thirty.

"Send, send, send, send," muttered Beulah to herself again. She wondered if Gareth would be angry with her. She also wondered why the ancestors deemed it necessary to send her a dream of a man carrying a huge credit card under one arm, and dragging a giant book on wheels behind him around a railway station.

That seemed a peculiar thing for the ancestors to know about.

Chapter 8 Saturday 08h30

Gareth Jones clicked the SEND/RECEIVE button on his email program for the third time in less than a minute — but nothing changed on the screen.

Jesus Christ! What the bloody hell is number four doing this morning? It's thirty minutes past deadline time and the feedback still isn't in.

He needed to do the analysis of last night's dreams, but he didn't like to start until he had the feedback from all three dreamers. He never knew which of them may contain a key element, and if he omitted looking at one feedback until later, then he subconsciously may give that feedback more weighting. And that might influence the interpretation.

Why the hell does number four have to be late today of all days? Gareth Jones referred to the dreamers by their number, as de-humanising them made the dream translations more objective. Also, no-one had ever referred to Gareth Jones as a *people person*, which was another indicator as to why he denoted the dreamers by number.

Gareth had recruited three dreamers so far. The first person he'd recruited was Lisa Harris, a librarian from Tyneside in the north of England. She was very good at specific details from her dreams. They may not have always been relevant, but they were very precise.

Then he'd found Bonita Milano. But she was dead now, so effectively there wasn't a number two.

The third recruit had been Patrick Harris, who'd been unemployed since leaving university two-years ago. When Gareth had met with him, his life revolved around online gaming and social networks, which had meant he was highly computer-literate. As he lived with his parents in north London, he had access to their computer whenever he needed it, which seemed to be all day long. Patrick had been remarkably good at putting context to his dreams and Gareth had noticed this from the first test they had done with him. While the others just wrote down their dreams verbatim as they recalled them, often producing disconnected elements and statements, Patrick was different. He'd give the key elements, but he could also experience feelings in his dream, which frequently enabled him to give context to what a specific dream was all about. Gareth found this to be a really useful trait.

Patrick was claiming unemployment benefit, and was receiving some money from his parents, both of whom worked full-time. Gareth offered him £700 a week to be one of their participants under the condition that he stop claiming the unemployment benefit —

for the weekly payments would be classified as income. Patrick told him not to worry about that, but he was concerned that his parents might find out he was earning so much money and want him to start paying towards his living expenses at home. Gareth said he'd arrange to pay it directly into his bank account. It would also be best if he told absolutely no-one about the payments, or what he was doing to get the money. Patrick had agreed to this immediately, which made Gareth sense there was a dishonest streak to him — which he'd have to watch closely. Surprisingly, Patrick had turned out to be very reliable, sending his dreams through each day by the required time.

Then there was number four. She was the blubbering, black woman in that crappy, little flat in Bristol. He couldn't complain too much, as she'd hardly ever been late in the past. And he'd got her at the real bargain price of just £350 a week. She was interesting because her feedback frequently contained unusual details and strange perspectives. These could be tricky to understand at first, but afterwards, they often validated some of the other dreamers' content, and helped to frame the overall understanding of the interpretation.

During the recruitment of these dreamers, he'd told them how the Peckham Institute was conducting a long-term study looking at the development of people's dreams over time. They wanted to monitor a small number of people, possibly over several years, to see how the type of dream, and the detail of their dreams, changed as people got older. This was just a ruse to make them think they could get paid for a long time, which would keep them active and responsive in the short-term. In some ways the longer-term plan might be true, as each of the dreamers was required to give a cheek swab. They were told this was for a health check, but in reality the samples were sent away for detailed genetic testing to see if the participants had any tendency towards chronic disease. Having dreamers with a long life-expectancy could be a great benefit for the Institute. Especially if the results continued to go as well as the first trials had gone.

All the dreamers were supposed to send in their dreams every day, and Gareth had made sure they understood this when he'd met each one. If they failed to send a dream in, then they risked being rejected from the programme. They also had to write down their dreams in the order in which they had them. For many people, even recalling one dream in any kind of detail would have been difficult, but for people who were active dreamers with good recall, this wasn't an issue at all. And of course, this was precisely the type of person that Gareth was looking for.

Typically, it was only the feedback from the dreamers that came in on a Tuesday morning that mattered. And even then, it was only the last one or two dreams of the night that would be of interest. In a normal week, Gareth would quickly skim the content of the emails on the days other than Tuesday to make sure the quality was there. He might send a reminder to add more detail if any of them started to become too brief in their feedback.

Today was Saturday, not Tuesday. It was an unusual situation, and today's dreams were very important. He needed to start the interpretation now. Finally he saw the email from number four arrive in the form of a bold entry at the top of his email inbox.

Just as different people spoke with different accents, people dreamed with different emphasis. Some of the dreamers tended to have a focus on what people were doing as part of a dream, while others concentrated on a place and its surroundings and environment. Some had a flow of a storyline to their dreams while others tended to capture more specific aspects such as names, numbers, and signs. Gareth had been picking this up over the last year or so and knew what the specific focus was for each of the dreamers. Knowing their styles helped with the interpretations.

Gareth would read one feedback at random and extract all the key pieces of information. He'd then quickly sketch an image of how he visualised what they were saying. Once he'd finished summarising one dreamer's feedback, he'd move straight on to the next, until he'd converted all the feedback into a mix of visuals and key-statements. Only then would he study what he'd produced and start to conclude the findings.

It took Gareth two hours from when he'd received Beulah's feedback to sketch out the dreams — and to understand what the consolidated picture was. It looked like Andre was going to have to be at Paddington station again early tomorrow morning.

Gareth Jones had studied psychology while at university and had stayed on to complete a PhD. He became a full-time researcher at the university with a focus on the psychology of sleep disorders. He started to use the quality of the recall of dreams as a proxy-measure for the deepness of the sleep that the participants had. He'd always ignored the actual content of the dream as he felt this was irrelevant, until, in a freak occurrence, two people happened to discuss the same dream they'd had the night before. When he questioned them, each could be prompted to complete the missing parts to match the dream of the other person. *They'd had the same dream from totally different perspectives.*

Gareth became fascinated with this — almost to the point of obsession — and had put in a proposal to research what he called parallel-dreaming. He discovered that very little work was being done in this area, and felt it was a field that he could be at the forefront of. He became passionate, almost to the extent of being obsessive, in his belief in the concept of parallel-dreaming.

One problem with parallel-dreaming that he hadn't considered, was how to find people who had the parallel dreams in the first place. He'd done extensive testing with the two subjects that had the initial parallel-dream, but they didn't seem to have any ability to repeat their skill, no matter what he tried. He didn't believe their dream was a fluke, but eventually the funding dried up because he was unable to produce any results beyond that solitary occurrence. He began to despair, but eventually was put in touch with someone who had an interest in dreams, and more importantly, who seemed to have money.

Gareth had several meetings with Paul Peckham, who explained that he was interested in sponsoring two fields of work. One was in the transmission of thought, and the other in the receiving of thought, with the receivers doing this through their dreams. Was Gareth interested in this? Gareth asked how this related to parallel-dreaming and Paul had explained that the transmitter would be sending the same information to all the participants — and as Gareth would be running the receiving end, it would be his job to interpret the dreams and to identify the issue that was being transmitted. Gareth said it sounded very interesting and Paul Peckham agreed to set up the funding through his own institute.

Gareth's role would be to recruit the dreamers and to run the programme with them. Paul had insisted that Gareth abide by two important conditions. The first was that there would be no papers or research published, and no public scrutiny of the institute for the first two years of operation. The second condition was that Gareth should not make any attempt to find out who was transmitting the dreams. Paul explained that if there was any interaction between the sending-party and the receiving-party, it could negatively impact the research programme. Gareth explained that his research protocols could manage any interaction between the transmitter and himself, as this was standard procedure for many kinds of research projects. But Paul Peckham had been adamant that this would not be allowed to happen.

Gareth had reluctantly agreed to take the sponsorship, but was pleasantly surprised to find that Paul had included a generous salary. Normally the recruitment of participants would only take a week or two, but Paul had insisted that Gareth create a comprehensive specification on the type of dreamers they were looking for. He said that he'd got some plans to extend the research and potentially run it for several years, so it was essential to get the best people from the start. It had taken Gareth over a year to find the dreamers and they'd only started the pilot-research the previous autumn. For some reason, Paul was in no hurry to get hard results from the research — which irritated Gareth somewhat.

It was around this time that Paul had also insisted that Andre work with Gareth. His role would be to ensure the overall security of the project in several different ways. Gareth knew that Andre had, as he described it, *freelance, military experience* and that he had worked for Paul previously in some capacity. Andre was amiable and helpful, but very guarded on his background. Gareth felt the phrase *hard bastard* may have been applied to Andre on some occasions in the past — and meant as a compliment too. He also felt that not knowing too much about Andre's background might be the preferred course of action.

Part of Andre's role was to *make things happen on the project*. Gareth had asked Paul what that meant, but Paul told him not to worry at this point in time.

One particular day about a year ago, Paul had asked for a strange webpage to be put up on the Institute's website, and that he wanted to know the dreamers' output the next morning. When Gareth asked why, Paul just replied he was running a test with the transmission group. Gareth gave Paul the feedback the next day and heard nothing more about it, until Paul came to see Gareth and Andre at their small office in central London, three months later.

He'd explained how the pilot-stage of the project was now at an end, and that the focus of the project was changing. Gareth had been worried when he heard this. Paul had gone on to explain what the focus of the project would be from then on — which blew Gareth's mind. He couldn't comprehend that what he was being told was possible.

Paul reminded them both of the special dreams of three-months earlier and informed them that had been the first test-run. It had been a very successful test-run too. So successful in fact, that Gareth and Andre would each receive a bonus of £250,000. Paul told them they would be receiving more bonuses in the future if things continued to go so well.

This was the moment when Gareth Jones' life-mission changed from being a leading and respected academic in his chosen field of expertise, to a simpler goal of wanting to be rich beyond his wildest dreams.

Chapter 9 Saturday 08h45

During his overnight flight to Johannesburg, Reece had mentally retraced his steps in Paddington station in an attempt to understand how the Post-it note could have got into his book.

Before he bought it, he'd just read the overview on the back-cover and had flicked through a few pages. He'd then swapped the damaged copy for the one which was in better condition. He hadn't noticed any Post-it note in the first book when he'd flicked through the pages. He'd then taken the book to the cashier who'd scanned the barcode with a hand-held scanner, and who then placed the book inside a small, plastic bag in full view of him. The cashier had seemed very much dis-engaged from his work, so he was sure he hadn't put the Post-it note inside.

Reece had then put the book in the side-pocket of his carry-on bag which he'd immediately zipped up. He'd bought the train ticket and then gone for coffee where the bag was by his feet for the few minutes he was there. There was nobody else around, which was how he'd had the opportunity to talk with the barista girl, and give her his card. He'd then got on the train and put his bag on the vacant seat beside him. The train was lightly loaded and there was no-one sitting anywhere near him. He'd taken the book out of his bag and seen the lime-green Post-it note.

There was absolutely no way that anyone could have put it in the book after he'd taken it off the shelf. So it must have been put in *before* he even touched the book. He considered the possibility that the Post-it note wasn't meant for him at all. He opened the book and rechecked it.

DON'T GO AHEAD WITH YOUR DREAM SHARING WEBSITE

Who the hell else but him could possibly be doing a dream-sharing website? Of course it was meant for him. Was it some kind of safety-warning that he was meddling in something risky? Or was it a threat?

A threat!

He recalled the comment that Mentat12 had made on the discussion-board when he'd announced he was going to set up the dream website. This was definitely a threat. And it was definitely meant for him.

But how did they know he was at Paddington station?

And at that *time?*

And that he would buy that specific *book?*

Who the bloody hell are they*?*

Why shouldn't he do this *website?*

Stop! Too many questions.

The taxi taking him from Johannesburg airport to the conference venue had left the main carriageway of the M1 De Villiers Graaff freeway, and was taking the off-ramp marked Sandton. Reece needed to focus on the presentation he would shortly be giving. He closed his eyes and started to visualise himself in a room, standing in front of the audience.

What was his opening statement going to be?

How should he run the presentation to get the message across with maximum impact?

He decided to use the same approach that he'd used successfully yesterday. He let the opening three-sentence visualisation run on in his mind.

Chapter 10 Saturday 11h25

Reece had presented to a large team of the bank's senior management in a more-relaxed environment than he'd done yesterday. This team were on a week-long, business planning exercise, and his presentation was intended to inspire them with examples of how the bank was looking to grow through new products in the future.

After the presentation, Lauren Harper, the person who'd coordinated his visit, came over to thank him.

"I know your flight back to London isn't until this evening, so do you have plans for the rest of the day?"

"I'm going to get a day-room at the airport hotel and do some work."

She explained that she'd only come in to see his presentation, and was heading home for an informal lunch with friends. She invited him to join them. Reece had been to South Africa a number of times before, and although he didn't like Johannesburg as a city, he did like the people. You could arrive as a complete stranger in a Johannesburg home, and leave with a houseful of new best-friends. Her suggestion was far superior to spending the afternoon working in a hotel room, so he accepted her offer.

Lauren drove him back to her house where he met her husband, Steve. She then offered him use of a spare bedroom, which had an en suite bathroom. There were towels and toiletries laid out on the bed.

"I know what overnight flights are like, so take the chance to freshen up. Come through to the kitchen when you're ready."

Reece undeniably felt overnight-grubby, and was grateful for the chance to clean up. After his shower he made his way to the kitchen, which was in fact, a huge entertainment area. The large kitchen opened out onto a dining area where a table for eight was laid. On the far side of the table, large sliding doors were open, leading out onto the garden that surrounded the house.

"Anything I can do to help?" offered Reece.

"Yes. Get yourself a drink, stand over there, and make scintillating conversation," said Lauren.

"Anything a little more useful I can do to help?"

"You're fine with that," she said, and proceeded to explain who would be joining them for lunch.

"There are two other couples coming. Kobus and Renata, and also David and Michaela. There's a good friend of ours called DD too. It's all very relaxed. The conversation can tend to get a bit boisterous, but I'm sure you can handle that," Lauren said with a smile.

"And what does DD stand for?" asked Reece, trying to fathom out whether this was a male or female name.

"It's a nickname he's had ever since we've known him. Apparently it stands for Drop Dead. He says it's because he's drop-dead gorgeous, but often it's due to people telling him to drop dead after some of the provocative things he says."

"Sounds like a character."

"He's more than a character. He's several characters. The stuff that goes on inside his head is impossible to come from just one mind. You'll see."

When everyone had arrived and introductions to Reece had been made, Steve ushered people towards the table. Reece found himself sitting between DD and the hostess, Lauren. He spent a little while explaining why he was in South Africa for only twelve hours, which even he thought a little bizarre.

"Oh, I forgot that I need to offer you ladies a pre-emptive apology," said DD.

"A what?" asked Renata.

"A pre-emptive apology."

"And what's one of those?"

"You know that if you say something wrong to someone, then you should always apologise for it afterwards?"

"Go on."

"Well, I'm apologising for it beforehand. I'm trying to be a more polite and sensitive person. That's all."

"Is this a general apology — or for something specific?"

"Something very specific."

There was a silence. DD liked to insert unnecessarily long pauses to build up the tension.

"What is it?"

"What's what?"

DD also liked to insert moments of amnesia in his conversation to raise the level of involvement of people with his story.

"What's the thing you want to apologise for?" came the impatient reply.

"I want to offer a pre-emptive apology just in case I happen to refer to any of you women as a hideously-repulsive, fat-arsed bitch. I wouldn't want you to take it the wrong way or anything."

"Not take it the wrong way?" said Michaela, gagging on the sip of wine she'd just taken.

"Of course not. I want you to take it in the most positive sense of the term."

"You use that term to me and you'll be in for a big surprise."

DD turned to Reece. "Not many men would be willing to apologise for something *before* it happens. These women don't seem to have it in their hearts to forgive."

"If it's not too personal a question, how come you're the only single-guy among all the married couples?" asked Reece provocatively, deciding to play with the fire DD had just lit.

"That's down to one of two reasons," he replied. "The first is that I've seen how the quality of women declines drastically as soon as they get married. I'm not sure I want to spend the rest of my life married to someone as unforgiving as the women around the table here."

"There'd better be a second reason coming pretty damn quickly," said Renata. Her lips pursing aggressively.

"And the second reason would be that there are only three truly-amazing women on the planet, and as you can see," said DD, gesturing around the table with his fork, "they've all been taken already."

"Definitely the second reason," said Lauren.

"You obviously all know each other well," Reece said, nodding his head towards DD in particular.

"The guys and I have all worked together in the past. And as for the women, I've known this one, this one and that one for over fifteen years," said DD, pointing to Renata, Michaela and Lauren respectively.

"Don't ever refer to me as *this one*," said Michaela firmly, shaking her finger at DD.

"Profound apologies, Michaela. I didn't mean to offend you. What I meant to say was I've known this one, *that one* and that one for over fifteen years," DD retorted, with an emphatic nod of his head towards Michaela in the middle.

"He was the best man at our wedding, weren't you DD?" said Lauren.

"And when was that?" enquired Reece.

"It'll be fourteen years in October."

"Jeez Steve, you'd better watch out. Apparently after fourteen years of marriage you can start to get quite attached to them — if you aren't careful," said DD with a straight face. "Anyway, I'm surprised that your marriage to Steve has lasted this long considering what he said to me about you on your wedding day."

Once again DD paused to let the statement hang. Lauren finally picked up on it.

"And what exactly did he say?"

"Just that he thought he needed to get married to help his career. And that you'd do as his interim bride — until he met the woman he truly loved, and wanted to spend the rest of his life with."

"Well, the fact is, I *am* his wife."

"Lauren, you should use your correct title when referring to your marital status."

"And what's that precisely?"

"Technically, your correct title is that you are Steve's first wife" replied DD.

"I'm his *only* wife."

"Technically, first wife. Just trying to be accurate. That's all," said DD.

Lauren decided not to rise to the bait.

"You seem awfully well-informed about women and marriage considering you're still single," added Renata.

"I've known you three couples for so long that I feel I'm effectively married to a third of each of you women. But I just get the best bits of you."

"You think that this is the best of us do you?" said Michaela in a mock-threatening manner.

"Yes, based on what your husbands say about you," said DD struggling to keep his tone as factual as possible. "Would one of you ladies please pass me the salad bowl?"

The salad bowl remained on the table.

"Come on," he said. "No need to be upset with me. Not yet, anyway."

Throughout the main course the conversation roamed over subjects far and wide.

"DD, how's the lasagne?" asked Lauren, spoon in hand, ready to dish him a second serving.

"Lauren, there's only one way to describe your lasagne." He paused for effect, noticing that Michaela had just taken a mouthful of food. "And that's to say it's just like making love to Michaela."

"Wha… Wha… Wha… What?" choked Michaela.

“Michaela, you should get that repetitiveness checked out. It sounds like you’ve got a problem there.”

“And how’s my lasagne like that DD?” asked Lauren.

“Like what?” said DD being deliberately obtuse, purely for effect.

“How’s my lasagne just like making love to Michaela?”

“Because when you’ve had it once, you just want more and more,” DD replied, offering his empty plate for a second helping.

“What! What! What! What did you just say?” exploded Michaela, almost choking again on her food.

“I do believe that I’m paying both Lauren’s lasagne, and your love-making capabilities, a great compliment. David, you’re her husband, am I right here?”

“You certainly are DD.”

“How can you say that?” exclaimed Michaela, smacking her husband’s arm.

DD leaned towards Reece in a conspiratorial manner. “David’s going to have a lot of explaining to do the next time he starts making amorous moves on his wife,” he chuckled.

“Hey Michaela, you know that if you ever want your husband disposed of, I have a friend who can do it for you,” interrupted DD, giving her a grossly-exaggerated wink. “And he pays a very good rate too.”

DD left the statement hanging while he took another mouthful of food. All present knew they were being set up for a line, but DD ate his food in the silence, knowing that eventually someone would rise to his bait.

“He would actually pay to do that?” said Renata.

Kobus shook his head, knowing his wife was being set up by DD.

“Yes, and he pays a really good rate of £30 per kilo of body-weight too.”

DD was building the set-up nicely, and again let the silence hang.

“What does he do with the body?”

“Actually, I’m not sure. But I do know that he owns a business that makes cook-at-home lasagne.”

“Thanks for that little gem DD,” said Lauren, firmly closing out that line of conversation.

“Have I told you about my brilliant idea for a new business? I’m starting my own company to launch it,” enthused DD.

“You being serious?” asked Kobus.

"Absolutely. It's a self-improvement programme for women that I've developed," said DD, waving his fork at the three women around the table.

"What's this programme called?" asked Michaela suspiciously.

"It's called *Unleash The Whore Within*," DD replied with a proud smile.

"That's charming," said Michaela sarcastically.

DD nodded. Reece noticed how DD held the pause, recognising this as his trademark characteristic when telling a story.

"Would you like to know more?" DD eventually enquired of Michaela.

"If we must."

"My research shows that beneath the prim-and-proper persona that every woman exudes, is a latent, whore-like tendency that wants to be unleashed. Women want an alter-ego they can use to vent unbridled sexual-lust on their husbands." He paused briefly to look around the table. Three pairs of female-eyes glared contempt at him.

"You'll like this," he continued, "because the programme is a single, two-hour lecture that you women attend. It's where I explain the principles that enable you to *Unleash The Whore Within.* At the end, I hand out an action plan of all the things you need to do to deliver the ultimate in sexual bliss for your husband. But do you know what the best bit is?"

The customary pause followed as DD took a sip of wine.

"It only costs £99!" he concluded excitedly.

"You seriously believe that women will pay £99 and then actually attend a lecture called *Unleash The Whore Within*?" asked Renata incredulously.

"No, not at all" said DD.

Silence again, as DD waited for someone to respond.

"How do you make money then?" asked Lauren in an exasperated tone.

"Of course women are never going to buy a product with a name like that. But imagine how many men will want to buy it as a gift for their wives and girlfriends. That's where I'm going to make an absolute fortune. But I still haven't come to the best bit of this idea yet."

He took another infuriatingly-long sip of wine.

"How many women do you think are actually going to turn up to a venue with a big banner at the front saying *Unleash The Whore Within*?" A pause duly ensued.

"None!" DD exclaimed. "I won't even have to run a single lecture," he proclaimed victoriously.

"You talk absolute crap," said Michaela, realising that DD hadn't been the slightest bit serious.

"It's absolute genius," said DD.

Reece put a hand on DD's shoulder, "I have to admit that's inspired thinking."

"Please don't encourage him Reece," begged Lauren.

"See, Reece recognises great thinking, and he's an expert in this area."

"And you're the greatest thinker ever aren't you DD?" said Lauren, tousling his hair as she passed behind him, clearing the plates.

"Sarcasm doesn't suit you Lauren. It's the lowest form of wit," said DD.

"Well it suits you because you're the lowest form of life," she responded matter-of-factly. "Why my husband chose a best-man at our marriage, who in reality is the worst-man on the planet is beyond me?"

"You know that a comment like that will definitely get you on the front-cover of Whore & Bitch magazine don't you?"

"Don't make me angry. You won't like me when I'm angry," yelled Lauren from the kitchen.

"I don't like you when you aren't angry, so it won't make much of a difference," DD yelled back, desperately trying to keep a straight face.

"Did you know that at one time I used to think you were hot, young, sexy and gorgeous?" he added.

"And when did that stop?" enquired Lauren.

"Just now when you started yelling at me. When you were a little girl, innocently playing with your toys and dolls, did you ever imagine that you'd grow up to be an absolute bitch?"

"No. I don't believe that thought ever crossed my mind DD."

"Fortunately, you're still a little way from getting there."

"How far?" asked Lauren.

DD held up his first-finger and thumb, showing the smallest of gaps between them.

"You know DD, during the moment of conception, when the male's sperm race to be the one to fertilise the female's egg, the particular one that is successful is considered to be the best out of the 120-million in the race to survive. If you were the best out of those 120-million, then there must have been some real crap in the ones that didn't make it!" Lauren hit back.

"Do you know that I get really turned on when a woman yells at me? And what's more, I think it will be a really good thing if you and Steve get divorced," said DD.

"Why?"

"Because then your ex-husband and I can spend more time out boozing whenever we feel like it. And as an added bonus, you could be my bit-of-fluff-on-the-side."

"If I ever become your bit-of-fluff, then my life will be in a very dire situation." DD and Lauren both laughed at this.

"If you think that any woman would ever want to be your bit-of-fluff-on-the-side, as you so articulately put it, then you don't understand women," said Renata.

"You think us men don't understand women?" asked DD. "It's the other way round. You women don't understand us men. And I have proof," he added.

"Really?" asked Renata.

"Really," replied DD. "Do you want to hear it?"

"Do we have a choice?" she said in a resigned manner.

"No, so listen closely." Once again DD paused, just to infuriate the women a little more.

"First, you women only have X-chromosomes, whereas we men have both X- and Y-chromosomes. So in actual fact, we men are half-women already. Which is why we understand you, but you don't understand us. And secondly," he continued, "every man was once a woman during an earlier reincarnation of our spirit."

"What crap is this?" asked Michaela.

"Guys, isn't this true?" DD appealed, motioning to the males around the table with his wine glass. The three husbands all gave restrained nods of agreement.

They had no idea where DD was going with this line of conversation but it was always amusing, and often gave them a new perspective on life. There was a very-high chance it was all bullshit, but DD was able to get away with saying things to their wives that they would never dare say themselves.

"Every man knows that reincarnation is a fact of reality, because we men evolved from women in a past reincarnation. Hence we know it to be true. You women haven't yet made this advancement of gender, which is why you all deny it. Of course this complete ignorance you all possess isn't really your fault." He paused to let the last comment sink in. "But eventually you'll understand the cause of it as you transcend through reincarnation."

"You're saying that when women die, we'll be reincarnated as men?"

"Absolutely not!" replied DD vehemently.

"But you just said that men are reincarnations of women." Michaela protested.

"Yes," said DD. "But you can't go from a woman to a man in one reincarnation. It's too big a leap for you to take."

"So what's the next reincarnation for a woman then?"

"A dung beetle," said DD authoritatively.

"A dung beetle?" repeated Michaela absentmindedly, not believing what she just heard.

"A dung beetle," confirmed DD. "It's a good move for you. It enables you start doing something useful with your lives. You might spend your short, dung beetle life pushing crap around — but at least you won't be full of it."

Reece was finding it hard not to grin. To cover up his struggle he asked "What happens after that?"

"The next reincarnation after the dung beetle is a pig, which again is a great improvement from being a woman. And then a dog, followed by an eagle, and then into a leopard, and onward to the final reincarnation where you transcend into that ultimate of all species — a man," concluded DD triumphantly, banging his fist on his chest for added effect.

The men sniggered quietly to themselves, wary of enjoying the story too much.

"This is why you're destined to remain single for the rest of your life," said Michaela. "You are such a misogynist."

"What's a misogynist?" asked DD.

"Someone who hates women, you ignorant pig."

"Actually, the ignorant pig was four reincarnations ago," said DD "Anyway, you know I don't hate you. This is just my way of showing affection for you without saying things that will get me into trouble with your husbands."

"You've got the weirdest way of showing affection for somebody," said Lauren.

"But that's the whole point of being different — not doing the same as everybody else. Life would be so boring if everything was always going to be the same. And so predictable."

"What do you say about that, Reece?" asked Kobus.

"He's got a point. Taking an interesting perspective always stretches your thinking," Reece replied.

"Talking about interesting perspectives, I've got a very topical one for you, considering we're having lunch," said DD.

"Stop. No more perspectives from you. Just be quiet for once," said Renata.

"Imagine you three married-couples are in a plane crossing the Andes and it crashes," continued DD unabated. Three pairs of female-eyes rolled in disdain.

"You three guys survive and your wives all die. There's no food, and after a couple of days you're starving — and you decide to eat the women. The question is this. *In what order would you eat the bodies?* I mean, would each of you want to eat your own wife first, last, or in the middle?"

"I can't believe you're asking this question," said Michaela, completely dumbfounded.

"It's lunchtime so it's topical. Anyway, shut up. The food doesn't speak" said DD nodding towards her, and instantly receiving a look-of-death in return.

"So, you guys. What's your answer? Who do you eat first?"

The three husbands all declined to respond for fear of incriminating themselves. Reece thought this the wise thing for them to do. He didn't know how he'd answer the question either, if it was asked of him.

"Reece, you're a creative thinker. How would you answer that question?" said DD turning toward him.

Reece found that if he thought about a problem that wasn't really his to answer, he usually couldn't come up with anything snappy, or out of the ordinary. However, when he was put on the spot and expected to say something instantly, he knew he could just let his mind go blank — and then say the first thing that came into his head. This was a peculiar, but useful, capability Reece knew he possessed.

"A stew," he said without a pause, "then you wouldn't know who was who in it. And I'm sure it would be tender, delicious — and very tasteful," he added as an afterthought to appease the about-to-be-eaten females.

"A very good answer," said Lauren. "Unlike DD's tasteless question."

"Nice comment man," said DD, giving Reece a gentle punch on the arm.

"So what's a good example of creative thinking in business Reece?" asked David.

"You might believe it's about big-picture thinking — the next new thing to change the world. Occasionally it is, but most of the time it isn't. Businesses usually want small changes to the things they already do — but something that will have a big impact for them. Often, the smaller the change, the more appealing it is to them, and that's where the creative thinking comes in. Looking at the same thing that everybody else looks at, but seeing something very different."

"I can give you an example of making small changes for a big difference," said DD. "Just using the keyboard of my computer, I've created the world's strongest online-password, that's absolutely impossible to crack."

The customary pause from DD before he continued.

"It's a sixteen-digit password that changes every time. It's so secure that even I don't know what it is."

"How can you have a password that changes every time — and that you don't know?" asked David.

"That's the clever bit, so listen up. I close my eyes and press six keys at random. To make a password more secure, you should incorporate unusual keystrokes that other people don't normally use. So I then press the backspace key six-times. I then press one, two, three and four — and it's done. How about that for a really secure password?"

"So your password is six random keys, six backspace presses, and then 1-2-3-4?"

"Certainly is," confirmed DD.

"In a slightly-perverse way you've got my point across," admitted Reece.

"DD, you are such an arsehole," said Renata. "Why is it you always have to take things to such extremes?"

"Because that's where things get interesting. If you have beautiful-black on the left side and wonderful-white on the right side, then who wants to be in the ghastly-grey middle-ground?"

That's an interesting approach for thinking about things Reece thought. Be at the edges, no matter where the edges are. Just avoid the middle-ground which is where the majority of people will be. He made a mental note to develop that into a thinking tool in the future.

"I say provocative things to dislodge people's thinking. If you're in the middle-ground then that's just existing. But being at the extremes — that's living. That's real thinking."

"Talking about not being the same as everyone else, someone seems to think that getting a personalised number plate for his car is a wonderful idea," said Renata, rolling her eyes in the direction of her husband. "I think it's a complete waste of time and money."

"Then maybe I can help you there," replied DD, pursing his lips in thought.

“Hey Kobus,” said DD in a loud-and-stern manner, that was clearly intended to get the attention of the whole table. “Renata says you’re looking to get a personalised number plate.”

“That’s right.”

“Man, I just want you to know that I think it’s a brilliant idea. Totally brilliant.”

“Thanks DD.”

“However,” said DD raising his finger for effect, “there is just one thing that we’ll need to consider.” The use of the word *we* was clearly intended to make this sound like a comment coming from the entire table.

“And what’s that?” asked Kobus, feeling justifiably concerned about what DD’s next comment would be.

“Well,” said DD, using the thumb and first-finger of each hand to form a rectangle in the air, the size of a car registration plate, “we’re going to have to use awfully-small letters to get *COMPLETELY USELESS WANKER* onto a number plate.”

The table dissolved into laughter. Renata laid her hand on DD’s forearm and said, “thanks for the help.”

After dessert, Reece and DD stood in the afternoon sun, talking. Reece had discovered that DD was an engineer who designed new products for a multi-national home-appliance manufacturer.

“How do you come up with all these things that you say?” asked Reece.

“Man, sometimes my mouth just starts saying something — and I have no idea how it’s going to end. I just trust that my mind will be able to finish it off in time. It also has to do with the fact that this is kind of a safe environment,” he said, waving his arm in the direction of the others inside. “I can say whatever I want — and get away with it. Well, most of the time. It sometimes feels like a chance to put my mind to the test to see what it’s really capable of.”

“Do you get the opportunity to think like this in your work?” asked Reece.

“When we’re developing new ideas for products, it helps to be very open and free-wheeling in thinking, to explore for new ideas and opportunities. How about you?”

“Same. When we’re opening up new opportunities, absolutely anything goes, and strange thinking is encouraged. Obviously outside of that time you have to behave, and think normally.”

“It’s sometimes hard to behave normally isn’t it?” said DD with a wink.

Reece tended to judge people quickly — sometimes too quickly — but now he sensed a bond of unspoken-understanding with DD. It felt intuitively comfortable to him.

"I believe that our minds are much smarter than we are. This may seem like a paradox, but I think many people expend a lot of energy restraining their mind rather than letting it do what it's truly capable of. Your *Unleash The Whore Within* programme might have a lot of success as an *Unleash The Genius Within* programme instead."

Lauren had walked over to join the two of them. "I hope this guy's not giving you too much grief," she said to Reece, affectionately squeezing DD's arm. "He's in London himself next week — aren't you DD?"

DD nodded.

"What are you doing there?" asked Reece.

"I'm attending a conference for four days."

"Is it the *Potential of the Human Mind* conference?"

"Yes, you know of it?"

"I'm speaking at it," said Reece.

"That's a weird coincidence!" exclaimed Lauren.

"It is," agreed DD. "Will you be there just on the day you're speaking?"

"No. They invited me to attend for the whole duration and to stay at the hotel on full-board too. They were really generous — especially as it seems to be a very over-priced conference."

"I know," said DD. "Fortunately, my company are paying, and that's the only reason I'm going. What subject are you speaking on?"

"The application of different thinking styles to create new opportunities."

"Sounds interesting. How did you get the speaking gig?"

"I wrote an article called *Popcorn and the Art of Fine Thinking* that was published a few months back. They must have seen that."

"I read that article." said DD. "And that's why you're speaking?"

"It must be. I got the invitation a few weeks ago, and that's all that I can think of that might have got the organiser's attention."

Reece didn't realise how wrong he was in this assumption…

Chapter 11 Saturday overnight

The leisurely lunch drifted on until the setting winter sun signalled the end of the afternoon. DD had offered to drive Reece back to the airport. On the way, DD explained that after five-years of service, his company allowed employees to attend any work-related conference of their choice, where all expenses were paid. Naturally, everyone chose an overseas event — and he'd chosen next week's London event.

Reece had begun to understand how similar his and DD's individual fields of work were. DD designed tangible products, whereas Reece designed the intangible business models and services. He'd felt surprisingly comfortable with DD's brashness, which contrasted with his own more-reserved and relaxed approach to life. He thought DD to be one of the most enigmatic characters he'd ever met, in the way that he could switch his thinking between a serious, work-related focus, and then instantly flip to the totally nonsense-related conversational topics he'd been hearing over lunch. Whichever way DD's switch was flipped, it always produced a very creative flow of conversation. Reece was looking forward to some interesting talk-time with DD at the conference.

Four hours later, flight VA218 was at its cruising altitude of 34,000 feet, heading due-North on its way to Heathrow. After a splendid three-course dinner, Reece opened up his copy of *Mind the Future* and skipped to the page with the Post-it note on. The way the message *DON'T GO AHEAD WITH YOUR DREAM SHARING WEBSITE* was phrased, could be read as a quiet statement, *and* as an active threat, both at the same time.

He realised the Post-it note was still on the original page of the book where he'd found it. He considered that this page had been specifically selected, but upon reading it, nothing seemed to stand-out in any way.

The stewardess refilled his wine glass for the third time as she passed.

Perhaps the Post-it note wasn't that important and he'd been over analysing it. Maybe he should just forget about it for a while. It had been a busy thirty-six hours. There was yesterday's presentation, last night's overnight flight, this morning's presentation, then a great lunch with an interesting series of conversations with DD, and now a flight back to London. Going to a different continent for a day always took its toll on you. He thought it amusing how his parents would go to a local seaside-town for a day out, and here he was, going to the southern tip of Africa for a day. With this thought going through his mind, and a slight smile on his lips, he fell into a deep sleep.

A little while later, flight attendant Veronica de la Rey walked down her aisle and noticed the passenger in seat 6F had fallen asleep. She took his half-full wine glass off the armrest and put his book into the seat-pocket in front of him. Reaching into the locker above his head, she removed a folded blanket. Standing in the aisle, and facing toward the other passengers, she held the blanket in her outstretched arms, and let it fall to unroll itself. She gently shook the blanket a couple of times before placing it over Reece's legs, just as she had been shown in her cabin crew training course.

She didn't know that Reece had worked with her airline in the past to develop innovative ways to boost the inflight customer experience. One of the minor items he'd recommended was this very subtle look-at-me-and-notice-what-I'm-doing tactic of shaking-out the blanket, to act as a subliminal-signal for the other travellers of how she was taking care of a passenger in her charge.

Veronica de la Rey noticed that her passenger had a slight smile on his face, and she wondered what he was dreaming about, before moving on down her aisle.

Reece had slept so deeply that he missed breakfast and had to be woken up to prepare for landing. They disembarked quickly and he walked out through the terminal and was soon on the Heathrow Express train heading back to Paddington. He reached into his carry-on to retrieve his book — but it wasn't there.

Damn!

He realised he'd left it on the plane somewhere when he fell asleep. It seemed a really interesting book, and he decided it would be easier to buy another copy rather than try to get it back from the airline's lost property.

The train slowed as it approached Paddington station, and he realised he could go to the same bookshop to buy a second copy. He walked into the WH Smith store knowing precisely where to go. There was only one copy of the book left. He suspected it to be the damaged copy he'd left behind yesterday, but was pleasantly surprised to find it was in pristine condition. He took the book to the check out.

"Can I help you?" asked the female sales assistant.

"I'll take this and be paying by credit card," said Reece, handing her the book. She processed the payment and put the book in a plastic bag.

"This seems to be exceptionally popular this morning," she said, handing him the bag and his credit card.

"Have you read it, Isobel?" he asked, quickly glancing down at her name tag.

“No I haven’t. But you enjoy it,” she replied, turning to serve the next customer.

Reece slipped the book into his carry-on and headed towards the underground station. A little while later, he was on the tube-train heading for home. With a twenty-five minute journey ahead of him, he got out the new book. On an impulse, he quickly flicked through the pages to make sure there was no Post-it note inside. As he did so, a flash of green in the pages caught his eye. He hesitantly turned back the pages one-by-one; rather hoping he’d been mistaken.

He was not mistaken. A square, lime-green Post-it note was stuck to one of the pages.

This time he knew without any doubt, that the handwritten message was meant for him. It read

REECE TASSICKER

DON’T MAKE THE DREAM SHARING WEBSITE

Chapter 12 Sunday afternoon

Reece exited the Fulham Broadway tube station, headed straight back to his apartment, changed, and went for a run to clear his head. But his head wouldn't clear. It was full of lime-green Post-it notes with his name on.

When he got back, he saw on his calendar he had an arrangement to meet a friend for lunch. He didn't feel like going out, so he called and cancelled. As he sat at the desk in his apartment, his eyes were drawn to the neatly-ordered stack of different sizes and colours of Post-it notes that he kept on the desk corner. What he'd previously considered as simple, but useful items of stationery, now appeared to him as a tapering, technicolour, tower of taunt. He realised he didn't feel like staying in — not alone with so many Post-it notes around him.

Truthfully, he wasn't quite sure how he felt. A sentence on a Post-it note seemed quite a gentle way of sending someone a message — compared to many other possible approaches. Like finding a horse's severed-head in your bed. Not going ahead with his dream-sharing website wasn't a big issue for him. If he didn't, that may well save him quite a lot of time.

He realised that what did concern him was the fact that someone knew precisely what he was going to do.

They couldn't possibly have put a Post-it note in every book in WH Smith.

No, the first damaged copy he'd flicked through didn't have one in, and he'd swapped it over for the good copy that did have a Post-it note in.

He'd made that choice.

He realised he was feeling totally unnerved. The fact that someone knew precisely what he was going to do and so could prepare something for him — even if it was as innocuous as a handwritten Post-it note — was deeply concerning to him. If he didn't go ahead with the dream-sharing website, he'd still be concerned that someone was able to know his every move. At least with a horse's head in his bed, he'd have known who it came from.

To take his mind off this line of thought, he went down to the nearby Westfield shopping mall which contained a multi-screen cinema complex — where he watched two movies. It comforted Reece to have so many people around him. He was also grateful that he had the conference to attend later that day.

The conference was unusual in having a late-Sunday afternoon registration with an evening social event. Despite it being residential, Reece still considered it to be an exceptionally-expensive conference to attend. As a speaker, though, he was given full-access for all four days, including the complimentary accommodation and meals. He'd appreciated the residential aspect as he found the evening-socials and meal-times to be excellent networking opportunities. It also avoided the need for commuting across London too. The Post-it notes had made staying in a hotel seem surprisingly more appealing than being alone in his apartment.

The venue was the five-star Churchill hotel on Portman Square. It was two blocks off Oxford Street, close to the Marble Arch end. The hotel was barely a mile away from Paddington station, the source of the bizarre Post-it notes. Reece thought this was a little too-coincidental, when the conference could have been anywhere in the south-east of England.

Registration was as slickly organised as any he'd seen. While one young-man from the conference team welcomed him, another was using his details to check him into the hotel, and within a few minutes he was in his room.

There was a conference welcome-pack on the desk, perfectly positioned, facing the chair. He sat down and opened it to find there was surprisingly little inside. Just an agenda for the conference, a list of attendees with their name, company and job title; a Conference Navigator Guide, and a bright-orange device that looked like a smart phone with a belt-clip attached. Usually, there was a vast amount of marketing blurb from the sponsors — but not here. He realised he hadn't seen any sponsors' desks or banners downstairs either — which was unusual. But given what they were charging to attend the conference, maybe they didn't need sponsors.

Reece flicked through the Conference Navigator Guide, relieved at not finding another Post-it note inside. It was a booklet designed to help conference attendees to gain maximum value from the speakers, and from each other. Given the four-days of time people were committing, he thought it an innovative way of collecting all the extracted-value from the conference in one convenient notebook.

He was browsing through the contents when there was a knock on the door. Reece opened it to find an attractive, dark-haired woman in a black, two-piece skirt suit.

"Good afternoon Mister Tassicker. Welcome to the Churchill. I'm Heather Macreedy, the conference director. I hope everything's in order for you?"

"Yes, thanks. And do come in."

She entered, and they sat down in two chairs by the desk, where the contents of Reece's conference pack lay open.

"As one of our speakers, I'd just like to explain the conference structure, and to check if there's anything you need. This is the first time we're running *The Potential of the Human Mind* conference, and it's been surprisingly popular. We're covering a number of different themes including the capabilities of the mind; extremes of usage; perspectives of human development; and also the application of the mind to design and creative thinking, which of course is your speciality. All of the main presentations will be in the large auditorium. Some of the other sessions are being run in parallel as separate streams. You'll need to choose which of those you want to attend."

She picked up the agenda from the table. "You're scheduled to speak on Thursday, the final day, straight after lunch. That may change if it's alright with you?"

"Of course," said Reece. "I'm staying for the full duration. But why might my speaking time change? I thought the schedule was fixed."

"If there's an issue with a speaker in an earlier session, we may call on you to present at short notice. Is that a problem?"

"No. My presentation is complete and I'm ready to go." In reality, Reece had barely started work on his presentation, but an earlier slot would mean a bigger audience than speaking after lunch on the last day. Heather noticed a very-slight reddening of Reece's cheeks and an increase in his blinking rate as he made this comment. She doubted its truth, but continued regardless.

"There's also your Contactor," she said, picking up the bright-orange device from the table. "It helps you find the people at the conference that you'd like to meet. And it helps others to find you too."

"How does that work?" asked Reece curiously.

"A problem at conferences is that you may know the name of someone you'd like to speak with, but you don't know what they look like. With the Contactor device, you select the names of the people you want to meet from the pre-loaded attendee list. When you are close to any of them, it will vibrate and display their name and photograph. The same thing happens on their screen with your name and photo. The vibration stops after a few seconds so not to irritate you. The interface is similar to any smartphone contacts-page and the instructions are here on the back of the attendee list," she said, turning the list over to show him.

"There is just one thing," she added. "We'd like to ask that you wear your Contactor at all times. Even if *you* aren't looking to meet other people, *they* may be looking to meet you. The battery will last the full four-days of the conference too."

"Sounds useful," said Reece, thinking he'd enter some names into the device later.

"If there's anything else I can help you with please let me know."

"Will do," said Reece, escorting her to the door.

He'd meant to prepare his presentation yesterday afternoon in Johannesburg, but a rather pleasant lunch had put a stop to that. Reece took a beer out of the mini-bar fridge, opened up his laptop and spent the rest of the evening creating his presentation.

Chapter 13 Monday 05h00

Reece had dialled a five o'clock wake-up call into the bedside phone. At that precise time, an automated message used a well-clipped, English tone, to wish him a good-morning and remind him this was his wake-up call.

He had no recollection of any dreams from the night before. This wasn't surprising, as last night's sleep was in a different bed, and the previous two sleeps had been on aero-planes. With no dreams to write up, Reece changed, and went out for his run. The hotel was close to Hyde Park, and he decided that would be his destination. A short distance along Oxford Street, past the Marble Arch, across Park Lane and he was into Hyde Park. With open spaces and good running surfaces, Reece was free to overlay some powerful thinking onto his running. Issue number one today for the Council's Counsel was…

Reece regularly did something that very few others ever did. He liked to *think about thinking*. Everybody thinks. We do it all the time. In fact we can't stop thinking. If we try not to think, then we are thinking by the very act of not wanting to think. Thinking takes very little energy, we can do it anywhere, any time and we can do as much of it as we want — all for free.

The problem with thinking occurred when you wanted to do some deep and focused thinking about an important topic. This was frequently hard to achieve due to the inces-sant chattering going on within your mind. Barely had you started to focus on your issue, when your mind would lead you off into some vaguely connected area. And within a few moments of that, it led you off into yet another area, which was now far from the original issue you wanted to focus on. Even when you recognised that this had happened, and you re-focused back on the original topic, your mind very quickly drifted into other areas, again and again.

Early on in his use of creative thinking, Reece had found his chattering mind to be a complete nuisance. Intuitively, it seemed a useful capability to let the mind wander, but the problem was that the mind would wander off and get lost. So he'd started to explore for ways to quieten his chattering mind. Ways that would allow it to focus solely on the topic he wanted to focus on.

One approach he used was meditation, where he was able to slow his mind down so the chattering became an unobtrusive whisper. His mind would still wander a little, as he wasn't expert enough to completely calm it. But the wandering was so slow and peaceful, that it was much easier to guide. Meditation was all well and good when you were in the privacy of your own home, but it wasn't a practical approach in the office or when with clients.

Another approach was a range of pen-and-paper thinking tools he'd developed, which had to be completed within a fifteen-minute timeframe. The intense concentration needed to achieve the set-purpose of the tool was a little like having to complete a test in just a few minutes. The time-pressure kept you extremely focused on what you had to achieve.

A third approach he'd discovered was the one he was using right now. Reece had found that running was the perfect way to quieten his chattering mind. While running, you had to be consciously aware of what was going on around you; where you were going; what the ground was like beneath your feet; were there any risks of twisting an ankle; and many other considerations too. Reece found that this seemed to still the chatter completely. It was as though the part of his brain that liked to start the chatter was so preoccupied with all these running related issues, it left the remainder of his brain free to think on his topic — without distraction.

Whenever his mind was engaged on a thinking issue while he was running, he could easily develop thirty or forty interesting thoughts. This was why he always carried a Sony IC digital voice-recorder with him. He got so many good ideas, that without his Sony IC, he'd never remember them all.

Reece found there to be a beneficial, symbiotic side-effect to thinking while running. The act of running allowed his mind to focus on the issue he wanted to think about, while the fact that he was deeply-focused on an interesting issue, took his mind off the exertion he experienced while running. With a good topic resonating in his mind, Reece felt that running was as relaxing as meditating, which considering he was covering ground quite fast, seemed paradoxical to him.

These approaches to thinking allowed him to achieve some unusual new insights and thoughts on big issues for his clients — and also for himself.

He thought about some of the things he'd changed with his running. He used to get knee and lower-leg running injuries a few years ago, and no matter how much he stretched beforehand, he couldn't prevent these injuries. Reece had accidentally found an article on *how stretching can be bad for you.* That didn't make sense to Reece, but he thought he'd try it anyway. He was surprised to find that not-stretching reduced the number of muscle pulls he had considerably.

Another article he'd read on running was about breathing patterns. He'd always been a two-two breather while running — which was two-paces to breathe in, and then two-paces to breathe out. The article showed how breathing in an odd-number pattern could help reduce injuries. It was based on the fact that when you exhaled while running, you emptied your diaphragm more than you did when breathing normally. This meant that when your foot landed during this maximum point of exhalation, there was less cushioning of the upper-body on the lower-body, due to the overly-empty lungs. With a two-two breathing pattern, this less-cushioned step was consistently being done on the same foot. By simply breathing in for three-paces, then out for the usual two, the least-cushioned step alternated between the left and right foot. Reece had adopted this style of breathing and found it eliminated his remaining knee problems.

Sometimes the most beneficial improvements in many aspects of life came from unexpected and relatively minor changes. This was the philosophy he used with his business clients too.

To boost his own thinking, and to discover fresh perspectives, Reece had created four imaginary personas in his mind, all of whom had very different styles of thinking. These personas formed the Council he'd elected to lead and govern him. He'd designed them to take differing views on whatever the issue was, and to make suggestions as to how to move the thinking forward. He would give them an issue to ponder, and then he'd just listen in to their discussion in his mind. The advice and ideas he received from them were their Counsel to him.

His Council's Counsel.

Reece trusted his Council's Counsel implicitly. They resided in his mind, and they were absolutely dedicated to doing the best they could for him and helping him to be successful in all that he did.

While Reece shared a lot with his clients about what he did and how his team worked, he didn't share the fact that much of his work came from his Council's Counsel. *That would have sounded too weird to them.*

On today's run, the first issue for the Council's Counsel was the matter of the two lime-green Post-it notes. As his feet covered path after path around Hyde Park, the Council's Counsel covered option after option, concerning the two Post-it notes.

You think the Post-it notes are a threat?

Mentat12's response was a threat, wasn't it?

Somebody doesn't want us to do the dream-sharing website.

Is it a big deal if we don't?

I suppose not.

All that the Post-it notes and Mentat12 want, is for us not to go ahead with it.

Why do we feel fear about this?

Maybe we should be intrigued by it.

Why don't they want the website to go ahead?

That's a good question.

Possibly they are setting up their own dream-sharing website.

Would competition drive this level of effort to dissuade us?

OK then. How did they get the Post-it notes in the books?

Was it a trick of some kind?

I don't see how they could do a trick like that.

Magicians do unbelievable tricks on television.

We've never been able to figure out how they do those things.

True.

These were just two Post-it notes.

And when did Post-it notes become the weapon of choice for anyone seriously considering harm to someone?

Good point.

Perhaps this is an opportunity.

For what?

Should we try to contact the Post-it note inserters?

Why?

To suggest that we could work with them together in some way.

Interesting idea.

Reece listened in as the Council's Counsel took many different directions. He captured the most interesting thoughts on his voice-recorder for consideration later. As he headed back to the hotel he was feeling surprisingly energised, and so he increased his running pace. He felt that interesting things were going to happen at the conference, and that today was going to be a great day.

Unfortunately, breakfast had other plans for Reece Tassicker.

Chapter 14 Monday 08h00

It was a glorious, summer morning in London, and at the end of his run, Reece spent fifteen minutes walking aimlessly around the garden in Portman Square to cool down. After that, he'd gone back to his room, showered and reviewed his presentation. He refined it until he was completely satisfied, and then headed down to the restaurant for breakfast.

After visiting the buffet table and filling a bowl with fresh fruit salad, muesli and yoghurt, he spotted a table set for six, with only three people on. A quick round of introductions, then Reece sat down to join them. He'd just taken the first spoonful of muesli when he heard his phone chirp. Entering his phone's access code, he saw there was one new text message. He opened the message. It read:

YOU WILL SHORTLY RECEIVE A CALL ABOUT THE DREAM WEBSITE YOU ARE BUILDING. DO NOT PROCEED WITH IT. YOU HAVE BEEN WARNED!

You have been warned!

Reece felt uncomfortably-hot, as a brief wave of nausea washed over him.

"Are you alright?" asked the woman sat next to him "You've gone white as a sheet."

The nausea passed.

"Sorry. Yes. I'm fine. I just got a bit of..." He couldn't finish the sentence because he didn't know how to. As he stared uncomprehendingly at the message on his phone, a rectangle appeared on the screen with the name Brad Berry centred in it. Two coloured squares appeared below the name, a green one showing ACCEPT and a red one showing DECLINE. He couldn't comprehend why the text message had suddenly changed to this. Then the phone rang loudly, startling him. The screen had changed because of an incoming call from Brad Berry. Brad was his friend who was building the dream-sharing website for him.

"Yes?" Reece answered nervously.

"Morning Reece, it's Brad. I just want to give you a heads-up on where I'm at with your dream website, mate. I was working on the visual styling yesterday and have started coding the HTML. It's very straightforward and I'm sure I'll be able to get it done to a demo-stage by this evening. What I need from you is..."

Reece was initially dumbstruck. He'd been reading the warning in the text message that he would receive a call about the website — when he immediately did. Somebody was messing around with him. Playing a joke that had gone too far. He'd regained his voice. And it was an angry voice too.

"Listen Brad. Are you behind all this? Why did you just send me a text and then call me?" shouted Reece into his phone.

"What? I didn't send a text. I've just called you."

"You're the only person in my phone contacts who knows about me building this website. So don't screw around with me!"

"I'm not screwing around with you. I'm just calling to tell you that I've done what you asked."

"When did I ask you to call me?" demanded Reece. "What game are you trying to play?" he added angrily.

"Listen mate, I'm sorry if I've got you at a bad time. You said you'd be at a conference for most of this week and that I should call you early Monday morning before it started. And that's what I'm doing. That's all."

Reece recalled that this was indeed true. He *had* asked Brad to call him.

"Listen Brad, I'm sorry for this. My mistake. I'll call you back later," and he pressed the red square on the screen to end the call.

He shifted his gaze slightly, and looked past his phone. He realised his bowl of muesli was now a couple-of-feet below his phone. He was momentarily confused, until he realised he was now standing up. He must have also been very loud while speaking to Brad, as many people in the restaurant were looking at him peculiarly. As he looked at them, they nervously turned away, avoiding his gaze.

"Is there a problem, Mister Tassicker?" enquired a vaguely-familiar voice from right behind him. He turned to see Heather Macreedy standing there. "You seem a little upset about something."

"No. I'm fine, really. Thanks."

A few people were still looking in his direction, so he gave them an exaggerated smile and mouthed the word *sorry* towards them. He did this several times in different directions. He realised he must have been speaking exceptionally loudly for so many people to have heard him.

"Would you like to come to my office for a minute — if that would help," Heather said to him discreetly. As Reece was feeling distinctly embarrassed about what had just happened, this seemed a face-saving course of action to take. He excused himself from the table, and followed Heather out of the restaurant, down a number of corridors, until they came to a door with a sign saying PRIVATE. NO ADMITTANCE. Heather held her access card against a touch pad on the wall, which caused a small light to change from red to green. There was a substantial click near the door handle, which allowed Heather to open the door, and to lead Reece into her office.

Chapter 15 Monday 08h30

They were in a windowless room, the size of a single-garage. The magnolia-painted walls were bare of decoration. It looked the kind of lifeless room that would be forever destined to store broken furniture. Near the door was a round table covered by a burgundy tablecloth, just large enough to accommodate the four burgundy-cushioned conference chairs around it. Behind that was a large rectangular table, also covered by a burgundy tablecloth. This table held several laptops connected to a bank of three large, flat-screen monitors. A spaghetti-mess of cables connected the laptops and monitors to some other small boxes adorned with connection-ports of varying types and small panels of flashing lights. Reece couldn't see what was on the monitors as they were facing away from him, and towards a man of Middle Eastern appearance, who was tapping away on one of the keyboards. Heather offered no introduction to the man.

There was another table with an open laptop on, that Heather appeared to be using as a desk. She went over, picked up a green folder, and then indicated to Reece to take a seat at the round table. She sat down on the opposite side of the table to him.

"I hope everything's alright? You seemed a bit concerned by something over breakfast," said Heather.

"I had to fly to Johannesburg and back over the weekend. The lack of sleep may have got to me," he said. "That, and the fact there's been some weird things happening over the past few days. Nothing for you to worry about."

"That sounds intriguing. What kind of weird things do you mean?"

"No, I don't want to burden you with them. I'm sure you've got a lot going on with the conference."

"Please, I'd be quite interested to know what these things are," she said.

"Don't worry. It's fine," said Reece firmly, in an effort to end the discussion. He didn't think she needed to know what was happening — and she probably wouldn't believe him, anyway. He'd end up looking more of a fool than he had just now in the restaurant.

"What if I told you that other people have also had some strange things happen to them over the last few days?" she said.

"Really?" said Reece in a high-pitched tone, which gave away the extreme level of surprise that this had raised within him.

"Like what?" he asked, trying to lower his voice without making it sound too obvious.

"I can't say, because they told me in confidence. But it's related to some of the conference topics in different ways," she replied. "If you want to tell me some basic details, then this might help us to see if they're experiencing similar things to you."

Other people had weird things happening too! How weird could their things be compared to his? Then again, his weird things were just two Post-it notes and a text message. What if other people had really strange things happening, which made his pale into insignificance? Now he was curious to know what was happening to others. At least if he told her, even just some basic details, he might learn something about the other people's events. And that might be very interesting. *So should he tell her or not?*

Reece didn't notice, but Heather had been watching his facial-expressions and body-language very closely. She realised he was hesitating about whether to tell her or not. If he'd already decided not to tell her — he would have said so by now. He was indecisive because he was at the tipping point. *Should he or shouldn't he tell her?* Heather recognised this was the moment to nudge him.

TELL ME NOW! she shouted. But no-one would have heard this. She was shouting at him from within her mind. Nudging him over his tipping point.

Reece had been hesitant about whether he should tell Heather the things that had happened over the last few days, when he got this sudden urge that seemed to say *tell her*. So he did. He told her about the two Post-it notes in the books, *and* the text message, *and* then the phone call. As soon as he'd said all this, he felt very foolish.

She just sat there staring at him, obviously thinking about something.

Probably how big of an idiot she thinks I am. This conference was turning into a nightmare. Maybe he should leave and only return on Thursday to give his talk.

Heather stared at him for a little longer, chewing on her bottom lip, obviously in deep concentration. *What the hell was she doing?* thought Reece.

She opened the green folder on her desk and passed a document across to Reece.

"Do you remember signing this?" she asked.

It was one of the original copies of the Official Secrets Act acceptance form he'd signed when he'd done some work for the Ministry of Defence two-years ago. They needed help to creatively overcome some logistical issues with the rapid movement of materials and supplies in a military deployment.

"Yes I do," said Reece, shocked. "What are you doing with it?"

"You also signed another document for the Supply Directorate. That was the area within the MoD you did the work for wasn't it?" She asked this in a flat, matter-of-fact tone that Reece associated with the evil-enemy types that James Bond always encountered in the movies.

"Yes."

Heather pulled a thin document from out of the folder and slid it across the table to him. The heading on the document read Supply of Services to Ministry of Defence: Counter Terrorism Science and Technology Centre.

"I need you to sign this, before I can tell you anything more," she said. "It's basically the same document you signed last time, but modified to suit a different area of work."

"What's this all about?" he asked. "Are you with the Ministry of Defence?"

"You've asked two questions. The first I can't answer until you sign this," she said tapping the document on the desk with her finger. "Your second question is answered by the fact that this document is in front of you." Her finger again tapped the desk.

"I'm not sure if I really want to sign this before I get it checked out legally. That's what we did before we signed the last one."

"Let me explain something to you," she said, leaning towards him. "We've been tracking you for a few months now, ever since you got involved with that website discussion forum on memorable dreams. You asked if anyone had dreams they knew they were meant to remember. You recall that?"

Reece nodded, momentarily too confused to speak.

"You were in discussion with two people whose usernames were Bonita1974 and SweetDreamer. Both said they had dreams they were meant to remember. Am I correct?"

"Y-y-yes," he stammered in response. He was both stunned and impressed by these revelations. She wasn't reading these details from anywhere; she was narrating them as facts, and with an absolute confidence in her knowledge.

He composed himself. "Yes that's right. But they stopped posting comments quite quickly as I recall."

"The reason they stopped posting comments was because they stopped living. They died within forty-eight hours of each other, both under suspicious circumstances. You are the only other person we are aware of that is a three-time dreamer. You are alive, and you are being threatened in a most unusual manner. If you want to know any more you will sign this document here, here, and here," she said pointing to three places on the document with a pen.

She offered the pen to Reece. He took it and signed the document in three places.

“Now I can explain things to you,” she said.

Chapter 16 Monday 08h45

"As far as anyone in the hotel is concerned, I'm the conference director for this event," explained Heather. "In reality, I work for the Ministry of Defence in the Counter Terrorism Science and Technology Centre, or CTS&TC for short."

"That's not an easy abbreviation to remember," said Reece.

"I'm an operations field-director for the Mind Capabilities Unit, which is a CTS&TC offshoot. Most of our work is around the sciences related to aspects of terrorism. How to spot and track any type of weapon that a terrorist might want to use, and how to mitigate the effects of those weapons on military personnel and the general public."

"What kind of weapons?" asked Reece.

"All kinds. From arms and explosives, through to biological, chemical and technology weapons, which include online computer attacks and virus development."

"What does your specific area do?" asked Reece, baffled as to how a conference could be considered the weapon of choice for an aspiring terrorist.

"At the Mind Capabilities Unit, we look at some of the more esoteric aspects of military-related science, including what the human mind and body are capable of. We're particularly interested in observing, guiding and developing mental capabilities."

"Are you talking about using mind control as a weapon?" Reece was struggling to keep his voice and manner composed under the onslaught of revelations Heather was making with each sentence she spoke.

"No. Not now. Back in the '60s and '70s, the Americans and Russians were heavily committed to that. While there were some minor successes, they found it impossible to scale anything up to the point where it became a practical weapon. When the cold war ended, the need for that type of research was considered unnecessary. The MoD was never really interested in the potential of the mind as an offensive weapon. We were more concerned with ways to understand if it was being used against us, and if so, how we could counter its use. In the '80s and '90s, the department's budget for this was cut, but we continued to support some university research programmes to develop deeper understanding in specific areas."

She continued with her explanation.

"There have always been individuals who claimed to have special capabilities. Many were false claims. However, some seemed to have certain skills that couldn't be explained by science. The military don't like things they don't understand, because if you don't understand it, you can't control it, and so it's considered a potential threat. At the time, they determined this threat to be minimal, especially as there were so few people with any capabilities. Over the last decade things changed dramatically. With the phenomenal growth of the internet, we became aware that a lot more people were involved with these special capabilities than we ever imagined. There was a proliferation of websites, discussion groups and newsletters discussing topics that were potentially of interest to us. They were also talking about activities they were trying — and being successful at — in their own way. To stay on top of what was happening, we developed special software that could automatically track activities based on the key-terms that we asked it to search for. All we had to do was ensure that we were up-to-date with all the relevant terminology and colloquialisms. From there, the software would pick-up any abnormal levels of activity or when something new started up. What became really interesting was some of the new things being discovered and discussed."

"Is that how you know about my online dream discussions?"

"Yes, it works very well," she said, with a smile. She took a sip from the bottle of water on her table.

"Universities and private institutions are always researching unusual and edgy topics in new fields. They frequently have expectations of what they anticipate finding — but occasionally they get some very peculiar results. Research projects are usually set up and run under rigorous conditions such that the results will stand up to scrutiny. We found that a number of people involved in these research teams were discussing strangely-anomalous results, which they couldn't account for. We were aware of some of these anomalies from the research that the MoD was discreetly sponsoring — but that was with only a few universities around the UK. When we started to monitor the discussions identified by the software, we were astounded at the number of anomalies being discussed *globally*. We started to take a much greater interest in these anomalies — more than we let people know about. We saw groups forming with the sole purpose to master the anomalies, and use them for their own purposes. The problem is that people's own purposes can rapidly change from a skill or capability being used as a form of fun, to it being used for self-gain, then for criminal activity, and then for other purposes like terrorism and warfare."

"Would using these skills for self-gain be a crime?" asked Reece.

"That's a very grey area. Let me give you an example. Imagine you own a shop and I go in to buy something for five pounds. As I hand you a ten-pound note for payment, I use a mind-control technique that convinces you I've just given you a fifty-pound note. You then mistakenly give me forty-five pounds change. Have I broken any laws? Effectively I could say that you, the shopkeeper, made the mistake, and that I wasn't paying attention when you gave me my change."

"I see your point," said Reece. He seriously doubted people had these kinds of skills, yet he felt perturbed by Heather's accepting tone of voice.

"You seem very matter-of-fact about all this," he said.

"I have reason to be."

"Why?"

"That, I'm not going to explain." She wasn't going describe her own capability to anyone, especially as she'd kept it a deep secret within her for years. She also thought Reece Tassicker wouldn't be very happy knowing she'd recently used it on him.

"We've been observing a number of people-of-interest for a good while. However, it's the individuals we don't know about that concerns us. We thought it time to be a little more pro-active, so we organised this conference. We're hoping it will draw out some people that we don't know of, who are involved in some of the activities that interest us."

"And do you think it's going to work?"

"Well, the conference hasn't even started, and you are in my office having found two miraculous Post-it note messages, and had a text message that predicted the future, all in the last 72 hours."

Reece thought she could fittingly have added the phrase *so what do you think idiot*?

She added, "So what do you think?"

Reece waited with a grimace. Fortunately, that was all she said.

Chapter 17 Monday 08h50

Heather Macreedy was good at reading people and understanding their behaviours, and she was reading Reece Tassicker quite easily now. It was a skill that had served her well for a long time.

At university, she'd obtained her first degree in mathematics and psychology, and had then studied for a Master's degree. She earned this for a project where she created a software tool to recognise and analyse online conversation patterns. She'd cleverly linked an algorithm to a series of web spiders, such that the algorithm would reprogram the spiders to look for different terms based on what they initially found. This formed an iterative loop that helped understand when conversational patterns began to evolve, and solidify, around any specific subject that was introduced as a search trigger. This project was how she'd come to the attention of the Ministry of Defence. With so many ways for the public to communicate on subjects potentially of interest to the military, Heather's program was found to be highly effective for identifying individuals and groups that may be deemed a threat to security.

She'd been offered a job by the MoD, and spent the first two years refining her algorithm to thc point where it was one of the primary tools for detecting suspicious online behaviour. It had been a version of Heather's algorithm that found the dream discussion-forum and picked up Reece's dream-sharing topic. She'd then spent three years supporting field operatives with real-time intelligence where she learned the full capabilities of the military intelligence network in civil operations.

Contrary to popular belief, which was frequently derived from spy movies, field agents didn't have access to vast amounts of information and services from their laptop. It was too easy for a laptop to be stolen. Instead, they got nearly all their support from highly-skilled analysts in safe and secure locations, who did what the agent requested, and who tried to pre-empt what the agent might need.

Heather had then applied to become a field agent herself, and completed ten months of intensive field-operations training. During this time, she'd learned skills, and practiced live-fire scenarios, that would give her dad a heart-attack if she was ever able to tell him — which of course, she wasn't. She'd been a field agent for four years before becoming a field director, where she was responsible for setting up and running active operations. She enjoyed the excitement when it happened, but also enjoyed the quiet times too — and there was a lot of that. She anticipated that running this conference was going to be one of the quieter times.

Heather was watching Reece now. *Closely.* She certainly wasn't going to tell Reece anything about her own background, but was carefully balancing what else to explain to him about the conference, that would help her achieve success from this operation.

"As I explained to you yesterday evening, the conference is covering a number of themes which represent key-areas that MCU are interested in. We believe that if an individual is developing capabilities in an area for personal gain, they may want to attend a conference where their subject is being spoken about. The speakers have been invited because of their expertise in these areas. They are the magnets to attract the individuals who may be of interest to us. As an incentive, the speakers have all been given full-board in this five-star hotel, just like you. This will help encourage casual interactions between the attendees and the speakers outside of the programme times. We're closely monitoring which sessions people attend, and who they meet with in the breaks."

"Won't you need an army of people to do that?" asked Reece.

"You know the Contactor device that we spoke about last night?"

"This?" said Reece, pointing to the bright orange device clipped to his belt.

"Asif designed the Contactor system," she said, pointing in the direction of the man behind the bank of monitors, "He's monitoring everyone in real time. The device continuously transmits its location, and is accurate to within a metre anywhere in the hotel. That's accurate enough for us to know who is sitting or standing next to who, and where they are at any given moment. The system also monitors who attends what conference sessions. All these inputs are analysed by a behavioural-algorithm in the software which helps us to profile how the people interact."

"Can you give me an example of this?" asked Reece.

"No, and that's because of your security level. There's an example I can tell you from a French mobile-phone company. They learned that in France, if a man used a mobile phone to call someone between the hours of five and seven on a Friday afternoon and spoke with them for more than four minutes, then he was probably speaking to his wife. However, if he did this and then sent a text message shortly afterwards, then he was most likely speaking to his mistress. So you can see how algorithms help us to understand people's behaviour."

"Interesting example," acknowledged Reece.

"The cost to attend this conference is much higher than a similar conference would be. We made it fully-residential to justify the high price, and that's worked well to keep out the general public. Anyone attending that we haven't invited as a speaker or guest, obviously feels there is something interesting here that they place a high value on."

"How did you attract the right kinds of people?" asked Reece.

"Anyone with an active interest in a subject tends to browse the web to keep up-to-date. We just placed adverts on relevant websites and discussion forums. That was easy."

"It all seems quite extraordinary," said Reece, "and you're running it well considering you aren't conference organisers."

"We have a professional conference company behind the scenes to organise and manage it. Which reminds me, it's almost nine, and the opening keynote address will be starting shortly. We'd better go," she said, rising from her seat.

"Just one thing," says Reece, apprehensively. "What exactly am I doing here as a speaker? I thought it was based on the article I had published in the Harvard Business Review earlier this year."

"Popcorn and the Art of Fine Thinking, wasn't it? said Heather.

Reece liked the way she instantly recalled the title. It must have impressed her.

"What did you think of it?" he asked.

"I haven't read it. Your invitation wasn't anything to do with that. You came to our attention as a three-time dreamer and we told the conference company to get you here one way or the other. They must have decided to use that as the hook," she said dispassionately.

Reece was speechless at her brazen candour.

"We wanted to see what you would talk about, and whether you would interact with anyone else who is interested in dreams. We've become very interested in you based on what you've told me in the last few minutes."

She paused with her hand resting on the door handle.

"That was a high-speed introduction of who we are and what we're doing here. You just signed a document and are now officially part of this. You do understand the implications of that don't you?"

Reece nodded.

"Now, shall we go through to the main auditorium for the keynote address?"

Chapter 18 Monday 09h00

The day which had started out so positively for Reece, had taken a dramatic turn in the last hour.

He felt nervous about receiving the text message just before Brad had called.

He felt intrigued by what Heather had told him about the MoD being interested in his dreams.

He felt worried that the other two people he'd been conversing with had died in suspicious circumstances.

He felt safer that the security services were running this event.

He felt hesitant about the fact that he effectively worked for them again.

Actually, he wasn't sure how he really felt. The only thing he knew was that there were too many things going on around him that he wasn't in control of.

Heather guided him to the main auditorium, and then left him alone. As he entered from the back, he saw the chairs arranged in rows, facing the raised speakers' platform. He walked down the centre aisle, noticing that each seat was numbered on the back with a temporary paper-label. The rows were numbered A to V, starting from the front, while the seats were numbered one-to-ten on the left-side and eleven-to-twenty on the right-side. Reece worked this out in his head to be a total of 440 seats. The room seemed to be about two-thirds full, and he took a seat in the middle of the room. He noticed an oversize seat-label on the back of the chair in front, identifying his seat as J9. Reece wondered why they'd bothered numbering the seats when all the sessions were supposed to be free-seating.

The conference chairman walked to the podium to introduce the keynote speaker.

"We are delighted to welcome Professor Sir Simon Bartlett to give our opening keynote address," said the chairman. He then proceeded to give some background on the Professor.

"Professor Bartlett started researching the psychology behind advanced motivation in sportsmen and women, while a post-graduate student at Cambridge University. It was his expertise in helping athletes to achieve their best through understanding the abilities of the mind, that secured him an associate professorship at Loughborough University. Shortly after that, he became a full professor there, and incidentally, one of the youngest people to be awarded a professorship in the UK."

"It was during his search for ways to develop advanced levels of motivation, that he became involved in some of the more unusual aspects of the mind, including many of the pseudo-sciences such as telepathy and mental projection."

"In 2002, he established the UK Centre for Extended Sports Capabilities. This centre identified individuals with enhanced mind and body capabilities, to help design mental programmes for sporting associations. This centre did so well in identifying the underlying physiology and psychology behind successful athletes, that ninety per cent of Team Great Britain's medal winners at the London 2012 Olympic Games had been through the centre's programme."

"Professor Bartlett was awarded a knighthood in the 2013 New Year's Honours list, and last week it was announced that he has been appointed to head the Prime Minister's special commission on intellectual development in education. His latest book *Mind the Future* is currently on the UK best-seller list. Ladies and gentlemen, please welcome Professor Sir Simon Bartlett."

A polite ripple of applause accompanied Professor Bartlett on his short walk to the lectern in the centre of the podium. The potted history of his background made him think back to the one overheard-sentence in a university cafeteria that had changed his life and put him where he was today.

Simon Bartlett, as he was then, was working as a researcher at Cambridge University. He'd become fascinated with the field of advanced motivation and what made some athletes able to achieve the most amazing successes. Unfortunately, he was struggling to get grants to fund his research area. Without grants there could be no ground-breaking research, and without ground-breaking research there was no way he would achieve the academic recognition that he so desired. At the time, his area of sport motivation wasn't of high-enough profile to get the attention of potential sponsors.

One day, he'd been sitting alone in one of the university cafeterias, when he happened to overhear a discussion by a group of journalism students. Their extreme-youth and naivety of conversation clearly marked them as first-years. He was idly listening in to their amusingly-idealistic discussion, when one young girl made the comment that changed his entire life. They had been talking about the fundamental purpose of the newspaper industry, and were deliberating truth and factuality — or the lack of it — in journalism. This girl had made the comment that news wasn't about what was right or wrong, or what was truth and fact. It was solely about writing three-word headlines that would catch peoples' attention.

As a researcher he'd been totally focussed on finding new truths and facts in his field of study. But this girl was right. It was about making headlines. From that moment on, Simon Bartlett had focussed on creating headlines, and making sure those headlines were associated directly to him. While some academics built a reputation through a solid base of consistent development, he'd leapt from headline to headline, creating a profile that was intended to gain him prime-attention whenever editors needed academic substantiation of some fact.

He'd had many successes. While some academics had studied dry, highly-specialised subjects, he'd focused on helping British athletes be the best in the world. And that was what the newspapers wanted to know about, because that was what the British public wanted to hear about. His success with the British team in the Olympics, his knighthood last year, and his recent appointment to the Prime Minister's commission, had boosted his public credibility to the point where his view would always outweigh those of any purely-academic expert.

While some people who were famous had an amiable and relaxed approach to their fame, Professor Sir Simon Bartlett did not. In his view, he was the absolute, authoritative figure on his subject. The dryness of his personality put across not opinions, but unassailable facts. He was ruthless in putting-down anyone who had the effrontery to criticise his approach. And today at this conference, these people would hear one of his positioning talks, intended solely to lift his own standing, even higher.

There were some other details regarding how Simon Bartlett had got to where he was today — but he tended not to dwell on those.

The overheard conversation of the first-year journalism students had caused him to speak to a colleague in the psychology department, who he knew was doing some unusual research in the fringe-field of telepathy and extra-sensory perception. This research was receiving regular funding from a backer who had a personal interest in the area. Simon Bartlett found out who the backer was, and created a research brief entitled *The desire for success as a driver of telepathic skills* which was designed solely to appeal to the backer. He pitched this brief without his colleague knowing, and subsequently received funds from the backer to do the research.

His colleague was furious when he found out what he'd done, but Simon Bartlett offered to do the research jointly with him. If it went well, Simon Bartlett would ensure that he personally would get the credit, but if it went badly, then he'd leave it with his colleague, as this was his area of expertise. Simon Bartlett felt the field of telepathy to be a complete waste of time as an academic subject, but it had the potential to get headlines, one way or the other.

While testing for certain mental-skills on the project, he found two volunteer participants who were quite unusual. They were a married couple who genuinely seemed to have slight abilities to know what the other was thinking. All they had to do was have a strong desire to tell the other person something, and the thought was transferred. Simon Bartlett thought this was an interesting area to investigate for athletes, as nobody wanted something more than an athlete did — and that was to win. For athletes, winning was the only thing that mattered. It was what drove them to spend countless-hours training. Was this a new field of motivation where an athlete could coerce other athletes to subconsciously recognise them as the superior athlete? *Mind control for athletes.* He realised that this could be a new aspect to the research area he was desperate to be involved in.

Simon Bartlett thought he could use the married couple for publicity, and he'd tipped off a red-top newspaper about their skills. The newspaper loved this — a married couple with telepathic skills. They exaggerated the story out of all proportion, even to the extent of asking whether any children they had would inherit these capabilities. The couple were very uncooperative with the journalists, and the story soon faded away. They were also very angry that their story had been told to the newspaper. Simon Bartlett denied being involved in any way. He said all he'd done was to give a neutral comment about the possibility of them having some skills, and that more funding was needed to continue with the research in the area.

Immediately after this publicity, Simon Bartlett was approached by a woman called Philippa-Jane, who told him she represented a number of organisations that funded research in unusual areas. They did it discretely, through her, as some of them were publicly-listed companies who didn't want to have it widely known what specialised areas of research they were funding. She'd told him at their first meeting that if he was willing to *absolutely discredit the supposed skills* of the married couple, he would be rewarded with an associate professorship — and a sizeable grant to explore his field of extreme motivation.

Without hesitation, Simon Bartlett took up the offer, and set up another battery of research tests with the couple. He altered the final results to show they had no capabilities at all, and leaked this conclusion to the News of the World, a Sunday newspaper known for revelationary-journalism. As a weekly paper, they were desperate to demonstrate their in-depth ability to uncover the truth over that published by their daily rivals. To achieve this, the story was printed as front-page news. It included several quotes from Simon Bartlett, who publically declared the couple to be frauds, with no skills over-and-above the levels of chance.

Two days after publication of the article, Simon Bartlett had received the offer of associate professorship, and funding sufficient to develop numerous streams of research into his field. He found Philippa-Jane to be a strong supporter of his work, and she consistently brought him funding for new areas of research. After a few years of this, he'd been talking with her over lunch one day, when she'd told him a full-professorship was available if he'd be willing to work on some new, related lines of research. All Associate Professor Simon Bartlett could think of was becoming Professor Simon Bartlett, and he agreed before he'd even heard her full proposal.

Philippa-Jane wanted him to build on the reputation he'd acquired from the News of the World article, and to de-bunk more of the pseudo-science claims to discourage research in those fields. They would be giving him regular funding to undertake research programs into this field and to investigate people who claimed to have these capabilities. Philippa-Jane insisted that the investigative research work was not to be interfered with under any circumstances, as her clients wanted to see what was, and was not, being achieved by individuals. She'd then said something which really appealed to Professor Simon Bartlett — that he was free to gain whatever publicity he could from the discrediting of the individuals or subject.

Publically discrediting the pseudo-science on one hand, while delivering positive results from the real-science on the other, all helped to significantly boost his profile. The one proviso from the sponsors of his work was that they reserved the right to state which areas of research on extreme motivation he should explore. There had been a few disagreements on this, but even though he had to make some concessions in the areas of the mind he investigated, two things happened; the funds kept flowing and his profile kept growing. That was all that mattered to Professor Simon Bartlett.

Philippa-Jane occasionally asked for his attendance at certain events, which she told him was requested by his sponsors, and he always complied. The only thing that irked him was that she absolutely refused to tell him who his sponsors were. Initially, this bothered him. Then he realised that as long as they kept funding his research, he didn't really need to know. Today was one of the events they'd asked him to attend. He'd agreed to give the keynote opening at the conference, and to stay for the morning sessions, and then leave immediately after lunch.

Philippa-Jane wasn't attending the conference but she knew all about it. It had been her idea. She worked for a front-organisation set up by the MoD to secretly-fund research that had potential military value. The MoD had an active interest in what was good for athletes, because what was good for athletes to compete at their ultimate capacity, was good for soldiers too. After all, the concept of *I'm going to kill you before you can kill me* was the ultimate sporting competition.

Professor Sir Simon Bartlett walked to the podium and put his notes on the lectern. He reached into his inside pocket, pulled out his reading glasses, and carefully put them on. He lowered his head to look over his glasses at the audience. He looked to the right side, and then the left, and then to the middle of the auditorium. While some speakers started their introduction by thanking specific people for the opportunity to speak, Professor Sir Simon Bartlett acted like he had a God-given right to be on the podium. Without any sense of beginning, he just started speaking.

"When it comes to the capabilities of the mind there should be no middle ground. Either the capability should be proved or refuted. The proven aspects should be applied to the best of our abilities and the refuted elements should be publically declared as drivel. This will enable us to focus on the areas that do add value, rather than wasting precious time and resources on those that do not".

He didn't give ideas or thoughts to encourage people to form their own opinions — this wasn't his purpose. Because he was always right, the only opinion that mattered was his, and there would be no discussion about that. His tone was matter-of-fact. Monotonous. Passionless. Like a lion methodically stripping the carcass of a dead antelope. Eating until its appetite was satiated and then, without a thought for the antelope, moving on. Many disagreed with his views, but Professor Sir Simon Bartlett knew how to use his position and reputation to bulldoze and discredit anyone wanting to contradict his viewpoint. Those who did contradict him usually ended up feeling like the antelope at the lion's meal-time.

Reece thought Professor Sir Simon Bartlett to be a totally-pompous ass. Unfortunately, a successful, pompous ass. Anyone who could claim to have helped Team Great Britain to do so well at the Olympics could ride that chariot for a long time. He put his points across using uncommonly long words, which Reece only expected to hear at meetings where experts were speaking to experts. Being told that *the proclivity of participants in reprehensible activities to infiltrate and subjugate capitalistic organisations to disenfranchise the stakeholders* was approaching Reece's vocabulary limits, especially when he could have simply said *the criminals want to put their people inside big companies to steal money.*

Professor Bartlett continued, "There are four key points that I'm going to focus on for the rest of my talk. The first is how we can extend our understanding of extreme-focus in athletes and apply it to the education of young people in our schools. The second point is how we will continue our research to discover the as-yet unknown capabilities of the mind. The third point is how we can develop countermeasures to alleviate the risks of terrorist organisations using mental-capabilities against our great nation."

Reece recognised that he was doing an excellent job of justifying further funding for his work from both the aspirationally, beneficial perspective and from arousing the fear-factor within people. He thought there wasn't one of these three points that didn't have the potential for front-page news in the tabloid newspapers. He had to acknowledge that Professor Bartlett was a very smart operator — even if he did have an insufferable level of arrogance.

I wonder if he appreciates the added extras I got when I bought two copies of his bloody book thought Reece sardonically.

"Finally, and most importantly," continued Professor Sir Simon Bartlett, "is point number four."

But he would never get point number four out…

Chapter 19 Monday 09h15

Anthony Thorpe had entered the main auditorium early. He wanted to be sure he got a seat with a clear view for the opening key-note address, and thought that an aisle seat would best suit his needs. He noticed that the rows had letters to identify them. *Row G would be most appropriate* he thought, and he sat down.

Some may have smiled at the irony of him being in row G, but not Anthony Thorpe. It had been fourteen years since he'd last experienced joy. Fourteen years since he'd been happy enough to smile at anything. For it had been fourteen years since Gail had died. *His Gail.* Who he had always referred to lovingly as *Gee.*

Anthony listened to Professor Sir Simon Bartlett drone on in an overbearing monotone. He heard him mention the four key points he was going to focus on. This would be an appropriate time to give the Professor's talk some well-needed assistance. He held up his smartphone in front of him, and selected the camera. He then pressed the movie icon to start recording video. The word RECORD appeared in red at the bottom of the screen, as the camera began to capture the Professor's talk. To anyone watching, it would seem like Anthony Thorpe was just recording a well-known person giving a speech.

Holding his phone steady in this position, he moved his head slightly to the right to get a direct view of the speaker. He focused his gaze intently on the middle of Professor Sir Simon Bartlett's face. He imagined the specific sensation that he wanted. An intense tingly-feeling, high up in the nose, near the sinuses. Holding this sensation in his mind, he used the phrase *PROJECT* as he imagined the sensation barrelling away from his mind, and right into the centre of Professor Sir Simon Bartlett's face.

Chapter 20 Monday 09h15

After barely fifteen minutes, Robyn Taylor's senses were going numb under the droning onslaught of Professor Bartlett's talk. It wasn't by choice that she was attending this conference; she was here as Samuel's minder.

Samuel passed her his pencil. He took another identical one from his pencil case and continued with his drawing. Robyn opened the zip-locked plastic bag on her lap, took out a pencil sharpener, and sharpened the pencil, allowing the shavings to fall into the open bag. She handed the pencil back to Samuel. He took it without a word, and put it back into his pencil case. She used to count the number of times she had to sharpen his pencils, but that activity soon stopped when she realised the number was going to be endless.

I'm fifty-four, she thought. *I have a loving husband, two wonderful daughters, and a nice semi-detached house that we own outright. I'm in a plush hotel conference room, being bored out of my mind, and sharpening pencils for someone who barely recognises that I exist.*

Don't drift! Stay focussed!

This was her first field assignment with Samuel for the Mind Capabilities Unit, so having a successful outcome was really important to her. Robyn told herself she was fortunate to be here today, as she recalled how it had happened.

She'd been working for the British Army, in a civilian capacity, as a human resources manager for many years. She counselled Army people who were having personal problems that affected their work. When the last of her two children had moved out of their home, Robyn decided she wanted a more interesting job. She'd applied for a position within the MoD's Counter Terrorism Science and Technology Centre, working as a field-operative with people who needed special support. She'd been offered the role, and accepted it. It was an unusual role too, and over the last twelve months she'd discovered it could be fascinatingly exciting — and excruciatingly boring — sometimes both in the same day.

The thought of field work had appealed to Robyn — and generally she enjoyed it. Right now though, this presentation was exceedingly tedious, as she couldn't understand many of the words being used. She looked at Samuel sitting next to her. His sketched page of arrows was almost complete and he'd be starting a new page soon. He never seemed to get bored, no matter where he was.

He handed her another pencil to be sharpened, without looking up or saying a word. He took a replacement from his pencil case and continued shading the arrows. Robyn opened up the zip-lock bag and sharpened the pencil. Again.

If the speakers are all going to be like this one, maybe today I will start counting the number of pencils I sharpen, she thought. She handed the sharpened pencil back to Samuel who again took it without saying a word. She looked at him. A man who was so amazingly-annoying in his behaviour, but so annoyingly-amazing in his capabilities. She wondered what Samuel thought of the speaker.

Samuel Gray didn't think anything about the speaker. To him, it was just part of the background noise in his head. Samuel Gray thought only about his arrows — and nothing else. On his lap was his clipboard, and on the clipboard was a pad of graph paper, covered in neatly-drawn arrows of different sizes, colours and styles. The arrows were artfully drawn, with varying thicknesses of line for the borders, and different styles of shading and in-fills for the bodies. The arrows were drawn solely from straight lines, with not a curved line to be seen anywhere on the page. And every arrow pointed from left to right.

Even though the page looked quite full to Robyn, Samuel was able to fit ever-smaller arrows into the gaps, until finally, the page was a mass of arrows; long and short; narrow and wide. The end result was really quite elaborate, the way the arrows filled every bit of space on the paper. Robyn wished there could have been a few curly ones, as she was a Laura Ashley and paisley-coils type of person.

She watched as Samuel turned to the next clean sheet of graph paper, and started on a new drawing. There wasn't even the slightest pause to review the work of art he'd just created. He simply finished one drawing, and started the next. But of course he had his routine to go through before he could start drawing…

a new sheet of graph paper so check the front cover of the pad is it Grosvenor House Papers Limited un-punched pale-blue graph paper yes it says Grosvenor House Papers Limited un-punched pale-blue graph paper this is the best colour graph paper the green graph paper lines resist wanting to be parts of arrows I know the blue lines want to help make arrows I can help them do it that's why blue is my favourite colour now are all the vertical lines going straight up and down yes are all the horizontal lines going straight across the page yes the lines are ready to be put in order they need to have the arrows on them to tell them which is the right way to be the horizontal lines are quite good as they go from left to right but also from right to left I will help them to understand that they need to point from left to right making them into arrows will help them the vertical lines don't understand that up and down is wrong and that left to right is the only way to be the vertical lines are useful as arrows need to have some vertical lines in them to emphasize the arrow head the lines are just waiting for him to help them point somewhere they are waiting for order I will give it to them by drawing arrows on them I need to draw the first arrow for this first arrow I want a blue Artline 700 Fine Bullet Tip Marker with the 0.7 millimetre fibre tip and the green six-inch plastic ruler the first arrow on the page is always the most important as it tells all the other arrows the correct way to point look at the way the pen seems to eat up a line of single green graph paper squares as it moves along the paper it is important to move the pen slowly so that the arrow knows it is growing look at the fascinating way the blue ink relentlessly fills in the row of squares as it moves across the page no matter how long the line is the ink fills up one little square after another the line seems to know what it is doing but the squares don't know what is happening to them until it is too late and they are all filled in how can something so long and straight come out of a small round pen DON'T THINK OF THE SHAPE OF THE PEN BECAUSE IT IS ROUND WHICH IS BAD BUT THE SIDES ARE STRAIGHT which is good why can't she find him pens that are square like she found him the graph paper without the little round holes punched in the long side THOSE HOLES DISTRACTED HIM AND SCARED THE ARROWS ROUND THINGS ARE BAD and straight things are good the Grosvenor House Papers Limited un-punched pale-blue graph paper has no round holes in it so it's very good the first arrow outline is finished but I need to do the filling in before the arrow gets cold use the Staedtler Tradition 2B pencil for the shading always do the darker shading first because that's the way that it should always be done oh no the tip has just broken she must sharpen it...

Samuel held out the pencil.

"Four," said Robyn quietly, as she took the pencil, opened the zip-lock bag and started to sharpen it. Without realizing it, Professor Sir Simon Bartlett's talk had made her start counting the number of pencils she sharpened.

Samuel heard Robyn murmur *four* quietly, and remembered when she'd given him his first box of Artline marker pens. He'd wanted to put all twelve into his pencil case, but Robyn had told him he could only take four at a time, as twelve was too many to carry.

she said only take four but why only four pens and not all twelve the smallest squares on his graph paper each had four sides the small ones were grouped into blocks of five-by-five with a slightly thicker blue line to surround the twenty-five squares these also had four sides and the four blocks of twenty-five squares formed another bigger square of ten-by-ten small blocks which had an even thicker blue line around it and that square had four sides and all these bigger blue squares were held tightly together by an even thicker blue line which formed the outside border of all the squares on the page and that had four sides too the page itself had four sides and the arrows had four sides because they had a top and a bottom and a left side and a right side and at school some of the other children had called him four-eyes because of his thick glasses and there were four directions up and down and left and right and right was the most important direction and whatever was pointing right was good four was good and right was good and four was right and she was right that four pens was good if four pens was good and she was right about that then he would want four pencils and four rulers and four pencil sharpeners and four became his favourite number because things that came in fours were good and if you wrote the figure four it looked a bit like an arrow which was good EXCEPT THAT IT WAS POINTING TO THE LEFT AND THAT WAS BAD as all good arrows point to the right from now on always write the number four the other way round so it points to the right and not to the left because right is good and good is right and four is the right number for everything...

As Robyn absent-mindedly sharpened pencil number four, she thought back to when she'd ordered those new Artline marker pens for Samuel. He'd wanted to carry the whole bloody box around in his pencil case, but she'd suggested he only take four. He'd paused to think for a few moments and then put four into his pencil case. She'd been surprised that he'd acquiesced so easily to her request.

As she reflected on this, it seemed peculiar that from that moment on, almost everything had to be done in fours. Every morning when he packed his pencil case, he would have to choose four different coloured markers, four pencils, four rulers and four pencil sharpeners. The time it took him to select which colours to take used to infuriate her. The way he would lay four of each item out and then start swapping colours, until he got the precise combination of colours of the items that he wanted. It was different every day too. And why he needed pencil sharpeners when that appeared to be her sole responsibility, she wasn't sure.

She did feel uncomfortable that ever since she'd suggested that he only take four marker pens, he'd started to write the number four backwards. Robyn hoped that she hadn't triggered this unusual behaviour.

She offered the freshly-sharpened pencil back to Samuel. At first he didn't see it as he tended to look away when Robyn was sharpening a pencil.

pencil sharpeners are small and rectangular in shape which is good because they have straight edges the hole at the end where the pencil goes in is BAD BECAUSE IT IS ROUND but the pencils aren't round because they are hexagons it's bad the way the pencil sharpener changes the straight arrow-like shape of the pencil into flowery and curvy wood-shavings when it gets sharpened she must do this for him LOOK AWAY WHILE SHE DOES IT LOOK AWAY LOOK AWAY it's good how the pencil comes back from her very sharp and pointy just like a good arrow should look she is good at doing that she mustn't use one of his pencil sharpeners she must always use her own she was good at bringing her own pencil sharpener he had special combinations of colours and if she borrowed his she may not return it which would spoil the pattern it can take a long time every morning to get the right combination of colours of Artline pens and rulers and Staedtler pencils and pencil sharpeners she used to get upset with him and tell him to hurry up but she doesn't know how important it is to bring the exact right things with you each day she knows now to leave him alone in the mornings while he works out what things he needs to take for the day to draw the best good arrows she liked to do things quickly but he liked to make sure he was doing something the right way that's how he was different to her he knew he was different to a lot of people...

Like any typical child, the young Samuel Gray heard what people said when they spoke. However, unlike any typical child, he sometimes heard a voice in his head when no-one was speaking. Not all the time, just occasionally.

When he was younger, he remembered that he seemed to spend a lot of time speaking with different doctors. When he told them about these voices, the doctors would tell him that they understood, and they would nod, knowingly, at whichever of his parents had brought him that day. The doctors told him that the voices weren't really there, and that it was just him speaking with an imaginary friend that he had in his head. They told him that many children like him had imaginary friends, and that they would eventually go away. He used to wonder what the doctors meant by *children like him.*

He also used to wonder why the voices he heard seemed awfully grown-up, and used grown-up words that he didn't understand, as though they were having a grown-up conversation with someone else. One doctor said the voices would go away quicker, if he tried to ignore them, and block them out. So he did what the doctor told him. Samuel Gray knew that doctors made you better. *Especially if you do exactly what they tell you.*

In his mind though, he couldn't tell which voices were the real, spoken ones, and which were imaginary, unspoken voices. So to be sure, and because he wanted to do what the doctor had told him, he started to block out all the voices. He found that if he focused intently on a toy, or a book, or anything for that matter, and looked at nothing else, then he was able to block out every voice. Strangely, this made him feel good. He learnt that if he could stare fixatedly at something for several minutes, then a kind of quiet-numbness came over him, and there were no voices.

What changed though, was that his parents started to touch him to get his attention, and they spoke with exaggerated words directly into his face to make him understand them. The sight of his parents' mouths moving in such an unnatural and exaggerated manner, along with their shouting, scared him, so he would avoid looking at their mouths by focusing on whatever item he had been holding at the time. This seemed to make things worse for them, as they would grab his shoulders and force him to look at them. To this day, he didn't like looking at people's faces. He preferred to keep his head down, looking at the wonderful arrows he was drawing. Nor did he like people touching him either.

Eventually, the doctors changed, and they started asking that he listen to what people were saying. They made him do exercises with his parents, which was a little better, for at least they stopped the exaggerated yelling directly to his face. Slowly, he learned to be able to listen to the noises and voices around him. The only difference was that it seemed the unspoken voices had been replaced by a kind of gentle, whooshing sound. He only heard it occasionally, but it seemed to be with about the same regularity as which he had previously heard the unspoken voices, so he assumed it was the same thing.

The whooshing sound was similar in nature to a car that passed by. It was heard approaching from a direction in one ear and then it continued past, and away, in the other. This was how Samuel could tell where the whooshing was coming from, and where it was going to. Whenever he did hear the whooshing sound, if he looked in the direction of the source, there was normally a person there. He therefore assumed that some people were capable of making the whooshing sounds. He never told his parents, or the doctors, about the whooshings. He was sure they wouldn't like it.

To save himself from having to turn round and risk having to look at someone whenever he heard a whooshing sound, he used to draw a big arrow on a piece of paper, pointing to the whooshing sound's origin. He enjoyed drawing the arrows, but his piece of paper would end up having arrows pointing in different directions. So he changed things, and once the first arrow was on the paper, whenever he heard the whooshing sound, he would rotate the paper to point to the source, and then when it stopped he'd rotate the page so the arrows pointed to the right, and he'd carry on drawing more arrows. He started to find this a very relaxing thing to do. He loved drawing his arrows. He loved it so much he now spent all his time doing it.

The one thing he didn't understand was why the people who were making the whooshing sounds didn't seem to know they were doing it. He thought this a little peculiar.

Robyn noticed Samuel would glance up occasionally at the big screen above the speakers' podium, to see if there were any PowerPoint presentations being given. Professor Sir Simon Bartlett didn't believe in visuals, and so the screen simply displayed his name.

Samuel loved watching PowerPoint presentations that had lots of arrows in them. Once, he made his own PowerPoint slide deck that he showed to Robyn. He'd created slides with arrows of all different types and sizes and colours. He showed her his first slide, and then his second, then the third, fourth and fifth slides. Robyn wondered how many slides of arrows she would have to look at, but she sat there patiently with him. Until she happened to glance down at the lower-left corner of the computer screen, and saw they were only on slide 17 of 628.

She'd excused herself, and had forgotten to return.

Samuel was severely autistic, which was obvious from his manner and appearance. The public-at-large generally believed that severely autistic individuals lacked certain mental abilities. While this was broadly true, what was not widely known was that many autistic individuals had very special capabilities. Sometimes these capabilities were so well-developed, that the individuals were described as savants; people with exceptionally-high knowledge or skill in a specific area.

Robyn had volunteered to be Samuel's minder, and to be involved with his testing from the start, because she had a personal interest in the condition. Her sister had a child with severe autism, and Robyn thought being involved with Samuel would give her some insights that may be useful for her nephew.

Samuel had been brought to the attention of one of the research groups that Philippa-Jane was allocating funds to. They were trying to understand the extent of the savant areas of expertise exhibited by people with severe autism. Samuel's medical specialist had contacted this research group to suggest him as an interesting research participant. She'd done this because during her tests of him, he'd demonstrated a consistent tendency to be distracted by something which she couldn't identify. He'd seemed different to her usual patients, and she'd hoped they might find something that would help her, to help him.

The researchers recognised Samuel had an unusual skill as soon as they started to test him. He was unable to explain to them what it was or how it worked — to Samuel, it was just a whooshing noise passing through his head. They documented him as having an unknown, anomalous capability that they couldn't identify. When Philippa-Jane heard about this unusual ability in Samuel, she sent a discreet message through to the head of the Mind Capabilities Unit suggesting they explore this subject's capabilities further, under the more secure environment of a formal MoD programme. This was when Robyn had first met Samuel.

Because of her background in helping individuals who needed support, she was appointed as a SPECCAB minder. SPECCABs were individuals with special capabilities. The MoD had a knack for creating abbreviated titles for roles — and in this case the title was SPECCAB. Robyn immediately despised the term. The people with special capabilities frequently seemed to be those who were also challenged in other ways, and in Robyn's mind the last thing they needed was yet another name that separated them from the rest of society. She was told there were three SPECCABS the MCU were running trials with, and that she would be the minder for two of them; Samuel and Jonathan. She'd spent most of her time so far working with Samuel in a variety of testing and training sessions.

Many of these sessions were run at universities around the country, often under the guise of a departmental research project, where individuals who claimed to possess some kind of mental capabilities would be tested,. The individual would be asked to perform the skill they claimed to be capable of, and the researchers would measure their success. Often their results would no better than those achievable by the laws of chance — or what guessing would deliver. The ones that did better were the ones that Samuel could hear a whooshing from when they were actually performing their mental activity.

Robyn had asked the psychologists at CTS&TC, what it was that Samuel could pick up. They explained he had the ability to detect if someone was using mental projection in some way. He only heard the whooshing sound when there was a projection of mental energy of some kind. They didn't know how Samuel detected it, other than what he'd managed to explain to them about the whooshes.

Using Samuel's amazing skill, the researchers had found that many people could exert an influence using mental energy, often without knowing it. In department stores, good shop-assistants had only a short-time to get you interested in buying something. Successful street-beggars had only the briefest of moments to convince you to give when they approached you. And when an actor performed a soliloquy in an emotionally-charged play, they would draw you into their plight in a highly-dramatic manner. In many of these scenarios, Samuel had been able to pick up mental-projections through the whooshes he heard emanating from the individuals performing the action.

In all these different scenarios, when the people who achieved the better results were asked how they did it, they frequently replied that *they could read people*, or that *they were a people-person.* They were unaware that they had any abilities around mental projection. *And the MoD certainly weren't going to tell them of this fact.*

Interestingly, at a children's nursery where three- and four-year-olds were playing, there was also a lot of very low-level mental activity occurring. The young children all seemed to *unknowingly* have this skill, for when Samuel sat in the middle of the nursery, he said there was so much activity, he couldn't point his arrows fast-enough.

The MCU had even set up a poker game, with some highly-experienced players. To make it an intensely contested event, they'd put up a £50,000 winner-take-all prize pot. In poker, the individual players were continuously trying to read the other players — to out-think and out-play them. Samuel had picked up a continuous, low-level of activity from some of the better players. This test scenario had been particularly effective in helping Samuel demonstrate his ability. Unfortunately, the head of the MCU had gone apoplectic when he found out he'd have to justify a £50,000 expense for a prize at a poker competition to his superiors.

One exercise did cause concern for the researchers though. They took Samuel to a classical music concert at the Royal Festival Hall. They had seats in the middle of the stalls where they let Samuel draw his arrows. At several times during the performance, he pointed quickly to one-of-three directions. During the interval, he told them the whooshes were very loud. One of the directions was off to their left, while the other two were behind them, all of which made it difficult to see where the projection was coming from. Precisely what the mental projection was, they didn't know, but it did prove that some people had a strong capability. The concerning question for the MCU was whether these people knew of their capability or not. And if they did, what were they doing with it — especially at a classical-music concert.

Robyn's other charge, Jonathan, was a savant who could recognize and recall tremendous amounts of detail about individuals when he was in a large group of people. They wanted to see if he could be trained to recognise the tiny giveaway-traits of suspicious behaviour exhibited when someone was about to do something untoward, or was feeling guilty about having done something.

Then there was the SPECCAB they had codenamed PAXO. She was lined up to be his minder in the future. She hadn't been told what skill he possessed except for the fact that he was truly exceptional. If they'd given him the codename PAXO, she dreaded to think what he might be capable of.

The research exercises with Samuel had provided Robyn with a level of excitement and intrigue she'd never experienced before, and today was their first, active field-assignment together. She wasn't too sure if a conference was going to provide any interesting activity though.

Chapter 21 Monday 09h15

"And point four," said Professor Sir Simon Bartlett, "is the pre-eminently, significant issue of… Aaaaaachoo!" An explosive sneeze emanated from his nose and mouth. It was picked up by the microphone, enhanced in volume by the amplifier, and boomed out to the audience through the loudspeakers. Everyone looked up. Their minds awakened from whatever mental slumbers they had been in by the deafening nasal-explosion. All except for Samuel, who just paused momentarily in his arrow drawing, before continuing.

"I do apologise for that," said the Professor, wiping his nose with a handkerchief, which he quickly put away.

"As I was saying, point four is the pre-eminently significant… Aaaaaachoo! Aaaaaachoo!" Two more huge sneezes were amplified through the speaker system. The handkerchief reappeared and then disappeared.

"Profound apologise again. As I was saying, point four is… Aaaaaachoo! Aaaaaachoo! Aaaaaachoo!"

Robyn's full attention had been on the speaker and his sneezing, but out of the corner of her eye, she saw Samuel start to rotate his drawing, and then stop.

"Aaaaaachoo! Aaaaaachoo! Aaaaaachoo! Aaaaaachoo!" Several of the audience had started counting the sneezes, and when Professor Bartlett did a four-sneeze count after a one-, two- and three-sneeze count, not all their sniggers and giggles were completely suppressed.

Robyn was now fully focused on Samuel, who had rotated his drawing to be pointing to the left and slightly forward. He then rotated the drawing back to the usual left-to-right alignment. He'd picked up someone projecting mental energy, but Robyn hadn't had enough time to see where it was coming from.

The speaker tried to deliver his fourth point one more time.

"Aaaaaachoo! Aaaaaachoo! Aaaaaachoo! Aaaaaachoo!" Then, with an almighty arching of his back, and throwing his head forward in the manner of a cobra striking at its victim, Professor Sir Simon Bartlett unleashed the most enormous of sneezes.

"AAAAAACHOO!"

It was loud despite the fact that the sound engineer had already muted the podium microphone. Two spotlights which illuminated the speaker's podium gave the geyser of mucus that was ejected from his nose and mouth the appearance of a blizzard of luminous snow. As Professor Bartlett tried desperately to retrieve the handkerchief from his pocket, the glistening streams of snot that covered his mouth and chin, glowed expansively under the bright lights.

As the Professor hurried off the stage, Robyn was leaning over Samuel's shoulder, taking a sightline along the direction his arrows were pointing. Her priority was to identify the end-marker, as she'd been shown in her training. At this moment, Samuel's arrows pointed towards a fire extinguisher mounted on the far wall, just to the left-side of the doorway with the fire-exit sign above it. She'd also noted the label showing that Samuel was in seat H14. She had her sightline established, which was fortunate, as Samuel was already rotating his drawing back to the normal left-right orientation. She now had time to see who was sitting along the sightline. There seemed to be a dozen or so potential people, several of whom were talking to the person next to them, no doubt about what had just happened, and a man who was holding up a phone, obviously trying to get a photo of the event. *He's probably missed it by now*, she thought.

This was an exciting start to the conference. It looked like someone had been projecting energy that made the speaker sneeze in a sequenced pattern. She'd better tell Heather about this immediately. They would want to identify who was sitting in the sightline seats. As Robyn gently led Samuel out of the auditorium, the chairman was explaining over the now re-activated microphone, that there would be a short break to allow the speaker time to recover.

Anthony Thorpe pressed the PAUSE button on his phone, and the video recording stopped. He had a slight smile on his face now. Not because of what had just happened, but because of what was about to happen. As he waited for Professor Bartlett to return, he noticed the number stuck to the back of the seat in front of him, G10. G — as in his Gee. His mind thought back through the years, to the time before she'd left him. And beyond that, to the time before she'd even met him.

As a little girl, Gail Canning's parents had bought her a puppy to keep her company. She decided to call him Floppy, due to his long floppy ears. Gail loved Floppy, and would talk to him all day, reading him stories from her books and getting him involved in her play activities. Whenever Gail called his name, he'd lift his head and come running towards her. Over time, Gail realised that she could get Floppy's attention simply by thinking his name out-loud. She had to think it very loud, above all the silent-sounds of other thoughts that fill a little-girl's head. Over time, she gave this loud thinking the name *mind-shouting*.

One day, when Gail was fourteen, Floppy was run over by a car and killed. She was devastated by Floppy's death. For months afterwards, she would mind-shout his name when she was in bed at night, wondering if he could hear her in heaven. Eventually Gail got over Floppy, as school work, music and boyfriends started taking up more of her time. She tried mind-shouting with some of her friends, and even with complete strangers, but to no avail. There was never any reaction from them.

When she was sixteen, Gail went on a school trip with her class to see Shakespeare's Romeo and Juliet as part of her English Literature studies. Her class was told to sit in specially-reserved seats at the theatre, and Gail found herself in the front row of the balcony. She was leaning forwards, watching the play, her palms flat on the edge of the balcony with her chin resting on the back of her hands. She was utterly entranced by the performance. Her mind drifted off and she imagined herself on stage playing the role of Juliet, standing on the balcony and uttering the famous line *O Romeo, Romeo! Wherefore art thou Romeo?*

That's not now dear, that's later, gently admonished a voice in her head.

Gail's whole-body jerked momentarily, and her eyes went wide. She hadn't actually said anything — but somebody had answered her back.

Can you hear me? she mind-shouted.

Yes I can, my dear, replied the voice.

Gail was frozen in place, not daring to move. She watched the first act, trying hard not to think of anything too specific. When the play resumed after the interval, she tried mind-shouting again.

Are you there?

Yes I am, responded the same voice in her head.

Gail didn't know whether having someone reply to your thoughts was a wonderful thing — or a terrifying thing. Either way, she wanted to think about it when the person who could hear her thoughts wasn't around. On the way back home, Gail recalled the good times she'd had with Floppy, when she used to mind-shout his name and he'd respond. This convinced her that mind-shouting was a good thing. She tried it occasionally over the last two years of her school life — but with no success.

When she left school, she'd got a job working for an insurance company, handling customer claims in the company's main processing centre. One day, she had to take some documents for shredding, which required her to walk through a part of the building she rarely went to. It was a cubicle maze, where several-hundred people worked handling motor accident claims. It was a lovely summer's day and she felt in high spirits. On her way back through the maze, she did a spur-of-the-moment mind-shout to the whole room.

Hello there. I hope you're having a nice day!

She got a response in her head from a male voice. All it said was *Uh?*

Intrigued, she started walking around the passageways between the cubicles, mind-shouting *Who are you?*

All she got was a series of partial responses which included

Wha...

Uh?

Who?

Shit!

And some assorted animal-sounding grunts.

As she wandered around the cubicle maze, she could hear the voice sometimes quieter, and sometimes louder. She followed the direction of the louder sounds, and eventually came across a young man with his back to her, frantically peering over the top of his cubicle.

She tapped him on the shoulder, smiled and mind shouted *Hello.*

In her head she heard him saying *What? Who? How?* in a range of different, but clearly-panicked tones.

"Hi, my name's Gail Canning," she said, sitting down next to him.

"Anthony Thorpe," he replied, completely flustered.

"I think you and I need to talk," said Gail, in as calming a voice as she could muster, putting on what she hoped, was her most disarming smile.

Privately, she mind-shouted.

Uh? Wha... was all she heard in her head. She realised that this was probably the first time this had happened to Anthony.

She invited him to the building's coffee shop, where they talked. She told him about her mind-shouting and he told her that occasionally, he'd heard strange voices in his head — but he'd never tried to answer them back. He explained that it seemed a bit weird to him. Over the following days, they'd talked a lot more. It transpired that Anthony's mind-shouting skills were very limited, as he'd never really used them. The coffee-times soon turned into dating, and in their spare time, they found that their mind-shouting conversations were limited to just a few words. He could clearly understand longer-sentences from her, but was only capable of sending a few short-words back to her. What they did discover, was that he could exert an influence over many of her feelings. For example, he could make her feel as though a part of her body needed to be scratched. With the few simple words that he was capable of sending, supported by the feelings he could transmit to her, they eventually began to share a love that was deeper, than had ever been shared by two people before.

They were both quite introverted, leading quiet lives as individuals and also as a dating-couple. Over time they became engaged, and a few years later, married. They loved making plans for the things they would do in their future, even though they lived a modest life. They also didn't feel any real need to develop their mind skills any further.

One evening, when he was idly browsing the internet, Anthony saw an advertisement looking for people to be involved in the research of psychic phenomenon — which included a payment as an incentive to participate. Extra money would be useful, so they submitted themselves for testing and were accepted. They were tested individually, but the results didn't indicate to the researchers any particular skills. When they were asked why they thought they had skills, they had each explained that they had unusual capabilities — but only with each other. The researchers then devised some new tests for them to do together, at which they did exceptionally well.

Things then got out of hand, as one of the daily tabloid newspapers somehow got their details and published an article about them entitled *The Psychic Couple*. They became minor public figures for a short time — but against their will. They didn't like this publicity, and they spoke to the person who was running the research with them, whose name was Simon Bartlett. He was most apologetic, saying he had no idea how the newspaper had found out about them. He asked if they would stay for another round of testing, and that he would ensure they received a much higher incentive payment for this next panel of tests, as a recompense for the unfortunate situation that had just happened. He'd then offered them a surprisingly generous amount of money if they'd continue. He also told them that they were to be the sole participants, to keep it private for them.

These tests were quite different to what they'd done before, but Anthony and Gail did their best for Simon Bartlett, who personally did all the work with them. He explained that he wanted to be absolutely sure that nothing was leaked to the newspapers again. All through the tests, he'd given them positive feedback on how well they were doing. When the tests were finished, he'd paid them their money and explained that he had to spend several weeks going through the results to analyse and write up the findings.

Barely a week later, Anthony and Gail were out for their regular Sunday morning walk, when they called in at the local supermarket on the way back to buy some milk. As they entered, Anthony cast his eyes over the Sunday newspapers to see what the headlines were. To his shock, on the front page of the News of the World were his, and Gail's, photographs. The headline above simply said *Psychic Frauds*.

Dazed, they bought the paper and read it thoroughly at home. The article told the story of how they had essentially defrauded a research organisation out of the exact sum of money that had been given to them. Numerous comments attributable to the research institute and lead-researcher Simon Bartlett, stated that additional research had proved conclusively they had no capabilities of any sort whatsoever, and that they were simply trying to waste valuable research resources for personal gain.

They tried in vain to contact the newspaper with their version of the story, but news moves on, and the paper wasn't interested any more. When Anthony tried phoning Simon Bartlett, he couldn't get to speak to him, and no-one would return their calls. A few days later, he was told that Simon Bartlett no longer worked there.

Anthony and Gail were quiet people who valued their privacy. They had never told any of their friends or family that they had these unusual ways of communicating — so they didn't receive any support from them. They felt isolated, publically humiliated, and completely betrayed by Simon Bartlett, whom they had trusted. Their loving-life together had been destroyed.

Gail fell into a deep depression, crying all day, and unable to go to work. She wasn't able to sleep, and so her doctor prescribed some sedatives. This didn't seem to help Gail. One evening, not long later, Anthony Thorpe came home to find all the pill containers empty. His Gee's lifeless body lay on the bed, arms folded across her chest like a sleeping angel. There was no note left for him. But he knew it was shame and humiliation that had driven her to take her life.

He couldn't understand why Simon Bartlett had discredited them so badly. He'd seen how they both had these unusual capabilities when he and Gee had demonstrated them to him. For some reason, Simon Bartlett didn't want to know the truth, and Anthony Thorpe had no idea why that was.

After Gee's funeral, Anthony knew he had to go on with his life.

He knew it would be desperately hard without her.

He knew it was through her mind-shouting skills that they had met.

He knew that Gee had been much better than he was with her capabilities.

He knew that the two of them hadn't lied about their abilities.

He knew that, somehow, he would vindicate Gail.

What he didn't know at this point in time, was exactly how he would achieve this vindication.

But he knew it would be through an indisputable demonstration of his own capabilities.

So Anthony Thorpe made an oath.

He committed that he would spend time every day, for the rest of his life, developing his capabilities. He would understand the full-breadth of what he could do, and then he'd learn how to do it to the best of his ability. And when he felt that he had achieved this peak of his capabilities, he would demonstrate them to Simon Bartlett. He wanted Simon Bartlett to be convinced — convinced beyond any possible doubt — that his, and Gee's capabilities, were real.

Only then would vindication be achieved for him and Gee. And if total humiliation could be achieved for Simon Bartlett at the same time, that would be an added benefit. This was the oath he made, and this was the oath that he mind-shouted to his Gee, hoping that she would hear it.

As he put his phone back inside his jacket pocket, Anthony Thorpe permitted himself another weak smile. The first stage of vindication had been quite effective, and he'd captured it all on video too. He was shortly going to bring the person he knew as Simon Bartlett, and who everybody else knew as Professor Sir Simon Bartlett, to his knees. His humiliation had only just begun.

Robyn was pleased at how calm she was considering this was her first time in the field on a real assignment. As she and Samuel made their way along the corridor towards Heather's office, Robyn was looking forward to her first official, field-debriefing. She was going to make sure it was fully detailed.

Chapter 22 Monday 09h35

Asif Tahir was Heather's field-systems operative. His role was to run all the systems that Heather needed to make her operation a success. He loved this role. It gave him access to some of the most extraordinary IT systems and hardware he could ever dream of handling.

If he'd been back at one of the MoD's main centres, then his time would have been fully occupied. In the field, however, there was always lots of downtime while you waited for something to happen. This tended to bore many people, but not Asif. He could access all the systems, explore them for interesting features, or even be doing some developmental work of his own creation. He'd designed the Contactor system when he'd had downtime on previous field-exercises, and was pleased to see this was the first time it was being deployed. He wanted to make sure it was a success.

At the moment though, his tool of choice was a piece of A3 paper which had the layout of the main auditorium on it. Heather, Asif, Robyn and Samuel were sat at the round table in their office-cum-storeroom. Samuel was busy drawing arrows, his clipboard inconveniently taking up over half the table, with Asif's sheet of paper squeezed onto the small remaining area.

"Samuel was sitting in seat H14," said Robyn.

"Here," said Asif, marking a dot on the seat marked H14 on his layout.

"I sighted Samuel's arrows toward a fire extinguisher on the wall by the fire exit," added Robyn.

"Which side of the fire exit?" asked Asif, pointing at the fire exit on his diagram.

"Left side," responded Robyn.

Asif put another dot on the layout and drew a straight line between the two. He recalled the fire extinguisher she was referring to from when he'd walked the room first thing this morning, looking for defining features. Even though he was a systems person, he was also extremely practical.

"Anything else you can tell me?" he asked.

"There were a lot of people in the sightline, maybe ten or twelve." Robyn started to describe some of the people she could remember. "There were…"

"That's all I need, thanks," said Asif, cutting her off abruptly as he stood up. "I can check the Contactor system to see who was sat where, and overlay that onto this layout. I'll get back to you when I have something." He told Heather he had to see the hotel's maintenance about a power-supply issue he was having, and with a brief nod of his head towards everyone, he left the room.

Asif had spoken and moved so quickly that Robyn was disappointed she hadn't had the opportunity to tell him more.

Heather, meanwhile, was observing Samuel as he created his picture of arrows, which was almost a full page at this stage. Though she'd never seen one of the SPECCABs in action before, she'd heard about Samuel, and his ability to detect mental-projection activity. Heather had asked if he could be at her conference, and her request had been approved.

"Tell me how the arrow-thing works," said Heather, moving her chair round to take up the empty space left by Asif. Robyn decided to give a full explanation to Heather. She started off with the initial research activities, then the training exercises, followed by the simulations in secure locations. She wanted to ensure she gave Heather all the details.

While she spoke, Heather was watching the arrows being drawn, and noticed how Samuel seemed oblivious to the two women and their conversation about him. His head was held low over his paper, his nose almost touching it as he continued drawing arrows, all pointing to his right and away from Heather.

While Robyn's narrative continued, Heather's mind drifted off. The conference had started barely an hour ago, and already she'd had two significant events happen. First, the Tassicker fellow had caused a commotion in the breakfast room, and then told her about the miraculously-appearing Post-it notes. Then secondly, she had a key-note speaker seemingly unable to speak any key notes at all, due to a peculiar sneezing fit — apparently caused by some mental projections.

That's a pretty powerful start, she thought. It could be a busy day after all. And now she was sat with a woman who talked excessively and wouldn't get to the point. Heather's patience had now gone beyond its breaking limit, and she had to get back to the conference. She needed to speed things up. She looked at Robyn, and focussed her mind.

GET TO THE POINT! she thought loudly, projecting it towards Robyn.

Robyn stopped in mid-sentence, her mouth open. She'd just been explaining some of the training validation-protocols they'd used during the testing of Samuel's skills, when she had this sudden urge to get to the point of what she was saying. She couldn't immediately make the leap from what she had been saying, to produce the framed conclusion that she felt the necessity to say. She stammered incoherently while her mind searched for that one sentence she needed.

She glanced down at the table. Her mouth, which had been open while she searched for the words she needed, opened a little more. Her jaw had dropped because of what she saw on the table. Robyn instantly realised what had happened and glared at Heather, her mouth now closed and tight-lipped.

Heather noticed the rapid change in Robyn's manner, and also glanced down at the table. Samuel had rotated his drawing so the arrows pointed directly at her.

DON'T YOU DARE POINT THAT PICTURE AT ME!

Without meaning to, Heather had reacted angrily and projected this thought directly at Samuel.

Just a few moments earlier, Samuel had been drawing his arrows, when he heard a whooshing in his head. As he'd been shown, he rotated his picture to point towards the source of the sound. It seemed to be coming from the lady across the table. Samuel didn't lift his eyes to look at her, as he didn't like looking at people's faces. When their mouths moved, it still reminded him of his parents shouting at him in that exaggerated manner. It was good to always be looking down at his arrows.

The whooshing stopped, and Samuel was just about to turn his picture back to its left-to-right orientation, when a massive whoosh came straight at him and filled his head with sound. Rather than pass by him, this whoosh came straight into his head and reverberated around the inside of his skull like a gunshot in a cave. He'd never heard a noise so loud in his life. It was the first whoosh that had ever been aimed directly at him, and he knew he needed to get away from it.

He instinctively straightened his legs to push his chair away from the noise's source, and he leaned back as far as he could. Rather than slide, the back-legs of the chair caught on the carpeting, and his chair started to topple-over backwards. Samuel was not a nimble man. His arms flailed wildly, but not enough to recover his balance. As Samuel and his chair passed the tipping point, his legs went up in the air and he fell over backwards, hitting the ground with a heavy *thud*, which dislodged his thick spectacles.

He didn't cry out. He didn't make a sound. He simply rolled sideways off the chair and lay in a foetal position, his knees tight against his chest. Robyn moved quickly to be by Samuel's side. He didn't seem to be hurt, just badly shaken. Considering Heather was supposed to be an experienced field operative, Robyn was surprised that she just sat there, seemingly stunned into immobility.

“It’s alright, Samuel. It’s alright,” said Robyn comfortingly. “Let’s go back to your room for a rest.” She offered her arm for him to take if he needed it. But he didn’t take it, preferring to get up clumsily by himself.

Heather was now moving, and had sprung around the table. She put her hand under Samuel’s arm to assist him to stand. “I’m so sorry about that. I didn’t mean to do anything to you,” she said.

Samuel pulled his arm away, recoiling from her touch.

“You don’t touch him,” spat Robyn venomously. “Never.”

She gently ushered Samuel back onto his feet, handed him his spectacles, picked up his clipboard and pencil case, and guided him out of the room. The door closed behind them.

Heather slowly picked up the fallen chair, and sat down on it.

She took a deep breath and put her head in her hands. As Samuel had pushed himself away and had started to topple over, she’d seen the look of absolute terror in his eyes. Given his appearance and the challenges he had, she imagined that those eyes hadn’t seen much joy in their life.

And then I go and do that to him.

She’d initially felt anger towards Samuel.

But now she felt ashamed of herself.

And then so guilty.

And suddenly so sad.

Her thoughts went back to the last time she’d felt so sad.

When Heather was eleven, she, her sister Sally, and her parents had lived in a small terraced-house in the centre of Colchester. There was a small paved yard at the back, which was all the outdoor-area that the girls had to play in. On sunny days, her mum would often drive the two girls to spend the day at their granny and grandpa’s house, a few miles away, which had a huge garden that the two girls loved to play in.

One glorious day, they’d decided to do this, and were preparing to go. Heather was busy with a paint-by-numbers picture which was coming along nicely. She wanted to finish it so she could mount it on her bedroom wall.

“Aren’t you getting ready Heather?” asked her mum.

“I’ve changed my mind. I want to stay here and finish this,” replied Heather, petulantly.

"Come on," said her mother. "Just a little while ago, you were really keen to go to granny and grandpa's."

"Well, I've changed my mind," said Heather, just wanting some peace and quiet.

"What do you want to do, Sally?" asked her mum of her sister.

"Maybe, I'll stay here as well," replied Sally.

That would not give Heather the peace and quiet she needed to finish her painting.

JUST GO NOW! GIVE ME SOME PEACE AND QUIET thought Heather to herself.

"Come on, Sally. Let's go now," said her mother. "We'll give Heather a bit of peace and quiet. I'll be back in twenty minutes, and your dad is just upstairs fixing a cupboard door." She kissed Heather on the head, and her mum and Sally went out of the door.

That worked out nicely, thought the young Heather, as she continued with her painting.

Her sister and mum were buried in adjacent graves. The vicar who led the service had said many things about life and death. Only one of which had stayed with the young Heather. He'd said, 'Even if God did have the power to prevent car accidents, it wasn't Him that caused them'.

Heather knew it was her who'd told them to go, even when her sister had wanted to stay. Well, she hadn't told them openly. She'd only thought about wanting them to go. But surely, thinking about something couldn't cause it to happen. *Or could it?*

It could.

For years now, Heather had been able to *move people along* as she described it to herself. If they were undecided on something, she was able to get them to make a decision, or take a specific action. She knew she couldn't make somebody do something they didn't want to do. But when they were at the indecision-point, she was able to tip them one way or the other. It was a skill she'd never told anyone about. She'd always convinced herself that she was just helping people to do something they wanted to do anyway.

The unfortunate incident with Samuel just now, where he'd simply pointed a piece of paper at her, had blown her self-delusion completely apart. And it was confirmed by the way that she had literally blown him off his seat with her thought.

She hadn't meant to do it. She felt the weighty cloak-of-guilt being placed over her shoulders and back. Heavy, to act as a reminder that it was there. Thick, to act like an insulating layer and prevent the guilt of what she'd done to that poor man from escaping.

She now realised something else she felt guilty about. *She* had sent her sister and her mum off to granny and grandpa's that morning, all those years ago. If *she* hadn't used her nudge, they wouldn't have gone. She knew she hadn't killed them — but she also knew she hadn't let them live.

And now, that waffling woman and her SPECCAB, both knew she had this capability — and they were angry with her.

What would they do?

Who would they tell?

She felt anger rising up within her again. Anger towards them. They could cause so much trouble for her. Then she realised that, actually, the anger she was feeling was directed against herself for the two lives that she'd destroyed all those years ago. All this time she subconsciously knew what she'd done. That she was responsible. That was where the anger needed to be directed.

At herself.

"Control, Heather. Control," she said quietly in her solitude.

All that the rambling woman and the SPECCAB had done was to point out a truth to her. She shouldn't be angry at them. They were just doing what they were supposed to do — their job. *And they'd done a good job too.*

Heather realised she'd been referring to them as the waffling, rambling woman and the SPECCAB. They were essentially good people and well-meaning. Their names were Robyn and Samuel, and they deserved due respect from her.

And she would give it to them.

It was barely a minute since she'd picked up Samuel's fallen chair and sat down on it. But in that minute, almost her full lifetime had gone through her thoughts. If Heather had reflected on what her mind had achieved for her in such a short space of time, she would have been astounded. The massive quantity of memories it had sifted through instantly, and the emotions it had combined with those selected memories, had enabled her to re-analyse part of her life.

Heather's mind had acted like a time machine, taking her back through the decades, and allowing her to change her view on what had happened in the past – both decades ago, and seconds ago. Her thoughts empowered her to be a different person going forward into the future. Such was the authority of the human mind. It had reviewed and re-assessed her life in sixty-seconds. And all this happened due to countless synapses firing for the first time in her brain.

Heather hadn't understood that her mind had performed like a personal time machine, solely for her own benefit. However, the next time this happened she'd appreciate it a lot more. *Because it would save her life.*

Chapter 23 Monday 10h00

After a short respite, Professor Bartlett had returned to complete his keynote speech without any further dramas. Reece expected him to come back with a little more humility and empathy toward the audience, but he issued the briefest of apologies, and then became even more pompous, as though this would recover any credibility he had lost.

Towards the end of his speech, some in the audience were hoping that the earlier affliction would return, just to put him in his place. But it didn't. What was good news for many, was that in order to get the conference back on time, the chairman didn't allow any questions.

The chairman thanked the Professor and then explained that all the speakers for the rest of the conference had been asked to summarise their top-three takeaway points at the end of their presentation.

The first speaker's title slide then appeared on the large screen behind the podium.

Chapter 24 Monday 10h05

Presentation #1

What we know is interesting.

What we don't know is fascinating!

By Dr Jean Rose PhD
Head of Scientific Knowledge Mapping
University of Surrey

Many academics like to impress you with what they know — and that's because the whole point of academia is to expand our knowledge. Beyond the existing boundaries of our current knowledge, are vast swathes of un-accessed, future knowledge. Things that science is busy trying to unlock right now, that when they succeed, will advance us a little way into this future. Converting some of the unknown into the known, that adds to the vast pool of knowledge that we have accumulated over the centuries.

In my studies of human knowledge, I look backwards over the shoulder of humanity. And what I find most amazing aren't the new boundaries that we are busy exploring — it's the significant gaps we've left behind us.

Some critical areas where we don't know the answers to things we should know. But more importantly, there are some things we don't seem to want to know.

A peculiar walk

Imagine you are taking a walk in the countryside. You are travelling a route that goes up hill, and down dale, and which will eventually bring you back to home.

At one point, you come to a wide river. You aren't sure how to get across, but in an instant, you find yourself on the other side of the river. You continue on your stroll without a second thought. The path suddenly stops at an impenetrable forest. Again, you pause, unsure of what to do, but in a moment you are on the far side of the forest, with the path stretching out in front of you. Then the path brings you to the top of a tall cliff, with no apparent way down. Again you pause, and then miraculously find yourself standing at the bottom of the cliff, with the path once again before you. This happens repeatedly for differing obstacles, and every time you inexplicably appear on the other side of the obstacle, with the path ahead of you.

When you finally get home, your spouse asks how your walk was, and you reply that you simply followed the path, and that nothing unusual happened. It might seem peculiar that in this story, you ignored all the weird things that happened. But are you aware that this is precisely what happens in your daily life?

In this presentation, I'm going to take you on a journey which will start at the vast scale of the cosmos, before passing down through the scale of human beings and our daily life, to end at the level of the fundamental building blocks of the universe, the atomic scale.

I'll show you some of the extraordinary anomalies that exist around, and inside, each and every one of us. Things that scientists tend to ignore, purely because they have no way to explain what is happening.

THE COSMIC SCALE

Our missing universe

Have you ever looked up on a cloudless night, contemplating the untold number of stars, twinkling like diamonds on a black, velvet background, and wondered what mysteries the universe holds for us? The biggest mystery is that the stars and planets in every galaxy only add up to about five per cent of the calculated mass of the universe. We don't know what accounts for the other ninety-five per cent of it.

The universe started with the big bang, after which it expanded rapidly, and continues to expand, in all directions. The force of gravity should tend to cause this expansion to slow down, stop, and then reverse direction, causing the universe to start to contract. By observing distant galaxies, cosmologists have confirmed that the expansion of the universe isn't slowing down — it's speeding up. The universe is expanding at a faster rate than it did in the distant past, and for this to happen, there must be some kind of force driving this acceleration.

The belief is that space isn't empty at all, and that it contains something that is exerting this accelerating force on the universe. It's an extremely weak force, but the fact that there is so much of it, enables it to have an immense effect. This force has been called dark energy — not because it is evil — but because it is an unknown entity. This dark energy is believed to make up seventy per cent of the missing ninety-five per cent of the universe.

Advances in telescope technology have enabled cosmologists to understand that the known mass of all the stars and planets in the universe is insufficient to account for the gravitational observations that they've made. There would need to be around twenty-five per cent more matter in space for the observations to make sense. We don't know what this missing twenty-five per cent of matter is, but we do know what it isn't. It isn't stars or planets or inter-stellar dust. It's something else that has mass, but which can't be seen. This unaccounted part of the universe has been labelled dark matter, purely because we can't see it and we don't have any idea what it is.

The dark void of space may be dark but it certainly isn't a void. There are vast quantities of unknown energy and invisible matter somehow hiding away out there.

The mystery of gravity

Gravity is the force which every single body exerts on every other body, and which is proportional to its mass. Gravity keeps our Earth orbiting the Sun, for without it, we would just slingshot into the deep abyss of space. Gravity keeps the moon orbiting our Earth, which in turn causes the movement of the tides. Gravity keeps you seated on the chair that you are currently in. Without gravity, you'd float into the air the moment you stood up.

The basic principles of gravity were identified and mastered hundreds of years ago when Sir Isaac Newton first observed a falling apple. Today, we understand them to such a degree and accuracy, that we can launch rockets into space and use the gravitational effect of the planets to slingshot them in specific directions. The mysterious thing is that we have absolutely no idea what causes gravity.

None whatsoever.

Constants that aren't constant

If you draw a circle, and then add a straight-line through the centre, this line represents the diameter. There is a fixed ratio between the circumference and diameter of your circle, for the circumference is always pi times longer than the diameter. The value of pi is approximately 3.141592 or 22/7. It never changes, no matter the size of the circle you draw, or where you draw it. Using this knowledge of pi, once you know any one of the circumference, diameter or area of a circle, you can work out the other two precisely. It has never changed over time and never will.

It is a constant.

But imagine if tomorrow, we discovered that the value of pi had changed. That in the distant past it was very slightly different. Do you think this is possible? It shouldn't be possible, because constants are supposed to be constant. That's part of their definition of being a constant.

In our universe there are numerous other constants which, just like pi, should never change. One of these is called the fine-structure constant.

If you touch two magnets together, you will be aware of two forces that feel different in nature, but which are the same force in reverse. If the magnets are arranged such that the north-pole of one is brought towards the south-pole of the other, the magnets are attracted to each other. If one magnet is turned around such that the same poles are pointing together, the magnets will repel each other. These forces of attraction and repulsion are opposite variations of the same physical principle.

In a similar way, a particle can have a positive or a negative electrical charge. Particles, like magnets, are attracted towards other particles with the opposite electrical charge, and repelled by those with the same electrical charge. This effect is called electromagnetism, and the strength of this electromagnetic force of attraction or repulsion is based on the fine-structure constant. The value of the fine-structure constant is approximately 1/137 — but it isn't the numeric value which is of interest — it's the fact that it is supposed to be constant.

Early this millennium, a team of scientists from the University of New South Wales in Australia, led by John Webb and Julian King, were analysing data received by radio telescopes pointed at some of the oldest galaxies in the universe. As these galaxies are so much older than ours, they are located in a very different part of the universe to us. This team's research discovered that in these distant parts of the universe, the fine-structure constant had a slightly lower value. Not by very much, *but definitely smaller*. This caused much concern in the scientific community.

Then a few years later, the same team was pointing their telescope in the opposite direction, and they again found evidence for a changed value of the fine-structure constant — but this time it was *slightly larger* in value. It appeared that the fine-structure constant has different values, in different parts of the universe. This finding that a constant can vary across the universe had an alarming impact on many aspects of the scientific community, because constants are supposed to be constant.

Let me put the issue of a changing constant into context. Two plus three equals five. It always has and it always will. But what if there was evidence that billions of years ago, two plus three actually equalled 5.01? Can you imagine the impact this would have on mathematics?

Or what if we discovered that the value of pi changed when measured in different parts of the universe? This would mean that a circle drawn in a distant galaxy, is different in some way, to a circle drawn here on Earth, But how could a circle be different?

The findings of the Australian team were based on the observation of distant galaxies. However, a confirmation of this varying fine-structure constant came from a most unusual source here on Earth. The fine-structure constant is closely related to the rate of a nuclear reaction, and if it were possible to examine the remains of a nuclear reaction from the distant-past, the value of the fine-structure constant could be calculated as it was, at the time the nuclear reaction occurred.

Around two-billion years ago, conditions on Earth were such, that a low-level, self-sustaining nuclear reaction took place over several hundred-thousand years in a discrete body of uranium ore. This reaction changed the molecular structure of the uranium deposit, leaving behind a tell-tale, geological fingerprint. This ore body now forms the Oklo uranium mine in Gabon, West Africa. It is unique, as the only place on Earth where a natural nuclear reaction has taken place. It was while mining this uranium deposit in the 1970s, that geologists discovered it to be the remnant of this ancient nuclear reaction. When the ore was analysed, it was discovered that the fine-structure constant of two-billion years ago was different from the value of today.

This shows that a generally-accepted scientific constant (in this case the fine-structure constant) can, and does, change. It differs in different parts of the universe, and it changes over time in any specific part of the universe, such as here on Earth.

A constant that isn't constant, potentially undermines vast areas of scientific knowledge that are held to be fact. It's a very disturbing concept for science. It's an anomaly. Something that shouldn't be able to happen — but has happened.

And we don't know how, and we don't know why.

THE HUMAN SCALE

The enigma in our DNA

At the moment of our conception, we humans start out as a fertilised single-cell, and inside this cell is a molecule of DNA — or deoxyribonucleic acid. Our DNA is like an incredibly-thin, very-long ladder with three-billion rungs that has been rolled into a tight ball. If you were to carefully unwind this DNA ladder, you'd find it to be about seventy-two inches long, but microscopically thin. This DNA ladder forms the blueprint of how each of us should be built to create a unique human-being.

Around twenty-four hours after conception, the first cell divides into two, and the DNA strand splits long-ways down the middle. The left-side of the split DNA strand grows a new right-side, and the right-side grows a new left-side. This ensures that both cells each have a copy of the blueprint to follow. These two cells will in turn divide to form two more cells, and the DNA splitting and re-growing process is repeated. This dividing process continues until, at birth, a baby is born made up of several trillion cells.

In this nine-month gestation in the womb, the seventy-two inch long DNA strand has been faithfully split and re-built trillions of times. However, of these seventy-two inches, only *one-inch* of the DNA contains instructions of who we are as an individual. Geneticists have no idea of the purpose of the other seventy-one inches. This used to be referred to as junk DNA, but there's something strange about it. If it had no purpose, then it would rapidly mutate and not correct itself. But long sequences of this non-coding DNA have remained essentially the same for over 100-million years.

So they must be doing something — but what? And why do we need so much of it?

The first heartbeat

I'm going to be very glib about possibly the most fundamental question of all — *How did life start?*

There are ninety-eight chemical elements that occur naturally on Earth. Imagine that you were provided with the ultimate laboratory, equipped with ninety-eight jars each containing one of these elements. Imagine too, there was equipment that could produce any combination of heat, pressure, humidity, gas-levels, lighting, and any other condition you needed. How would you turn a combination of those chemicals into some form of life? Intuitively this doesn't feel like it's possible, and to date it has been scientifically impossible to achieve in the laboratory.

I'm not taking the formation of life question any further, as there's an extension to this which is even more perplexing.

How did we become intelligent?

In this ultimate laboratory, if you did somehow manage to create a living thing, it would most likely be an extremely basic life form. Let's assume that your life form starts to evolve and even manages to mutate and create a brain — or some other organ — that it can use to think. How do you create that first thought? And then the second thought? And how does your life-form learn to combine thoughts one and two to create a third, totally new thought? Let's call this process of thought generation *intelligence*. How do you create this intelligence in your laboratory?

We have no idea where intelligence comes from. And while we are talking about what's going on inside our heads, we don't know how thinking works. We know physiologically that the brain is sending millions and millions of signals every second between different combinations of brain cells, as we can observe this by the use of electrocardiograph machines. But we don't know how the brain actually processes and stores information. Additionally, we have no idea on how the brain comes up with new ideas, or where flashes of inspiration originate.

We have absolutely no idea — and yet we call ourselves the intelligent species.

Where are your memories kept?

Think back to when you were a child, to a time in the past when you were playing on a beach with a bucket and spade. Many of you have just been recalling an experience you had as a child which happened decades ago. You may recall considerable detail of that event including how you felt, the people who were with you, the sounds, smells, weather and so on. How are you able to store all that information for decades inside your head? How are you able to instantly recall it and re-live it as a multi-media, technicolour, seemingly-real experience in your mind?

Science has no idea about how this is possible.

Dreaming shouldn't happen

Many of us dream at night — some of us in surprising levels of detail too. Again, we have no idea why we dream. Common sense dictates that the brain should switch off and re-energise itself at night, like the rest of our body does. But not so. For some reason that we don't understand, the brain engages itself in a series of dream cycles each night, where it creates mini-scenarios and sequences of activities that it pretends we are involved in. Sometimes dreams are so real that they can disturb our sleep.

Dreams aren't unintentional by-products of the mind — we are intended to dream. The body has even created a mechanism whereby the brain releases chemicals during dreaming, that stop the motor neurons from sending out signals, which effectively paralyses the muscles in our body. This enables us to dream about walking without our arms and legs starting to move.

We all have several dreams, every night of our lives. We don't recognise this fact because we usually don't remember them when we wake. We are clearly meant to have dreams, but what purpose they serve is unknown to us.

THE ATOMIC SCALE

We've considered some things we don't understand at the grandest scale of the universe, and at the level of daily activity of human life. Now, let's drop down to the scale of atoms and particles.

Things that change because you watch them

Quantum mechanics is the study of matter itself. How atoms, and the fundamental particles that they are made of, behave.

Matter usually behaves in one of two distinct ways, either like a particle or like a wave. To understand the difference between the two, imagine a stone dropped in the middle of a pond. Before the stone is dropped, it has potential energy due to its vertical height above the water. When the stone is released, it speeds up as it falls, and the potential energy it had due to its height is converted into kinetic (or speed) energy. This is particle-motion, where something with a physical mass moves in a straight line to end up in a new position.

As the stone hits the water, its kinetic energy is converted into a small amount of sound energy (you hear a splash) and a lot of pressure energy, which causes waves to move out from the impact point in concentric circles. With wave-motion, the water in the pond is lifted each time a wave passes by, but once the wave has passed any particular part of the pond, the water level returns to where it was before. There is no net movement of the water, whereas the stone has physically moved from its original position, high above the water.

We can recognise there is a clear distinction between particle-motion (the falling stone) and wave-motion (the ripples in the pond) in the normal course of life. In quantum mechanics, however, this distinction between particles and waves doesn't exist. Things that normally behave like particles start to act like waves in certain conditions, and things that are normally observed as waves, seem to act like particles.

There is a well-documented demonstration of this effect called the double-slit experiment. It consists of a firing-mechanism, like a gun, that shoots very-small, very-light particles called electrons, through two extremely-narrow slits in a screen. Behind this screen is a wall which is capable of measuring what happens when the electrons hit it. If lots of these electrons are fired through the two slits and they behave like particles, then the back wall should detect a pattern that looks like two vertical lines where the electrons have come through the slits. However, if the electrons were to behave like waves, then they would spread out as they left the gun, and go through both slits. As they pass through each slit, they will again spread out like a wave and leave a widely-spread pattern on the back wall behind the slits. This pattern would be very different in appearance to the two vertical lines seen when the electrons behave like particles.

Now, let's imagine we are running this experiment. When the first slit is blocked off, and we start firing the gun, the electrons go through the second slit and we see a vertical line on the wall behind the second slit. When this second slit is blocked off and the first slit is opened, a similar vertical line appears on the wall behind the first slit. So, based on this, when we open both slits and fire the electron gun, we would expect to see two vertical lines on the back wall, one behind each slit. Strangely, this isn't the case. When we open both slits something very bizarre happens. Rather than getting two vertical lines on the back wall, we get the pattern associated with waves coming through the slits.

When only one slit is open the electrons behave as particles. By opening the second slit, we cause the behaviour of all the electrons to change from a particle to a wave. What is even more interesting is that if we now close the second slit, the behaviour of the electrons immediately reverts back to that of a particle. So whether the second slit is open or closed, dictates how the electrons passing through the first slit will behave. This double-slit experiment isn't just a scientific theory, it's an easy laboratory demonstration to set up, and it has been observed and validated many times.

Something as outrageously un-scientific as electrons arbitrarily changing the way they behave, obviously demanded an explanation. In the 1920s, in an effort to clarify the situation, an eminent group of scientists led by Danish physicist Niels Bohr, developed what is termed the Copenhagen Interpretation to address how something can be both a wave and a particle. They determined that what is passing through the experiment is not a particle or an actual wave at all. *It is a probability wave.*

This implies that the electron does not have a specific location, but has a probability of being anywhere on a wave-front. Some locations will be more probable than others, and some will be less probable. Their interpretation was that an electron not being observed doesn't exist as a particle at all, but has a wave-like property covering the areas of probability where it could be found. When the electron is actually observed, the wave-function collapses and the electron becomes, and acts like, a particle.

This interpretation very neatly explains the observed change in behaviour of the waves / particles in the double-slit experiment. When we aren't looking at a specific particle, the probability wave of that single particle spreads out and passes through both slits at the same time, and is picked up by the back measuring-wall as a wave. If we observe the electron by placing detectors at the slits, the probability wave collapses and it is forced into revealing its location which causes it to be observed as a particle.

That something so fundamental as the properties of an electron passing through a slit being dependent upon whether it is being watched or not, definitely stretches the expectations of normal behaviour. This weirdness of quantum mechanics doesn't end here though.

Faster than the speed of light

Quantum entanglement is an aspect of quantum mechanics that Einstein himself referred to as *spooky action at a distance*. With quantum entanglement, two particles are forced together to interact, so that they produce a shared end-state. Electrons can possess and share a number of different end-states, one of which is known as *spin*. For convenience of explanation, let's assume that this state of spin can be either clockwise or anti-clockwise. Getting pairs of electrons to interact and entangle is straightforward in a laboratory, so let us imagine that two electrons have been entangled — and then separated from each other.

Initially, we don't know what the direction of spin is for each electron, as both could be spinning either way. However, when one of the electrons is observed, and measured to be spinning in a specific direction (e.g. clockwise), the other electron in this entangled pair will, from that moment on, be found to be spinning in an anti-clockwise direction. Measuring one electron influences the state of the other, even though they may be separated over a relatively large distance.

In August 2008, Nature magazine reported an experiment undertaken by the University of Geneva using photons instead of electrons. They placed a photon source at the exact mid-point between two villages, located eleven-miles apart, and which were connected by fibre-optic cables. For twenty-four hours, they sent separated pairs of entangled photons over the fibre-optic cable; the first to one village and the second to the other village. As the photons arrived at each village, they observed one of the pair of entangled photons and measured the speed with which the other adopted the corresponding state. The time taken for the second one to change showed that the two were communicating in some way, at over ten-thousand times the speed of light.

Consciousness and quantum mechanics

The number of things we don't understand about quantum mechanics is vast, and at this level the principles of common sense and normality seem to collapse completely. The physicist Richard Feynman won a Nobel Prize for his work in this field, and even he said that 'If you think you understand quantum mechanics, you don't understand quantum mechanics'.

Essentially, the Copenhagen Interpretation suggests that nothing is real unless it has been observed. Referring to this perspective, renowned physicist Stephen Hawking is concerned that if this is true, then perhaps there must be some outside body observing our universe; otherwise our universe would just collapse back into its own wave-function. British physicist Sir Roger Penrose believes that even consciousness itself is linked into the strange and wonderful world of quantum mechanics, as none of the known laws of science can even begin to account for the concept of human consciousness.

With quantum mechanics we have reached the point where physics and human-consciousness seem to meet. It's an area that many physicists like to avoid, as it appears there's a direct link between the conscious choice to measure something through experiment, and the outcome of that experiment.

THE ANOMALIES IN LIFE

I started this presentation by taking you on a walk along a path in the countryside, where you suddenly appeared on the far side of a wide river, impenetrable forest and tall cliff. What we've considered so far aren't the peculiar transitions across obstacles — these represent *the regular path on your journey.*

We're now going to consider those strange transitions. *The weirdness on your journey is about to start.*

Evolutionary cycles that don't add up

Mankind has been moving along a particular path for a long time, and that path is evolution. Many of us might think that it's been a steady path of continuous improvement, stretching all the way back to when we were pond scum. Each generation of life being a little more advanced in some way, than the previous one. Generally this is true. However, there are some big exceptions — or anomalies — in the evolutionary process where it all seems to fall down.

Research into human evolutionary development can be a slow process. To make useful discoveries in practical timeframes, and to stop themselves from dying before their studies are complete, researchers need to move faster than the twenty-odd year breeding cycle of the human race. To achieve this, they study faster reproducing species like fruit flies and bacteria for their research. A fruit fly generation is around twelve-days, which gives thirty generational-evolutions in a year. With some bacteria the generation time is twenty-to-thirty minutes, which practically delivers around 2,000-generations in a year. Scientists have been using these two species for over twenty-years, aiming to prove how the evolutionary process works in different ways.

University of California, Irvine researchers found that after observing 600-generations of fruit fly evolution over twenty-years, all they managed to develop were fruit flies that were marginally different — but that were sterile, so they died out. Michigan State University evolutionary biologists didn't do much better with their bacteria. After 40,000-generations all they had achieved were bacteria with degenerative mutations, and few positive mutations at all. What's interesting to consider here, is that researchers often try to accelerate the results by picking only the stronger examples of each generation to take to the next stage. So, even with this evolutionary assistance, few beneficial results were achieved.

Too much change in an unrealistic timeframe

It's a fact that we are descended from apes. Homo habilis was one of our ape-like ancestors who lived around two-million years ago. Without meaning to offend our revered ancestors, Homo habilis looks decidedly more ape-like than human. With a big assumption that the average evolutionary-generation is fifteen-years based on it being around twenty-years now and only ten-years then, our evolution from ape-like man to GQ front-cover model took around 130,000 evolutionary cycles.

So in 40,000 evolutionary cycles, the bacteria barely advances itself while in just three times that number of cycles, we have improved from ape-like, to modern human. Personally, I like to consider myself a higher life form than bacteria — which means I'm a lot more complex an organism. Surely this complexity would tend to make human evolution a much slower, and more involved process than the bacteria?

It seems that our evolutionary achievement is strangely peculiar, in a very positive sense. How is it that the human race has managed to become a remarkably, well-developed diverse species in such a short number of cycles compared to the retrograde evolution that has been observed in the laboratory in simpler life-forms?

Evolution: An almost-right theory

In his book *Evolution: A Theory in Crisis*, Michael Denton states 'The concept of the continuity of nature has existed in the minds of man, never in the facts of nature. Nature, in short, appears to be profoundly discontinuous'. These discontinuities are so-widely prevalent in the field of evolution that they have their own term. They are called saltation, and the definition of this term is 'Abrupt evolutionary change or sudden large-scale mutation'.

Charles Darwin's theories of evolution have generally been shown to be correct for relatively minor developments within species, but they can't account for the relationships between classes and orders of species. Darwin's classic text *On the Origin of Species* was first published in 1859 and at that time the fossil record was poorly known. Darwin himself described the perceived lack of transitional fossils as 'the most obvious and gravest objection which can be urged against my theory'. He dismissed this by explaining the extreme imperfection of the geological fossil record.

Over 150-years later, those fossils still haven't been found.

The Cambrian explosion

Around 580-million years ago there was a sudden explosion of life on Earth. For no obvious reason, the previously steady progress of evolution accelerated for a period of around 30-million years to produce an immense array of new development and variants of existing life-forms.

Science has no explanations as to why this explosion of life would suddenly start. And then just as suddenly stop.

Eyes that see

Human organs are extraordinarily-complex things, but the one that causes most concern for the evolutionary biologists is the eye. The eye is one (or two) of the fascinating items that suddenly appeared out of the Cambrian era. It may well have evolved from a light-sensitive spot on the skin of some life-form. Each component of the eye such as the lens, retina, eyeball and optic nerve has scientists baffled as to how they developed.

But this mystery is nothing compared to what would have to happen inside the brain to process the signals from this newly developed organ. And also to be able to understand and interpret what was being *seen* for the first time.

How the eye evolved is one mystery. But how the brain understood what the early eyes saw, is much more confounding.

Instant feathers

Military fighter planes may be impressive due to the speed at which they fly and their airborne capabilities, but this is nothing compared to the miracle of the feather. Feathers, of course, are what help birds to fly, keep warm and dry, colour or camouflage them, and are unique to birds and bird like species.

We do not know the origin of the feather as there are no traces of anything evolving into a feather. Feathers just seemed to appear from nowhere in the evolution process.

Monarch butterfly mystery

The Monarch butterfly demonstrates an interesting evolution through four different stages in a short space of time. It starts life as an egg, and then hatches into a caterpillar which uses its powerful, chewing jaws to eat its own weight in leaves each day for about two weeks. It then wraps itself in silk, and becomes a chrysalis for another two weeks. During this time phenomenal changes occur, such as changing its chewing-mouth into a straw-like tongue, which is the necessary tool for sipping nectar from flowers. It uses enzymes to dissolve all its internal organs, and then grows beautifully-decorated wings before finally emerging as a ready-to-fly butterfly. And it achieves all this in around twenty-eight days.

In a typical year there are four generations of Monarch butterfly. The first three have a lifespan of four to six weeks. However, the fourth-generation live for six-to-eight months and actually migrate to a warmer climate over the winter period, before returning to their home-territory to start the annual cycle again.

How does every fourth-generation manage to live so much longer, and how does it know it should migrate to warmer areas?

These examples are just a few of the major anomalies that exist along the path of evolution. These are the points were species have come across some obstacle, and have miraculously appeared on the other side — and we have no idea how it happened.

ANOMALIES AND DISCONTINUITIES

Nature has supported the consistent development of our species over time by creating order, in a disorderly universe. By following this consistency back through time, we have formed the theory of evolution. However, there are specific points in the past where we observe that a discontinuity occurred, and the consistency was disrupted. Subsequent to this discontinuity, the consistency restarted — but aligned in a slightly different direction.

An anomaly occurred which disrupted the seemingly ordered sequence of our existence, and the discontinuity effectively acts as the marker of the anomaly happening. Our theories and scientific laws are valid for the consistency before and after the anomaly, but they can't account for the anomaly itself.

It isn't just in evolution that this happen, as we've seen that anomalies occur in other scientific fields too.

We like consistency in science, because much of science is based upon consistency. Science can't handle the disconnects. Perhaps the map of universal development consists of a series of wonderfully-straight highways, miles and miles in length, with occasional bends that slightly change the direction of travel. The straight parts of the highway are where everything comes together to work as it should, while the bends are the brief moments in our universal development where an anomaly occurs to re-align us for the next super-long straight section.

The unfortunate thing with scientific laws and theories is that they have to be valid on absolutely every occasion. If they aren't consistent in this regard then the theory must be wrong — *go find a new one*. The converse of this is when a theory seems to be valid for a particular aspect of nature, and then we discover an anomaly, then the anomaly needs to be discredited as the theory has to be seen to be correct. Especially when large numbers of other theories may have been built on an initial base-theory, that is now potentially at risk.

Anomalies have clearly happened in the past which triggered discontinuities in the development of the universe, nature and the human race. We don't know what causes them. We don't know why they happen at those specific moments. And we don't know how they happen.

It's alright to be all wrong

Holding two contradictory views is not perceived acceptable for scientific theories, as a theory is intended to have a definitive answer. But in our lives, on our world, in this universe, we need to acknowledge there is an element of uncertainty in our reality. We need to have scientific flexibility to acknowledge that occasionally, something unusual can, and does, happen to help our development. At the two extremes of scale in our universe, at the level of quantum mechanics and at the cosmic level, we are already seeing how the scientific rules and laws are falling apart.

When it comes time for the caterpillar to change, it wraps itself in a cocoon and it then produces enzymes that dissolve its own organs and body into a gooey pulp from which its butterfly form is created and emerges. Why is it that as a race we are so reluctant to accept discontinuities? If we were caterpillars in a caterpillar universe, would we deny the potential for us to become butterflies — because butterflies don't comply with what seems normal to caterpillars?

As academics, we spend our time looking for the new consistencies in the patterns of life. There is a whole different world of investigation and discovery that we pay very little attention to — and that's the field of anomalies. It's the anomalies that cause the discontinuities we've seen which, I believe, are the most fascinating opportunities for us to explore.

If anomalies occur at the smallest and largest of scales, then they must surely occur at the intermediate scale too — the human scale. I'm sure that many of us have experienced things we can't account for in our daily lives. Unexpected peculiarities. Things that seem oddly out-of-place.

These anomalies are the things that we should recognise, acknowledge and explore. If anomalies occur in our lives in small ways in one area, then why shouldn't they occur in potentially bigger areas of our lives too?

Let me reiterate some of the key gaps in our knowledge:

- We don't know what ninety-five per cent of the universe is made of
- We don't know what causes gravity
- We don't know what the bulk of our DNA does for us
- We don't know how life started
- We don't know where intelligence comes from
- We don't know where memories are stored
- We don't know why we dream
- We don't know how complex humans evolve so quickly when lesser life-forms evolve into junk
- We have many inexplicable mysteries in nature including the Cambrian explosion, eyes and sight, feathers and the Monarch butterfly
- We have energy that communicates at ten-thousand times the speed of light
- We have constants that aren't constant, and
- We have things that change just because you observe them

Is this giving you a new perspective on life? Are you beginning to see that not everything is as solid and pinned down as you thought?

Nick Bostrom is a Professor in the Faculty of Philosophy at Oxford University, and also the director of the Future of Humanity Institute there. He suggests that there is a significant chance that almost all civilisations at our level of development, become extinct before they become technologically mature. Knowing this would be about to happen, our future descendants may decide to create an ancestor-model so that humanity can stay alive in a computer simulation. He estimates that there's a twenty per cent chance that we are living in a Matrix-type simulation. If we were, would we ever be able to know it?

In the Matrix movie, there was a moment where Neo sees a black-cat twice, and that was a sign there was a glitch in the Matrix. What I've hopefully demonstrated to you is that there are glitches in our reality. These are the anomalies in our lives and in our history.

This conference is about the potential of the human mind, and there's so much that we don't know about what happens inside our heads. We don't know how we think, how we store memories or where original thought comes from. Over and above this, many people claim to be able to do incredible things with their minds. Unfortunately, science tends to debunk many of these abilities — but perhaps these abilities are anomalies — the things we should be exploring.

Many of us experience unusual things and occurrences in our personal lives. Anomalies that we can't explain. Because they are happening to us, we have a right to believe in them. *We shouldn't be told what's right, by people who can't explain what's wrong.* And there's a lot wrong with life and the universe that science just can't explain.

IN SUMMARY

As a conclusion, I've been asked to put the three essential points that I'd like you to take away from my presentation. They are:

1. If anomalies exist at the grandest-scale of the cosmos and at the scale of the fundamental particles that form us as human beings, then by default, they exist at the human-scale too. We should learn to observe the anomalies that happen to us, because that is where the truth and fascinating knowledge lies, and not in the consistent patterns of our daily existence.

2. There are so many things that we can't explain about how we developed into who we are — and yet we get on with our lives and achieve amazing things every day. This proves that we don't need to understand something before we can use it to our benefit. Perhaps we should be more believing in the anomalies that we experience in our lives, and learn to appreciate, enjoy and use them without being too analytical about their source.

3. The double-slit experiment proves that observing and measuring something can cause it to break down from an indeterminate state to become a known-form. What if this principle was valid at the human scale too? What if there are indeterminate anomalies all around us, and to make them known to us, we have to find our own way to observe them? We own the anomalies that happen to us, and we have the right to explore them. Don't be told otherwise. This should not stop us from believing in the anomalies and achieving amazing things through our mind and with our thinking.

Thank you for your time.

Chapter 25 Monday 11h05

It was the morning tea-break. Reece was standing near the front of a queue for refreshments when an overly-loud, and heavily-accented, voice called out to him.

"Hey man, howzit?" DD walked up to Reece and shook his hand warmly. DD smiled to the people behind Reece and offered another *Howzit* to them. In DD's mind, if he could engage them in conversation, it would justify his pushing in almost at the head of the queue. "I didn't think they'd put a synchronised-sneezing cabaret act so early in the conference," he said. The people immediately behind Reece in the queue laughed at this, so DD turned to them.

"Didn't you think that woman's talk was sensational? The bombshells she dropped were staggering," he enthused.

"Yes," said one of them, "there do appear to be some discrepancies around us."

"Discrepancies? *Discrepancies!*" said DD in a tone of incredulity. "Discrepancies are what you find in your change when you pay cash at a dodgy supermarket. There shouldn't be discrepancies in nature. If we found one, we should stop the bus and not move on until it's been resolved and understood. We're living in a world surrounded by massive anomalies, and the front page of today's newspapers talk about some politician who's screwing his secretary."

Reece and DD helped themselves to coffee and moved away.

"He called them discrepancies!" said DD, waving his biscuit in the direction of the coffee queue.

"If that professor had sneezed himself inside out and disappeared up his own arsehole, you Brits would express mild-surprise and then suggest a cup of tea while they sorted out the speaker roster," DD continued, oblivious to the fact that the majority of people within earshot were British.

"Reece, I'm having a brilliant insight here. You know what this reminds me of?" said DD.

There was a long pause. Reece recalled DD's tendency to use pauses to engage people in his conversation.

"No, I don't," he replied dutifully, to restart DD's conversation.

"There's a kids' joke," he said. "What goes ninety-nine, donk; ninety-nine, donk; ninety-nine, donk?

"I don't know."

"A centipede with a wooden leg. That speaker was saying that this is essentially how evolution works. It goes all the way from one to ninety-nine in perfect order, then there's a donk, and the perfect order starts all over again, until the next donk occurs. She's actually saying it's the *donks* that we need to understand, not the orderly one to ninety-nine part. She is so right, man."

Reece saw that DD was getting steadily more animated with each sip of coffee he took.

"And did you hear her refer to anomalies happening in our personal lives, too. I'll bet that because she's attuned to these anomalies, and she's experienced some fascinating things herself." He paused for a brief moment as something obviously clicked in his head. "I need to go and speak with her."

"You experienced any anomalies yourself?" asked Reece, suspecting DD had.

"Of course, man. Weird shit happens a lot. Hasn't it happened to you?

Reece thought that lime-green Post-it notes and future-predicting text messages weren't quite on the same scale as the evolution and quantum mechanics examples he'd just heard. But they certainly fell into the category of *weird shit*, as DD so eloquently put it.

"I suppose it has," admitted Reece.

DD finished his coffee in one gulp. "I needed that for a boost," he said, "I'm getting another coffee and then finding that speaker. See you later man."

DD with a double-dose of caffeine in him would certainly be an assault on that speaker's calm manner, thought Reece, as the bell sounded for the start of the next presentation.

Chapter 26 Monday 11h30

Presentation #2

Are we too lucky?

By Dr Richard Saunders
Department of Meta-Physical Sciences
Durham University

I'd like to introduce myself to you. I'm Richard, a thirty-two-year-old male of the Homo sapiens species. I weigh seventy-kilogrammes, and I have the same component-parts as most others of my species.

My body and organs are made up of many different types of cells. These cells are formed of molecules, which in turn consist of atoms — or chemical elements. If you were to take my seventy kilogrammes of body mass and break me down into my individual chemical elements, you'd find that I consist of around:

43 kg oxygen;
16 kg carbon;
7 kg hydrogen;
1.8 kg nitrogen;
1 kg calcium and
0.78 kg phosphorous.

The remaining 420-grams of me consists of a large number of different elements — all in very small quantities.

Now you know who, and what, I am.

YOU ARE MADE OF NOTHING

Every chemical element is made from just three different components; protons, neutrons and electrons. Protons and neutrons are about the same size and join together to make up the nucleus of the atom, while the electrons are much smaller and they whiz around the nucleus in a fuzzy, three-dimensional orbit. Each chemical element is distinct from any other due to the different combination of protons, neutrons and electrons it has. For example, my carbon atoms each have six protons, six neutrons and six electrons while my phosphorous atoms have fifteen protons, sixteen neutrons and fifteen electrons.

Let's look closely at the structure of an atom, and for convenience we'll consider a simple atom like helium. This atom consists of two protons and two neutrons bonded together to form the nucleus, with two electrons whizzing around this nucleus. If we take five-million helium atoms and place them side-by-side on a piece of paper, then this line of atoms would be the width of a full stop. Again to get a sense of scale, if the nucleus of this helium atom was the size of your thumbnail, then the electrons would be orbiting your thumbnail-nucleus at an average distance of around one-kilometre (or two-thirds of a mile) away.

An electron doesn't orbit a nucleus in a prescribed circle. Instead, it whizzes around the atom in a three-dimensional way, sometimes closer, and sometimes more distant. Because the distance isn't fixed, the nucleus can be described as having an electron-cloud around it, as the electron could be almost anywhere in this cloud at any moment. Given the relatively massive gap between the nucleus and the electrons (for their size), and the approximate volume that the electron-cloud takes up, a typical atom is effectively 99.9999999999999 per cent empty space.

Because an atom's structure consists of so much empty space, if we could extract all the protons, neutrons and electrons and fit them into a neat pile next to each other with no gaps between them, the matter of the entire human race — all seven billion of us — would fit inside a ping-pong ball.

ABSOLUTELY EVERYTHING IN SEVEN SENTENCES

I'd like to take you back in time to a Tuesday afternoon. Just before half-past three. About 13.8 billion years ago. It's just a couple of moments before the universe was created.

Now to be truthful, Tuesdays don't exist; neither do afternoons; or even half-past three's. Because at this moment of creation, there was absolutely nothing.

And there was absolutely everything.

Our Earth is one of eight planets that orbit the Sun. Our Sun is one of around 400-billion stars in our galaxy. There are an estimated 100- to 200-billion galaxies in the universe. That's around sixty billion, trillion stars in total. Now imagine this colossal number of stars, and the planets that orbit them, all compressed together so tightly, that they fit into something smaller than this full-stop. It may seem absurd, but that is how things were just before the start of time.

And then, 13.8 billion years ago, there was the big bang.

A lot has happened since then, but I'll summarise by giving you the history of absolutely everything, in seven sentences:

1. One-millionth of a second after the big bang, the first protons and neutrons have been made.
2. A second later, the first helium nuclei are being formed.
3. Four minutes after this, the universe has a temperature of around a billion-degrees and consists entirely of unstable helium-nuclei, with lots of spare electrons and protons around.
4. After 380,000 years, the universe has cooled down sufficiently, that every bit of matter that will ever exist in the universe, is created over a period of a few-thousand years, in the form of hydrogen and helium atoms.
5. At around 400-million years of age, these hydrogen and helium atoms begin to coalesce to form the first stars.
6. A few-billion years later, these early stars explode to create all the other chemical elements through a nuclear-fusion process, and spew them out across the universe.
7. After 13.8 billion years you are watching this presentation.

The fascinating thing is that for the first few-billion years, the universe consisted exclusively of hydrogen and helium. The other chemical elements didn't exist and were only created when the early-stars ran out of hydrogen and destroyed themselves in massive explosions called supernovas. These explosions were so powerful that nuclear fusion occurred, and the protons, neutrons and electrons from the helium atoms were forced to join together in new-and-different combinations to form all the other chemical elements.

Apart from my seven-kilograms of hydrogen, which has been around almost since time began, the rest of my chemical composition has come from those supernova stars that exploded billions of years ago. The fact is that we humans consist, quite literally, of stardust.

In this presentation, I'm going to show you how extraordinarily lucky we have been in the last 13.8 billion years. And while you consider the things I'm about to tell you, please bear in mind these two extraordinary facts: You are stardust, and you are mainly empty space.

OUR FINE-TUNED UNIVERSE

As the previous speaker showed us, pi has a value of approximately 3.141592. Why it should happen to have this particular value is a bit of a mystery in itself. But that value was defined at the instant of the big bang. Perhaps in a different universe, pi could just as easily be 2.9 or 3.3 or 12, and it would still be possible to draw a circle. However, if some of the other fundamental constants of physics in our universe were even just *slightly different*, we wouldn't exist.

Exhibit 1

In the few seconds after the big bang, the newly-formed entity expanded at the most phenomenal rate, to grow from a microscopic-crumb, to form the universe as we know it today. The speed at which this was achieved is almost incomprehensible. However, this speed was actually critical to our existence.

In his book *A Brief History of Time*, Stephen Hawking states 'If the rate of expansion one second after the big bang had been smaller by even one part in a hundred thousand million million, the universe would have re-collapsed before it ever reached its present size'.

On the other hand, if the rate of expansion had been just a fraction greater than it was, the helium and hydrogen atoms wouldn't have coalesced to form the early-stars. Which means the subsequent supernova explosions wouldn't have occurred, and all the other elements wouldn't have been formed — so we wouldn't be here.

Exhibit 2

The force that bonds the protons and neutrons together in the nucleus of an atom is called the strong nuclear force. This force is the basis of atomic explosions and nuclear reactions, where protons and neutrons are forcibly separated and the energy in the bond is released. Even though this force is extremely strong, it is also highly-sensitive in value. If the strong nuclear force was just two per cent larger, then all the hydrogen would have been consumed in the first few-minutes after the big bang. As stars typically contain around seventy per cent hydrogen, the formation of the early stars would have been very different — if it happened at all. Which potentially means the supernova would not have occurred, and hence the carbon and oxygen elements would not have been created. As we are carbon-based life-forms who breathe oxygen, this would have prevented our creation.

Exhibits 3, 4, 5, 6…

We are extremely fortunate that the rate of initial expansion of the universe, and the value of the strong nuclear force, are what they are. But it isn't just these two values that appear finely-tuned. The values of a number of other fundamental constants and forces of physics were similarly, and fortuitously, defined at the moment of the big bang.

Constants such as the weak nuclear force, gravitational force, ratio of electron-to-proton mass, ratio of neutron-mass to proton-mass, and the decay-rate of protons, all lie within critical ranges for our survival. Other measures such as the average distance between stars, and between galaxies, aren't formal constants but if their value was much different than it actually is, life could not have formed.

If you were a scientist who believed in God, you might expect this degree of fine-tuning in the creation of the universe. But to the non-religious, this is an extreme set of coincidences. Again quoting Stephen Hawking, who himself is an agnostic, 'The remarkable fact is that the values of these numbers seem to have been very finely adjusted to make possible the development of life'.

The delicate balance between these fundamentals, each sitting within a precariously-narrow range, ultimately provided a very-small window through which our existence was conceived.

Is this perfect combination of these fundamental values just a fluke of nature? Or have we had fortune on our side?

THE RIGHT PLACE AT THE RIGHT TIME

There's a limited temperature range that we humans can endure for extended periods and still feel comfortable. Woolly-fleeces when it's cold and sun-hats when it's hot, all help us now, but our primitive ape-like descendants were different. They didn't have the ability to make and wear clothes, so they had to live on the parts of the Earth where the climate was *just right*. Not too hot and not too cold.

For complex life (like us) to develop, our planet needed to be located at a distance away from the Sun that was also *just right*. Too close to the Sun and we would roast and be subject to intense radiation and solar flares. Too far away, and Earth would be excessively-cold. This limited range of distance from the Sun at which complex life like ours can form, is known as the Goldilocks zone. If Earth were four per cent closer to the Sun (and so warmer), the water which makes up our oceans would not have condensed out of the atmosphere. If Earth were just two per cent farther away from the sun, then we would be in a permanent ice-age.

There are other crucial factors which also dictated whether life like ours could develop and survive.

- The Earth has to be within an appropriate size range. Big enough that the gravitational effect is sufficiently strong to retain the water we need for life, but not too big (like Jupiter), that the gravitational effect retains too many of the gases that are detrimental to advanced life development.
- The speed of rotation also needs to be just right. If the Earth rotated much-quicker, our atmospheric patterns would create consistent, and extremely-violent, storms, which would not be conducive to the forming of life. If Earth rotated slower, then the days would get too hot, and the nights too cold, for sophisticated life to develop.
- The Sun has to be at the right stage of its own lifecycle to support the development of life on Earth. Three-to-four billion years ago, when the sun was younger and smaller, it was not strong enough to sustain liquid-water on the Earth's surface, and without water, life on Earth could not develop. The sun will continue to grow in size and temperature to such a degree that in around a billion-years from now, the surface of the Earth will become too hot for

liquid water to remain, which will end all life on Earth. So there is a limited window in the lifecycle of the Sun where species can survive on Earth.

- There mustn't be too many large meteors and comets around while life is developing, for the effect of these on Earth could be disastrous. One meteor-impact caused the extinction of the dinosaurs some 65-million years ago, and plunged the world into an ice-age. Having smaller meteors is a positive aspect as there are theories that the water on Earth arrived in the form of ice entrained in these meteors.

We are very fortunate to be living in an extremely-narrow patch of space, on a planet that is rotating at just the right speed, orbiting a Sun that is at just the right stage in its lifecycle, and with just the right number of comets and meteors in our vicinity. A significant number of variables that have miraculously conspired to create a situation that has been ideal for our development and survival.

Are we just the fortunate race in the universe, when so much could have gone against our development? Or again, has some lucky force been on our side?

LIVING ON THE EDGE

Paradise means different things to different people. Whatever form your particular paradise takes, it has something in common with everybody else's paradise. It happens on the outer-surface of a blob of molten rock whose inner-temperature is 5,500-degrees Celsius. We are protected from this heat by a thin crust all around the surface that has solidified and upon which we live. Around this crust is a thin layer of gas known as our atmosphere, just sixty-miles thick. This thin layer of gas is all that prevents the vastness of space from killing us by asphyxiation, freezing us to death with its extreme cold, letting our blood boil due to the vacuum, bombarding us with lethal micro-meteorites, cooking us alive by solar-radiation and blinding us through the glare of the sun.

This interface where the atmosphere makes contact with the thin crust of our planet, is the surface on which we live — and where all of our versions of paradise happen.

When you consider the many ways in which the conditions of outer space could wipe out every living thing on the planet, then we appear — once again — to be extremely fortunate.

OUR MOON

One event that has enthralled — and terrified — mankind throughout history, and that will never fail to go un-noticed, is a total solar-eclipse. This occurs when the moon passes directly between the sun and the Earth, to temporarily block out the full-disc of the sun, and it's an awe-inspiring sight. There are a number of circumstances that perfectly combine to produce solar eclipses on Earth, including the size and position of both the sun and the moon from Earth, and the inclination of the orbit of the moon relative to the sun. If any one of these parameters was even slightly different, then this amazing event would not occur.

Another interesting feature of the moon is that it always keeps the same side pointing towards us — which is why we can never see the back of the moon. This happens because the rotation of the moon on its axis is precisely synchronised with its period of orbit around the Earth.

Are these just more freak coincidences, or is the moon's behaviour a primitive sign to us every-night, that luck is on our side?

THE DO-IT-YOURSELF DNA KIT

The last presenter described our DNA as a three-billion rung ladder, so let's stay with this analogy. The information in our DNA is in the form of a code made up of four different chemical bases, referred to as A, G, C and T. Each rung of the ladder is formed of one chemical base on the left-side and a different chemical base on the right-side.

Ikea is a highly successful company selling Scandinavian-designed, flat-packed furniture that you assemble yourself. Think of a strand of your DNA as the ultimate piece of Ikea do-it-yourself furniture, scaled up so that the rungs of the DNA are the same width as a household ladder. You unpack this rather large box to find there are two very-long side-frames to the ladder, and three billion rungs, which you carefully lay out on the floor of your lounge. Great care is needed when you assemble your DNA ladder, as any rung can fit in any place — and the rungs can also be fitted the wrong-way-round if you aren't careful. So you have to ensure that each rung is fitted in the right location and the right-way-round too — otherwise you will be building a mutation.

If you take just ten seconds to fit each rung, and you work without taking a break, then in around 950 years you will have assembled your DNA ladder. During this time, if you make any mistake at all during the assembly, this error — or mutation — could be fatal to you. So it's essential you build your DNA ladder with absolute accuracy. Do you think you'd be able to do it? Could you follow the instructions perfectly?

The interesting thing is that you, a prime example of the most intelligent species on the planet, don't assemble your own DNA. It assembles itself without your knowledge or involvement. Nature does this all of its own accord, and it gets it right most of the time too.

Just because you have the instructions, all three billion pieces, and the Allen key tool needed for your Ikea DNA ladder-kit, what are the chances of the components coming to life and the ladder assembling itself correctly? If just two components somehow managed to move and put themselves together, then your Ikea ladder would find itself a degree-of-fame comparable to the Shroud of Turin and statues that weep blood.

If Ikea furniture isn't your thing, then imagine your DNA strand as a three-billion piece jigsaw puzzle. With regular-sized pieces, this jigsaw would measure a kilometre on each side, and again you'll need to assemble every piece in exactly the right place.

The rungs of our IKEA ladder each represent a chemical base pair, which is equivalent to the left side of a particular rung being red in colour and the right side being green. To divide, the ladder starts to separate itself vertically down the middle — just like a zip being undone. As soon as the ladder separates, enzymes start to rebuild the DNA by adding the missing parts. The red left-side of the divided rung needs to create a new, green right-side, while the part of the ladder that had the original, green right-side of the rung now needs to create a new, red left-side. As each rung is different, this needs to happen correctly three billion times to the left-side of the ladder and also three billion times to the right-side of the ladder.

A cell will typically take around twenty-four hours to complete this dividing process, which means that in just one cell, there are 34,700 rungs being un-zipped every second! Now this may seem quite impressive, until you understand that there are approximately 100-trillion cells in the human body. The three-billion base pairs need to be replicated 100-trillion times before you are even born.

Because of the risk of damage to our genes caused by DNA-mutations, we have a DNA-repair mechanism to proof-read, and correct, our DNA during the replication process. Our bodies have enzymes that recognise structural imperfections in our DNA and which repair it by cutting-out the wrong-parts and putting the right-ones back in their place. However, errors can sometimes get past, and in these cases the repair-mechanism may no longer recognise them as errors and they become permanent mutations.

Our DNA replication and repair process is an amazing, biological phenomenon — like a checking mechanism with intelligence. Studies of fruit-flies indicated that if a DNA mutation changed the way that a protein was produced by a gene, then about seventy per cent of the mutations had a damaging effect, while the remainder were neutral, or slightly beneficial. Considering the complexity of the replication process, and the sheer number of times that it occurs in the human body, the process seems to strangely allow just enough positive-mutations for evolution and advancement of ourselves as a species.

This remarkable practice of dividing, rebuilding and repairing our DNA at phenomenal-speeds with amazing-accuracy, is just one of countless, similarly-extraordinary processes that occur within our body. This was seemingly all created by random acts of nature and development.

Does this seem intuitively to be a right-and-real thing to happen naturally? Again, if it is, we appear to be an exceptionally-lucky species.

THE DICE OF LIFE

Pick any number between one and six. Now imagine yourself rolling a dice and you need to roll that number to live — get any other number and you will die. You only have a one-in-six chance of being alive after the dice has been rolled.

Let's further imagine that there were just twenty key-stages in the development of the universe and the evolution of mankind. At each of these key-stages, there were just six possible directions that could be taken. One is essential for the creation of a universe supportive to life, and the subsequent existence and development of mankind — while the other five directions would be unfavourable and would lead to our non-existence. Whatever number you initially selected therefore has to show at each of these twenty-stages when the dice of life is rolled.

The odds of your number being selected at each one of the twenty dice-rolls is only one in 3,656,158,440,062,976. Translated into betting-talk, the odds of you being alive today are only one in approximately 3.6 million, billion. Now that's poor odds indeed.

But only having a one-in-six chance at just twenty decision-points isn't anywhere near reality. When we look back at the route taken by evolution, there have been far more than twenty decision-points, and there are many more developmental routes that could have been taken than just six. In reality, it's impossible to work out the number of different things that you overcame in your development to be here today. The number would be too huge to consider. Whatever the number is though, congratulations! You've overcome tremendous odds and are so lucky to be here today.

BREAKING THE LAW

Thermodynamics is a field of science that studies how systems are affected when energy is applied or taken away. There are a number of laws which govern this field, and the second of the laws of thermodynamics states that *energy will always tend to move from a localised, higher energy state to a lower energy state*. What this means in reality is that water will spray out of a high-pressure hose pipe, flow to the lowest-point on the floor, and remain there. Similarly, a house of playing cards will tend to collapse until all the cards have fallen to the lowest possible level — where they are all lying flat on the table.

Energy in a closed-system will always move from order to disorder, and never the other way around. If you had built a house of playing cards on your desk and they had all fallen down, they would remain that way, as the cards lying on the desk are effectively a closed-system. If, on the other hand, you opened a window and allowed a strong wind to blow over your desk, the wind may blow some of the playing cards away — but this is no longer a closed-system as the wind has acted as an external energy supply.

At the moment of the big bang, all the energy in the universe was at its most concentrated and highest level. From that very first instant, as the universe began its expansion, the energy started to dissipate to lower levels. There is still the same total amount of energy in the universe, but it is now spread out and at a lower, average energy-level. Just as the orderly structure of a skyscraper will become a disorderly mound of rubble when it collapses, so the same should be happening to the universe since the big bang. Except that it isn't. It's actually getting more ordered rather than less.

Looking at the rubble of our collapsed skyscraper, would we ever imagine that long after the dust had settled from the collapse, a time would come when the dust starts to cluster itself into small lumps, and these lumps will merge to form bricks and these bricks will start to stack themselves up into the most beautiful structure ever seen? Would we ever in our wildest dreams imagine that something like that could happen?

From the moment of the big bang, we, the seven-billion incredibly-complex life-forms, living on a paradise planet, with our immense abilities to think, dream, create beautiful works of art, and to fall in love — are the proof that our evolution is going against the second law of thermodynamics.

IS MATING NATURAL?

One of the most remarkable developments of the human body is that which maintains our existence — our reproductive mechanism.

Our distant ancestors were pond-scum. Single-celled creatures that simply divided to create more of themselves — very much like a bacteria reproduces today. The problem with this kind of growth is that the pond-scum is simply cloning itself, for the split entity is intended to be a mirror of the original. Cloning doesn't allow for any new variants to be incorporated into the proliferation process. The fertilisation of one-thing-by-another to produce an offspring, allows for the strengths of both the participants to be incorporated, which increases the degree of positive-mutation that can be created. Hence sexual-reproduction is a better way of developing than simply dividing to produce species-growth.

At some point in the distant past, the basic creatures that are our ancestors began to develop organs that were capable of sexual-reproduction. This was a monumentally-important direction for a species to take, and it has clearly worked very well in getting us to where we are today. But how they managed to achieve this success is most intriguing, and a few interesting questions remain.

Why change?

If these ancestral-creatures had a perfectly good way of reproducing themselves then why spend millions of years steadily developing another set of organs that couldn't be guaranteed to work? And even if they did work properly, the newly-produced offspring might be less-viable life-forms than the ones produced by the cloning process. How was this long-term change-programme initiated in the first place?

What decided that there would only be two genders involved?

In hindsight it makes complete sense that only two genders are required, as this is the simplest approach to take. However, what primitive impulse within some pond-scum recognised that this was the best approach and initiated the whole process of sexual-reproduction between two different genders? The pond-scum most likely didn't possess any intelligence, emotions or even feelings. So how did it get the urge to start creating reproductive organs and to allocate the physical components in a matched-way between the two genders? Especially when the different genders didn't exist at the time?

Why weren't the first attempts at organ development recognised as negative mutations?

If any single- or multi-celled organism could replicate itself efficiently by dividing, then it wouldn't have any need to develop new, embryonic organ-growths within itself. If it did start to do this, the first few changes would surely have been recognised as mutations and should theoretically have been corrected by whatever primitive DNA correction mechanism was present at the time. This obviously didn't occur and the initial-growth continued to build and develop over vast numbers of cycles.

How would the different sets of reproductive organs know if they'd got it right?

Given that two genders were deemed necessary, then each gender needed to produce its own specific reproductive organs over a vast number of generations of change. These two different sets of organs needed to work perfectly together when the time came to use them. How was this achieved so effectively when there was no opportunity to test them beforehand? The chance of them working successfully early on was extremely low. So, how was any feedback given on what was working well and what didn't work properly?

Reproduction is a very complex process, with so many elements that need to be *just right* for it to work. But in the trial-and-error early-stages there must have been many facets that were incomplete or incorrect. How did the creatures know which facets needed major-change over tens of thousands of lifecycles — and which not to change? Especially when the feedback-loop of success for each element was of extremely-long duration.

What motivated both genders to start using these new organs?

At some transitional point, just before the reproductive organs were ready for use, the splitting and cloning process must have still been used. What prompted the creature to switch and use the new method of reproduction rather than continuing with their individual dividing, which had been very successful throughout the past?

How were the specifics of each gender's reproductive system determined?

Of the many different ways that a new form of reproduction could occur, it was somehow decided that both an egg and a sperm would be required for the successful reproduction process. How was it determined that the female of the species would be born with all the eggs she will ever produce inside her at birth, while the male would create their part of the process on an as-required basis? Similarly, before the first egg was ever fertilised, the female somehow was identified as the vehicle for the gestation period, and so all the necessary physiological-needs of that stage of the process needed to be developed too.

Did these initial reproductive developments simply take this one direction, or did we have a vast number of false-starts and dead-ends? If we assume that not every evolutionary development is correct and successful, did we develop a number of alternate reproductive techniques in parallel, or were we extremely lucky in everything going just right with the one we selected?

And what happened when we decided to use the new organs? Did it work perfectly the first time? Did it work at all? How were we able to keep reproducing during the transition period? Were the first offspring from this new reproductive system viable life-forms?

Surely the first multitude of created-offspring must have been failures — to put it politely. Where would any specific, positive-feedback from these failures be coming from to encourage continued commitment to this process of development? There are so many variables to consider in the development of a new reproductive system, with so many ways for them to go wrong — and only a very limited number of ways that they could be right.

Imagine if four card-players sat at a table represented those distant creatures that we are descended from. Two of the card-players decide they each want to get a perfect-hand with all the cards from one-suit, as this represents each of them developing a new, and perfectly-functioning, reproductive system. This will allow them to mate with each other and to produce new, healthy card-playing offspring.

If each of the four players is dealt a thirteen-card hand from a normal deck of fifty-two playing cards, then the odds that any two of the players will receive a perfect-hand of thirteen-cards of the same suit is approximately 430 million, million, million-to-one against. And this is just two people and a pack of fifty-two cards!

When we think of the almost-inconceivable number of hurdles that we've overcome to be here today, through a reproductive-system developed from scratch — and the number of ways things could have gone wrong, what are the odds against this actually happening naturally? Surely many times greater than the chance of two people getting a perfect-hand of cards.

But, we are here today — and this is a fact. Once again, we have overcome seemingly insurmountable odds that were stacked against us.

A FREAKY STREAK OF LUCK

I started this presentation by asking the question *Are we too lucky?* There have been some quite remarkable and fortuitous occurrences along the 13.8 billion year timeline from the big bang to today. Has there been the hand of a deity involved? Or are we the output of the longest, freaky streak-of-good-luck imaginable?

As scientists continue to gain new understandings of the inner-workings of the cosmos, mankind and the fundamental particles that we all consist of, we can expect to find more examples of aspects of our existence that are wildly-surprising and totally against the odds of expectation.

SUMMARY

This conference is all about the potential of the human mind and so I'll conclude with three takeaway points to get you thinking differently about your place in the universe:

1. We have the capabilities to perform sensational scientific, engineering and technological feats, but when we try to understand how the universe was able to create us out of nothing, there are many aspects that don't seem to make sense. Why does nature tantalise us with the unbelievable way that fortune has been on our side in the past? Perhaps we aren't meant to be analysing our past as much as we do. Perhaps we are meant to be looking forward and using our good fortune for our future development.

2. Our imaginary three-billion-part Ikea DNA-ladder is still lying on the floor of our lounge in pieces. If a psychic claimed to be able to use her mind to move one piece of this ladder just a small distance, many people would doubt this ability and would deride her as a charlatan. However, when nature creates this DNA-ladder millions of times a second inside every human being — then we accept this without question. We need to be more open-minded about what we are capable of. Too many unbelievable and remarkable things have occurred in the past to enable us to be where we are today. They are probably occurring now, and certainly will in the future too. We need to be more open to accepting unbelievable and remarkable things in our lives.

3. At the start of time, just before the big bang, everything in the universe was compressed into something smaller than a full-stop. And right now, the matter that makes up the entire human race will fit inside a ping-pong ball — if it wasn't for unseen-forces that exist in our lives that magically seem to be of just the right size for our development. We live in an exceptionally-lucky universe where the odds of us being here today are so phenomenally remote as to seem unreal. *What if it isn't just good luck?* Or what if luck is one of the forces-of-nature that are part of our lives? Truly appreciate this fact in your life and recognise it and use it in any way that you seem fit. You are the fortunate species and luck is definitely on your side. *You are meant to be lucky.*

Thank you for your time.

Chapter 27 Monday 13h05

The conference chairman had wrapped up the morning session, thanked the speakers, and then given directions on where lunch was being served. Reece followed the crowd into an adjacent area which had been laid out with a number of large buffet tables, which held the same selection of food options on both sides to speed up service.

DD caught up with Reece, who was near the back of a long queue.

"Man, you must love queuing. Let's go over there," he said, pointing, and led Reece to a table on the far-side of the room which had a shorter line of people. As they walked, DD told him of the things he'd spoken about with the first presenter.

"Jean was saying that if you point out peculiar occurrences at the cosmic and microscopic extremes of scale, then people seem happy to accept that. But if you point out something peculiar that occurs in your personal life then it's doubted or actively-derided because it can't be proved. She surprised me with that one — but it's so true, man."

"Did she give you any examples from her personal life?"

"I asked her straight-out."

"I thought you might." Reece was beginning to get a good handle on DD's style.

"She told me of three incidents that happened to her in the last few-months. A psychic gave her a reading and seemed to know far more than he should have about her personal life. Apparently the guy was hearing the information from the spirit world. She also talked of having a sudden impulse to call a friend she hadn't spoken to for a long time — and that person had called her later that same day. Then she also said that someone showed her how to use dowsing twigs to search for water, and that the twigs kept twitching uncannily as she held them. She said these weren't big issues in the course of the universe, but they were peculiar things that had happened to her, which were significant at a personal level."

"What's interesting is that those examples wouldn't have been noticed by another person, even if they were standing right next to her. Maybe these anomalies occur at a very personal — almost intimate — level," said Reece.

"There could be things like that happening to many people. But we keep quiet for fear of looking like knob-heads," said DD.

They reached the buffet table. DD handed a plate to Reece and took one for himself. On the other side of the table, and moving in the opposite direction, were Professor Bartlett, Heather Macreedy and the morning's chairman, helping themselves to food.

"Looks like we're at the VIP table," said DD.

Reece noticed that the Professor seemed to have fully recovered from his earlier sneezing affliction, and had entered into a new, overly-loud monologue with, or rather at, Heather and the chairman. Reece didn't notice Anthony Thorpe standing up against the wall-drapes, in line with the advancing dignitaries, appearing to be doing something innocuous on his phone.

Anthony Thorpe was in a state of mental bliss. He was caught in that most-pleasurable of places where something that had worked well was giving him immense satisfaction, while he had the knowing-anticipation that something even better was guaranteed to happen very shortly. He'd left the last presentation early and made his way to the dining area, where he'd stood by the main doorway waiting for the guest speakers to enter. When they had, he'd observed which buffet table they were using and had then taken a position against the wall, so that they would be advancing towards him as they made their choice of food.

He was holding his phone vertically in his left-hand while pretending to press things on it with his right. In reality he was setting up the best viewing-angle of the queue of approaching dignitaries — and preparing for what was about to happen.

Reece was busy reading the small triangular-cards that identified the various dishes that were on offer for lunch. In front of him were three large platters, the first of which contained soy-glazed, wild-salmon slices, neatly arranged in parallel rows. The second displayed crayfish tails meunière, all beautifully arranged in circles with the tail-ends pointing towards the centre, while the third platter contained small bowls of Keralan fish curry.

He noticed the Professor was continuing his monologue, while helping himself to one of the soy-glazed, wild-salmon slices. He placed it on an already rather-full plate. With two more appetising platters facing the Professor, Reece was curious whether he would try to fit even more food on his plate.

At that same moment, Anthony Thorpe pressed the RECORD button on his camera. Keeping his phone held steady, Anthony Thorpe imagined the feeling of something warm and gloopy inside his stomach, with large bubbles of gas rising rapidly up through it.

When he had the feeling in his mind he thought *PROJECT!* and he sent the thought racing towards the centre of Professor Sir Simon Bartlett's head.

Reece was watching the Professor reach for one of the crayfish tails when he stopped, mid-motion.

He'd probably realised that he was taking too much food, thought Reece.

He saw the professor's out-stretched hand suddenly pull-back and grab his stomach. The other hand lost its grip on his plate of food, which fell onto the metal cover of a serving-tray, which had the effect of significantly amplifying the loud clatter.

The conversation in the dining-room dropped noticeably as many heads instinctively turned to face the source of the noise.

CRY OUT! projected Anthony Thorpe, and the professor let out a bellowing-grunt which seemed to emanate from deep within his gut. Now, the whole room was completely silent, with everyone looking in the direction of this unexpected and alien sound.

EJECT! thought Anthony Thorpe, using every ounce of mental-force he could muster to send the thought towards the Professor. There was a hot, gurgling sound before a stream of vomit spewed out of Professor Bartlett's mouth, completely covering the platter of soy-glazed, wild-salmon slices.

Reece, DD, and the people on either side of them, sprang backwards in a move so-perfectly choreographed it was worthy of any leading corps de ballet.

A second stream of technicolour vomit then gushed out of the Professor, engulfing the crayfish tails meunière, which was the dish that Reece had unfortunately decided was going to form the basis of his meal.

There was a static, stunned silence for a moment, as the professor dropped to his knees and clutched his stomach.

And then a polite-panic ensued.

A desperate-few hastening to leave the area before the stench of the vomit started to make *them* gag, bumped into those hastening to assist the professor. They also bumped into the hotel staff hastening towards the incident to clean up the situation as their training dictated.

"Excuse me, please!" said the ones with delicate stomachs.

"Are you alright?" said those trying to assist the professor.

"Would you like to move into the room next door?" prompted the hospitality staff.

"Bollocks. Let's go back to the queue that you were originally in," said DD, in a matter-of-fact tone that seemed completely incongruous to Reece.

As DD and Reece relocated to the other-end of the dining-room, a few decisions were made with a finality rarely seen in everyday life.

Anthony Thorpe pressed PAUSE on his phone's camera and knew he'd captured to perfection all that he needed.

Heather Macreedy knew instinctively that this was a malicious act by someone at the conference.

Professor Sir Simon Bartlett knew that his reputation as a speaker at conferences was shattered.

And Reece Tassicker knew he would never be able to eat crayfish tails meunière again in his life.

Chapter 28 Monday 13h25

With remarkable efficiency, the catering staff ushered everyone into an adjacent room and were carrying the platters around, offering most of them as finger-food, which Reece thought to be quite a creative response. They informed everyone that the afternoon session would be delayed by thirty-minutes to allow people enough time to eat. Though not many seemed to be eating.

DD made a number of derogatory, yet humorous, comments about Professor Bartlett and his lack of table-manners, while he tucked into one of the soy-glazed, wild-salmon slices. Reece was impressed at how heartily DD could eat this when not fifteen-minutes ago, they'd observed the same dish as a set of neatly-arranged rectangular-islands floating in a sea of vomit.

"I think I prefer the soy-glazing on this wild-salmon as opposed to the Professor's choice of sauce," said DD, "you should try some. It's really good."

Reece tried hard not to think about how the buffet-table had looked after the Professor's outpouring, but he knew it was likely to become a hot topic for his chattering mind in the near future. He also tried hard not to think about connections between his mysterious Post-it notes, and the Professor's unusual sneezing and vomiting — but he had a nagging-feeling that they were related in some way.

DD wandered off to look for dessert, so Reece turned to another attendee standing nearby eating his lunch, and asked what he'd found exceptionally interesting so far. What *others* found exceptional, invariably gave Reece a fresh-perspective on things.

The man replied in a clearly-Boston accent. "In any talk I look for three-key things that I'll actively do something about. After this morning's sessions, though — I'm screwed. It feels like so many things I thought were hard facts have been turned upside-down. Especially the issues with evolution. It's like coming home to find a new door has mysteriously appeared in the hallway of your home. You're curious to know what's behind it, but at the same time nervous of what you might find."

"Anomalies."

"What?" said the American.

"Your door is an anomaly. It's what the first speaker was talking about," stated Reece. "If you want to ignore the new door, then your life will continue as normal. She was effectively saying that new-doors are appearing in many people's homes, and she wants us to open them to see what's there — not to ignore them."

“And what about those long-odds against our existence that the second guy mentioned?”

“More doors. Makes you think there’s been an extreme run-of-luck giving the evolutionary process a helping hand. There’s too many significant flaws for it to stand up by itself,” said Reece, speaking more to his own thoughts than to the question the American had asked.

“Significant enough, that back in the States, there’s a growing belief in Intelligent Design.”

“What’s that?” asked Reece.

“Intelligent Design? It’s a movement which claims there are so many faults in the story of evolution, that it’s impossible for it to be a truly-plausible explanation of how we, as a race, came to be here today. They believe there had to be some kind of supreme intelligence involved — which they state was the Christian God. They use the inconsistencies of evolution as their core argument to prove the existence of God.”

“I can see how they think that, based on what we’ve heard,” said Reece. “Playing the God-card must make it difficult for the evolutionists to argue against them.”

“Surprisingly not. One of the main arguments against Intelligent Design is that humans — and other species — have some basic design flaws. We aren’t perfect. Which is something you’d expect if God were involved in our evolution.”

This seemed like an extremely valid point to Reece, which opened up a dilemma in his head: *Which is correct; Evolution or Intelligent Design*? He launched a visual-thinking technique in his mind which he used to help him understand unusual issues. He imagined a straight line with Darwin’s theory of evolution at one-end and Intelligent Design at the other. Based on the lectures this morning, the ascent of man due to pure-evolution seemed highly-implausible. On the other hand, a god that was involved in our design and who factored-in design faults, and who let innocent children suffer pain-and-hardship as a result of his errors, also didn’t sit well with Reece. *There must be something between the two extremes* he thought.

A bright-red door instantly appeared on his imagined continuum and started sliding up-and-down the line between the two ends, not knowing where to stop. As it reached the evolution-end of the line, a hand appeared in Reece’s mind, pushing it away. Evolution is the wrong cause — the presentations have shown there are too many anomalies for it to hold fully true. As the red door reached the other end, representing a God-driven Intelligent Design cause, another hand appeared, again pushing it away. A benevolent god causing the world to be the way it was, also didn't stack-up as a valid cause.

Reece watched the door slide between the two opposing perspectives, being continually repelled by each end. A second, slightly-curved continuum appeared above the first, and the bright-red door started to move back-and-forth along it. The mid-point of this second line moved away from the initial straight line and formed an arc, then a semicircle, and finally an ellipse. The door was now oscillating, in decreasing-steps, around the uppermost point of the ellipse.

The door had found the place where it was meant to be — located between the two ends of the straight line, but high above it — at a position that had no known name. Reece realised he needed to find out what this position represented. This was a door that he'd definitely have to open.

"This morning's put dozens of new doorways in my mind," said the American, "and I'm fascinated to know what's behind them."

"Me too," said Reece, absent-mindedly watching his imagined door make its last few oscillations, before finally locking itself into its new position.

Chapter 29 Monday 14h15

Presentation #3

Human evolution: Where to from here?

By Dr Mahesh Rajbansi
Head of Medical Futures
University of Edinburgh

A common perception is that evolution is making us steadily better as a race, generation after generation. But how do you measure *better*?

Perhaps an interesting way to understand if humans are getting better, is to consider the people who want to be the best. People who commit to the ultimate-levels of personal development because their reputations depend on it. The Olympic athletes.

These select individuals are pushing the limits of human capacity in the very-public, and closely-monitored, environment of the Olympic Games. By setting a world record, they are acknowledged as the best in the world at their event — the crowning glory for an athlete. So the study of how athletic records have improved may be a good indicator of how the human body has improved in specific, and measured, ways over recent times.

FASTER, HIGHER, STRONGER

The Olympic motto is *Citius, Altius, Fortius*, which is Latin for faster, higher, stronger. This is a tacit-acknowledgement of the traits that helped man to stay alive when being pursued by a predator seeking its next meal in the dim-and-distant past. Whether one of our ancient-ancestors was panting his lungs out while being pursued, or was trying to reach the first branch of a suitably-high tree, or was wielding his club at the predator's head, the phrase faster, higher, stronger probably defined which of our ancestors survived — and which did not.

But how much faster, higher and stronger have we got in recent times?

Geoffroy Berthelot is a researcher at the French National Institute of Sport and Physical Education. He analysed official world-records and found that for track and field events, peak-times didn't improve in sixty-four per cent of events from 1993 through to 2007, the date of the study. He claims that the peak of athletic achievement was reached in 1988, and that in the 1990s we started to see a *decrease* in performance.

Another researcher Giuseppe Lippi, an associate professor at the University of Verona, studied the International Association of Athletics Federation world-records from 1900 to 2007 in nine Olympic sports — the 100-metres, 400-metres, 1,500-metres, 10,000-metres, the marathon, long-jump, high-jump, shot-put and javelin. He concluded that improvement had essentially stopped — or reached a plateau — in several events.

Records in relatively-new sports such as mountain biking and the winter sports are still being beaten regularly, but that's only because these sports are still quite young, and that being newer, they tend to involve equipment that allows science to have an impact, for example in the bicycles and ski-equipment used.

What is of particular interest are some of the issues that are driving record performances today. All sports require equipment that has been improved by engineering and science over time. A simple pair of running shoes, the fibreglass pole used by pole-vaulters, and the highly-complex archer's bow are just a few examples of improvements in sports equipment. The issue of science assisting athletes through the kit they wear and use is interesting. According to Berthelot's research, the high-tech swimsuits worn by swimmers were the deciding factor in twenty-one of the twenty-two world-records set at the 2008 Beijing Games. In 2009, the International Swimming Federation decided to ban the high-performance swimsuits that helped Michael Phelps win eight gold medals in Beijing.

Another demonstration of technology helping athletes, relates to the cycling event where riders have to cover the greatest distance in one hour. In 1973, the Tour de France legend Eddy Merckx set a record distance of 49.931 kilometres. In 2000, British cyclist Chris Boardman used a similar type of bicycle and added just eleven-metres to Merckx's record. Boardman then switched to a state-of-the-art bicycle and used a modern, aerodynamic cycling helmet to beat the record by almost seven-kilometres.

If world-record performances start to plateau, and the use of new technology is closely limited by the sporting control bodies, then there becomes only one option left to improve records — the super-athlete.

SUPER-ATHLETES

The rapid rise in sports television coverage over the last few decades, combined with the glamour and associated fortunes that arrive with professional sport-success, means more and more people have been embraced by the search for super-athletes. Whether you are a youngster from a Brazilian-slum showing off some amazing skills with a ball, or a bare-foot, long-distance runner from the plains of East Africa; a video taken on a mobile phone, and uploaded to YouTube is a means to display your talents to the world. And you can guarantee there's always a talent-scout not very far away.

Because of this wider search for potential sporting stars, it has become much easier for researchers to identify what they call *extreme outliers*. These are individuals who have the right mix of genetics, skill, metabolism and desire-to-excel, and who have the potential to push the envelope of sporting records to new limits. In some sports — like basketball — being exceptionally tall can be the primary-contributor to being a successful player, while other sports need a different variety of physical attributes for world-record success.

Michael Phelps is a sixteen-time Olympic gold-medal winner, and is a prime example of an extreme outlier — or a super-athlete. Phelps is 6 feet 4 inches tall with a 6 feet 7 inch arm span, a broad back, comparatively-short legs and huge feet. The perfect combination for competitive swimming.

Several countries have programs to spot the extreme outliers who may have a natural potential to excel in their sport. In Britain, UK Sport's Sporting Giants talent-identification program looks to identify outliers in body-size, which effectively means men over 6 feet 3 inches tall, and women over 5 feet 11 inches who are in the age-range sixteen to twenty-five. Similarly, the Australian Institute of Sport is also looking for outliers to bring into its sports programs, where potential athletes from the age of twelve are assessed using sophisticated techniques.

While typical athletes try their utmost to squeeze every advantage from their coaches, training and diet, they are inevitably going to be outdone by the extreme outliers. These super-athletes will be the ones who will be making-and-breaking records in the future. However, there are several super-athletes around now, and one of them is Usain Bolt.

Bolt is a once-in-a-generation athlete who breaks the records that have become static, and brings fresh excitement into athletics. The record for the 100-metre sprint back in 1909 was 10.5 seconds. At the 2008 Olympics in Beijing, Bolt set a new world-record of 9.69 seconds, and just a year later he knocked a further 0.11 seconds off that, to record a time of 9.58 seconds. To reduce the 100-metre record by that margin was a phenomenal performance, but that's how records will continue to be broken — by waiting for these extreme outliers to come along to advance the sport. But just how much more can the records be reduced — even by super-athletes like Bolt?

Whether we are watching the Olympics live in the stadium, or on television, we all love the excitement of seeing new world-records being set. But what happens when it gets to the stage that this rarely occurs, and that all we can do is watch to see who wins? To find out who the fastest person is today, and not necessarily the fastest person ever, just isn't as exciting. Maybe technology will have to come to the rescue, and we will see race-times being measured — not to hundredths — but to thousandths of a second, and this will be the incremental improvement for new world-records. Similarly height and distance records may be measured incrementally by the millimetre rather than by the centimetre.

Or perhaps in the future, the best athletes will be the offspring of an extreme outlier athletic-couple, or they may come from a genetically-engineered foetus. Then the distinction between what is natural-talent and what is artificially-enhanced will be a very difficult line to define.

ANIMAL ATHLETES

Some interesting comparisons in this area can be obtained from the world of animal sports where selective-breeding has been practiced for many years. In greyhound racing's premier event, the English Oaks, there has been little improvement in the winning times since 1966. In the horse racing world there are three premier thoroughbred events on the international calendar; the Epsom Derby, the Kentucky Derby and the Melbourne Cup. Over the last fifty-years there has been no clear trend of improvement in the winning times of these leading races. Similarly, the winning time for the British Grand National horse race hit a plateau around 1971.

Harvard evolutionary biologist Andrew Berry attributes this to the fact that you can only breed horses with ultra-light-and-thin bones to a certain limit. Past that point, the bones tend to break under stress. If dogs and horses are at their upper-limit, even with sophisticated breeding techniques, perhaps humans are getting there too.

MIND OVER BODY

It's been tens of thousands of years since an ability to flee from predators was key to our survival — and maybe evolution is aware of this. There isn't any driving need for us to be faster, higher and stronger any more. If we need any of these attributes for any reason, we now apply our intelligence so that faster, higher and stronger become the use of bicycle, ladder or lever.

So, is there any real need for further evolution of these physical capacities, except for the sake of our interest in sporting competitions? Possibly not. Perhaps our evolutionary potential is being focussed on other areas of our body instead.

In April 2011, a two-year-old British boy, Alfie Clamp, made the news when he was announced as the first diagnosis of a chromosome condition where he has an extra-strand of material. Unfortunately, Alfie was born blind, and with severe disabilities which initially confounded doctors. It was only when they carried out detailed tests that they found out about his most-unusual DNA structure. This condition is so rare that it doesn't have a name. Alfie's parents had their DNA tested, and were not found to be carrying any faulty genes.

Our DNA has the amazing ability to read-and-copy itself, to fix errors in itself, and to evolve itself for the future. Unfortunately, not always beneficially.

We have to accept that the evolutionary process of allowing changes to our DNA must occasionally result in things going wrong, and that sometimes these developments are so wrong that death, or severe-deformity prevail, in which case the gene-line doesn't continue. Sometimes evolution gets it wrong in unusual, but not necessarily fatal ways, where an interesting development occurs whose immediate benefits may not always seem obvious.

SUPER-NORMAL HUMANS

Sometimes humans are born with, or develop, conditions that are not normal. These developments are often referred to as *abnormal*, which is technically correct as they aren't meant to be normal — they are evolutionary developments.

However, the term *abnormal* has negative connotations, so even if some of the developments are negative in nature, perhaps these developments should be seen as *super-normalities* instead.

Some of these super-normalities have the medical profession baffled because they cannot account for the condition. Here are a few interesting examples:

Brooke Greenberg, was an American born in Maryland in January 1993 who didn't age normally. According to specialists, different parts of her body aged at different rates. When she tragically died at the age of twenty, her brain was only as mature as that of a new-born infant and she had a mental-age of a one-year-old. She stopped growing when she was just five-years-old and maintained this appearance until she died in October 2013. Some in the medical profession believe that her genes may hold hidden secrets to preventing aging.

Gabby Gingras, a young-teenage girl from Minnesota, has a condition whereby she feels no pain at all. Though this may sound like a blessing, it means that she tends to injure herself a lot — and often quite-severely too. She is one of only sixty recorded cases of this condition around the world.

Natalie Adler, a woman in her mid-twenties from Melbourne, Australia lives in a world where she can't open her eyes for three days at a time. She finds that her eyes clamp themselves shut for this period, and afterwards they open as normal for three days — before the cycle repeats again — incessantly.

Harry Raymond Eastlack died of pneumonia in 1973 at the age of forty. He was also known as *The Stoneman* as he suffered from an extreme case of the rare disease Fibrodysplasia Ossificans Progressiva. This is a disease that causes the muscles and tendons in the body to solidify and turn into bone. When he died, the only part of his body that he could move were his lips. The first case of this was identified over 300-years ago and doctors still can't explain what causes all the body's soft-tissue to turn to bone.

These are some examples of unusual developments in the human body where evolution didn't get it quite right. There are some other interesting examples of people where evolutionary development might have delivered some traits that appear to be more beneficial in nature:

A German boy born in 2000 was identified as being unusual from the moment he was delivered. Even on the day of his birth, the special tone of his muscles was obvious to the doctors and nurses present. This baby is the first documented case of a human with a double-dose of a mutated-gene that is known to cause incredible strength in mice and cattle. Before he was five, the boy was able to hold three-kilogram weights with his arms extended — a feat that many adults can't manage.

John Perry, a sixty-two-year-old from Essex in the UK, can eat whatever he likes — because he never gets fat. He has a condition called lipodystrophy which means that irrespective of how much junk food he eats, his body just burns off all the fat immediately.

Wim Hof from the Netherlands, has earned the name of *Iceman* due to his ability to withstand cold. Scientists are baffled about how he is able to endure the conditions to which he exposes his body. In 2009 he ran a marathon in Finland in temperatures of minus-twenty degrees Celsius wearing just a pair of shorts. In 2010 he broke the ice-endurance record by standing fully-immersed in iced-water for 1 hour and 44 minutes.

These are examples of human capabilities that that are readily observable. But what about things that aren't obvious unless they are specifically tested for? The human liver, for example, is responsible for over five-hundred different functions within the body, including the production of bile, the decomposition of red blood-cells, and the general detoxification of your body. What if somebody's liver can perform one of these five-hundred functions, but with a significantly-greater efficiency? Or what if their liver has an additional, and useful, function that we don't even know about?

There could be many evolutionary developments occurring within our own bodies that we may have no insight of whatsoever. We can spot people with super-developed brains because we can readily test them to see the output, but what if people have a super-developed heart, gall bladder or pituitary gland? How would we know?

As a species we may be approaching our limits regarding our sporting prowess, but there still seems to be room for our bodies to evolve in other physical ways that may be of benefit. I've shown you some interesting physical capabilities that evolution seems to be exploring — but none that seem to have immediate and mass-benefit to the human race. So could the future-evolution of mankind be based around our minds and mental capabilities rather than our physical abilities?

Let's take a look inside our heads.

ADVANCED MIND STATES

Let's imagine ourselves in Tibet. A beautiful, far-off land, where our first mental-associations might revert to mountains, orange-robes and meditating-monks. Due to its high altitude, Tibet's climate ranges between cool, and cold, and as meditation generally requires sitting-still for a considerable time, this can tend to make it uncomfortable for the monks. However, there is one particular meditation technique practiced by Tibetan Buddhist monks, known as *gtum-mo,* which enables them to warm their own bodies. Under scientific conditions, monks using gtum-mo have demonstrated an ability to raise their own body temperature, especially in their fingers, by up to eight-degrees Celsius.

Another experiment using the same technique, took place outdoors when the air temperature was only four-degrees Celsius. The monks each had a large sheet soaked in cold water placed over their shoulders. For most individuals this would likely produce uncontrollable-shivering and potentially result in death. However, for the monks using gtum-mo, their increased body temperatures *dried the sheet within an hour.* Assistants working with the monks removed the dry sheets and replaced them with wet ones. Eventually, each of the monks had dried three sheets over a period of several hours. For the monks, this isn't a party-trick — it's proof they can achieve a deep-level of meditation, and that they are fully in control of their minds — and ultimately their bodies.

Herbert Benson, an associate professor of medicine at Harvard Medical School, is interested in bridging the gap between western and eastern medical-practices. He has been studying gtum-mo for more than twenty-years and states *'There's another reality we can tap into that's unaffected by our emotions, by our everyday world. Buddhists believe this state of mind can be achieved by doing good for others and by meditation. The heat they generate during the process is just a by-product of gtum-mo meditation'.*

But Buddhist monks aren't the only ones who demonstrate extreme-capabilities with their minds. Hyperthymesia is a condition where people have the extraordinary ability to remember almost everything that has happened to them in their lives. One well-documented case is that of American school administrator Jill Price. She was born in New York in 1965, and can recall every day of her life since the age of fourteen *in extreme detail.* It isn't just the detail of particularly special events in her life — it's *every* detail — even seemingly trivial things that were going on around her. She simply remembers everything — and she's not alone either, as there are at least six other confirmed cases of this condition.

Autism is a condition where the growth and development of the brain is impaired in some way, and individuals with autism often have diminished social-interaction and communication skills. Some autistic people, however, display amazing capabilities in drawing, mental calculations, playing an instrument, or in a variety of other ways. These individuals are described as autistic-savants.

As the cause of autism isn't known, we can't be sure how the autistic-savant condition develops. Some claim that their amazing levels of performance are achieved because they practice their skill for endless hours. However, this doesn't explain how they can demonstrate their abilities right from the start — before they have spent time working on their gift. What is known for certain is that autistic-savants do have a non-standard brain organization — but where it develops from isn't known.

Stephen Wiltshire was born in London in 1974 and has been diagnosed with autism. His particular skill is his ability to draw a city skyline in amazing detail after seeing it just once. In 2009, he took a twenty-minute helicopter ride over New York City and then proceeded to draw a five-metre panorama of the city landscape from memory. He has since repeated this ability in numerous cities around the world.

Leslie Lemke is an American born in Wisconsin in 1952. He was born with eye-defects and brain-damage and had to have his eyes removed when very young. During the first seven-years of his life, he made no sound or movement, and showed no emotions at all. He only learned to stand-up at the age of twelve, and was fifteen before he could walk. As a sixteen-year-old he sat with his family one Sunday evening while a movie was on television, which included Tchaikovsky's Piano Concerto No1. In the middle of the night, Leslie's mother heard music in the house. She found Leslie at the piano, playing the piece without having had as much as a single piano lesson.

Derek Paravicini is a British autistic-savant born in 1979, who is also a musical prodigy. Coincidentally, he is also blind due to the oxygen-therapy he was given when he was born extremely-prematurely. This therapy affected his underdeveloped brain which means he has a severe learning disability. Derek has the ability to play a piece of music after hearing it once. He started playing the piano at the age of two, and gave his first concert at seven-years-old. When he was nine, he gave his first major concert at the Barbican in London.

Daniel Tammet is another British autistic-savant, also born in 1979. He has particular capabilities in memory, mathematics and languages. His feats include finishing fourth in the World Memory Championships in 2000, reciting the digits of pi from memory to 22,514 places in just over five-hours, and learning conversational-Icelandic in just seven days.

Daniel is a different savant for a very-special reason. Whereas most savants can't explain how they do what they do, Daniel can explain, and has spent time with researchers explaining how he does what he does. With regard to numbers, Daniel explained to researchers that each positive-integer up to 10,000 has its own unique shape, colour, texture and feel. When he multiplies two numbers together, he sees two shapes which change and evolve into a third shape — which is the answer. He performs mathematics through mental-imagery. When Daniel recited the digits of pi, he said he found it easy because he didn't see pi as a string of digits, but as a story, projected like a film in front of his eyes.

Does it not seem strangely-peculiar how these individuals are able to perform these feats that are so unusual? It may seem like a storyline from a fantasy-novel, or a science-fiction movie. But no — this is an odd aspect of our reality. These are natural capabilities where the individual has acquired the competency with very little, if any, effort.

Allan Snyder is director of the Centre for the Mind at the University of Sydney, Australia. He has studied Daniel Tammet in particular, and the capabilities of the human-mind in general, and he's confident that everyone has the same extraordinary potential that savants like Daniel Tammet have. He also estimates that ten per cent of the autistic population, and around one per cent of the non-autistic population, actually have savant-abilities.

The competencies we've just listed are natural, or latent, capabilities. These individuals didn't spend hours of their childhood, learning or practicing how to do these things — they simply had the natural-ability to do them. On the other hand, a different approach is where specific techniques are learned with the sole-aim to acquire such skills. This is often most dramatically demonstrated by young children — or child prodigies.

CHILD PRODIGIES

A child prodigy is someone who masters a particular skill at an early-age to a level which would normally be expected, only when they are much older. We have no idea how child prodigies come about. Is it nature that produces a prodigious-ability to learn a specific activity, or is it the nurturing-environment in which they are brought up that helps their talent to develop?

Child prodigies aren't just a modern occurrence; they have been recognised for centuries, especially in the fields of music and the arts. Mozart may be the most well-known as he learned to play the piano at the age of four, composed his first musical pieces at five, and by the age of eight had written his first symphony.

Modern child prodigies are usually associated with academic-related activities, so let's look at some interesting examples of these young-people's achievements:

Kim Ung-Yong was born in 1962 in Korea. He started speaking at just four-months, and could converse fluently by six-months. He could read Korean, English, German and Japanese by his second birthday, and needed about one-month to learn a new language. At the age of five, he could solve complicated differential and integral calculus.

Mohammed Hussain Tabatabai was born in 1991 and by the age of two could recite the thirtieth-sura of Quran by heart. He memorized all the Quran by the age of five, and was awarded a doctoral degree from Coventry University, UK, at the age of six.

Arran Fernandez was born in June 1995 and broke the age-record for gaining a General Certificate of Secondary Education (the English academic qualification usually taken at the age of sixteen) by sitting the examination at just five-years-old.

Sufiah Yusof was accepted by Oxford University in 1997 to study mathematics at the age of thirteen.

In a sporting capacity, *Tiger Woods* was introduced to golf before the age of two, and first broke the eighty-handicap at the age of eight.

Perhaps the really-interesting question isn't around the specific quantitative-aspects of their successes, but around the qualitative-abilities of the mind to achieve them. What else can the mind do — and how are our minds evolving as we speak?

FRENCH AND SWISS BRAINS

Did you hear about the Frenchman who had no brain? While this may sound like the start of a really-funny joke, it's actually true. Or almost true, as the Frenchman concerned had almost no brain at all.

Our brain is surrounded by a liquid called cerebrospinal fluid, which acts like a shock-absorber. By floating in this liquid, our brain is protected from impacts to our head, and from bouncing around inside our skull when we walk or run. Normally we produce around a half-litre of this fluid every day, but occasionally we produce too much, and develop a condition called hydrocephalus, which is colloquially referred to as *water on the brain*. Individuals with this condition will often have a tube inserted through their skulls to drain off this excess fluid. This is where our Frenchman appears.

As a child he was diagnosed with hydrocephalus, and had a tube inserted into his head, which was subsequently removed at the age of fourteen, when doctors thought the condition had cleared. But it hadn't. Thirty-years later, the man was feeling unwell, and in 2007 was examined by Dr Lionel Feuillet, a neurologist at the Mediterranean University in Marseille, France. After performing a number of brain-scans, they discovered that his skull was full of cerebrospinal fluid, and that the pressure of the fluid had squeezed his brain to form a thin-layer of brain tissue around the inside of his skull.

The man was married with two children, and worked as a civil-servant in the French government. They ran some intelligence tests and he displayed an IQ of seventy-five, which is below the average figure of 100. If it had been any lower, he would have been categorised as being *mentally challenged*. He effectively was living a normal life but with very little brain in his head.

A century before our French civil-servant's condition was discovered, there lived another man, who coincidentally also worked as a civil-servant, and who also had a most-unusual brain. He worked in the Swiss patent office in the early 1900s, and was the man that Time magazine labelled as the most-significant-figure of the twentieth-century. His name was Albert Einstein, and though regarded as one of the most intelligent individuals of all time, there are some very-peculiar facts regarding his genius that most people are unaware of.

Einstein failed his initial entrance examination for the Zurich Polytechnic, but successfully passed it on his second attempt. He enrolled on a teaching diploma in maths and physics, but apparently didn't distinguish himself in the eyes of his lecturers while he was there. He finally graduated, and then spent two-years unsuccessfully applying for university assistantships and permanent teaching positions. During this time, he held several temporary-jobs teaching mathematics at Swiss schools, until a friend's father helped him get a job in the Swiss patent office, where he spent several years working as an assistant patent-examiner.

In 1902, he fathered an illegitimate child, a girl named Lieserl, who is mysteriously unaccounted for in any records after her first-year. A year later, in January 1903, Einstein married the mother of his child, and subsequently had another child with her in May 1904. He also completed his doctorate-studies at this time, and in 1905, at the age of twenty-six, he submitted his technical theses and was awarded a PhD from the University of Zurich.

Considering the tumultuous period that had occurred in his life during the conservative, early twentieth-century, Einstein then proceeded to have what is described as his miracle year.

In 1905, in addition to submitting his PhD thesis, and without having convenient access to scientific reference materials, Einstein wrote and submitted four papers to the highly-respected, academic publication Annalen der Physik (Annals of Physics) which subsequently published them the same year. These are the four papers and the dates he submitted them:

18 March 1905. Paper on the Production and Transformation of Light. This covers the photo-electric effect and eventually earns Einstein a Nobel Prize.

11 May 1905. Paper on the Motion of Small Particles. An explanation of Brownian motion, or how particles in a gas, travel in random paths based on the impact of atoms and molecules upon them.

30 June 1905. Paper on the Electrodynamics of Moving Bodies. Also referred to as the special theory of relativity, which explains the dynamics of bodies when moving close to the speed of light.

27 September 1905. Paper on the Inertia of Bodies and their Energy Content. This introduces the relationship between matter and energy through the iconic equation of $E=mc^2$.

These ground-breaking papers, which were actually submitted in a period of just over six-months, are referred to as the *Annus Mirabilis*, or *Miracle Year* papers — and it's easy to understand why they are so-named.

If you were to write a fictional-story based on a twenty-six-year-old character, who had produced no notable work, and who suddenly writes four amazing scientific papers in six-months, it certainly wouldn't feel like a plausible plot. How was Einstein suddenly able to unleash his mind to discover these ground-breaking new concepts? How did he achieve his phenomenal Miracle Year out of the turmoil in his personal life?

Maybe he just decided to put his mind to the issue!

YOU AND YOUR PHENOMENAL CAPABILITY

Imagine yourself sat at a desk, with a computer in front of you, which is connected to a printer. You open a new Microsoft Word document and you select Calibri font, and set it to font-size eleven. Now you are ready to start typing — but what are you going to type?

You are going to type everything you know.

All your memories, all the people you know, the members of your family, your friends, your work-colleagues. What they look like, what their voices sound like, all the things you've done with them in the past, what you have planned to do with them in the future. The places you've been, the events that have happened in your life, your sixth-birthday party, how you felt, what you ate, where it was held, who was there. All the knowledge that you have, the things that you learned in school, the masses of general-knowledge that only comes in useful in pub quiz-nights, all the skills, information and knowledge you need to do your job. All the songs you know, the lyrics, the chorus, the music that you like to sing-along to. The books you've read, their plots, authors, and your favourite parts. The films you've seen, what your favourite actors look and sound like. Your favourite food, how you cook it, the parties you've been to with your friends, who was there, the funny jokes that were told, and how you met your loved-one.

And the list goes on, and on, and on. You are going to type everything you can remember — in full, multi-media detail. The sounds, visuals, smells and tastes that are associated with every one of these memories — and how you felt about them at the time they happened.

Assume that time isn't an issue, and that your fingers won't get sore while you type-out this gargantuan document. As you finish a page, you print it out, and add it to the stack of pages which grows steadily higher and higher. When you've finished typing out the full details of every thought and memory you have, you take all the printed sheets to a row of filing cabinets. These metal, four-drawer filing cabinets are the type you frequently see in older offices. You open the top drawer, fill it with the typed-sheets and close it when it is full. You open the next drawer below this and do the same, and then again with the third, and fourth, drawers. This filing cabinet is now full, so you move on to the next filing cabinet.

How many of these filing cabinets do you think you will need to store the typed-out details of everything you can remember? A hundred? A thousand? Ten-thousand? More? Whatever number you choose, this is the store of the *conscious* memories that you have.

There's another level of memory that hasn't yet been accessed — *the subconscious-level*. At the conscious-level are the things *we know that we know*. The memories that we can recall immediately. At the subconscious-level are the things *we don't know that we know*. This is the bank of knowledge and experiences that we've forgotten — or that we *believe* we have forgotten.

An example is to think of the lyrics to the second-verse of the song *Yesterday* by the Beatles. Off-hand I don't know what they are — but give me time to quickly sing the first-verse and chorus in my head and I'm sure I'll get it. Another example is to think what were you doing on the day you were fifteen-years and seventy-nine days old? You probably have no idea, even though you lived through every second of that twenty-four hour period. However, if you could look back at your teenage-diary for that day, you may have made some notes that would bring that whole-day flooding back to you. Your diary entry may include some places that you used to frequent that you haven't thought about in years, together with the friends you had at the time, and the things you did. If you thought about this event in detail, and all the things that were happening in your life at the time, you may see that you could quite easily fill another fifty printed-sheets of memories that are triggered by this one stimulus alone.

Can you ride a bicycle? Do you remember how hard it seemed when you were a child trying to master the art of balancing on two-wheels? It may have been twenty-five years since you last rode a bicycle — nonetheless, you could get on one tomorrow and ride away. How would you describe to someone what they needed to know to ride a bicycle? This is detail that your conscious-mind often doesn't appreciate, and yet needs to be stored in your subconscious, so that you don't need to learn how to ride a bicycle again the next time you use one.

While you ponder the bicycle issue, what about explaining how to drive a car, how to throw a ball, how to swim, or even how to tie your shoelaces? These, and many more things, are the forgotten, subconscious content that we also want to type and print out for filing away in your memory filing cabinets.

It's a very-approximate number, but neurologists estimate that our subconscious-memory may be 10,000-times larger than our conscious-memory. This means we may well have *10,000-forgotten items* in our subconscious mind, *for every single-remembered item* from our conscious mind. So, whatever the number of filing cabinets that you had filled with your printed-out memories, multiply this by 10,000. This much-bigger number of filing cabinets, all filled with the collection of your memories, is sitting somewhere inside your brain *right now*. If you manage to live long-enough, your brain may even store this information for over a century too.

It seems unbelievable that this phenomenal-volume of detailed memories can be readily stored inside your head — and in a way that is easily accessible too. It's an amazing feat of nature — but what's really interesting is that nobody knows just whereabouts inside your brain this vast quantity of information is actually kept. We know that certain parts of the brain, such as the hippocampus, are used in the accessing and recall of memory, but how, and where, our memories are stored is a complete mystery.

BRAIN POWER

Another interesting area is in the capacity of the brain to process information when compared to a computer. Computers are far superior to the human-brain in working out numeric calculations, as they are able to calculate millions of equations in a fraction of a second — and with perfect accuracy. When it comes to interpreting qualitative-streams of information, the human-brain can be far superior.

If we assume our eyes take the role of closed-circuit television cameras and our ears are microphones that pick up the audio-stream, a human can watch some behaviour on the cameras, and listen to the associated audio-track and know that a person is breakdancing in a public-place to a particular music-track, which is just audible above a background-hubbub of conversations. For a computer to be able to interpret the visual inputs, and to separate-out the various elements on the different-planes to identify an upside-down human is dancing against a back-wall being lit by projected images — and to ignore the conversations and to relate the person's movements to the music, would require a vast amount of computing power.

While this understanding of the breakdancing-scene is going on, the brain is also subconsciously taking in sensory-inputs from all over the body, and analysing these in the background. From this continuous input-and-analysis of information, the brain simultaneously coordinates the 650-or-so muscles in your body to make all the necessary movements you need as part of the activity you are involved in at any given moment. The brain also operates all your bodily-functions such as making sure your lungs inflate and deflate, and that your heart keeps beating at an appropriate-rate for the activity you are doing.

Interpreting all the nerve-inputs from around the body to produce the feelings you have, while understanding and interpreting the world around you — moment by moment — are other activities the brain handles for you in the background. All this occurs in a seemingly-effortless manner, and your brain is also ever-ready to instantly handle any other task you decide to give it too.

Kwabena Boahen is associate professor of bioengineering at Stanford University in the US. He started out in the fields of electrical and computer-engineering before moving into the areas of biology and the brain. He's estimated that for a supercomputer to be able to do the things that a human-brain can do, would require sixty-million watts (or sixty-megawatts) of power. To put this into context, a typical UK nuclear power-station produces 1,200-megawatts, which would only be enough to power *twenty* of these human-brain equivalent computers.

As an indication of this, early in 2014, a team of German and Japanese- scientists used the K-computer (which is the world's fourth-most-powerful supercomputer) to map how the mind works. They modelled what happens in just one per cent of the brain over a period of just one-second, yet it took the K-computer forty-minutes to undertake this task. The K-computer has over 700,000 processor-cores, 1.4 million gigabytes of RAM, and consumes ten-megawatts of power.

As you comprehend the contents of this presentation, your brain is consuming just twenty-watts of energy, which is one-third of the power of a desk lamp. The K-computer needed 500,000 times this amount of power to do just one per cent of what your brain is doing right now. And it took the K-computer forty-minutes to do what you do in one-second. This supercomputer was designed by a large team of highly-skilled engineers using complex equipment, and it needs a significant infrastructure to operate correctly. Your brain is just a series of *freak accidents of nature* caused by the repeated, and random, mutation of cells from generation to generation. And we all get one for free when we are born.

Makes you think doesn't it?

MIND GAMES

We've already seen the abilities some individuals have, but let's look at some additional capabilities of the human mind.

The Russian psychologist Alexander Luria documented the case of Solomon Shereshevsky over a period of thirty-years in the middle of the twentieth-century. Shereshevsky could memorise complex maths formulas, giant number-matrices, and even poems in foreign languages that he did not speak. He could achieve these feats in a matter of minutes due to the memory process he used, which was based on mnemonics. Mnemonics is the association of the things an individual wants to remember, to a specific framework that is meaningful to the individual.

What is peculiar is that Shereshevsky could remember almost anything he wanted to, whereas Jill Price wasn't very good at memorizing anything at all, except for the events that happened to her — and which she remembered in absolute detail.

One of the most interesting of all numbers is pi, which many of us know as approximately 22/7 or 3.142. However, it's unusual because the digits after the decimal-point go on forever, without any recurring-patterns as far as anyone has discovered to date. Akira Haraguchi is a sixty-five-year-old Japanese engineer, who is known for memorising and recalling the digits of pi. He set the world record of 100,000 digits in October 2006, which took him around sixteen-hours to complete. He relates each digit of the number to one of the kana (syllables) of the Japanese language and he creates a story around them. The first fifteen-digits of pi are 3.14159265358979 and Haraguchi's story (when translated into English) starts *The wife and children have gone abroad, the husband is not scared.*

There are also some interesting records that incorporate both *speed* and *memory*.

Imagine these nineteen-digits were flashed on a screen for one-second. How many would you be able to recall?

4 0 2 3 8 7 7 2 5 1 6 8 3 6 5 2 3 1 9

And here are forty-four binary-digits. If they were flashed on a screen for only one-second, how many would you remember?

101	010	1110	1001	0111
100	110	0110	0111	1111
				1001
				0000

Ramón Campayo of Spain holds the record for recalling both decimal and binary-numbers after seeing them for one-second. The binary-digits are particularly interesting as Campayo uses three different storage techniques, and the way the numbers are laid-out is designed to help him recall them. In the space of one-second, he *looks* at the first two-columns as numbers; the next two-columns are translated into images; while the final-column is just *said into his mind* at the last-moment. When he recalls the numbers, he writes the final-column down first, as this is the one that is held most-delicately in his mind.

Campayo acknowledges that he uses speed-reading and speed-memory techniques, and has published do-it-yourself books and software on the subject.

How it is done isn't too important here — it's the fact that it *can be done* which is interesting.

QUALITY THINKING

We've seen some of the capabilities people have, which demonstrate the amazing potential of the mind. If all these feats were only achievable by geniuses with extremely-high IQs, then we — the average people — might feel disappointed with ourselves. But this isn't the case. With the exception of Albert Einstein, the people I have mentioned in these examples are ordinary people — or are individuals who are challenged in some way, either mentally or physically.

This tends to indicate that many of us may possess the potential to do something amazing with our own minds. We aren't aware of this because we just haven't tried to apply ourselves as yet.

But the future of our minds may not necessarily be about the amount you can remember, or the speed with which you can learn a new skill. Perhaps it's about something more *qualitative* rather than *quantitative* in nature. Like Einstein, potentially we all have the latent-ability to switch our minds into over-drive for specific periods or purposes, and to apply them to considering some of the biggest issues which we face today.

SUMMARY

The three closing thoughts that I want to leave you with are these:

1. How do you know that you personally haven't got any spectacular mental-capability? Have you tried to test yourself or demonstrate your abilities? They don't have to be in the fields that I've mentioned here, they could be in any way, shape or form. *You don't know what you don't know* — so try out different things to understand the special capabilities that you may have hidden away in the depths of your mind.

2. Einstein had his Miracle Year. What if we all had the ability to flip a switch and have, maybe not a miracle year, but a miracle month, day, hour — or even a miracle moment? Why not explore what you need to do to switch yourself on mentally, the way Einstein did?

3. You can't evolve yourself physically, but you can evolve yourself mentally. For your benefit, and for the benefit of everybody else too. *If you believe you can do it, then you can do it — and if you believe you can't, then you can't.* It's entirely up to you.

It's your choice to do whatever you put your mind to. Thanks very much and good afternoon.

Chapter 30 Monday 15h00

Part-way through the last presentation, Reece had felt a gentle-tap on his elbow, and turned to find Heather crouching by his side.

"I want to move your presentation from Thursday, to four o'clock on Tuesday. Are you okay with this?"

"Sure," replied Reece.

"I need you to announce the launch of your dream-sharing website then to see if this elicits any response from the attendees."

"Do I have a choice?"

"No, and thank-you." She'd then left his side, walked up to the stage, and handed the chairman a piece of paper. Obviously the message had been pre-written. The launch of the dream website was going to be announced whether Reece had agreed to it or not.

At the end of the presentation, the chairman thanked the speaker and then made the announcement about a minor change to the conference agenda — and that a new dream-sharing website would be launched tomorrow. He'd then announced a break for refreshments.

Reece's anxiety over the lime-green Post-It notes returned. Was there some risk to him from going ahead with the dream website? Perhaps Heather was being a little too-nonchalant about putting people's lives — or more importantly, his life — at risk. Reece walked out of the auditorium, not noticing that Gareth Jones was frantically typing on his laptop's keyboard.

Gareth had found the last presentation on the evolution of the mind fascinating. It was a pity the speaker had missed-out the most phenomenal capability of the human mind — what it can do when we sleep and dream. And Gareth knew more about this, than probably anyone else on the planet. One day, in the not-too-distant future, he imagined himself on a stage, talking about the ground-breaking work he was busy doing. The standing ovation he'd receive at the end would be overwhelming. He was still engrossed in his imagined future glory, when the chairman had announced the change in timings and the launch of the dream-website. This abruptly terminated Gareth's reverie as he realised that was going to be a problem for them.

He checked the time. Just after three o'clock. He'd need to be quick to catch the afternoon deadline. He moved to find a quiet space at the back of the auditorium, opened up his laptop, and quickly created a new webpage for the Peckham Institute's website. It took a few moments to calculate the name of the webpage in his head, and he entered the title as he worked out each letter. The page name was VIIGI-XEWWMGOIV-4.

He created the location of the new webpage on their website and set the go-live date and time.

DATE: 14-JULY-2014
TIME: 15:14:15
URL: HTTP://WWW.PECKHAMINSTITUTE.ORG.UK/VIIGI-XEWWMGOIV-4

He was able to create the webpage quickly because — just like all the others he'd done recently — there was no content on it. He clicked the UPLOAD button with barely a minute to spare.

He was unsure of what the output from the dreamers would be. They may want something more-drastic to happen.

Chapter 31 Monday 15h10

Reece was standing in line for coffee and discussing the last presentation.

"For Einstein to develop just one major-piece of work when he was that young, would have been amazing. But to come up with the four most ground-breaking theories of his life within a six-month period is almost beyond belief."

"Like he somehow managed to boost his mind for that period," said the man Reece was talking to in the queue.

"You know how it's possible to get into a downward health-spiral, where you become run-down and ill, so your body becomes more susceptible to other ailments which compounds the situation. What if it's possible to get into an upward-spiral around thinking?"

"What do you mean?"

"When your mind is engaged in hard-thinking work, can it break-through to access parts of the brain which deliver better ideas, which further stimulates your thinking, which in-turn allows you to break into more parts of the mind?" suggested Reece. He was using the man as a sounding-board for some of his own thoughts, and not just making idle conversation.

"We supposedly only use a small-percentage of our brain. Maybe Einstein accessed some of the untapped-potential of his mind as part of an upward-spiral."

"He obviously did something unusual. Have you heard of the concept of *flow*?"

"By the guy with the unpronounceable-name?" said the man with the unknown name. His name-badge was twisted-around so that Reece couldn't see it.

"Mihaly Csikszentmihalyi, yes," said Reece. "He defined flow as being completely immersed on an issue. Like being totally in-the-zone when you're so focused on a subject that you can think with absolute clarity. That would help achieve an upward spiral I'm sure."

"Does that ever happen to you?"

"Flow? Sure it does — especially when I'm out running. And you?" asked Reece.

"In the shower, or when I'm out walking the dog. It's odd that your best ideas seem to happen when you're alone. Why don't they come up when you're brainstorming at work — when you need them most?"

"Did you know that brainstorming is a really inefficient way of thinking?" said Reece.

"No?" said the man, clearly surprised by this fact.

"How often do your brainstorming sessions give you those brilliant, yet practical ideas that you need?"

"Hardly ever — I must admit."

"Research has shown that getting the same people from a brainstorming session to work individually *instead*, would have delivered a greater quantity, and quality, of ideas than they did as a group. The fact is, brainstorming was developed in the early-1950s by Alex Osborn, an ad-agency guy. It's a grossly-outdated process, but many companies still use it because they don't know any better."

"I didn't know it was so old," said the man.

"Certainly is. It's peculiar that companies have moved on to embrace new technologies and processes in other aspects of their business, but when it comes to thinking about growth, they stick with a process that's over sixty-years old."

"How come you know so much about business thinking?"

"It's what we do as a company — help organisations to think differently," answered Reece.

"So, how do you do that?"

"Our Ingenious Growth teams use techniques that align to the way new ideas are formed in the mind."

"Can you give me an example?"

"Sure. Have you noticed that when a new idea comes to you, it's often very-fleeting in nature? If you ignore it — then you'll lose it?"

"That's true, yes."

"In a brainstorming session, it's difficult for an individual to get their fleeting, new idea to establish itself when you've got a continual stream of people talking — and trying to get you to focus on their ideas instead."

"How can you get around that?"

"Much of our work is done in silence to power-up individual thinking. We often have a leader who whispers a continuous stream of thought-provoking triggers — which you listen to when you need it — but which you can easily tune out when your mind is working on a specific idea."

"A novel approach. Does it work with groups?"

"Of course — but the people work as individuals within the group. With brainstorming there are too many ways that a group can get into downward-spirals when emotions or personalities come into play. The techniques we use are shaped to help individuals get into their own flow-zone instead," Reece replied.

"Maybe groups unconsciously destroy upward-spirals when they start," suggested the man. "I don't imagine Einstein ever bothered being part of a brainstorming-group."

Reece thought it quite amusing to imagine Einstein standing at a flipchart in a brainstorming-group. As Reece had gone quiet, the man thought he was waiting for him to make another comment, and so he continued.

"Also, why do people need a group for good thinking? Why don't we have the confidence to do our own thinking and then get feedback from the group? Given what you say about brainstorming groups being so ineffective, maybe we need to switch our approach to thinking and switch back to using our individual minds."

The man had just used the word *switch* twice in one-sentence. It seemed to jump out at Reece, and his mind started to wander. The Council were back.

Switch. Switch.

The man said switch.

What if there's a switch in the mind?

To turn on powerful thinking?

Like a light-bulb?

An Einstein Switch.

That's a good name.

It's a switch that actually turns on an upward spiral.

Is it an attitude you adopt?

Or a process you use?

Don't know.

Maybe savants, child prodigies, and people with amazing mind-skills have learnt to somehow turn on their Einstein Switch.

Interesting thought.

The man was still talking and Reece realised he'd missed some of what he'd said.

"...I mean, if evolution can break the second law of thermodynamics, then why can't individuals?"

"But we do — all the time," said DD, who at that moment had walked up to join the middle of the queue again.

"I'm not sure I completely understand the second-law thing," said Reece. "You're the engineer DD, explain it simply."

"Energy naturally flows from the highest form of structure to the lowest. The tallest mountain will eventually crumble to the finest dust. Landslides go down-hill, right? Remember that example of the three-billion piece jigsaw? A square jigsaw with that number of pieces would measure over a kilometre on each side. Now imagine you had a box that was so big, you were able to assemble the entire jigsaw inside it. When it's complete, you put the lid on — and give it a really-good shake. What do you think will happen?"

"It'll come apart," said Reece.

"Of course it will. That represents the mountain crumbling to dust. If you carried on shaking the box what are the chances of the jigsaw rebuilding itself? Perhaps by extreme-chance, a few pieces might happen to join together correctly, but as you keep shaking the box, they'll tend to fall-apart again, rather than more pieces joining on to them. Is this making sense?"

Reece nodded.

"The big-bang represents the highest-form energy-structure, and since then we should be falling to lower-form energy-structures. But for some particular reason we, the inhabitants of this planet, aren't. We're actually getting more complex, and that was the example of the three-billion part DNA ladder. This wouldn't be expected to happen in the natural course of our evolution. But that's the issue with evolution as a concept — the whole thing goes against the second law of thermodynamics, man."

"And that's the key point, isn't it?" asked the man.

"Does the pope shit in the woods? Of course it's the key point!" DD's arms started waving around — almost to the point of injuring the nearby people as his over-animated explanation continued.

"Now a similar thing has happened with intelligence. At some point in the past, we crossed a certain threshold where we developed intelligence of a sufficient-level to become clever. *And then cleverer*. At this point we had the ability to make ourselves more efficient. Whether it started around the time we first used basic flint-tools, or when we learned the benefits of fire, or even when we developed the first wheel — isn't that important. Because by that time our minds were primed and we had the ability to do more. We were basically smart. But how we actually *became smart* — that's where we went against the second law. Intelligence shouldn't have happened by chance. That's not things decaying into lower energy-levels by any means. And whether its intelligence, reproductive systems, or the DNA replication-and-repair system — they're all examples of us going against what should be expected to happen." DD was now in full flow with his explanation.

"Have you heard of the Universe in a Box scenario?" he asked.

Reece and the man both shook their heads.

"Imagine that soon after the big bang happened, someone put all the bits-and-pieces into a huge cardboard-box and kept shaking it. Every so often they'd look inside to see what had happened. What's the chance of them opening the box at some point, and finding the human-race all looking up at them saying *Hello there, fancy a cup of tea?* According to the second law of thermodynamics, we shouldn't be here. It's that amazing," he said, finishing with a flourish.

"Anyway, why's this queue not moving?" asked DD, peering forward.

"It looks like they've run out of tea," said the man.

DD put his hands to his temples and loudly cried-out, "nooooooo!" He stopped as something caught his attention. "Reece, wait here," he said, and dashed off into the crowd.

He returned a few moments later, guiding a woman by the elbow. Reece recognised her as the presenter of the first-session — Dr Jean Rose.

"Reece, this is Jean who gave the first lecture. Wasn't she sensational?" enthused DD.

Reece introduced himself and agreed that her lecture had indeed been sensational.

"You said you'd got something to ask her," said DD, looking expectantly at Reece.

Reece had anticipated he'd have to somehow fabricate a chance-meeting in order to speak to her, but here DD had dragged her across the room like a dog carried a toy back to its basket.

"I'd like to know why there isn't more research being done on the anomalies you mentioned?" asked Reece, remembering his question at the last moment.

"That's the big question — and it's one that I'm passionate about. Do you mind if I tell you a story?" Jean replied.

"Please do," said Reece.

"Throughout civilisations, there have been insightful-people who had a natural curiosity about the world — why things are the way they are, and what causes them. These people have created and extended our knowledge, and over time have shaped the various fields that form the over-arching term of *science*. The physics, biology and chemistry we are taught in school rely on the basic premise that what happened last-time, will happen the next-time too. This premise of absolute predictability is the foundation of scientific laws. These are the laws that apply to everybody and everything. They never change — and you can't get an exemption from them. Because of this constancy, they form the foundation stones for the advancement of new learning."

Her soft-Scottish accent was pleasing on the ears, and as she wasn't holding a drink, she was using her well-manicured hands to emphasise the points she was making. Reece noticed that DD seemed peculiarly transfixed by her hands. Or maybe he was just staring at her breasts. *With DD, you couldn't be sure* thought Reece.

"As many of these basic principles had been tested for centuries without any observable deviation, the scientists of the time used this initial set of laws as a platform upon which to build new, and more advanced, theories. In the early-1900s, scientific thinking and the available experimentation technology, had advanced to such an extent that scientists like Einstein, Bohr and Planck could postulate new-theories stating that some of the basic laws weren't actually valid in every situation. Retrospectively, it was brilliant theoretical physics by individuals who would be acknowledged as the best in their field. However, at the time it was really-bold thinking to contradict centuries of accepted scientific belief."

"Today, there are tens-of-thousands of diverse research areas being meticulously and passionately explored by hundreds-of-thousands of scientific researchers. Occasionally, in one of these fields of study, an individual will discover something that appears to violate an accepted scientific truth. Now this is a tricky situation for the individual, the individual's team and for their organisation, because to challenge the accepted theories can be risky scientific ground. Countless scholarly-minds have been consolidating these theories over the centuries, and building new-ones based on the old. To challenge this structure risks debunking a vast amount of work that has been done in the past, and probably puts at risk research being undertaken in the present. For every new research hypotheses being put forward, there are likely to be other researchers committing significant time and effort working on a contrary viewpoint. As it's most unlikely that both can be correct, this means one party will be shown to have been pursuing a wrong direction."

She paused, and asked, "have you heard of the internet term of *flaming*?"

"Isn't that when someone receives a hostile response for something they say online?" offered Reece.

"Exactly," she said. "It's also the academic, Rottweiler-type response that an edgy scientific theory can receive. It makes the most articulate internet-flamer seem akin to a two-year-old's babbling. Even deciding to undertake research in a particularly esoteric field — such as extreme capabilities of the mind like telepathy, clairvoyance, and extra-sensory perception — can be deemed areas to be avoided by serious researchers. It's unfortunate, as these are potentially some of the more-interesting areas that would benefit from investment in time and resources. As a result, many of these esoteric areas of research are left to relatively low-funded institutions, which, due to their lack of main-stream research credibility, will always be open to ridicule by better-funded individuals. Even if something unusual is discovered in one of these fields, gaining acceptance of this research-finding by academia and main-stream research bodies may be an arduous task."

"So if someone took the risk and investigated an anomaly, and actually found something interesting, even then it's likely to get condemned by the people who need to maintain the status quo for the sake of their own work?" asked DD.

"Precisely," replied Jean. "Sometimes, the potential impact of these findings is so radical, that most scientists would rather not address them, as they have no idea how to integrate these concepts into their own work. In fact, many researchers are probably quite grateful that findings of this nature were made in fields unrelated to their own, which allows them to pursue their research in a state of fortunate scientific-ignorance. Findings of this nature don't fit our model of normal expectations. They are anomalies. And they are problems as far as research goes."

Jean paused, and took a deep breath. "Sorry if I got carried away with this. But it sometimes feels like the whole of science is looking at the wrong things, and that you can't get their attention to this fact. Does that answer your question?"

"It certainly does," said Reece. "It's a tragedy that the anomalies have less attraction to academia than you'd imagine they should."

"Some of the issues are very tough-nuts to crack. You could spend your whole life investigating just one of them, and either you won't be able to find the answer to it — or if you do, it may not be accepted by others," she said. "It's a big risk for an individual to take."

"Maybe the anomalies don't want to be answered," added DD flippantly, flashing her what he hoped was his most-enigmatic smile.

That's a strange thing for DD to say thought Reece, as he felt the phone in his jacket-pocket begin to vibrate. The call was from his office.

Chapter 32 Monday 19h50

Reece missed the remainder of the afternoon presentations. Some weeks-ago, he'd proposed a project to a client where his company would provide a thinking support service to help them with their business growth in one area. The managing director had called his office saying she wanted to proceed — but across the whole business — and he'd spent the rest of the afternoon and early-evening revising the proposal. After he'd emailed the response back to the client, Reece headed down to the hotel's restaurant.

There hadn't been any obvious individual or group that he could join, so he was sitting alone at a table, awaiting the arrival of a medium-rare sirloin steak. He'd not asked for any sauce as he wanted to avoid anything vaguely-resembling the image still in his mind of the lunchtime buffet platters.

A woman approached, and in a mild-Australian accent said "you're at the conference too, aren't you?" She waved the name-badge lanyard that hung around her neck.

"I'm Jennifer Goddard, from Mindwerx International. We're an Australian company who train people in mind-skills. Mind if I join you?"

"I'd enjoy the company," said Reece, introducing himself. They spent their main-course, dessert and a bottle of Graham Beck Railroad Red, discussing their different approaches to thinking techniques. They'd moved on to the relationship between thinking and memory, when Jennifer mentioned that she was the organiser of the World Memory Championships.

"One speaker gave the example of the Spanish-guy who could remember nineteen-digits after seeing them for just a second," said Reece. "Is that what you do?"

"That's rapid recall rather than memory development," Jennifer corrected him. "They're quite different."

"Then perhaps you'd better explain," said Reece.

"Our World Memory Championships are held every year and incorporate ten challenges to test the extent of an individual's memory in a number of different formats. These include memorising the order of decks of playing-cards, matching names to faces, memorising the order of random words and number lists," Jennifer explained.

"And how good are the winners?"

"It's sometimes better to see it visually," she said, reaching inside her bag and removing some A4-sized sheets of paper from a folder.

“The current record for the number of random digits memorised in fifteen-minutes is 937,” she said, placing one of the sheets on the table in front of Reece.

“Here’s a list of 937-digits.”

5 7 7 0 1 2 0 5 8 6 3 0 0 4 0 1 3 3 9 2 7 7 2 4 6 1 5 1 6 9 4 9 2 0 4 1 5 2 4 5 4 7 0 3 4 4 6 1 0 5 6 2 3 7
9 7 3 2 2 2 2 0 1 2 5 1 0 4 2 2 1 5 1 7 6 3 1 5 3 1 4 6 2 2 0 0 5 7 9 5 8 4 9 3 5 3 2 1 4 4 8 5 7 8 8 0 3 3
7 8 9 4 0 6 9 5 6 0 2 0 6 5 5 5 6 3 1 3 9 4 1 4 5 5 4 9 4 0 7 6 4 8 6 4 7 9 6 6 3 0 6 0 2 5 2 5 2 3 8 6 5 4
3 2 7 1 6 7 6 8 9 2 6 6 8 0 9 4 7 1 5 9 8 6 2 3 3 3 4 1 0 1 7 0 9 3 3 4 2 7 0 9 5 2 2 6 2 3 5 7 1 4 2 9 4 8
8 4 0 3 1 1 6 2 4 3 6 5 0 4 9 7 7 9 2 5 9 7 8 3 2 8 8 4 8 9 1 9 5 7 7 6 7 2 3 4 0 3 3 6 6 7 5 0 3 2 9 5 6 0
5 6 9 8 5 7 2 2 7 9 1 7 1 7 1 5 0 5 7 6 9 6 0 7 9 0 0 2 5 8 0 0 2 6 5 1 1 7 9 2 4 2 8 7 7 7 8 5 6 8 1 6 6 9
7 7 6 1 6 2 2 8 6 0 8 6 9 1 8 8 5 5 0 2 5 0 4 0 4 8 0 8 7 6 0 9 4 0 2 4 3 5 8 9 3 3 5 9 6 1 4 1 2 6 7 5 1 0
0 0 1 8 7 8 4 9 6 9 0 1 9 4 9 5 2 1 9 3 1 0 2 4 1 1 8 6 1 5 8 0 7 0 8 8 3 1 1 9 3 2 7 1 6 7 6 8 9 2 6 6 8 0
9 4 7 1 5 9 8 6 2 3 3 3 4 1 0 1 7 0 9 3 3 4 2 7 0 9 5 2 2 6 2 3 5 7 1 4 2 9 4 8 8 4 0 3 1 1 6 2 4 3 6 5 0 4
9 7 7 9 2 5 9 7 8 3 2 8 8 4 8 9 1 9 5 7 7 6 7 2 3 4 0 3 3 6 6 7 5 0 3 2 9 5 6 0 5 6 9 8 5 7 2 2 7 9 1 7 1 7
1 5 0 5 7 6 9 6 0 7 9 0 0 2 5 8 0 0 2 6 5 1 1 7 9 2 4 2 8 7 7 7 8 5 6 8 1 6 6 9 7 7 6 1 6 2 2 8 6 0 8 6 9 1
8 8 5 5 0 2 5 0 4 0 4 8 0 8 7 6 0 9 4 0 2 4 3 5 8 9 3 3 5 9 6 1 4 1 2 6 7 5 1 0 0 0 1 8 7 8 4 9 6 9 0 1 9 4
9 5 2 1 9 3 1 0 2 4 1 1 8 6 1 5 8 0 7 0 8 8 3 1 1 9 3 2 7 1 6 7 6 8 9 2 6 6 8 0 9 4 7 1 5 9 8 6 2 3 3 3 4 1
0 1 7 0 9 3 3 4 2 7 0 9 5 2 2 6 2 3 5 7 1 4 2 9 4 8 8 4 0 3 1 1 6 2 4 3 6 5 0 4 9 7 7 9 2 5 9 7 8 3 2 8 8 4
8 9 1 9 5 7 7 6 7 2 3 4 0 3 3 6 6 7 5 0 3 2 9 5 6 0 5 6 9 8 5 7 2 2 7 9 1 7 1 7 1 5 0 5 7 6 9 6 0 7 9 0 0 2
5 8 0 0 2 6 5 1 1 7 9 2 4 2 8 7 7 7 8 5 6 8 1 6 6 9 7 7 6 1 6 2 2 8 6 0 8 6 9 1 8 8 5 5 0 2 5 0 4 0 4 8 0 8
7 6 0 9 4 0 2 4 3 5 8 9 3 3 5 9 6 1 4 1 2 6 7 5 1 0 0 0 1 8 7 8 4 9 6 9 0 1 9 4 9 5 2 1 9 3 1 0 2 4 1 1 8 6
1 5 8 0 7 0 8 8 3 1 1 9 3 2 7 1 6 7 6

“How many do you think you’d be able to recall — in the correct order of course — after being given fifteen minutes to memorise them?” she asked.

“*Bloody hell!* Barely any.” exclaimed Reece.

“Or, if you prefer words, then the record for recalling random words after ten-minutes to memorise them is 170. Here’s a list of 170-words if you’d like to have a go,” and she handed him another sheet of paper.

impossible, animal, tyre, frightened, loutish, adhesive, descriptive, well-groomed, eatable, wealth, humdrum, childlike, explain, wonder, slimy, ashamed, stingy, meek, abrupt, unsightly, cast, flagrant, defective, lush, deafening, brass, nebulous, shaggy, acrid, needy, nosy, angry, enchanted, turn, grateful, cumbersome, twig, poor, anger, blushing, force, certain, touch, toothsome, curly, filthy, decorous, enchanting, expensive, behave, expect, extra-large, yell, two, fair, ladybug, flat, forgetful, deliver, giant, second-hand, past, glorious, humorous, innate, jewel, sin, understood, irritating, jaded, move, jagged, question, new, order, shade, overt, possessive, productive, babies, sister, truthful, profuse, public, rude, rural, quartz, shaky, remain, simple, victorious, cycle, smoggy, sweet, memory, thumb, talented, truculent, rule, unbecoming, uttermost, violent, branch, camera, bubble, tree, business, cakes, chess, club, mist, request, tax, corn, cough, crow, distribution, claim, replace, flavour, flesh, bless, geese, hat, home, interest, loss, mailbox, month, passenger, picture, vacation, truck, position, ski, search, shame, week, sheet, silk, stage, star, value, stocking, substance, snow, toes, back, boast, cheat, cough, decay, treat, detect, develop, float, fool, sparkle, improve, jam, mix, paddle, pour, refuse, rely, risk, shrug, signal, surprise, waste

"And this next one is particularly impressive," she said, showing him a third sheet. "Here's a list of 4,000 binary digits arranged into groups of eight. You have just thirty-minutes to memorise all these."

01010100 11100111 10110001 10111001 10011010 11100010 11100011 10011011 01001011
01110010 01101010 01110011 00111111 01010100 00010100 11110010 10010001 00000100
00001111 01010001 00000001 10101111 10100111 01100000 11010111 10100001 01101100
10111010 11000001 01101111 10101111 00001000 00110000 01101100 01001011 01000111
00011110 10111100 10111010 01011001 10100001 00101010 11001101 11111100 10011000
00000000 10010011 00101100 00110010 00000001 11011110 10101000 10011010 11110010
10110010 11001100 01101011 11101000 00100010 00000101 00001010 11001111 11010000
00100000 11010000 01001100 10010110 10101110 11010001 00101001 11000110 10100000
01100011 10111001 11011001 11101001 01000011 10010110 10111111 00100101 10011011
01011001 10010101 01011001 01100010 11011100 11110000 00110111 00011110 11010000
00101100 01100001 01011011 00010110 11010101 10110110 00001100 01000000 11010001
01001101 01000100 01100001 10101100 11010001 11011000 10001110 11010010 01101111
00011100 10000011 00001010 00111011 11110111 01111011 10111110 10011111 00000101
10111110 10010000 00100011 01001101 00011000 10010011 00001001 10000110 11111010
01011110 10100100 00111101 11011110 01101001 10011111 11010010 10101000 10011010
10110101 10011010 00011011 01110101 10011011 11111100 10101000 11001111 01000000
01010100 01101111 10010010 01001011 10001101 00110110 10101010 01010001 01001110
01011011 00110000 10001101 01011001 01001111 10001100 01000001 01011100 01000010
01110100 11000011 11000001 11101000 11000111 01111011 01001101 10010111 01000001
00011001 11000011 00110111 00110010 01100011 11100000 10001001 11001110 11110001
01111011 00110010 11001110 00011001 11100010 11110000 00100001 00111101 11010110
01101000 00111110 10111111 01010001 10011000 11110101 01111111 10001001 01100100
10101010 01011001 00100101 01110101 01000110 11010000 10010100 01110001 00011111
10000100 01100000 10001010 11110001 11101101 01100010 10011010 00000000 11110101

10011101 00100000 01011001 00100000 10010100 00110110 01101111 10001101 11010011

01100010 11111111 00101101 10001010 00100000 10000010 01001010 10101100 11100111

00000010 01101001 01100000 01011010 10001110 11101011 01101011 11111001 01000101

10111110 00010101 00011010 10001111 10001111 01100110 10011001 10011100 00110010

11001111 11111001 11110001 00011001 00010110 11000100 10011111 10100100 01001001

01001100 11001110 00010111 00101100 00100111 01000110 00110101 10110010 01110111

11100000 01011111 00111000 01100001 11001111 00111110 11100011 00001100 10010001

10000101 10011001 00100010 00100000 11010110 00111101 10000001 10000010 10101001

10100111 11100100 11110111 11111000 01001111 00011011 00111101 10000001 10111010

01010001 10111001 11011011 00011111 11000100 00110110 10111101 00111111 11100101

10100101 11111011 11111100 11001001 01010100 10000010 00101000 00001011 00100000

00100111 10010000 01101101 10100011 10101111 10111001 00000110 11001010 01000110

00001000 01000010 10110111 01000001 00001011 01001000 00000010 01101110 10101000

11010110 11011110 01110000 10100110 10100111 01111001 00001011 00111110 00011110

11000101 11010111 11000101 01011001 00111110 00000010 01000010 10111010 10010110

01011001 11110111 01100110 11001001 01111100 01000111 11010101 10110100 10000101

01000000 10101001 01001010 10011111 10111001 10011110 11110101 10000011 11000010

01110111 11011110 01100011 00100100 00110001 11001110 11000101 00110110 00111100

11011101 10000000 11110110 10011100 00100011 01011101 10011000 01010000 00001101

10110111 00110001 00101101 11010010 01011101 00100010 00000111 10001110 10100011

01110101 10011011 00100101 10001100 00000110 00100001 00010100 11000101 11111100

01101111 00111000 10000010 00010011 10001001 01010011 01101010 11100011 01000001

00111001 01111111 00000000 01001011 01101010 11101011 00011000 11011101 10111010

11011010 11001101 01110011 01111111 11010101 00111000 00010110 11011110 01010000

01111100 11000011 11111010 01110000 00000100 00001000 11100001 00110101 10000101

01101001 00111010 11101101 01110101 00100011 01111010 11000100 11101000 11010111

11010101 00011111 10011000 01011000 01101000 11110001 01011010 11001111 11101100

01000100 11101110 11010100 11110001 10101101 11011000 10000010 01110010 10001111

00001110 11101101 11101010 10000001 11010010 11110110 00000100 11010111 01101101

00100001 10001100 00111110 10010001 11010111 01101010 10101100 01111001 11010101

00101100 11100110 11011000 11010110 11000101 10101001 01101000 11011111 10100001

01111101 10011000 10100010 00000010 10110001

“Someone can really do this in just thirty-minutes?” asked Reece, incredulity filling his voice.

"The current thirty-minute record is actually 4,140-digits. A few more than on this list," she replied, with a laugh. Reece stared at the sheet of ones and zeros on the table, shaking his head in disbelief.

"As a last example for you, if you want to break the record for shuffled playing-cards, then you have sixty-minutes to memorise the correct order of twenty-eight full decks of cards. That's 1,456 playing-cards," she added.

"This is phenomenal," said Reece. "What kinds of people are able to achieve these feats? Is it about having a photographic memory?"

"The people who do this are ordinary people, sometimes just kids in their early-teens. And surprisingly it isn't about having a photographic memory. They use a range of techniques to help them remember the order of things," she replied, "but they have to spend a lot of time practicing to achieve this level of competency."

"Are there any mental-arithmetic calculations involved?" asked Reece.

"No, not in the World Memory Championships. However, there's a different event for numeric mental-competencies. It's the Mental Calculation World Cup and it's held every two-years. Do you want to see the level of skill required to win that contest?"

"Certainly do," said Reece, intrigued.

"Here are some typical questions, along with the performance of the winners," she said, extracting more A4-sheets from her bag.

"One of the tests is to add up ten, ten-digit numbers as quickly and accurately as you can. Here's an example." She passed him a sheet which displayed a column of numbers.

2074981337
3007381320
5629013653
1429722945
8847012993
6288010775
7193740266
2968016438
9577633028
4482061118

"The best calculators will typically need about three minutes for ten such tasks. That's an average of eighteen seconds for each one."

Reece let out a quiet-whistle as he imagined the skill involved.

"Then there's the ability to multiply two, eight-digit numbers together without writing anything down. Here's an example," she said, passing him another sheet of paper.

48639471 x 92058341 =

"The winner will achieve ten correct answers in just under thirty-seconds for each one."

"They work that out in their head in just thirty seconds?"

"There are other mental-challenges involved too. What's impressive is that in 2010, the overall winner was Priyanshi Somani from India. She was the youngest participant in the competition and was just eleven-years-old at the time."

"That seems unreal," said Reece. "How do they do these things?"

"Obviously this isn't about memory. It's about techniques for doing calculations rapidly, all of which can be learned, but it also requires plenty of practice. Anyone can improve their memory dramatically, and their mental-calculation skills too, but I think it takes a certain type of mind to achieve what the champions do."

"But where will it stop? I mean, how fast can people get at these activities?" asked Reece.

"I don't know," Jennifer replied, "but isn't that one of the interesting and exciting things about the mind?"

"Do the individuals who win these memory and calculation contests understand how their minds really work? Do they know a truth that the rest of us aren't aware of?"

"Probably not. They just try different techniques until they find the one that works best for them. They likely understand how the technique works, but not the physiological-mechanics of their brain. You're aware that we don't know how the brain works, or how it manages to come up with specific thoughts. But it does — all the time. And we trust our thoughts. Maybe we shouldn't question what we're capable of, as much as we do. We should just get on and do it. Try to see how much, how fast, and how far we can take it. That's what the World Memory Championships are all about."

"That's a stimulating thought," said Reece.

It occupied his mind for the rest of their dinner.

Chapter 33 Monday 20h45

Asif entered the restaurant and headed directly to where Reece was dining with Jennifer Goddard. He knew exactly where to find them.

"Mister Tassicker, apologies for interrupting your dinner, but the conference director would like an urgent word," he said. Reece recognised Asif as the man who'd been partly-hidden behind all the computer-monitors in Heather's office from this morning. He excused himself and followed Asif back to their office. Heather was holding the hotel landline-phone to her ear and had a confused-look on her face. She waved her free-hand towards two chairs on the other side of her desk, indicating they should sit down.

"I'm really sorry but I'm unable to comment on that."

A pause as Heather listened to the voice on the phone.

"As I just said, I'm unable to comment on this in any way."

Another pause as the voice on the other end of the phone spoke again.

"Look, I'm very sorry, but I have to go," she said, and put the phone down to end the call.

"Something's happened. I've had four phone-calls put through by the hotel's switchboard asking about a video of Professor Bartlett on YouTube. I need to see it now."

Asif quickly returned to his desk, and his fingers rattled like machine-gun fire on the keyboard.

Heather's mobile-phone vibrated loudly on the desk in front of her. She picked it up and looked at the screen.

"My boss," she said to Reece, and grimaced. "Yes John?"

"What the bloody hell is going on down there Heather?" The voice known as John was obviously yelling into his phone, for Heather had moved the phone away from her ear. This enabled Reece to hear it clearly from where he sat.

"I've just seen a video of Professor Bartlett humiliating himself twice at your bloody conference. What the Christ is going-on?"

"There was an incident this morning, and another at lunchtime. We've only just found out about it going public ourselves."

"They're more than bloody incidents. Professor Bartlett is an important person for us, especially since being appointed to the PM's task-force," yelled the voice called John. "And make sure nothing else happens," it added. The voice stopped abruptly. The call had ended. Heather held the phone where it was and looked at Reece for a moment, her lips pursed tightly.

"Being part of the MoD, I presume you use secure communication channels," said Reece. "Maybe yelling down them doesn't help. I heard that entire conversation."

"My boss seems to have a few problems," said Heather. "Which means if I don't get answers, I'll be having problems too. Asif, what do you have?"

"I've just searched YouTube for the term Simon Bartlett and found a video uploaded today that's had over 35,000 views already." Asif replied. "Want to see it?"

Heather moved around behind Asif to look over his shoulder.

"Mind if I see?" asked Reece.

"Sure," said Heather, "you're cleared to watch YouTube."

"This is it," said Asif, opening the video on one of his larger-monitors and clicking the play-button.

The video started with a static-screen displaying the text

PROFESSOR SIR SIMON BARTLETT AT THE
POTENTIAL OF THE HUMAN MIND CONFERENCE
LONDON 14 JULY 2014.

After a few-seconds the screen disappeared, and a video of the Professor standing at the auditorium's podium appeared. He was speaking about his *fourth-point*, when he sneezed four-times, and then produced his monstrous, and extremely-repulsive fifth sneeze.

"This is being taken from an aisle-seat on the left-hand side. You can see the central walkway here," said Asif, pointing to the screen.

The video paused on a still-image of Professor Bartlett's face, covered in mucus. It then cut to a different-view showing the Professor holding a plate of food at the head of a queue of people. As they all watched the monitor, he suddenly clutched his stomach and dropped his plate. Both Heather and Reece know precisely what was going to happen next.

"Oh my goodness," said Asif, as he saw the first-projection of vomit over the buffet table.

"Holy shit!" he exclaimed, as the second explosive-spew from the Professor decimated the beautifully displayed food on the table. As the Professor dropped to his knees, the video held on this frame, before fading-out to show the same introduction screen that it started with.

"This must be the video that's been sent to the press," said Heather, "The four calls I've just had were from different journalists who all knew my name, the location, the details of the conference, and that Professor Bartlett was our keynote speaker. Someone's obviously making some kind of statement here."

She turned to Reece. "You were at the buffet table when this happened — I saw you in the queue. Did you see anybody filming this?"

"No," replied Reece, "my attention was on the Professor."

"I can check the Contactor system to see what that shows," offered Asif.

"Do it," instructed Heather.

Asif tapped on the keyboard. Two screens changed to show a heading entitled CONTACTOR SYSTEM with a list of clickable-options down the side. Reece saw that these were obviously locations within the hotel. On the first-screen, Asif clicked the MAIN AUDITORIUM option, and a layout of the auditorium appeared, showing the rows of seats and the podium. On the second-screen, he clicked the DINING ROOM option, which showed the layout of the long serving-tables.

Reece noticed that the style of display on the two new-screens matched the existing-one on the third-screen in the row, which indicated HOTEL RESTAURANT at the top. Whereas the first two-screens simply showed the room layout, the third-screen showed the layout of the restaurant tables, and also some white-dots adjacent to the tables. He recognised the location of the table he was sat at, and next to it was a white-dot in the position where Jennifer sat while they had dinner together. As he watched, this white-dot slowly moved from the table, through the restaurant and off the side of the screen.

"How did you know where to find me just now?" asked Reece suspiciously.

"You were on the restaurant-screen sat with another attendee," said Asif.

"Jennifer Goddard, right?" added Heather, more as a factual statement than a question.

"We're monitoring the location of the Contactor devices," she added. "That was how Asif knew you were in the restaurant just now."

Reece's hand unconsciously dropped to his waist and touched the device still clipped to his belt.

"The lunchtime-event happened around five-past-one, so let's move the timeline to just before then," said Asif. Using the mouse, he dragged a slider along a timeline located at the bottom of the DINING ROOM screen, until it showed 13h00. The black floor-plan showed the outlines of the rectangular buffet-tables in grey and that was all. Then, an army of small white-dots started moving onto the screen through the doorways, and they formed wavy-lines on either side of the buffet-tables. A few of the dots had different colours and Reece asked Asif what this meant.

"The white-dots represent individuals wearing their Contactor devices, while the coloured-dots are those people of special interest to us."

Asif increased the timing run-speed which caused the seconds display on the screen's digital clock to advance more rapidly. The dots on the screen began to dance in a seemingly-agitated manner. A red-dot appeared on the left-side of the screen and moved to the right in an animated-dancing motion. Asif moved his mouse to position the cursor over the red-dot, and a box appeared displaying the name Professor Sir Simon Bartlett.

"This is Bartlett. And this is you," said Asif, moving the cursor over an orange-dot, which caused Reece's name to appear in a box adjacent to it. Reece's orange-dot was following a white-dot which obviously represented DD. The red-dot of Professor Bartlett was at the head of a wavy line, while Reece's orange-dot was in the middle of another snake-like line on the opposite side of the table.

"Slow it down to real time," said Heather.

Asif responded, and the digital clock now advanced second-by-second in real time, as the red-dot and the orange-dot slowly approached each other on opposite sides of the table. At the instant they were directly opposite each other, the line that contained Reece's orange-dot suddenly moved to form an almost-perfect semicircle opposite the red dot.

"It just happened then," said Asif, pausing the playback.

The time showed 13:06:47, the moment that Professor Bartlett's reputation had erupted all over the buffet table. To the right-side of the two stationary lines of dots was a solitary white-dot, backed-up against the wall of the room. Asif rolled the mouse-cursor over the dot — and the name Anthony Thorpe appeared in a box next to it.

"Anthony Thorpe. That name isn't on our watch-list," said Heather. "He's standing in line with the end of the serving tables, roughly in the middle. Let's assume he's not facing the wall but facing into the room. He should have the Professor on the right-hand side with the food table dead-centre as he looks at it. Asif, run that YouTube video again."

Asif clicked the replay button on the still-open YouTube page. He fast-forwarded past the Professor sneezing, until it showed the buffet table view. The positioning of the Professor in the video matched the viewpoint from where Anthony Thorpe had stood.

"So Anthony Thorpe took this video," said Heather aloud. "Continue playing the video Asif."

They all watched the remainder of the video again.

"Remarkably steady camera work considering what occurred," said Heather. "Almost as though he was expecting it to happen. Where was Thorpe sitting for this morning's sneezing episode?"

"Let's see," said Asif, rewinding the timeline on the screen marked MAIN AUDITORIUM to show 08:55. White dots moved furiously around the auditorium before settling into seats.

"This is easier as there's relatively little movement happening," said Asif. The red-dot was stationary in the centre of the stage, and was clearly the Professor speaking. Asif clicked on a toolbar at the top of the screen entitled ATTENDEES, and a dropdown-list appeared. He scrolled down the list and clicked on Anthony Thorpe's name causing a grid to appear which contained twelve different colours. As Asif clicked on the purple-box, the list and box disappeared, and one white-dot on the screen changed to purple.

"He's next to the aisle on the left-side. Seat G10." stated Asif.

"Does it line up with the SPECCAB'S detection?" asked Heather.

"What's a SPECCAB?" enquired Reece.

"Sorry, you might be cleared for YouTube, but you aren't cleared for that." replied Heather.

Asif picked up the diagram he'd made at Robyn's debriefing session this morning. It showed the seats and sightline that Robyn had given them.

"G10 is directly on their sightline. The viewpoint of the YouTube video also corresponds too," said Asif.

"Then let's get some background on Anthony Thorpe before we speak to him," instructed Heather.

"I'm on it," said Asif.

Heather guided Reece away from Asif's work area. She didn't want Reece seeing anything he wasn't supposed to see. The hotel phone on Heather's desk rang again. She picked it up, listened briefly, and then slammed the receiver down hard.

"That's my damn comment," she said irritably towards the phone. "I seem to be exceptionally popular this evening".

Bah-whump!

Reece felt the peculiar pulse of a single, massive heart-beat inside his skull, as his mind switched from a passive observational-mode into hunting-mode. This happened whenever his mind received a significant stimulus of some kind. He'd obviously just received one *subconsciously* and his mind wanted to connect to it.

It must have been something Heather had just said, and he re-wound her voice in his head to recall the words she'd used.

That's my damn comment.

He paused for a moment. No, there wasn't anything there that attracted an idea.

I seem to be exceptionally popular this evening, was her other remark.

Exceptionally popular. Exceptionally popular. Exceptionally popular.

The stimulus that started his mind hunting was *exceptionally popular.* His mind repeated her words to itself.

Exceptionally popular this evening. Exceptionally popular this evening.

That's what Heather had said.

But that's not quite right.

What needs to be changed?

No. Not 'this evening'. It was 'this morning'.

Exceptionally popular this morning.

Yes, that was it.

The connection was forming.

"You alright?" asked Heather with a slightly-concerned look on her face. "You've gone…"

"Ssshhhh!" Reece cut her off, holding the palm of his hand towards her face.

The Council were back to assist him.

Exceptionally popular this morning. Exceptionally popular this morning.

That phrase is meaningful.

We've heard it recently somewhere.

Definitely.

A female voice said it.

Yes!

Where?

In a public place.

In this hotel?

No. Before then.

In a shop?

Yes!

A book shop?

Yes.

WH Smith.

Yes! The cashier.

We used her name when we bought the book.

What was it?

Isobel.

She used that phrase.

Yes!

"I've just remembered something," said Reece. "Yesterday morning at Paddington station, I bought my second-copy of the Professor's book with the Post-it note inside. I took the last copy off the shelf. When I paid for it, the cashier said the book seemed to be *exceptionally popular this morning*. Her name was Isobel, and I thought it seemed an unusual comment to make at the time, because she said she hadn't read the book herself."

"Which shop was it?" asked Heather.

"The WH Smith at the end of the platforms."

"That could be interesting to follow-up. I'll ask Asif to get onto it after he's uncovered what our Anthony Thorpe is up to."

Heather looked at the watch on her wrist. "Thanks for the help," she said. "Is there anything you need from me right now?"

If there was a tone of voice that indicated *leave now,* then that was it.

"I think I need a drink," said Reece.

"Sorry, none here," replied Heather.

Chapter 34 Monday 21h05

Reece made his way to the hotel bar, ordered a glass of the house red-wine, and waited while the barman poured it.

There had been a continuous assault on his mind since breakfast this morning. It started with the text message predicting a call; then he was drafted back into the secret service; then there was the sneezing event, which escalated into the lunchtime vomiting display. That bit of drama he would rather not have seen.

At the intellectual level, there was also the content of the presentations he'd heard today. They'd taken the world that he thought he knew, sliced it, diced it, and thrown it back in his face with a smug *so what do you think now, smart-arse?*

He just needed a little quiet-time to consolidate it all in his head.

"Another Beck's and a glass of dry-white over here barman," said a strong South African accent. "And I'll get that too," added DD, pointing to Reece's newly-arrived drink.

Obviously, this new world order didn't intend to let him consolidate things right now, thought Reece.

"It's your company that's getting this, isn't it?" queried Reece.

"And a damn fine company they are too," said DD, clinking Reece's glass with his bottle.

"I gather you've been in the bar for a while then?"

"It's a fine bar — one of the best in the hotel. And when I can legitimately put a bar-bill on my expenses, then I'm like a lion tearing apart a baby octopus."

"That's an unusual metaphor."

"It's a five-beer metaphor. Anyway, come over here and join us, we're having a great discussion."

"On what?"

"On everything we've heard today, man. What else is there to talk about?"

DD led him over to a small group which included Jean Rose. DD handed her the glass of wine.

"You remember Reece from the break time?" DD said this more as a command to her rather than a question. "Reece was queuing," he added. DD also made this sound like it was Reece's full-time occupation.

"What else do you do besides queuing, Reece?" asked Jean.

"I help companies to think differently about important issues," Reece answered.

“And how are you thinking differently after today’s presentations?”

Reece paused for a moment as the image of a 1950s science-fiction hover-car flashed across his mind.

Over time, Reece had noticed that when he was asked a question, an often-unrelated image would pop into his mind. He never knew how or why that specific image would suddenly appear, but he’d learned to use it — for it usually helped in getting his point across.

“Imagine that a hover-car mysteriously appeared, floating effortlessly at waist height. No-one has ever seen one before. It’s got the ignition keys in, an energy gauge that shows maximum capacity — so it’s ready-to-go. But instead of strapping ourselves in and having the ride of our lives, we start to take it apart. We become focused on trying to understand what each component is supposed to do. And when we’ve taken it apart, we re-assemble it, and analyse how the various parts interact with each other. Then we become curious about what each component is made of.” Reece flicked his glass with his fingernail so it made a loud *ting* sound.

“Then we’d be studying the wrong things, and missing the obvious fact that we could use the vehicle to go somewhere — or do something we’ve never done before. It seems to me that we’re analysing our existence too much, rather than moving on and achieving remarkable things with the minds and abilities we have.”

“Sum that up in one short-sentence,” said DD provocatively.

Reece hesitated, took in a deep-breath, and decided to let his mind enunciate the first-thought that came into his head.

“Are we missing the whole point of life?” were the words that came out of his mouth.

“I think we are,” said Jean emphatically. “That’s precisely what’s happening in research in many ways. We have a herd-mentality as to what constitutes valid research, and what doesn’t. There are too many really-interesting areas of research being labelled as risky or inappropriate.”

“Have you heard the white-washed baboon story?” asked DD.

Nobody had.

“In Africa, a troop of baboons can do a lot of damage to a farm’s crops and property. One day, a farmer decided to do something different to get them off his property. He caught one of the baboons, painted it head-to-foot with white-wash, and then let it go.”

DD took his customary long-pause while taking a drink from his bottle.

“Because the baboon was distressed by this ordeal, it rushed to re-join its troop where it knew it would be safe. However, the troop sees this highly-agitated white thing running towards them — which scares them — so they run away. The faster the troop runs away, the more the white-baboon tries to catch up with them, which in turn causes the troop to run faster. Eventually all the baboons are a long way from the farm — which is precisely what the farmer wanted.”

“And in our case Professor Bartlett is the white baboon. He’s chasing others away from interesting areas of research,” said Jean Rose, with an inebriated-giggle.

“It’s an appropriate description of him,” said the man standing next to Reece. “But does what we’ve heard today fit in with some of society’s biggest beliefs?” he asked.

“You mean like religion?” provoked DD. “Where does God fit in to all this stuff?”

Reece was beginning to understand the subtleties of conversation didn’t always sit-well with DD. But then again, maybe that was a good thing, as he got straight to the meaty-bits of the conversation. Reece thought this was something he should try for himself. *These people have a few drinks inside them already — and I don’t — so maybe now’s a good time to give the blunt question approach a go.*

“I’m an agnostic,” said Reece. “I believe that some kind of supreme power or force is behind everything — but not necessarily a religious deity. A lot of what we heard today fits well with my way of thinking, but isn’t this a difficult conundrum for a devout believer in God?”

“Not at all,” replied the man again. “One view of the things we’ve heard today is that they are the fingerprints of God. He left them around for us to see. Perhaps rather than casting doubt on God, it’s confirmed my belief in Him,” said the clearly-religious man.

“An insightful answer,” acknowledged Reece, raising his glass to the man.

“Or another way to view it,” said DD, “is that God cocked it up by leaving his fingerprints everywhere.”

“Only you could use a term like *God cocked it up* in a religious conversation,” admonished Reece.

“Sayeth unto me the truth. And the truth shall be sayeth as it is,” quoted DD authoritatively. “Corinthians seventeen, verses five and six,” he added.

“A man who knows his bible! That’s impressive DD,” said Jean, putting her hand on his arm.

“That sounds remarkably like a reading from the book of bullshit rather than the Bible, if you ask me,” warned Reece, with a wink to Jean.

"Man, she believed it. It's not often my bible-quotes hit home like that," protested DD.

"So, DD, tell us your view on the true nature of the universe," teased Jean.

"There's a women's joke, that men are just a life-support mechanism for a penis. But what if the universe is just a life-support mechanism for intelligence?"

"Continue," prompted Jean.

"Perhaps we are supposed to be looking forwards-and-inwards at ourselves as a species. Using our minds to develop the intelligence of the future. Instead we seem focussed on looking backwards-and-outwards, expending our precious resources exploring the cosmic and microscopic limits of our universe. Maybe the limits will always be tantalisingly just-beyond the extent of our scientific ability to perceive them."

"We sometimes say that we aren't seeing the big picture," said Jean, "and based on what we've heard today, I wonder whether we're all missing the biggest-picture in the history of the universe."

"Man, that is such a powerful statement," said DD. "Reece, doesn't hearing a perspective like that, give you a pineapple-feeling in your arsehole?"

Jean's comment certainly had given Reece a peculiar feeling. He doubted that it was in anyway aligned to DD's anal-pineapple sensation.

Chapter 35 Monday 21h30

Asif had just debriefed Heather on what he'd found out about Anthony Thorpe. It hadn't taken long.

"So there's nothing at all suspect about him?" asked Heather.

"Not even a speeding fine. He's been a maths teacher for the last twenty-eight years. He moved around a few schools to get to where he is now, as head of maths at a private school in Birmingham. The only link with Professor Bartlett was when Thorpe and his wife were in the newspapers regarding some research he was doing with them. That was twenty-two years ago — but it's all I can find."

"Show me the articles."

A few mouse-clicks later and Asif had brought them up, one on each screen. The first was from one of the daily red-top newspapers, and the second from the News of the World, five-weeks later.

Heather speed-read both articles in a matter of seconds. "Anything else?"

Asif knew he had to be sharp and responsive around Heather, as she had a reputation among the MoD techies of being direct and demanding. *And impressive too* thought Asif, considering how quickly she'd read the two articles.

"Apparently his wife died not long after the second article was published."

"How long after?"

"Nine-days. There was an obituary in a local newspaper."

"Cause of death?"

"Didn't say. But it did use the word *unexpected.*"

"This seems too coincidental. The second article was really-harsh on them — and attributed to Bartlett too." Heather folded her arms and stood beside Asif slowly-rocking her hips from side-to-side as if in a gentle-stretching routine. Asif knew to keep quiet — he'd learned she was thinking when she did this.

"Where's Thorpe now?" she asked, breaking the silence.

"He's in his room, and has been since lunchtime. The hotel says he ordered from the room-service menu at lunch and again this evening for dinner."

"Leave him for now, but keep an eye on him."

Heather's rocking of her hips continued. She didn't know why, or how, but it helped her concentrate when she was thinking — and she was thinking about the two newspaper articles now. Doctor Bartlett — as he was then — had significantly changed his view on

Anthony Thorpe and his wife as research participants, from the first to the second article. It was also bad-practice to disclose the identities of individuals involved in research projects too. *So how had the press got hold of their names?* Something was nagging at Heather's mind and she couldn't identify what it was.

"Why did Bartlett suddenly change his view in the press of what Thorpe and his wife were doing?" she asked aloud.

"Don't know," replied Asif.

"What was the date of the News of the World article?"

"Eighth of March."

"Pull Bartlett's biography up on the system. Let's see what was happening around that time."

Asif tapped on his keyboard and the biography appeared on a monitor. He scrolled through the list of activities until he found the relevant month.

"Look here," he said, using the cursor to highlight some text. "On the eleventh of March, Bartlett was appointed an associate professor, and received funding to develop a centre for extreme motivation."

"That's three-days later. There's another coincidence I don't like. What if he needed to discredit them to be sure his promotion and funding went through?"

"You think that Bartlett deliberately set up Thorpe and his wife to be fall-guys?" said Asif.

"Could be. And Thorpe has come back to get his revenge on Bartlett."

"But why wait twenty-two years to do it?" Asif asked.

"I don't know. But it was a pretty convincing revenge."

"Ironic that he did it at our conference isn't it?"

"It is," replied Heather. "But what if he's not finished yet?"

"What do you mean?"

"He didn't know that he was going to be detected by a SPECCAB in the auditorium. And neither would he know he was being tracked by the Contactor system."

"So he thinks he's got away with it un-noticed, doesn't he?" concluded Asif.

"He does."

"Then why not go home if he's done what he came to do?"

"That's what concerns me. What else is he capable of doing — and maybe planning to do?" said Heather. "Which organisation is paying his fees for the conference?" she added as an afterthought.

Asif tapped the keyboard. “Looks like he paid for it himself.”

“How is a school teacher able to pay for this conference, especially at the rates we’re charging?” asked Heather of no-one in particular. “And what’s he doing taking four-days off work during school term-time?”

Heather had stopped swaying her hips and had now started pacing up-and-down as she thought around these issues.

“Asif, who provided the funding for Bartlett to set up that motivation centre?

More keyboard tapping from Asif. “It was an organisation called the Scientific Research Development Board.”

“Run a cross-check on who was funding that organisation at that time.”

More tapping and a set of financial returns appeared on a monitor.

“Looks like they were a charitable operation, so they had to disclose the source of their own revenues. There’s several small commitments by private individuals and companies, but the largest-by-far was a Government grant under a scheme from the Department of Science and Education — as it was at the time. The scheme apparently stopped shortly afterwards.”

“A Government grant you say? Chase the budget-source of that grant on our system,” instructed Heather.

There was a short pause, then Asif responded, “it came from a budget with the code 6604-007184.”

Heather’s pacing immediately stopped.

“That could be a problem for us,” she said, warily.

“Why” asked Asif.

“6604 codes relate to a CTS&TC discretionary budget. Looks like we were the ones who funded Bartlett’s motivation research centre.”

Chapter 36 Monday 22h05

When Reece realised the discussion in the bar was going to continue well into the evening, he'd excused himself and returned to his room. He realised there were too many things that he'd heard today jockeying for prime-position in his mind.

Lying in bed he attempted to clarify some of them to himself. The anomalies and discontinuities that science couldn't explain were phenomenal in size and nature. Jean Rose was right in saying that more investigation of them needed to be done. But she'd made a good point that someone could spend a lifetime researching just one of the anomalies, and still have no idea what caused it in the end. Some of them, like the start of life and intelligence, seemed to be questions where the only conceivable answer involved some kind of external-contribution.

The anomalies and discontinuities were step-changes.

The Council were back. Reece let them run with the issue.

Would a god cause these step-changes to happen?

No

Why not?

A god wouldn't need to make step-changes.

Why not?

Because a god would have made sure that the normal flow of things didn't require any step-change corrections.

So 'normality' would, by default, be perfect?

A god could do that.

True.

Did evolution cause the step-changes?

But isn't the whole premise of evolution focussed around steady change?

True again.

So where did the external-contribution come in?

Through the red door.

What red door?

The red door we thought about earlier today, sliding along the continuum.

That's right.

It found a new place to stop.

Somewhere off the continuum.

The place where it stopped represents this external-contribution then?

It must do.

So how do we describe this external-contribution?

It must be some kind of driving force that influences things.

What do you mean by 'influences'?

Being helpful to us in different ways.

Perhaps in many ways.

Yes.

The second presenter spoke about the freakiest streak-of-luck in the universe.

He did.

Is this force random in the way it influences us, sometimes helping us, and at other times hindering us?

No — it's always supportive.

Consistently beneficial.

Some of the things this force influenced were monumental in potential and impact.

But done in an ever-so-subtle and delicate way.

The force caused life to form on Earth.

Did it cause it — or help it — to form?

Does it matter?

No, not really.

An all-powerful force — like a god — would have simply created a male and a female of the species.

And given them names like Adam and Eve.

But this force isn't all-powerful.

It's more restrained.

It helped life to start, but not in a complex way.

No, it was in a discreet and simple form.

Something really primitive — like pond scum.

Even before that. The life-form would take tens of millions of years to evolve even to become pond scum.

Did this force only form life?

No. This force has influenced the very nature of the universe.

Surely not?

How could it influence things on such a vast scale?

Over a universe billions of light-years in size?

And over billions of years in duration?

That would need to be a monstrous-force of colossal power.

Not necessarily.

What do you mean?

What if this force was everywhere — and had been there forever?

You're saying it's been constantly exerting its influence?

Yes.

Guiding and shaping us?

Yes.

And everything else in the universe?

Yes. This force was so pervasive in form that it didn't need to be colossal in power.

It was simple and delicate in nature.

A Delicate Force.

A Delicate Force that was all around us.

Correction — is all around us.

And in us.

A part of us.

Washing silently over and around us, like a wave.

Something we are unaware of.

But exactly what is this force?

Don't know.

Does it matter that we can't define it?

No.

It's like the hover-car we spoke of in the bar.

Don't worry about the model, colour and year.

Just get in and drive-the-hell out of it.

Don't try and examine and investigate it.

Just accept it.

And use it.

Use it?

It must still be around.

So maybe we can use it for ourselves.

Use the Delicate Force?

That's an interesting thought.

Reece felt himself falling asleep. He had a new understanding of a delicate force all around him. It was quite likely washing over him in waves right now. Waves moving forward over him, and then back. Forward and back. Like the waves on a beach. Forward and back. Forward and…

Chapter 37 Tuesday 01h55

Reece stands on a beach, staring over the ocean, watching the waves roll in. Initially, they seem to be exactly the same, but as he watches, he sees patterns in the waves. Some come in sets-of-three, closer together, with a pause before the next set-of-three arrive. Bigger waves arbitrarily spoil this pattern, barging their way in, and announcing themselves with a louder-roar than the others.

As each wave approaches, it curls-up on itself to gain height, as if to appear menacing and threatening to the beach. It silently builds, then launches its assault to crash down with a fearsome WHUMP! The wave shattering into a milky-foam that scampers up the beach. It travels as far as it can, getting thinner and thinner, before it says to itself 'enough, enough, get back, get back'. And in unison, all the water-molecules that made-up that wave, scurry back to the safety of the ocean as fast as they can.

Each wave makes its own advance-and-retreat on the beach, unaware it is part of a bigger tidal movement. The waves perform in the same manner, regardless of whether the tide is coming-in or going-out. The waves don't know this, but it's the gravity of the moon that causes the tides to ebb and flow several times a day. And it's the gravity of the Earth that makes the water molecules seem so desperate to get back to join the rest of the ocean.

Every time a wave recedes, it reveals a fresh arrangement of shiny, wet pebbles that all seem to be moving, as if alive. Some of them appear to be chasing the water away, telling it to go back into the sea. Others behave as if they are desperate to follow the water, wanting to see where it goes to.

Pebbles can't move of their own accord. They lie there immobile, as if in death. But when a wave engulfs them, they come to life for a few brief seconds. They are re-born. Able to move forward and backwards. To tumble over themselves. To lie on their backs to gain a different perspective of their ocean-world. To socialise, and to bump into other pebbles that they wouldn't normally ever know existed. If the pebbles were capable of religious belief, they would surely worship the mighty power of the ocean, that sends forth these waves of energy. The waves that re-birth the pebbles every few seconds.

Reece looks down at the pebbles all glistening and smooth. From jet-blacks to pure-whites, with a thousand shades of grey in-between. Then Reece notices a pebble of a different colour. A muted-orange pebble which seems unusually vivid, lying among its monochromatic neighbours. How does an orange pebble end up strangely out-of-place in a land of grey, black and white ones? As though it wants to stand out. To be subtly noticed. When he looks carefully, Reece sees there are other muted-orange pebbles too, scattered infrequently around.

The tide has advanced such that the incoming waves now cover his bare feet. For the brief time it takes each wave to rush back to its family, he can feel the pebbles all moving under his feet. His toes, soles and heels all feel the frenzied activity happening beneath him, with each wave that rolls-in and scurries-back.

Reece lifts his gaze to look far-out over the ocean. The big picture. Looking into the distance he can barely see any movement on the water at all. It looks so still. The pebbles on the ocean floor out there don't get brought to life by the waves. In the deeper ocean, every pebble acts as a gravestone for its own death. He looks down at his feet again to observe the busy world of the beach-pebbles. Being brought to life and moved back-and-forth by their deity, the sea.

The waves on the ocean. The pebbles on the beach. All living out their lives in complete ignorance of the force of gravity that makes all this happen for them.

But they didn't need to know about gravity.

How would knowing about it make the slightest change to their existence?

If he were a pebble, would it change his existence if he knew about it?

He wondered if the pebbles were happy.

He hoped so.

Chapter 38 Tuesday 05h00

The telephone rang three times before Reece picked up the receiver. He put it down immediately. He didn't want to hear the cheery, digitised voice wishing him an insincere good-morning.

Reece liked to get up quickly, but he did allow himself a morning-stretch in bed. He made tight balls with his fists, and pushed them as far up the bed as he could, while pushing his toes as far down the bed as possible. He held the stretch — and then relaxed. He wondered what made his body enjoy the sensation of a good-stretch in the morning. It was strange that the enjoyment was felt in the mind and yet it was the muscles experiencing the stretching-pleasure.

Once the stretch was over, Reece rolled out of bed, opened the curtains with a flourish, and looked out of the window. He noticed the curtains swayed back and forth like waves.

Waves?

Reece stood still. A connection was forming in his mind.

Waves on the beach.

The Council were back.

A dream.

We had a dream about waves and pebbles.

Why?

We fell asleep thinking about the Delicate Force which is guiding everything.

This must relate to the Delicate Force.

Did those pebbles know about the force of gravity that created the waves — which in turn caused them to move around?

Probably not.

The orange pebble stood out from all the other pebbles.

Did it know of the force that was driving its world?

Was the orange pebble supposed to represent us?

Mankind?

No! Us — Reece Tassicker.

If it was, would we know of the force that was influencing every aspect of our life since time began?

Probably not.

We'd likely be ignorant — like the pebbles.

But we do know of the force now.

So can we use it in some way?

Can we direct it?

Possibly!

That's worth investigating.

How can we use something we don't understand?

No. Stop right there. That's the old-fashioned hover-car way of thinking.

We don't have to understand something to use it.

If the orange pebble represents us, me, Reece Tassicker, then I'm being influenced by the Delicate Force directly.

How do you know that?

Because all the weird things that we've heard in the presentations have happened to our ancestors in the past.

How can we be sure?

Because if we trace our bloodline back, we must ultimately have ancestors who were pond-scum.

True.

And before that one of our single-celled ancestors must have been one of the first to be given life.

If not the very first one.

All this is in our historic bloodline.

We, Reece Tassicker, and the rest of humanity, are the living-proof — the outcome — of the Delicate Force's influence.

Has it stopped influencing us?

Why should it stop?

So, if the force is still influencing us now, where is it taking us?

Like it has always done in the past — beneficially forwards.

Beneficially forwards — what does that mean?

Moving us on to a better place.

And are there any ways in which we can actually use the force?

To do what?

To make the forwards-movement to a better place happen quicker.

Now that was a very interesting train of thought to follow. Reece was on autopilot as he got dressed into his running kit, for the Council were still busy in his mind.

How can we use something that we know nothing about?

Don't know...

Not sure...

We need to think harder.

Faster! Higher! Stronger!

Where did that come from?

That's the motto of the Olympic Games — from the presentation on evolution.

The speaker said our physical abilities may be peaking.

Yet our minds seem to be capable of ever more amazing feats.

How practical is memorizing the first 100,000 digits of pi?

Not very.

But it shows us what the mind is capable of.

The Buddhist monks raising their body-temperature.

The savant skills.

Child prodigies.

Memory and mental calculation champions.

They all seem unnatural — but in a positive way.

Science doesn't understand how these individuals do these things.

But that's not important at this stage.

Isn't it?

No. What's important is that there is absolutely no-doubt-whatsoever that these things can be done.

They seem beyond belief

Maybe that's their purpose.

What do you mean?

It's absolute, factual evidence — which seems peculiarly un-natural and unreal.

Is that where this Delicate Force is guiding us next?

Don't know.

Maybe it's just showing us that it exists.

By producing strange occurrences like these?

How else can it demonstrate its existence without doing some frighteningly-huge reveal?

Good point.

Reece closed his room door and headed towards the elevator.

Chapter 39 Tuesday 05h10

As Reece left the hotel's main entrance, he recognised a woman from the conference who was also dressed for exercise. She was stretching against one of the oversize flower-boxes that lined the hotel's short driveway.

"Going out or just back?" asked Reece.

"Going out. Want to join me?"

"Depends how-far and how-fast".

"About five-miles, easy pace?"

"Let's do it," said Reece.

"I'm Sarah. Want to run the park or some streets?"

"Reece. I did the park yesterday, so streets would make a change."

As they ran, they spoke about the insights they'd gained from the conference.

"Have you seen the film *The Man With Two Brains*?" asked Sarah.

"No, why?"

"It's a comedy with Steve Martin and Kathleen Turner from the early-eighties. There's one-part that's particularly relevant to what we heard yesterday. In the film, Steve Martin's wife had recently died, and he meets Kathleen Turner's character — who's a devious, scheming woman looking to find rich-men for their money. Steve Martin is besotted with her. He goes home, looks at a portrait of his dead wife, and asks it whether he'd be doing the right thing if he were to marry this woman. Everything in the room starts shaking, the lights flash, the curtains billow and the wife's portrait spins on the wall, while a loud *Noooooooo* fills the room. Eventually, everything stops moving and Steve Martin says *I'll keep watching for a sign from you.* He turns his wife's portrait around to face the wall — and walks out to marry Kathleen Turner."

"Sounds funny."

"It is. But the point is *are we behaving just like Steve Martin in the movie*? Are we ignoring these signs — all these signals — that there's something out of place in our universe?"

"I think we are. But why did you use the term *signals* just then?" asked Reece.

"Maybe these things are there deliberately — to get our attention."

"That first speaker pointed out that we tend to focus on the predictable patterns of continuity — and discount the anomalies. I think she's got an interesting point as those anomalies are so significant."

"When you consider the amazing good-fortune we've had in evolving to where we are today, it seems odd that these things stick-out like a thousand sore-thumbs," said Sarah.

They turned a corner. The early-morning sun was directly behind them, projecting their elongated-shadows on the pavement ahead.

"And at different levels too," she added.

"What do you mean by *different levels*?"

"There are the big things that have been around forever. The speaker had examples at the cosmic and atomic levels of the changing constants and that amazing stuff about entangled-photons communicating at ten-thousand times the speed of light."

"Yeah," agreed Reece.

"Then there's the stuff at the human level that individuals are capable of. Where our memories are stored, and the fact our brains need only a tiny amount of power to operate, and the skills autistic people have."

"Okay," agreed Reece, again.

Sarah went silent.

"Are there any other levels?" prompted Reece.

"I believe there's another one — but you may think it a bit odd."

"Try me," said Reece, thinking it couldn't be any odder than finding Post-it notes with your name on in books you bought.

"Well, there are some things which seem to happen at the personal level which seem peculiar, or out of place," she said, hesitantly.

"I completely agree with you there," said Reece, supportively.

"Let's turn right, down there," said Sarah, as they came to a road junction. They were about to run across the road when Reece grabbed her arm.

"Watch out! Orange traffic light." he said.

The traffic lights they were facing had just turned from red to orange. A late-running EasyBus coach with a destination-board indicating Stansted Airport, was already setting off across the junction. With a whoosh from its air brakes and a squeal of tyres, the bright-orange coach abruptly stopped, as a small delivery-truck crossed in front of it, clearly having driven through a red-light. It shot across the junction, swerving to barely miss the front of the EasyBus.

"Close!" said Reece, as the EasyBus set off again on its journey.

"But interesting," said Sarah. "Both drivers reacted wrongly to their orange traffic-light. The coach was in the bright-orange EasyBus brand colours. And did you notice the delivery-truck had a big advert on the side for Fanta orange. An interesting *orange* coincidence."

"Synchronicity at work," said Reece.

"Now that's creepily-weird," Sarah said conspiratorially. "Synchronicity — which we were just talking about is one of the signals that happen at the personal level."

"We were talking about synchronicity and an example happens at that precise moment," laughed Reece.

"But the more you are open-and-aware to these signals, the more frequently they seem to happen."

"And potentially, they're happening with the same frequency to everyone. It's that some people don't want to see them," said Reece.

"True. Have you noticed how synchronicity tends *not* to happen directly, or actively, between two-people? It happens with your surrounding-environment or in a passive-interaction between people."

"What do you mean?" asked Reece.

"That little orange-event could have happened to *just one of us,* if we'd been running alone. Or, on the other hand, if I hadn't pointed it out, would you have noticed it?" she asked.

"Possibly not," he replied.

"It happened to us together, but passively. We may both have had a different-interpretation of the same event — or one of us may not have noticed it at all. Synchronicity is a highly personal occurrence, and perhaps there are highly-personal signals that happen at this level."

"So we all have these signals, but individually?" suggested Reece.

"Everyone on Earth is connected to everyone else. Like pebbles on a beach. Every pebble is separate from every other pebble, as that's part of the definition of what a pebble is. But simultaneously, every pebble on a beach is connected to every other one, by nature of contact. Not directly — but by physical-contact through a chain of pebbles. Now pebbles can't move of course, but humans can. And this gives us a greater potential for creating and observing these synchronous signals," said Sarah.

Reece was distracted as the thought of the solitary orange pebble from his dream came flashing back to him. A reminder that synchronicity did *indeed* work on many different-levels. *Was his dream of an orange pebble a signal to him now?*

"There are many other types of personal signals too," Sarah continued. "Some people experience deja-vu or premonitions for example. Things that are meaningful specifically, and solely, to an individual. Perhaps even intuition is a signal too?"

"You know what stands out about what you're saying here? All the signals you mention are fuzzy, or vague, in some way."

"I don't follow."

"Whether it's that double-slit experiment where things change from a wave to a particle, just because you observe them, to the changing cosmic-constants, to the unfathomable-questions about our existence — and to the things you mentioned now at the personal level. None of it can be shown to the man-in-the-street as hard-and-clear proof of anything."

"Perhaps that's the way things are meant to be. Imagine what would happen if it *was* possible to prove something really weird." Sarah paused while she thought of an example.

"What if someone had the ability to think of something — and it materialised *right in front of you.* Like a white rabbit. Whenever someone requested it, this person could make a white rabbit appear in their arms. Now that would be scary. What else could that person make appear? A plague that would wipe out the world? Huge wads of banknotes? How about a continuous supply of food to feed the hungry?"

"Go on," encouraged Reece.

"Whatever it was that this person could do, businesses, governments, churches, criminals, and a host of other organisations, would all try to coerce the person to be on *their side.* To help them develop whatever things best-suited their ulterior motives."

"I can see that," said Reece.

"If only one person could do this, what sort of public uproar would be created around this person, who was capable of producing one specific miracle on an as-required basis? Or, what if other people saw this on television and tried it for themselves — and were successful? Suddenly we find there are dozens, or even hundreds, of people that can perform this feat. What would happen then?" said Sarah.

"That's a good point. Do you think these signals are *intentionally* hard to prove?" asked Reece.

"Maybe the different kinds of signals you pick up, whether they happen to you directly or because you learn about them, are meant to create a personal-perspective in your mind. This perspective will always be different to anybody else's, because others can never experience the same personal signals that you have. This ensures you create your own personal belief on the signals, which will be different to everybody else's. Does that sound a bit weird?" she added guiltily.

"No, not at all," said Reece. "If all these anomalies we've heard about *are* signals, and *were* proven to be an inherent-part of our evolution, then we could all sit-back and do nothing. Just wait for whatever our next-stage of evolution was. However, if we needed to *believe* in some way to achieve this next evolutionary stage, then we've made a change to ourselves — and perhaps that's how we'd be different to the people who *don't believe*. The ones who do believe in the signals, then start to see things differently to those who don't. They begin to understand more, develop more, create more, and ultimately evolve their mind more. Maybe that's the selection-process that evolution puts species through, and that's how we have the survival of the fittest concept."

"You are aware that Darwin's theory around survival of the fittest was actually the survival of those most able to adapt," said Sarah. "Perhaps the ability to change your mind and believe in something new, demonstrates your ability to adapt."

"The first presenter spoke about nothing being fixed until you observe it. It's as though the hard-facts of reality break-down a little, and become fuzzy at the edges. And this is where these signals lie — at the fuzzy-edges of reality. The purpose of the signals is to stretch the capacity of your reality to contain them. And once you accept that your reality has fuzzy-edges, you start to see the signals more readily," said Reece.

"Belief in the signals might be the evolutionary-hurdle that individuals need to clear, to open their minds for the future," suggested Sarah.

As they turned the corner onto Wigmore Street, they saw the hotel straight-ahead of them, acting as their five-star finishing line.

Chapter 40 Tuesday 06h10

Back at the hotel, Reece had taken another of his life indulgences, which was an overly-long, tinglingly-hot shower. This made his morning shave difficult — for the mirror was steamed-up. His mind was occupied, curating all the thoughts from his run with Sarah, when he absent-mindedly reached out to wipe the mirror with his finger. It created the shape of a snake on the steamed-up surface. He drew another snake-shape. And then he added a circle around them. He imagined a child drawing a similar picture with a crayon, on a piece of paper. When the child finished the picture, the crayon was a little-bit shorter, a sheet of paper had been used up, but a new piece of artwork had been created in the universe. And for the rest of eternity, that small-advancement in the form of a child's crayon drawing could never be taken away.

In the ultimate journal of the universe, this picture-event of that day would exist until the end of the universe itself. He imagined the universe writing its diary, noting down all the interesting things that were going on. Even here on Earth, there would be some unbelievable happenings, never mind what was occurring in strange-galaxies far away. In his mind, the diary evolved into a timeline — with everything marked on it for the duration of which it lasted.

Some things would stretch for the full duration of the universe, from the very-first day to the very-last day. Things like gravity, time, the value of pi, and a trillion other things. Then there were the things that lasted for just a brief-moment — like the orange truck almost crashing into the orange bus earlier. The universe would smile as it wrote that little entry into its diary.

There were now two timeframes for the diary. Events that lasted for an eternity, and events that lasted for a moment. Reece thought there should be a time-frame somewhere between these two. *But what?* He watched his reflection in the mirror carefully as he shaved.

He looked at his eyes.

The eyes in the mirror looked back at him.

He imagined himself as the observer of his wave-front — as the first presenter had discussed. *Our world only exists because some outside body is observing us.* If they stop observing us, then potentially, our whole universe collapses back on itself — until someone else starts watching. Imagine if you stopped reflecting in a mirror, and this was the signal that you would die shortly-afterwards.

How and why his mind came up with these strange thoughts Reece didn't know.

He smiled to himself in the mirror, in acknowledgement of an insight he'd just had. In the timeline of the universe, he was the third timeframe.

The lifespan of a human.

In some ways it was the ultimate measure of time. The three-score-years-and-ten that we were supposed to have on this planet. Now there were three relevant timescales in the diary of the universe. Eternity, momentary, and sitting between the two, a lifetime.

As Reece imagined these three durations on a timeline of the universe, an overlay started to appear. An overlay of signals. Some of the signals endured forever, while some lasted for just an instance, like the synchronicity that had occurred during this morning's run. And in between, were the signals that were the almost-unnatural capabilities that some humans were capable of.

Three words came to mind for Reece. *Enduring, Capability*, and *Instance*. The signals that Sarah had spoken of on their run, seemed to fit neatly into these three categories. Enduring signals were those things that lasted for a very long time. Capability signals were those peculiar capabilities that humans possess during their lives, and the Instance signals were those which occur in a moment and then pass. This seemed to be a framework that succinctly captured the signal types that Sarah had talked about.

Good thinking! Now it was time for breakfast.

Chapter 41 Tuesday 08h30

Gareth Jones was in his room, deciphering the morning's feedback from the dreamers. All the dreams had included shops, and people shopping in different ways. Patrick had dreamt of a line of shops on a road. Big shops, and lots of them. Lisa had dreamt that one of them was numbered 1507. He assumed the number was actually the time of interaction, 15h07, which was how she'd given them a time previously. At the end of the road with all the shops on, was a structure that — from the dreamers' descriptions — seemed very much like the Arc de Triomphe. This confused Gareth for quite some time, as he wondered what reason Reece had for going to Paris today. It took him a while to realise that Lisa's description wasn't of the Arc de Triomphe at all. It was of its smaller, and much less impressive cousin — the Marble Arch.

Once Gareth had Marble Arch identified, he checked a street map of London to see that the road with the big shops on was clearly Oxford Street. Probably one of London's most well-known streets, and famous for having most of the major department stores located on it, and at the western end, where it met Park Lane, was Marble Arch. This made more sense to Gareth, as it was very close to where the hotel was located.

Part of Beulah's dream was that many people were buying bright-yellow squares. This also took Gareth some time to understand, until he realised that the people in Beulah's dream weren't actually *buying* the squares. The squares were the large carrier-bags used by the shoppers to carry away their purchases. In London, there was only one store that used bright-yellow carrier bags — and that was Selfridges.

Gareth wondered how disturbed Reece Tassicker was getting by the seemingly bizarre events that were happening to him. He grinned to himself as he dialled Andre's number. There would be another event happening to Reece in Selfridges store later on today.

At 15h07 to be precise.

Chapter 42 Tuesday 10h00

Presentation #4

How real is reality?

By Professor Ken Callum
Department of Philosophical Sciences
Aston University, Birmingham

Reality is merely an illusion, albeit a very persistent one.

Reality is that which, when you stop believing in it, doesn't go away.

Seeing is believing.

Quotations by Albert Einstein, Philip K. Dick and anonymous

THE APPEARANCE OF REALITY

Are you comfortable in your reality? You may feel that you are sitting peacefully, nicely-relaxed and quite still. But in reality, you aren't.

You know that the earth is spinning, but you probably aren't aware that the speed at the equator is approximately 1,000 miles an hour. Planet Earth is also orbiting the sun at a speed of 67,000 miles an hour, and our entire solar system is moving towards another star, called Vega, at over 40,000 miles an hour.

We are part of the Milky Way spiral-galaxy, which *itself* rotates, and where we are located, the speed of rotation is about 480,000 miles an hour. And just for an added bit of fun, our galaxy is moving at 1,300,000 miles an hour across the universe. The only aspect of this cosmic, roller-coaster ride that you notice are the sun, moon and stars moving slowly across the sky each day due to the Earth's rotation.

It may seem hard to believe that you are moving in so many different directions at such amazing speeds — and yet you probably feel quite stationary. So what's the reality here? Are you sitting still, or are you rotating and tumbling in a frenetic combination of cosmic-motions?

You don't sense this movement because everything around you is moving in *the exact same manner*. There's no fixed-point that allows you to identify your relative speed. It's similar to being in an aeroplane in mid-flight. Despite flying at 500 miles an hour, it doesn't feel as if you are moving, because everybody, and everything you can see, is moving in the exact-same, steady-state way. If you didn't look out of the window at the ground below, you wouldn't even know that you were moving. It's only when you move relative to everybody else — when you stand up from your seat and walk down the aisle — that you notice the difference. Because then, you are moving differently to everybody else.

We all share the same planet — at the same moment in time — so we might assume that we are all part of the same reality. In the physical sense this is true

— but unfortunately reality doesn't exist in the physical world. *Reality only exists in your mind.*

Everyone sees the world differently, but we falsely assume that we all see it the same way. Before you can appreciate reality differently to everybody else, you have to look at it — and understand it — in a way that you might never have done before. The problem is that we don't know how to look at, and how to understand, the world differently, for we unknowingly deceive ourselves in numerous ways. Once we truly understand how our own perspective is so unique, then we can use this to create our own individual futures and choices — in our own personal reality.

What does reality consist of?

Do you believe that other alien-races exist somewhere in the universe — or do you believe that we are all alone?

If you *do* believe that aliens exist, then in some distant galaxy there is a star that our telescopes cannot see. Around this star orbits a planet whose name we do not know, and on this planet live a race of aliens, going about their normal lives. We don't know what they are doing right now — or whether they are enjoying whatever it is they are doing. But the fact is they must be doing something. *At this very moment in time.* They are part of the universe in exactly the same way as us. But are they part of our reality?

If you believe that we are alone in the universe, then imagine the Hilton hotel in Sydney, Australia. In particular, imagine room 703. Whatever is happening in room 703 right now, at this moment in time, is that part of your reality or not?

Whatever is happening on that distant-planet, or in room 703, is part of right now. *Part of this immediate instant.* These things may not have any impact on our reality, because we are unaware of them. Like so many other things happening at any given moment on Earth — or in outer space — only a tiny number will have any material impact on us. However, it's this incredibly-small number of things that form the extent of our reality.

Reality doesn't simply refer to the physical things that you can see, hear, feel and smell in your immediate vicinity, as your reality can stretch into other dimensions too. For example, you may be relaxing in your lounge watching an enthralling tennis-match on the television. This tennis-match being transmitted live to your television is also a part of your reality. While watching the tennis, your phone rings. It's your best-friend calling you from a Paris restaurant to tell you she's just got engaged. For both the crowd at the tennis-match watching it live, and for your best-friend in Paris, their experiences will be very different to yours. They will probably believe that their experiences of each of these events are *more-real* than your experience of them.

But for you, where is the reality of the tennis-match happening? On some distant tennis-court? On the surface of your television-set? On the retina of your eyes, where you perceive the light emitted by the television-set? Or in your mind, once you convert the electrical signals that your optic-nerves brought in from your eyes?

Our physiological links to the outside world

In your environment right now, you can see, hear, feel, smell and possibly taste a multitude of things. All these sensations were perceived by your various sensory-organs, and converted into electrical signals which travelled along nerves to your brain. In your brain, these electrical signals were decoded and assembled together to report-back the representation of your immediate environment at this moment in time. Even though there is something happening in the physical environment around you, which you are a part of, the way it appears to you is actually created inside your head. Your mind is like an ultra-real, multisensory, three-dimensional movie theatre, and the film that's now showing is a copy of what's going on around you.

So which is the true reality — the one that is happening all around you, or the one going on inside your head? This may seem counter-intuitive, but your true reality is the one happening in your mind.

The acid-test of this is to imagine that you are brain-dead. You would be a part of the physical reality that was occurring all around you in some hospital intensive-care unit. However, you would have no awareness or sensation of this at all. Without the interpretation of your reality that your brain provides — there is no reality.

You can influence and change your reality very easily though. If you close your eyes for a few-seconds, you can still hear, smell, and feel what's going on around you, but you may have missed something that happened that was purely-visual in nature. Perhaps somebody walked past the window and you didn't see them. The action of somebody walking past the window is a fact, and was part of the external, or physical, reality of the moment, but you were completely ignorant of this. Your view of reality is different because you don't know that this happened.

Another consideration is the electrical impulse conversion mechanism that we use inside our heads. When I see a fire engine going by, the paint on the vehicle absorbs all the different wavelengths of the sunlight, except for that corresponding to red, which it reflects. This red light enters my eyes and is converted by the retina into nerve-impulses, which are transmitted by the optic-nerve to my brain. My brain then converts these impulses into the colour I see as red. This is why the fire engine appears red to me. But who can say whether the way that I perceive the colour red *is the same way you do?*

Whenever I see the colour red, I get the same consistent trigger in my brain. So whether the red is from a fire engine, a woman's lipstick, a bowl of cherries, or the top light at a traffic signal, I recognise this as red. But what do I actually see in my mind? Is it the same reality as others see? I know that I must see something different to a person who is colour-blind. But are there other ways in which my reality is different to that of somebody else sharing the same experience as me?

FILTERS IN YOUR REALITY

It isn't just your senses that create your reality around you. Your frame of mind — the momentary belief system that you have — also influences your reality.

Frame of mind

Imagine two parents and their young child walking down a road at night. The child has just read a scary story, and fears there are monsters hiding behind every tree. The mother read the local newspaper and learned about the increase in crime at night, and fears there could be a mugger nearby. The father is taking in the evening beauty of the town when all is quiet. Three different perspectives of the same situation, at the same moment in time, and all due to the frames-of-mind that each individual had.

Also, in this same scenario, imagine if the mother sees a man walking towards them, and she glimpses his face as he walks past a street-lamp. She recognises the face from the local newspaper that morning. Was it the face of the escaped convict who is to be considered armed and extremely dangerous? Or was it the picture of the new vicar at the local church? Whichever view she adopts will influence the actions she takes in the next few-seconds, which will impact and shape the reality for all three of them over the next few moments.

External inputs

Your interpretation of reality can also be influenced by others, and unknowingly by yourself too. A great example is from the movies, when towards the end of a film, the sorrowful-music wells up to a climax — just as the lead actor dies in the arms of their loved-one. The appropriate use of the music pushes a sad-and-poignant moment into the tear-jerker arena that the director was striving for.

Or, imagine that you are waiting for your bus to go home, and you suddenly hear a loud bang. Was it a gunshot — or an explosion? If you believe so, then your reality is suddenly transformed into a nervous-awareness. When you realise it was just a piece of metal dropped by a worker on the nearby building site, then your reality changes again. These are two examples of external influencers that shape the way your reality reveals itself to you.

Belief shapes reality

Everyone has beliefs that cover many aspects of our lives. Sometimes these beliefs are momentary and soon forgotten. Other times these beliefs are deeper in nature and consistent over long periods of time, in which case they start to define your behaviour. A basic example of this is that people of a happy and positive disposition, tend to see the up-side in a given situation, while those of a negative disposition may tend to see only the faults and problems in that same situation.

Some beliefs are influenced by personal taste too. Imagine yourself in an art gallery, looking at a piece of artwork with someone else — who thinks it to be amazing. You might think it to be awful. This picture is the same reality for the both of you — but interpreted differently. If the other person explains what they think is amazing about this particular piece of art, you may then see it differently. You may begin to like the piece, for you are seeing things that you hadn't noticed before. Your belief system can change from moment to moment, and just by changing your attitude, you change the way you see your reality.

Your nerve-system brings in a range of electrical inputs from the various sensory-organs around the body, which the brain converts such that you are able to use these inputs as part of your mental-processes and thinking. However, the mind applies a range of filters from your knowledge, beliefs and emotional state to produce your personal version of reality — at that particular moment in time. You may believe that you are being impartial and factual as you create the reality around you, however, you can't help but apply the biases which are present at that point in time.

Reality is actually a lot more complex than you think. It isn't just happening to you — *you are creating it*, and that creation process has so many different variables to take into consideration. If your thinking influences your reality, then you have to ask the question *How good is the thinking that you are using to do this?*

TIME AND REALITY

Try this simple experiment. Scratch your big toe with your left hand and scratch your cheek with your right hand — just once — but at the same time. Notice how you feel the sensations in your toe and cheek both at the same time? That shouldn't happen, because the nerve impulses take longer to travel from your big-toe to the brain than they do to travel from your cheek to your brain.

Your brain knows this, and so it compensates. It can't anticipate the sensation from your big toe, or make it go faster, so what it does is to delay the sensation from your cheek, so they appear to arrive at the same time. But it isn't just your cheek-impulses that are slowed down. The brain compensates by slowing everything down, so it can process nerve impulses from anywhere on the body *at the same instant.*

Your brain delays everything by about eighty-milliseconds, which is just under one-tenth of a second. Whatever happens in the real world, you experience second-hand in your head, one-tenth of a second later.

False things in our reality

Ever used the phrase *If I see it with my own eyes then it must be real?* Or how about *I'll believe it when I see it*? Let's see how real these phrases actually are.

Imagine you are holding a coin in your hand and you close your fist tightly around it. You open your hand to see the coin has vanished! You feel something odd behind your ear, and reach-out to scratch it — and you find the coin that was in your hand just a moment ago. If this ever happened to you in real life, it would be extremely disconcerting.

When a magician does this trick to you, even though you know what's going to happen, it's still quite impressive. Magicians make tricks look so easy, and so natural, that it almost seems like magic. But as we all know, it's just sleight-of-hand with a good dose of deception on top. Even when you anticipate the trick, and you watch the magician's hands closely, they still manage to deceive you. But that's okay — as you know it's just a trick. But what happens to you when you are unaware that you are being tricked or deceived?

Subliminal advertising is a marketing technique whereby images of products are flashed on a screen too-quickly for the eye to recognise, but long-enough for the brain to register. It's often done surreptitiously with logos or words-within-images to attract attention. It can also be achieved with sub-audible sound, where the jingle associated to a product is played to stimulate you into buying that product. We are bombarded with so many advertising messages every day, that our minds are becoming more adept at blocking-out the billboard posters, website banners and also print, radio and television advertising. But how can you block something if you don't know it is happening?

Subliminal advertising is banned in many countries, but how would you know if you suddenly felt the urge to do something, that this was your own internal desire, rather than being drive by some external influencer? How would you know what is your opinion — and what is being forced upon you?

You have no free will

For close to fifty-years, Dr Benjamin Libet was professor of physiology at the University of California, San Francisco, and in the 1970s he conducted research into free will in the mind. He connected research participants to an electroencephalogram (EEG) which measured electrical activity in the brain, and then asked them to make a motion by flicking their wrist or pressing a button. He asked the participants to indicate the moment when they *first became aware* of their desire to make the movement.

Naturally, the *intention* to make the movement preceded the *actual* movement itself, but the EEG revealed that the brain activities relevant to the movement started half-a-second *before* the participant was aware that they wanted to make the movement. At the time, this research was extremely controversial, as it seemed contradictory to the notion of free will within mankind.

These results have been reproduced many times since then, and advanced brain-scanning technology has allowed more-accurate readings of the brain's activity to be undertaken. In 2008, researchers at the Max Planck Institute for Human Cognitive and Brain Sciences in Leipzig, Germany discovered something even more unusual. When participants were asked to press a button with either their left-hand or their right-hand, the areas of the brain associated with making the decision and the movement, would indicate activity *up to ten-seconds* before the participant was aware that they wanted to make a movement.

Additionally, the researchers were able to predict with a sixty per cent accuracy, whether the participants would use their left, or their right-hand to press the button. Again, this was up to ten-seconds prior to the participant being aware of having made their choice.

The Bem experiments

Daryl Bem is a renowned social-psychologist and professor emeritus at Cornell University. In the 1960s he developed the theory of self-perception, which is now a standard element in the study of psychology. His current studies focus on investigating the unexplained transfer of information between people, and also between people and machines. In 2011, he published the findings of research he undertook in a paper entitled *Feeling the Future* in the Journal of Personality and Social Psychology by the American Psychological Association. For this research, he involved over 1,000 participants and ran a series of experiments to test for their ability to perceive a future event.

When doing research exercises with members of the public, it's normal to pay them a monetary incentive for their time, which can add considerably to the total cost of undertaking any research. As universities perform large numbers of research projects, this could cost a significant amount. To overcome this in the university environment, students are frequently given course-credits if they volunteer to be participants in research. This is a mutually-beneficial arrangement which gives the researchers a wide pool of potential participants at minimal cost. The participants are still given a monetary incentive — but a very modest one for their time.

One of the additional incentives that Bem's research team offered, was to show the student-participants explicit erotic-images, and they could choose the type of image they would prefer to see, dependent upon their sexual preference. Once it was clear what type of images interested the students, they were then shown a computer-screen with a picture of two curtains. They were told that behind one of the curtains was an erotic picture, and they had to click on the curtain that they thought covered it.

The participants assumed that the tests were trying to detect their clairvoyant capabilities, as they had to think which curtain was hiding the picture. In truth there was no picture behind the curtain when they made their choice. It was only *after they had made their choice*, that a computer programme using a random-number generator, determined which curtain to place the image behind. The participants weren't trying to detect the outcome of a decision that had already been made (clairvoyance); they were trying to detect the outcome of a decision that had *not yet* been made (precognition). In effect, the test was to predict the future.

Over one-hundred sessions were run using thirty-six images each time, which delivered more than 3,600 test instances. The participants correctly identified the future-position of the erotic images 53.1% of the time — which is significantly above the 50% expected rate for any pick-one-out-of-two choice selection. When the same experiment was run using a variety of non-erotic images, the test results did not differ significantly from the expected chance rate of 50%.

Type of image	**% choosing the correct curtain**
Erotic images	53.1%
Neutral pictures	49.6%
Negative pictures	51.3%
Positive pictures	49.4%
Romantic, but non-erotic pictures	50.2%

One of the reasons that Bem ran the experiments using erotic imagery was that previous research by others, had shown that abilities around precognition appeared to be most prominent when tested on erotic or emotionally arousing imagery, as opposed to neutral imagery.

The second Bem experiment

Another of Bem's experiments was based around people's recall of a list of common words. The participants were shown forty-eight words on a computer screen and asked to form a mental-image of each word as it appeared. An example word might be *tree*. Each word appeared individually on the computer screen for three seconds. After all the words had been shown, the participants were given a surprise test, and asked to type in as many of the forty-eight words as they could remember. The number of words correctly recalled was noted-down, and the testing was essentially finished at this point — but the participants weren't told of this — and they were given another exercise to do.

In this next exercise, twenty-four of the words that had been used in the first-stage of the experiment were selected at random by a computer, and the participants worked through a series of exercises where they had to sort these twenty-four words into groups and re-type them into boxes on the screen. These exercises were helping to reinforce the selected-words in the minds of the participants, while the other *unused* twenty-four words acted as the *unpractised* control-group.

What's very clever about the set-up of this experiment was that the participants were being helped to remember twenty-four of the words once the test was over.

The overall results showed that the participants had a 2.3% better-recall of the twenty-four practiced words than they did of the twenty-four unpractised words, even though the practice took place *after the testing was complete*.

Both of these experiments — one using imagery and the other using words — seemed to indicate that the participants somehow managed to beat the odds that would be expected due to the laws of chance. Daryl Bem stated that this could be evidence of *time-leakage*, as the research could be interpreted to show that people can consciously access the future in some way.

In this research, the participants didn't know the true purpose of the tests they were involved in. They were ignorant to the concept of time-leakage, and weren't consciously trying to predict the future. This is how Bem can state that time was leaking from the future — into the present — and helping them to make more right-decisions that wrong-ones.

What is most fascinating about these experiments, is that they weren't run using people who claimed to have clairvoyant or extra-sensory perception skills. These were a mixed cross-section of regular university students; unsuspecting participants who simply volunteered to take part in some research activities — and who somehow managed to access a future event. If *they* were able to access the future, then perhaps we all have this capability to some degree.

Daryl Bem believes that his experiments provide evidence that human physiology can anticipate erotic stimuli before it occurs. He states that 'Anticipation of this nature would be evolutionarily advantageous for our reproduction and survival'.

It isn't just Bem's research that has shown this natural capability among people. In 1989 Charles Honorton and Diane Ferrari of the Stanford Research Institute reported on their research that analysed all the forced-choice precognition experiments appearing in English-language journals between 1935 and 1977. Their analysis covered 309 experiments conducted by sixty-two different researchers using more than 50,000 participants. They reported a small, consistent, and highly-significant success-rate being achieved across this multitude of experiments.

Energy and time

There's an alternative view of reality that incorporates the way that energy brings time to life.

Consider a timeline at the highest generic level, containing the three time-phases of past, present and future. The past is devoid of energy for it is finished and gone, while the future is devoid of energy because it hasn't yet happened. From a time-perspective, all we have is a series of nows that occur incessantly, one after the other. The next future-now comes into the present, and then in the briefest of moments, is gone and becomes the past.

This is very much like a movie-projector, where every frame before and after the current-one, is dark and invisible. All you can see is the current frame that the projector's-light illuminates. Energy has a similar effect on the now, making only the current-now be alive and real. There is no energy in the past or in the future. The *now* is how you convert the future into the past.

In physics, there is a continued belief by many academics that time doesn't exist. It is a non-natural dimension that has been created by humanity out of a need for convenience. There are many varied-and-valid scientific arguments as to why time does not exist. While this is a very interesting aspect to consider, it's not something I want to focus on now. I just want you to be aware that the concept of time isn't as fixed as perhaps you may believe it to be.

One of the laws of physics is that energy cannot be destroyed and it cannot be created — it can only be converted from one form to another. This opens up an interesting concept around time and energy. Does the passage of time — the inexorable-conversion of infinite moments of the future into moments of the past — create the energised-and-alive moments of the present? Or does the energy within the universe need the concept of time to be valid? If the sole purpose of the energy in the universe is to cause change, there needs to be a before-and-after situation — which by default needs some duration of time to occur. Whether that time is milliseconds or millennia, is immaterial — it's the fact that it requires two distinct and separated points on the time continuum.

Let's look at two examples of energy conversion over different time-periods. There is one energy-related equation that we all know, and that's Einstein's mass-energy equivalence-equation or $E = mc^2$. This equation shows that the total internal-energy of a body (E) is equal to its mass (m) multiplied by the speed of light (c) squared. Because the speed of light does not change, the internal energy of a body is directly proportional to its mass. This was unfortunately, but effectively, demonstrated by the atom-bomb which was dropped on Nagasaki in August, 1945. This atom-bomb contained 6.2-kilogrammes of plutonium, almost all of which fissioned into other elements in a fraction of a second when the bomb was set off. Just one-gram (1/28th of an ounce) of the plutonium did not convert into another element. Instead, it was converted into energy in the form of heat, radiation and kinetic energy, with the explosive power of 21,000 tons of TNT. This is the astonishing effect when we convert mass into energy.

There's another less-dramatic way that we convert energy — and we all do it every day. If you eat a bowl of cereal for breakfast, your body breaks down the cereal, sugar and milk you consumed and converts it into the energy you need to get you through your day. The amount of food-energy available is labelled on nearly all food products in the form of calories or kilojoules. As the body converts your breakfast cereal into energy, approximately twenty per cent of it is used for brain-functioning with the rest providing power for the rest of your body.

Internal energy

We all have changes in our energy-levels, even over a relatively short periods of time. We may eat chocolate for an energy boost, or have a cup of coffee to stimulate us for a little while. The chocolate and coffee are affecting our physiological energy levels.

Similarly we all have days when we feel mentally *down* — even if we aren't feeling ill, we feel illogically-negative towards particular aspects of our daily lives. And of course the opposite is true, as sometimes we wake-up and feel that today is going to be a great-day when we will take on any challenge that comes our way and make it a roaring success. This energy level reflects our attitude of the day or moment. This represents the frame of mind we are in, which translates to how effectively we apply and use our available energy.

But there are many different forms of energy, and these are just two examples at the physiological and attitudinal levels. Let's look at some more *unusual* energy levels which we possess.

Levels of energy & layers of reality

I mentioned that the brain converts energy into the thinking and mental processes which help us create the reality in which we exist.

There's another type of energy we can feel, and that's the energy of the world around us. It's very difficult to measure this energy in the laboratory, and it's hard to define academically, but I will give you some examples on a personal-level that you may be able to relate to yourself.

I enjoy running, and I frequently run to and from work. Part of my run takes me through central-London which I cover at around seven-thirty each morning. Most days I have to carefully think-ahead to make sure I'm running around the people who are potentially in my way — which is an accepted part of running in a busy city. Some days though, strange things happen — like everybody knows I'm coming and they move out of the way for me. This provides me with a clear run on the pavements and while crossing roads. Occasionally, the opposite is true, when I'm constantly bumping into people, or they change direction immediately in front of me. Then I can spend the entire run dodging from side-to-side. Whether it's my energy level which is different — or whether something is changed in the energy levels of the people around me, I couldn't say.

A particularly unusual, and ultimately tragic, event occurred on 14th March 2007. I was working with PDD, a leading UK design-company who are based in Hammersmith, West London. That afternoon I left their offices around five o'clock to walk to the local railway-station on my way home. It had been a very useful day with them, and I was feeling upbeat and positive. However, as soon as I left their offices I felt a strangely-negative energy around me. On the walk to the station it seemed abnormally-quiet, except for a solitary person shouting to themselves on the opposite side of the road to me. This person must have been suffering from some kind of mental problem — but it added to my unease. Something told me to be wary of my surroundings and to be careful in what I did. I got home without any further-incidents and I discussed this with my wife. We agreed it was probably me feeling peculiar in some way.

However, when I returned to PDD's offices the next morning, my way was blocked by police. It turned out that just thirty-minutes after I'd left, the previous afternoon, a sixteen-year-old boy, Kodjo Yenga, was stabbed and killed in a gang-related incident, immediately outside their offices. For the rest of the day, reporters and police stationed themselves outside the window of the office I was using.

I have no idea how I was able to pick-up this sense of negative-energy in the area around me. It happens several times in a year — and fortunately most times, nothing significant happens. However, I do believe that I'm not the only person who experiences strange situations like this. Perhaps we all have the potential to access similar *intuitive feelings* towards the environment around us.

Energy in the moment

The projector of life is shining its light on now — *on this very instant in time.* What is peculiarly-coincidental is that many of the unusual-capabilities that the mind has, are things that occur in very-short durations. The flashes of inspiration that we have, the ideas that suddenly pop into our head, the moments where extreme coincidences or synchronicity occur, or feelings of déjà vu — they are instances that happen with little or no warning.

These sudden-moments aren't that plentiful — and they aren't always obvious. Often we may not notice them unless we're paying attention and really want to see them. When you have an intuitive feeling of some description, it isn't a hard, unyielding feeling, it's much gentler — often difficult to describe — and it can easily be over-ridden and ignored if necessary.

Hunches and glimmers are other interesting mind-occurrences that happen *in a moment.* A hunch is an intuitive-guess or feeling, while a glimmer is a dim-perception or inkling. With a hunch, you intuitively feel that something is right or wrong in a particular situation or with a facet of reality. You don't have any proof, but something tells you that your view is different to what is conventional wisdom — or to whatever you are reading, hearing, seeing or understanding at any particular moment. A glimmer could be a brief-flash of enlightenment, where something triggers a new, and potentially-contrarian thought to you. It may be very tenuous and fleeting, but it is the first-sign of something interesting that may be worth exploring in some way.

Another example of a momentary occurrence is synchronicity, which is the area of unexpected occurrences that seem to be more than just coincidences, or which seem to defy the odds of normality in some way.

All of these examples where a mental-connection is made in an unexpected or sudden moment — are very tenuous in nature, but they do happen. Perhaps we should be paying more attention to what we can do to stimulate increased numbers of these *magic mind moments*.

Connecting to the energy / reality levels

There are several levels at which we connect with reality. The one which we experience for the vast majority of our time is being present-in-the-moment. Paying attention to what is going on around us and interacting with events as necessary to create and continue living in our base-perception of reality. However, we are able to detach ourselves from reality in a number of different ways.

1. *Daydreaming* for a few moments, or becoming transfixed on something, is where we take a brief break from reality. We don't consciously decide to do it, as our mind just *drifts-off* for a short-while.

2. *Meditation* is where individuals create an island of peace and solitude for themselves, and remain still for relatively-long periods of time as they focus their minds in a specific and personal way.

3. *Unthinking-moments* occur when we are preoccupied on a relatively-menial task, that somehow allows our subconscious to connect with our reality. Examples are when you are having a shower, driving the car, or playing solitaire on the computer. You aren't thinking about anything specific, but an idea, or the answer to a question you had, suddenly pops into your head.

4. *Distracted exercise* is when you can put your mind into a distracted-state while you are participating in vigorous, individual exercise. As a runner, if you start to notice how tired you feel, and how there are various aches-and-pains in your body, then you may want to stop and walk. However, if you can distract your mind with some kind of thinking, then the miles seem to pass effortlessly-by.

5. *Out-of-body-experiences* are where individuals feel they have left their own body, and can look down on themselves. When I've got an interesting issue to think about, I occasionally experience a strange kind of light-headedness while running, where it feels like I'm floating above myself as I run.

These are all different levels at which we can use our mind to detach ourselves from reality. They only happen when our mind is actively and deeply focussed (or distracted) on a topic — or an exercise. But they are examples of some relatively straightforward ways in which we can remove ourselves from reality for varying periods of time.

You may not know this fact, but a mobile-phone is actually a two-way radio, as this is the basis of the communication process. If you own a smartphone, it consists of a number of different radios that operate on different frequencies. It may have separate radios for a 2G-connection, a 3G-connection, a 4G-connection, Bluetooth, Wi-Fi, FM radio, GPS and potentially more. You may disable certain ones if you don't want to use them — or sometimes you may have your receiver turned on but no-one is transmitting on that channel, so you don't receive any signals. This happens when you are out of the coverage area for your mobile network provider.

Potentially the mind is the receiver for different types of mental-transmissions. Perhaps we all have the necessary pieces of transmitting and receiving equipment in our heads — but some of us haven't turned it on — or tuned it in. Possible some of us are only receiving and some are only transmitting. It requires two or more people to follow the protocol of transmitting and receiving on the same wavelength, at the same time, and within an appropriate range for anything meaningful to happen.

To have this ability to be *tuned-in* with our immediate environment would be a highly-practical skill to have — a useful capability for our mind to develop — if this were possible. If we could determine how we evolve, this is one direction that we may choose. As I said earlier, our mind is the sole-conduit to our reality. An enhanced mental-agility can help us interpret and interact with our surroundings in richer ways; helping us to experience a greater sense of reality. Potentially these additional dimensions in our reality are already there — it's just us who haven't tuned in those specific radio-receivers as yet.

The example I gave where I had the highly-negative energy feeling of the Kodjo Yenga gang-murder was unusual. In some ways it might have made more sense if I'd had the negative-feeling when I was in the proximity of the attack *after* the event. If it was possible for me to pick up the residual negative-energy in some way that might have made some kind of sense. But how was I able to pick up the energy thirty-minutes *before it happened*? Was it an example of Daryl Bem's time-leakage?

When you meet someone new, occasionally you may have a good feeling — or a bad feeling — about them. Sometimes the reason why you make this judgement-call isn't obvious to you. You may rationalise it by saying they *seemed like a good-person* or they *gave off a good-energy.* There just maybe more to these kinds of statements than we give ourselves credit for.

Realities are very personal and very different

Our individual realities are all so phenomenally different. Even if you feel that you are the same as everybody else, that isn't the case. The filters that we use to shape our interpretation of what's happening around us have been developed over our own lifetimes — each of which has been significantly different to everybody else's. Additionally, all the things that we've done, and that have happened to us in our lives, also impacted who we are today. These are what help shape and develop our personalities and make us individuals.

We may think that we are very similar to other people, doing the same kind of job as them, living in the same kind of house as them, going to work on the same bus as them and drinking in the same pub as them. From an external perspective, yes, we may be perceived as very similar — but what is inside of us, in our minds and in our version of reality is very different indeed.

Many people may keep things they've experienced locked up inside themselves. Things that they feel embarrassed about sharing with others. These may be strange things that have happened to them through their lives, things that they feel would sound silly to someone else. Well, what if everybody has experienced these things — and no-one is talking about them? Or what if everyone has the potential to experience these things — and more? Shouldn't we be talking about them to encourage a wider-acknowledgement that they exist, and to encourage a wider exploration of the possibilities?

Perhaps many might feel they are part of something bigger, and are destined for greater things — but they don't know what. Perhaps this is our latent evolutionary-capability getting restless.

As the neurons in our brains make new combinations of connections to spark a new idea, our personalities and who we are, contrive to ensure that we will never think of something in the *exact same way* that somebody else will. No two-individuals have the same experience, and so we all have the potential to look at the same issue and to come up with a new idea that is different and potentially-better, than anyone else can. Your personal background and your personality are the keys to a differentiated advancement from anybody else's.

SUMMARY

My three takeaway points are:

1. *Augmented reality*: Digital cameras and iPads allow you to put special effects on to images that allow you to see the image differently. You can add filters to your imagined reality to see it differently or to enhance it in some way. We heard earlier that Daniel Tammet sees numbers as coloured images, and there's a phenomenon known as synaesthesia, where people see sounds as different colours. Just because we both see a fire engine and recognise it as red doesn't mean we are actually having the same experience in the reality inside our heads. So what stops *your* mind applying more layers to *your* imagined reality than mine does?

Your reality doesn't happen to you. You create it, filter it, interpret it and then experience it in your imagination. You experience augmented reality all the time. The interesting question is *What else could your mind do to enhance it in more interesting ways?*

2. *Transmit yourself*: Our minds start to signal our intention to act some ten-seconds before we are even aware that we want to do something — so is it possible to detect this potential in others in some way? The additional dimensions in

our reality are already there — it's just us who haven't tuned in those specific radio-receivers as yet. Like a smartphone, it requires two-or-more people to follow the protocol of transmitting and receiving on the same-wavelength at the same-time and within an appropriate range for anything meaningful to happen. Explore the different mental-radios you have in your head; see what you can receive from others; and start transmitting yourself!

3. *The 53%-effect*: If it's possible for us to access the future through time leakage, how is that going to influence your life from now on? How can you use this to enhance your possible realities? At the 50% level, if there's a choice of one-of-two things happening, then equal-chances of either happening are possible. If you increase the probability of one-event over another, then there is a greater chance of that desired one occurring. We can refer to this beneficial support as the *53%-effect.* Even though it may not actually be 53% — it is indicative of a favouring in a specific direction. Learn to appreciate and use this advantage that's available to you to shape your future reality.

I started this presentation with the question *Are you comfortable in your reality?* Your reality isn't a passive entity — you have the opportunity to influence it in ways that you may never have thought possible before. Are you comfortable with it now? Tom Clancy, the fiction writer of many military and espionage novels, once said that the difference between reality and fiction is that fiction has to make sense.

Thank you — and enjoy your new reality.

Chapter 43 Tuesday 11h00

Asif had been following up on the sales assistant's comment from when Reece had bought his second book.

"I found out who the cashier was and I spoke to her. Surprisingly, she remembered making the comment."

"She did? How come?" It was Heather's turn to be surprised.

"Because shortly before Tassicker bought his book, another man had bought four copies of the same book — which she thought peculiar. That's why she made the comment to him."

"And?" prompted Heather.

"And the store's payment system showed that nine-minutes before Tassicker made his purchase with a credit card, someone bought four copies of the book, but paid with cash."

"What did the store security cameras show?"

"There's an unclear shot of someone taking the books off the shelf, doing something to one of them — and putting it back on the shelf. They then move to the tills, and pay."

"Any identity?"

"Male, average height, wearing dark clothing with no special identifiers. They kept their face down the whole time."

"Sounds like someone who knows how not to be recognised," said Heather.

"Definitely. However, because he bought four books, the cashier put them in a large WH Smith bag — which made it easier to track him afterwards when I accessed the station's CCTV system. The cameras lose him for a short period until the ones covering the tube-station entrance pick up both Tassicker and our bag-carrying target going through the ticket barriers."

"Were they together?" asked Heather.

"The target was behind Tassicker and appeared to be following him. I tracked them into the tube station but they split up, with Tassicker taking the Bakerloo line while the target took the Circle line."

"How did the target get through the barriers?"

"He used an Oyster travel-card. All Oyster cards are mailed out to a physical address when you first apply for one. I'm still working on finding the address the target's card was sent to. Our access into the London Underground payment programme requires a decrypter that I can't use from my laptop. I've got Cheltenham working on it," said Asif.

Asif was referring to Cheltenham Spa, a quiet town on the edge of the Cotswolds in the West of England, where the Government Communications Headquarters was based. GCHQ, as it was generally known, was a British intelligence centre located within a huge doughnut-shaped complex, that monitored all communications and signal intelligence for the military. It also monitored huge volumes of digital and telephone communications by business and the general public. This fact wasn't widely-known by the public until mid-2013, when the existence of the Tempora program was revealed by Edward Snowden, an American intelligence contractor, who leaked the information to the press. By intercepting the data carried over the fibre-optic cables that form the backbone to the UK's — and the world's — communications infrastructure, GCHQ had access to vast amounts of information on people, and what those people were saying, viewing, and doing.

"Tell me when we get something. What's Anthony Thorpe been up to?" asked Heather.

"He hasn't left his room. I've been watching through the corridor security camera. He ordered room service breakfast — but that was all."

"I'm concerned about him."

"Why?"

"There had to be some kind of connection between what Bartlett did to them in the newspapers — and his wife's death. Now, twenty-two years later, he gets public revenge on Bartlett — and then goes and sits alone in his room for a day. He's also personally paid a lot of money to attend this conference."

"So?"

"So I think he's at risk of self-harm — and the last-thing I need is someone killing themselves in the middle of the conference."

Heather paused, and considered her options.

"I'm going up to see him," she said finally.

"Is that safe without backup?" asked Asif.

"Get Samuel and his chaperon in here for when I get back. I'll only be gone a few minutes. I'll try to set up a meeting with him in a public area." Heather slipped her Contactor device into her jacket-pocket and stood up.

"Keep a watch on me with the corridor camera — just to make sure nothing goes astray. What room is he in?"

"Six-fourteen. And don't go inside the room," warned Asif. "I can't see you there."

Heather knocked on the door to room 614. She was fully-expecting Anthony Thorpe to be dishevelled in appearance, but when he opened the door, she was surprised to find herself facing a tall, relatively-slender man with a well-groomed, but greying beard. He was dressed in pale-brown trousers, a white shirt with a maroon tie, brown patent-leather shoes, and a matching belt. She could immediately see his clothes were inexpensive and quite well-worn — yet meticulously-laundered. A man who kept a smart appearance on a modest budget.

"Good morning Mister Thorpe, I'm Heather Macreedy, the conference director. I wanted to check that you were alright, as we haven't seen you in the conference since yesterday morning."

"There's something on my mind that I need to think about," he said courteously.

"I know the events that happened over lunch yesterday were quite disturbing to some people," said Heather. "I'd like to help you. Can we talk downstairs in the hotel's coffee lounge?"

"Thank you for your kind offer, but I doubt that you can help me with this issue," said Anthony Thorpe politely.

"It's about Doctor Bartlett."

"I believe it's Professor Bartlett, actually" he said, gently correcting her.

"Not when you and Gail first had dealings with him."

There was an unmoving-silence from Anthony Thorpe. Heather held his gaze, looking for any emotional signals from him. There were none.

This is a man in total control of himself she thought.

"How do you know about Gail?" he replied, in a measured tone.

"You probably want to hear what I have to say," she said.

Heather used a silent nudge on him.

MEET ME. HEAR WHAT I HAVE TO SAY.

Anthony Thorpe did hear the nudge. *Very clearly*. If Heather knew how clearly he'd heard it, she might have understood how vulnerable she was at this moment.

He stood silently for a moment, deciding what to do; watching her eyes, which remained firmly focussed on his.

"Thank you for that thought," he said finally. "I'll be down in ten minutes."

Heather nodded her agreement, then headed back to her office. She had an uneasy-feeling in her stomach. What had he meant by his comment *Thank you for that thought*?

Samuel and Robyn sat at the table in her office. Samuel was working his way through another drawing of arrows, while Robyn was waiting for an apology for yesterday's incident with Samuel.

But none was forthcoming. It wasn't in Heather's nature to apologise. Apologising was going backwards — not moving forward, in her opinion. Heather sat down and explained how she was going to be meeting with someone in the coffee lounge.

"I want the two of you close-by to check for any mental activity while I'm speaking with this man. Robyn, wear your mobile phone's earpiece. I'll call you just before the meeting starts, so you can listen in. If I give you any coded instructions, just respond to them."

"What do you mean by coded instructions?" asked Robyn.

"You'll know when you hear them. Just act natural that's all," said Heather. "And if Samuel picks up any mind activity happening, then your signal to me will be you standing up and looking for something in your handbag," she added, pointing at Robyn. "Is this clear?"

Robyn nodded, taken-aback by Heather's attitude, as if nothing had happened yesterday. But she was also looking forward to this new development.

Samuel continued drawing arrows. He hadn't looked at Heather once.

As Heather walked into the coffee lounge, she took two RESERVED signs from the serving staff's equipment shelf, and then dialled Robyn's mobile number. She held the phone with the screen pointing down, so it couldn't be seen by anybody. Heather took a seat at a table and placed the RESERVED signs on the tables on either side. She sat with her back against the wall; a solitary chair facing her, ready for Anthony Thorpe.

Heather had a clear view of Robyn and Samuel sat against the opposite wall. Their small table seemed entirely taken up by Samuel's drawing pad. Robyn was looking casually around the coffee lounge, but avoided looking directly at Heather. *She's following her training well* thought Heather. *Know your surroundings thoroughly, but never look directly at your mark.*

On the other hand, maybe she still thinks I'm an absolute cow second-guessed Heather.

Anthony Thorpe entered the room, looked around, acknowledged Heather's wave, and came over. He'd added a navy blazer to complete his attire, which Heather knew wasn't necessary within the hotel — but he was obviously a man keeping up an appearance. She noticed the handkerchief in his breast-pocket was the same pattern as his tie. He spoke in quiet, yet confident tones.

Just as he dresses thought Heather. He appeared relaxed in manner, with no sense of gloating — which was something she might have expected, given his success of yesterday.

They ordered coffee from the waiter, and made small-talk about the hotel until he'd brought their drinks, and left. Heather had decided that given what Anthony Thorpe was capable of doing, she needed to take an approach that would disarm him quickly, to minimise the threat to herself. It was a risky approach — but she had no alternative given the timeframes she was working to.

"May I call you Anthony?"

"Please do," he said.

"Anthony, I'm more than just the conference director here," said Heather in a hushed, and overly-moderated tone.

"Is that so?" replied Anthony Thorpe.

"You and I share a special capability."

"And what might that be?"

"I can make people do things that they don't expect to do," said Heather.

"Really?"

"Just like you can."

"I have no idea what you're talking about," he said calmly.

"Would you like me to give you a little demonstration?"

"That would be most interesting," he said curiously.

"Turn around discretely, and look behind you. See that woman sat over there?"

He turned around. "The lady in the blue-paisley top?"

"That's right. Now watch this. I'm going to make that lady put her hand to her mouth and yawn."

Robyn was listening to the conversation through her ear-piece and nonchalantly put her hand to her mouth and yawned, in a slightly too-exaggerated manner.

Heather started breathing again.

"How did you do that?" enquired Anthony Thorpe.

"Just by thinking about it in a special-way," said Heather. "I believe you did something similar yesterday to Professor Bartlett. Twice, in fact."

Anthony Thorpe paled visibly.

"I made that woman over there yawn. You made Professor Bartlett sneeze and vomit." Heather said this in a flat, factual tone, while holding his gaze. She could see Anthony Thorpe was shaken at this revelation from her.

"But he deserved it, didn't he?" she said, slowly nodding her head. "Because we both know it was his appalling behaviour. What he did to you with the newspapers. All those years ago. Isn't that right?"

Anthony Thorpe nodded quietly.

"And that led to the tragic death of your wife, didn't it? She paused, and changed from slowly nodding her head to slowly shaking it.

"Poor Gail," she added, after a pause.

Heather could see his mind was trying to grasp its next thought — but couldn't. His jaw twitched as his mouth knew it needed to say something — but his brain was beginning to falter, and disconnect, as it entered a state of mild shock.

She leant forward over the small table and placed her hand on his arm. "Anthony, I'm here to help you," she said quietly.

"Am I in trouble?" he eventually said.

"Not at all," she replied. "In fact quite the opposite."

He looked at her quizzically.

"I think you've been preparing for yesterday ever since Gail died, haven't you?"

"Yes," he answered.

"You could have done something much worse to Professor Bartlett couldn't you?"

Anthony Thorpe nodded.

"But you didn't want to kill him. You just wanted to destroy his reputation, which was *his* life. Just as he destroyed *your* life." She paused before adding "And Gail's."

"Yes."

"I think you're feeling lost and confused right now, aren't you?"

He leaned forward, placed his elbows on the table and covered his eyes with the palms of his hands. Heather cast a concerned glance towards Robyn, looking for a signal from her — but Robyn didn't move. She saw that Anthony Thorpe's chest was heaving. Then she noticed drops of water falling onto the table from his hands.

He was sobbing to himself.

She looked over his lowered-head towards Robyn, who shook her head slowly. Heather waited for his sobbing to subside, and then handed him a serviette from the table. He took it and wiped his eyes.

"I'm so sorry," he said.

"That's completely fine," she said soothingly — and then firmed up the tone in her voice considerably. "Anthony, please look quickly at what's on the table, but don't say anything."

She moved her down-turned palm to one side to reveal her Ministry of Defence ID card. When he'd seen it, she deftly slid it back across the table and into her pocket.

Anthony Thorpe had then started talking. He told her his story, and how it wasn't about vengeance or revenge, but about vindication. That he and Gail *genuinely* did have unusual abilities. He'd initially considered that when the moment of vindication arrived, he'd like to be standing directly in-front of Professor Bartlett, to remind him of who he was. But he'd realised that would just get the newspapers interested in him again. All he really wanted was for the news media to be interested in the embarrassment of the Professor — so he realised he had to stay in the background.

He explained that on Monday afternoon, he'd uploaded the video to YouTube and emailed the link to all the newspapers and news bureaus from a disguised email address. That night he'd gone to bed with an overwhelming sense of achievement.

This morning though, had been a different matter. He'd awoken for the first time in many years, without a sense of purpose in his life. He felt lost and without direction for his future.

"Anthony, you've spent many years helping countless boys and girls to learn mathematics, haven't you?"

"You seem to know a lot about me," he said.

"I'd like to know a lot more about you. And your special skills."

"Why?" he asked.

"Do you want this country to be a better, and safer, place for all those children that you teach?"

"Of course I do."

"Would helping to make that happen be an interesting new purpose in life for you?"

"Yes. But what would I be doing?"

"Before I can tell you that, I need you to sign some papers," said Heather.

Chapter 44 Tuesday 12h30

At the end of the morning session, the conference chairman had reminded everyone there would be an early lunch, followed by an exercise between 13h00 and 15h45 for anyone wanting to take part.

"This is an experiential exercise to discover if you — as individuals — have any interesting mental skills or capabilities. For those taking part, there will be simple tasks handed out at random. These tasks will involve you performing a set of tests in a location within a short-walk of the hotel," he explained.

"After dinner this evening, there will be a debriefing to discuss your successes and any interesting learnings from the exercise. Please be back here by 15h45 and ready for a prompt start at 16h00 when Reece Tassicker will be giving his presentation — and will also detail the launch of a new dream-capture website. Thank you."

Reece felt concerned there'd now be a much-greater expectation from the website than he'd initially planned. However, right now, he was more interested in the upcoming exercise. He was keen to explore whether he had any unusual skills, and headed for lunch with DD, who also intended doing the exercise.

In an attempt to eradicate the memories of yesterday's lunchtime fiasco, the hotel catering had changed the format of the food, its presentation and the manner in which it was served. Rather than rich individual servings in a buffet style, they had prepared large trays of traditional British food, with waiters who dished out the meal for you.

Reece had taken the steak and kidney pie with boiled potatoes and steamed vegies while DD had taken the cottage pie.

"I thought this was called shepherd's pie'" said DD, poking at his meal with a fork.

"Different dish," said Reece. "Shepherd's pie is made with lamb while cottage pie is made with beef."

"And this is traditional British food at its best, is it?" said DD, stirring his fork around in his food.

"I'm sure the best of British chefs were involved in its making," answered Reece.

"If this is their best, they must be from a pre-historic era. Is it a requirement that to be a British chef you have to still be able to walk and shit at the same time?"

Reece said a silent prayer hoping that DD's comment never got back to the kitchen.

“Cottage pie and shepherd’s pie you say. You Brits have a funny way of naming things.”

“They could have served toad-in-the-hole or bubble and squeak,” replied Reece.

“What?”

“Never mind.”

“Why don’t you people name your food the same way you name your streets,” suggested DD.

“What do you mean?” queried Reece.

“In smaller towns, the street names seem based on what was located on them, like Church Street, Market Street and Baker Street. I suppose there must have been a Prostitute Street at some time — it’s a pity names like that don’t exist anymore.”

“I know there’s a Virgin Street in St Ives in Cornwall,” said Reece. “Does that help?”

“It’s a good start. Talking about names, how come in the mid-sixties you could make a movie and call the lead actress Pussy Galore and get away with it? If you did that today you’d get lynched.”

“Changing times,” said Reece.

“I thought we were supposed to be more liberal these days than back then.”

“That was being sexist — not liberal,” corrected Reece.

“Talking about being sexist, you know how we heard that our reality only truly exists in our minds?”

“Go on.”

“Well, you see those three good-looking women over there?”

“Yes,” said Reece, a little concerned about where this thought stream of DD’s was heading.

“Right now, I’m imagining them naked in my mind — and it’s quite a sight.”

“Is there a point to this?”

“Can we ever really know how many different perceptual filters we’re applying in the interpretation of our reality?”

“What do you mean?”

“If we strip away all the filters and got the raw-feed coming in, for those people who don’t have many filters, then that would be close to normal. But for those people who apply lots of filters — and don’t know it, they will suddenly see reality in a new-light. The question is — can you ever be truly aware of the number of filters you are layering over your reality?” concluded DD.

"Sounds like the question of whether you see your reality as the glass being half-full or half-empty."

"I've never understood the thing about the glass. Surely it's whatever you want it to be," said DD.

"Okay, bad example. Similar situation though. The Bem experiments about being able to see the future; do you believe it's possible for you to do that, or not?"

"If average people without any special skills could do it, then I'm sure I could too."

"What was interesting about that was how the people being tested *didn't know* that the test was to see if they could access the future. They went into it without any preconceived ideas of whether they could do it or not."

"A-ha. They had no filters in place."

"Now imagine if they knew beforehand that they were testing an ability to see the future. Do you think they'd have got that fifty-three per cent success figure then?" said Reece.

"Interesting. If the participants knew what the aim of the experiment was, and they subconsciously believed that seeing the future wasn't possible, then maybe they wouldn't have been able to achieve that fifty-three per cent success rate."

"They would have put up a filter-of-doubt around their perception of reality. That would have made them fail at something that they would achieve *without* the fail-filter," said Reece.

"Our eyes can change from looking at a finger held in front of our face — to gazing at a distant galaxy, in a second," said DD, "but our minds find it impossible to do this once a filter is in place."

"That's deep," said Reece.

"Our reality is based entirely on what we perceive to be normal — but everyone has different views of want normal is. So there's many different interpretations of the common reality"

"Give me an example." said Reece.

"Let me demonstrate with an African story. One hot day, a lizard was sat on top of a rock. He noticed that from the left-side of his rock a snail was approaching, while from the right-side, a tortoise was approaching. The lizard watched the snail moving slowly from the left, as the tortoise moved ponderously from the right. As the sun got higher in the sky, the snail kept approaching from the left, while the tortoise was approaching from the right. As the sun passed its noon high-point, the snail and the tortoise were very close now, one coming from the left-side and one coming from the right-side of the rock. Suddenly, the lizard realises what's going to happen, and before he can shout a warning, the snail and the tortoise crash into each other. It's a catastrophic smash, with bits of shell everywhere.

In the animal ambulance on the way to hospital, the lizard asked the snail what happened. The snail replied *I don't know, it all happened so fast.*"

Reece shook his head slowly, as DD took the last forkful of his cottage pie.

"So you see, our interpretation of reality is based entirely on what we accept as our norm."

"Nice story — but what's it got to do with those three naked women of yours?" asked Reece.

"Maybe I have a fortunate filter in place that does that for me," grinned DD. "Anyway, you'll see me walk out of this hotel for the last time as we do this exercise."

"Really? Are you leaving today?" asked Reece, surprised.

"No. But when I return I shall fly back in like Superman — to demonstrate my newly-acquired powers."

"It's a revolving door so mind your cape."

"We'd better get moving," said DD putting his plate down. "Have a good one — and don't get into any trouble."

"I won't," said Reece.

But he would.

Chapter 45 Tues 13h00

After lunch, Reece and DD found there was a box of sealed envelopes on the table, each of which contained a personal task for the exercise. They both selected one at random.

Reece opened his envelope and discovered the specific task he had, was *to attempt to interact with a stranger and mentally read / influence them in some way*. The instruction sheet gave some examples of the things that could be attempted — such as trying to get them to say something specific or to influence them in some manner. Reece had been allocated Selfridges department store on Oxford Street, which was a short walk from the hotel.

He set off, nodding a silent greeting to Heather who was standing in the foyer as he left.

When Heather had been designing the conference agenda several months ago, she'd thought this might be a useful way to let the attendees experiment for themselves. It would lead to interesting issues being discussed in the evening's debriefing session. As Heather watched the people leave for their individual exercises, she felt unnerved by what the afternoon's exercise might bring — especially in the light of what had happened yesterday to Professor Bartlett.

Andre had also taken an envelope, but he had no intention of participating. He wanted to see how the exercise task was structured, as it would make his afternoon's work easier if he knew what might be happening. He followed Reece at a distance. He already knew where he was supposed to be going, for Gareth had briefed him on the dreamers' feedback this morning. Wherever Reece went beforehand, Andre knew that he would definitely be in Selfridges at seven-minutes-past-three this afternoon.

In anticipation of this, Andre had called Selfridges earlier in the day to get the name of the store's head of security, which turned out to be a Mister Jepson. He'd need this information for later, and he'd entered the details on a spare mobile phone he carried, which he used solely for making calls that he didn't want traced back to his own phone.

Andre smiled to himself as he followed Reece. Here were people trying to test if they had any unusual powers, while both Andre and Gareth knew from the dreamers *precisely where and when* something would happen to Reece at a future point in time. These people were such amateurs compared to what they could do.

Reece made his way directly from the hotel to Oxford Street, and turned left. Walking down two blocks, he passed Russell & Bromley and then Marks & Spencer, before entering Selfridges through the main doorway.

Andre smiled again. *This was so easy.*

Chapter 46 Tuesday 13h10

Reece walked through the double-set of doors which formed the main entrance to Selfridges, and found himself immediately in the women's perfume and cosmetics area.

As good a place to start, as any he thought.

He ambled past numerous counters where the assistants were busy with customers, until he came across the black and white-branded Chanel counter. A slender and stunningly-beautiful woman in a white clinician's outfit, was discreetly trying to make eye contact with people passing by.

Reece walked up, offered her an engaging smile, and explained that he was looking for a gift for his wife. This seemed to him the most straightforward way to start a discussion. Reece had never spoken with a beauty product sales assistant before — and found he was feeling uncomfortable because he couldn't pigeonhole her. Her shoulder-length, brown hair was the glossiest he'd ever seen, and it was pulled back off her face in a ponytail. As Reece spoke, he realised she could be anywhere between twenty-five and fifty-years of age. He could see she wore lipstick, mascara and eye-liner — but it didn't seem like she wore any other facial cosmetics at all.

Perhaps that's the way it's meant to be he thought. He found it disconcerting not to be able to figure out who she truly was. She started asking him questions about the type of fragrances his wife liked, what particular ones she was using at the moment, and what she wanted the perfume for.

Reece realised he was in trouble.

He wasn't married. He never had been. He wasn't even in a steady-relationship. He had never bought perfume before. He knew very little about perfumes, excepting for a few top-line house names. He immediately found himself focusing all his efforts on making up hopefully sensible facts about an imaginary wife with imaginary preferences for perfumes in different imaginary activities. He felt he was describing what characteristics his ideal partner should have for a dating matchmaker service.

Unfortunately, the fact that his mind was focused on creating a mythical woman, complete with a fantasy lifestyle — *on the spur of the moment* — meant he couldn't focus on trying to influence the assistant. He realised the more that he spoke, the bigger the perfume-scented hole he was digging for himself. He eventually admitted that he'd never bought perfume before — and that he needed to go and find his wife. He raised his index-finger and rotated it in a horizontal circle, as though to indicate that his wife was elsewhere in the store.

He then exited the perfume area rapidly. He hadn't really lied to the woman, for theoretically he was looking for his wife — he just didn't know who she was at the moment.

He stopped by the escalator to study the store floor-directory and considered a few options. Lingerie and swimwear sounded tempting, but Reece thought he may have even-more difficulty keeping focused there than at the perfume counter. Womenswear also seemed equally problematic. Menswear would likely lead to having to try items of clothing on — which he certainly didn't want to do. The food-hall was going to be exceptionally busy at this time of day. Home appliances and electrical goods had potential — and without the need to get personal with the sales people. With a boosted feeling of confidence, Reece took the escalator down to the lower-ground floor.

Meandering through one of the largest varieties of home appliances he'd ever seen, he noticed a woman mulling over an espresso machine. As she wore a pale-lilac jacket rather than the dark-blazer of the store staff, she was obviously a customer. He casually wandered over, and stood near her. He examined a digital alarm clock, as if considering buying it. He thought he would try to listen-in to the thoughts that were going on in the woman's mind. He knew the subject of her thinking, and considered that should help him in this, his first real attempt at mind connecting.

This area of the store was reasonably quiet, and Reece lowered his head as if focusing intently on the clock in his hands. He closed his eyes and stilled his mind, as if meditating. He then opened his mind to receive all nearby mental activity. He listened closely for cues in his head, allowing his mind to become a magnet to attract her thoughts. As he started to focus, he realised there was the sound of distant voices. A salesperson was in conversation with a customer somewhere to his right — and they were discussing a sandwich toaster. He put up a mental filter to ignore these voices. He tried to draw the woman's thoughts out of her head — but there was nothing. Reece turned his mind magnet up to full power, in a final attempt to hear the thoughts going through her mind.

But without success.

He opened his eyes and discretely turned towards the woman. She wasn't there! What had he done? Momentarily surprised by her disappearance, he looked around just in time to see her lilac-jacket disappearing up the escalator.

Not having achieved the success that he was looking for, Reece wandered out of home appliances and headed towards the book area. *This should be easier* he thought.

His attention was caught by a promotional poster for Professor Bartlett's book *Mind the Future*. He reached out for a copy — and hesitated. The last two times he'd done this, there'd been a lime-green Post-it note inside.

But he knew it had to be done.

Reece removed the book from the shelf and carefully flicked through the pages — but saw nothing. He did it again, a little more slowly, going through it from cover to cover.

Nothing.

He felt relieved, yet at the same time, disappointed.

He became distracted by the book and forgetting the exercise completely, spent a considerable time reading it. Reaching the end of a chapter, he remembered the task he had to do, and committed himself to having one more attempt at exploring his skills. Unfortunately, the only person in the book area was busy behind the payments till. Reece looked around for another department in which he could attempt his task, and noticed the adjacent photographic area.

Reece used to enjoy photography as a hobby, and he felt mildly confident with the subject. A sales assistant with *Janice* on her name-tag approached him.

"How can I help you today, sir?"

"I'm looking for a new camera," said Reece.

"What type of photographs will you be taking, sir?"

"I enjoy taking portraits," said Reece, grabbing at the first subject that came to mind.

He imagined a wave leaping from his head — into Janice's head — and engulfing her mind with the phrase *TELL ME YOU LIKE TAKING PORTRAITS TOO!*

"Lovely," said Janice, "I'm more into landscapes myself."

"That's interesting," said Reece, as he imagined another wave flowing into her head and flooding her brain with the phrase *TELL ME MORE ABOUT YOUR LANDSCAPES.*

"This Canon PowerShot is on a promotion at the moment and is great value-for-money. What sort of budget are you considering?" she enquired.

"I'm not sure. What kind of budget do you think I'll need?" he said, recognising this as a perfect opportunity to influence her. Another wave was sent thundering towards Janice.

ONE HUNDRED POUNDS!

ONE HUNDRED POUNDS!

ONE HUNDRED POUNDS!

“That depends on you. Can give me any indication at all how much you’d like to spend?” she said, looking at him expectantly.

Reece sent several waves into her mind.

ONE HUNDRED POUNDS!

ONE HUNDRED POUNDS!

ONE HUNDRED POUNDS!

“I can see you’re not sure. As I mentioned this Canon PowerShot is on a promotion.”

Reece sent yet more waves over Janice.

ONE HUNDRED POUNDS!

ONE HUNDRED POUNDS!

ONE HUNDRED POUNDS!

“It’s selling for four-hundred and twenty-five pounds. Is that within your budget, sir?

The phrase *catastrophic failure* wasn’t one Reece used very often — and never in relation to his own abilities.

It seemed entirely appropriate to him at that moment.

Chapter 47 Tuesday 13h50

"I got the Oyster-card information from Cheltenham earlier, and some interesting things came out of it," said Asif.

"The card was registered to a false name, but it had a real delivery address. It was sent to the Peckham Institute, which appears to do research on sleep and dreams. What's interesting is that Gareth Jones from the Peckham Institute is attending our conference."

"Is he the person who followed Tassicker?" asked Heather.

"I traced him on the Contactor system and then went to observe him in the auditorium. No, he's much shorter than the man in the WH Smith store video."

"What else?"

"His history on Contactor shows he's met several times with one other person at the conference — a Vernon Slater. This person's name and details that we have are clearly false, and he doesn't spend much time in any of the presentations. He's either in his room or out of the hotel — where we can't track him."

"What do we know of this Peckham Institute?" asked Heather.

"I'm busy on that. Give me twenty-minutes and I'll have something for you."

"Where are these two people right now?"

Asif clicked their names from the Contactor drop-down menu. "I'm not picking them up. Possibly out of the hotel."

"What about Tassicker?"

Asif clicked on Reece Tassicker's name. "He's not showing either. There's an exercise on now, so they may have all left the hotel to do that."

She'd forgotten about the exercise. Heather paused to think.

"Show me the list of people Tassicker entered into his Contactor. The ones he wants to meet."

A few mouse-clicks later, a list of names appeared in a column on the screen.

"Now let's see the lists for Gareth Jones and Vernon Slater."

As Asif tapped the keyboard, two more columns were added to the screen. In each of these columns there was only one name listed that Gareth Jones and Vernon Slater wanted to meet. It was Reece Tassicker.

"Now that's interesting," said Heather.

"Should we be concerned?" asked Asif. "Tassicker is supposed to give his lecture at four o'clock and announce that new website."

“If he’s not back in time — then we get concerned,” replied Heather.

Chapter 48 Tuesday 14h15

"Heather, I've got the background on the Peckham Institute. Want to hear it?"

Heather rose from her desk and went to stand behind Asif, looking over his shoulder. Seeing information visually on Asif's multiple monitors helped her merge and connect small details within the overview he was telling her.

"Okay, go."

"It was first registered as a business two-years ago and operates from a leased office in central London. It has two full-time employees registered on the payroll, Gareth Jones and Andre Konarski. I called their office number, but it's answered by a secretarial service who take a message and pass it on."

"Only two people? That's not many for a research organisation."

"They have three people registered on their payroll as contract staff. I accessed their backgrounds through GCHQ and found that all were previously claiming benefits of some kind, and were in low-paid jobs or not working at all. They're all now being paid significant sums of money every week. Interestingly, one of them is still claiming unemployment benefit at the same time as being paid by the Peckham Institute."

"That's useful to know. What else?" prompted Heather.

"There's no income being generated by the Institute, yet it seems to have quite a high operating budget. There're no published papers by the Institute, and no sign of any academic research activity at all. They seem to keep a very low profile."

"Seems unusual for a research institute. Normally they'd try to attract publicity to help get funding."

Asif continued. "Their website shows a holding page that says *under construction.* It was last updated over a year ago. That tells me it isn't under construction at all — they just don't want any public attention."

"True," said Heather, nodding.

"I was digging deeper into their website to see if there were any non-indexed pages and I found something peculiar. There are numerous webpages which aren't visible to the public and which are completely blank. The latest one was uploaded yesterday afternoon. I made a list of all of them and it doesn't make sense. Look here," said Asif, pointing to a monitor.

Domain name: HTTP://WWW.PECKHAMINSTITUTE.ORG.UK/

WEBPAGE ADDRESS	UPLOAD DATE / TIME	
EOIG-2	07-JAN-2014	03:14:15
PFTY-1	14-JAN-2014	03:14:15
GEX-4	21-JAN-2014	03:14:15
MQM-3	28-JAN-2014	03:14:15
QCZJ-1	04-FEB-2014	03:14:15
KW-4	11-FEB-2014	03:14:15
CXA-2	18-FEB-2014	03:14:15
NDE-1	25-FEB-2014	03:14:15
VL-3	04-MAR-2014	03:14:15
TXJ-1	11-MAR-2014	03:14:15
XWPE-4	18-MAR-2014	03:14:15
XPVX-2	25-MAR-2014	03:14:15
FHO-1	01-APR-2014	03:14:15
EEP-4	08-APR-2014	03:14:15
HWQ-3	15-APR-2014	03:14:15
FWID-1	22-APR-2014	03:14:15
PBT-1	29-APR-2014	03:14:15
LVLV-3	06-MAY-2014	03:14:15
ZFMQ-1	13-MAY-2014	03:14:15
SVGP-4	20-MAY-2014	03:14:15
JRRJ-3	27-MAY-2014	03:14:15
VYZ-2	03-JUN-2014	03:14:15
FSRMXE-EYVIPME-QMPERS-4	07-JUN-2014	03:14:15
CNGZCPFTC-LGUUKEC-HQTF-2	09-JUN-2014	03:14:15
PD-3	10-JUN-2014	03:14:15
EEO-3	17-JUN-2014	03:14:15
TTE-2	24-JUN-2014	03:14:15
YPN-1	01-JUL-2014	03:14:15
XSV-3	08-JUL-2014	03:14:15
TGGEG-VCUUKEMGT-2	10-JUL-2014	03:14:15
SFFDF-UBTTJDLFS-1	11-JUL-2014	15:14:15
UHHFH-WDVVLFNHU-3	13-JUL-2014	03:14:15
VIIGI-XEWWMGOIV-4	14-JUL-2014	15:14:15

“Explain this to me,” instructed Heather.

“This is the log of all the webpages that have been added to their website this year. The first column is the suffix of the webpage name. The next column is the date and time it was uploaded. Let’s look at the first webpage on the list as an example.”

Asif typed the page address HTTP://WWW.PECKHAMINSTITUTE.COM/EOIG-2 into his internet-browser and then tapped ENTER on the keyboard. The screen took a brief moment to refresh itself before showing a clear, white screen.

“And this is what we get,” said Asif.

“But there’s nothing on it,” replied Heather.

“Precisely. I checked more of them out, and there’s nothing on any of them. I thought there might be something hidden that was written in white text on a white background, but no. I went and checked the properties of each of these webpages, and their page sizes all show as zero. There genuinely is nothing on the webpage. There's nothing on any of them."

"Why do the webpages have such strange names? I thought the page address was generally descriptive of the page's content."

"That's normally the correct practice," answered Asif. "The purpose of creating these webpages seems pointless, unless the webpage address itself was all that was relevant. But look at the dates the webpages were uploaded. The short ones are weekly but the longer ones break the pattern."

Heather leaned over Asif to point towards the bottom of the monitor. "There have been four new pages added in the last five days. These latest ones seem different again. Longer names — but still in gibberish."

"It's a strange website. No public-facing pages, yet lots of hidden ones that have no content — and with unusual page names. I've never seen a site like this before.

Heather knew Asif to be a sharp and experienced techie, as she'd worked with him several times before. If he thought it strange, then she had concerns too.

"Asif, did you say the Peckham Institute is a registered business?"

"Yes."

"I thought these research institutes normally registered as a charity or not-for-profit organisation for tax reasons."

"That's right, but this is definitely registered as a business."

"Then who owns it and where do they get their income from?"

"The Peckham Institute is owned by a company called Somnium Trading, which in-turn is fully-owned by a Paul Peckham. I checked both company's bank accounts and every month the running expenses for the Peckham Institute are covered by a payment from Somnium Trading."

"Tell me more about Peckham."

"Paul Patrick Peckham, sixty-one-years-old, was in merchant banking for many years before becoming a stockbroker for the last fifteen-years or so. He seems a low-profile type, living in Devon with his family, but he's rich — very rich. And he got even richer three-years ago when he sold his stockbroking business for £380 million. That's when he set up Somnium Trading. It's unusual, as the company doesn't seem to employ any people. For the first two-years there was no turnover in the business at all, but in the last year it has done exceptionally well."

"Doing what?" asked Heather.

“They do stock market derivatives trading. I’m a bit out of my depth here, but when GCHQ saw I’d requested a background on Peckham, they sent my request onto one of their business analysts, who sent me some additional info. The analyst said there was something quite interesting about his trading too,” added Asif.

“Go on.”

“Peckham changed from trading shares, to trading derivatives in shares,” said Asif hesitantly.

“Explain the difference to me,” said Heather.

“Okay. Now bear with me on this,” said Asif, taking a deep breath.

“Let’s say that a particular share is worth £10 and you have £1,000 to invest — then you can buy 100 shares. If you own these for a month, and over that time the price of the share increases to £12 — and then you sell them, you’d have £1,200 and have made a profit of £200 pounds. If the share price dropped to £8 and you sell them, then you’d have £800, and would have lost £200. So in this scenario, for your original investment of £1,000, after a month you’d have £1,200 if the price went up and £800 if it went down. That’s how you make, or lose, money with shares. Okay?”

“Carry on,” said Heather.

“With share derivatives, you have the option to buy or sell a share at a specific price at an agreed date in the future. If the share that you have the option for moves the right way and you are in the money, then you exercise the option which forces the other party to buy, or sell, a specific share at the predetermined price. If it goes the wrong way for you, then you obviously don’t enforce the option and you just lose the money you paid to take out the contract. Is this making sense?”

“Yes, but how much more money can you make this way compared to buying and selling the share itself?” asked Heather.

“Let’s say that you believe the same share that I spoke about just now was going to rise in value from £10 to £11 over the month. You essentially take a bet with another trader who thinks that *isn’t* going to happen, and you place a bet — or fee — of say twenty-pence per share to be able to buy those shares in one-month at £11 each. So at twenty-pence fee per share, you can afford to buy 5,000 bets with your £1,000. Clear?”

“Clear,” Heather responded.

“Now if the share price falls, or only rises to £10.75, for example, then it hasn’t got to the agreed £11 level. Then you lose all the bets, and you’ve lost your £1,000 completely. However if the share gets to £12 — like in the example where we bought the shares, then you win your bet, and can make the person who took your bet sell you 5,000 shares at £11 each. Now you don't have to pay for these shares, as you immediately trade them for the £12 that they are worth. So you've made £1 per share on 5,000 shares which is £5,000. Take off your initial fee of £1,000 to buy the bets — or options — and you have made a profit if £4,000."

"So if we bought the shares we'd either make £200 or lose £200. But if we bought these options we'd either make £4,000 or lose £1,000. That's a big difference," said Heather.

"Yes," agreed Asif, "but very risky."

"So what did GCHQ say was interesting about his trades?"

"Derivative trades are closely monitored by the stock-exchanges on which they occur, and so GCHQ were able to see all the trades he'd made. He hasn't done many trades, but the ones he did always made considerable money. *Every time*."

"Really?" said Heather in a surprised tone. "How considerable?"

"Somnium Trading made a profit somewhere between seventeen million and fifty-eight million pounds — on every trade they did."

"That is considerable," said Heather, making an absent-minded whistling sound. "And Somnium Trading is funding the Peckham Institute. Do we know why?"

"There's very little public information on either company, but I did find one short news article from two-years ago. The essence is that Paul Peckham believes that we underestimate the value of good sleep. Apparently, this is how he has been so successful in life — by getting a good night's sleep and waking refreshed each morning. The article states his belief that good dreaming is part of good sleeping, and if he can get people to understand the value of good dreaming they would sleep better, be more productive the next day, and ultimately be making the world a better place. Peckham himself is quoted in the article as saying *He knows the power of dreaming as he started doing it when he was at university*. This is the reason that he established the Peckham Institute."

"That sounds like bullshit to me," said Heather. "From what I've heard, you don't have to dream to have a good night's sleep. A good night's sleep though, does help you have better dreams."

Heather chewed on her lower lip as she thought.

"Paul Peckham is sixty-one now, and he had this insight into dreaming while at university — right?"

"That's what the article says."

"It was about forty-years ago when he first understood the power of good dreaming. Then two-years ago, he sets up and funds the Peckham Institute." After a pause she asked, "what's the name of his trading company?"

"Somnium Trading."

"What does Somnium mean?"

After a few seconds on Google, Asif responded. "It's Latin for *dream*."

"Really?" mused Heather. She started rocking her hips slowly, while both their minds churned this information over.

"You know what I think..." said Asif.

"That he's a multiple-dreamer himself?" finished off Heather.

"I think he had a dream forty-years ago, and then had another, two-years ago. That's why he's invested money into exploring dreams through the Peckham Institute," said Asif.

"Let's back-track," said Heather. "The person who put the Post-it note into the book Tassicker bought at Paddington station, works for the Peckham Institute. Why are they threatening him to prevent the start-up up his dream website? Surely they'd want to reach-out to him to potentially work together."

"It's one thing to put a Post-it note in a book that someone buys, but how do you know they are going to buy *that particular book*, in *that particular store*, at *that particular time*? For me, that's the crucial point," said Asif.

There was silence as both of them considered these issues.

"What if they've found something out about dreaming?" suggested Asif slowly.

"Like what?"

"I don't know. But whatever it is, they don't want Tassicker to find out the same thing."

"You might have something there." She paused. "Did you say that one of the contract people on the Peckham Institute payroll is also claiming unemployment benefit?"

"Yeah," said Asif, rapidly tapping his keyboard. "Patrick Harris, male, twenty-four, lives in Willesden, North London. I've got full details for him on the system."

"North London? Get someone for a face-to-face with him quickly. We'll squeeze him to find out what he does with the Peckham Institute. If he doesn't talk, we'll make sure he loses his income from them — and that he'll have a hard time ever claiming benefits again."

“I’m on it,” said Asif. “And those strange webpage addresses that have been posted. I think that because there’s nothing at all on the page, then the information must be in the address itself. They maybe in some kind of code,” suggested Asif.

“Then you’d better get cracking,” replied Heather.

“You seem in a good mood.”

“What?” snapped back Heather.

“Not like you to make a joke,” said Asif, smiling.

“And what joke was that?”

“My mistake,” said Asif sheepishly.

Chapter 49 Tuesday 14h55

Reece had extricated himself from the disastrous situation with the photography sales assistant by saying he needed to get a sugary-drink as he was diabetic. This was a lie — but it was the only response he could come up with on the spur of the moment. As he walked away, he'd despondently determined that he had no abilities in the field of mind reading or mind projection whatsoever. Realising he still had an hour before he needed to be back at the hotel to give his presentation, he decided to put the time to good use and buy a gift-card for his nephew's upcoming birthday. He'd earlier seen a sign pointing towards customer services, and he set of in that direction.

Andre had been shadowing Reece's exploits in Selfridges from a distance, and realised that his behaviour could easily be construed as suspicious — if it was put into an appropriate context. It was this context that Andre's mind has been working on since they'd both entered the store.

Andre was stood in front of a row of high-definition, large-screen televisions. If anyone observed him, it would seem that he was watching the shared-programme that was running silently on every screen. In truth, he was looking through a narrow gap between two televisions, watching Reece speaking with the sales assistant in the photographic department. The context that Andre had been looking for now finalised itself in his mind. He checked his watch — it was almost three o'clock. Reece Tassicker was supposed to be at the designated-place at seven-minutes past three. It was unfortunate that Andre didn't know what the designated place was — except that it was in the store somewhere. The time was getting close, and Andre decided to make the call to start things moving. Using his second phone, Andre dialled the number he'd entered earlier for the store's head of security.

"Mr Jepson? Commander John Tooley of the Metropolitan Police Counter Terrorism Command here. We have a potential situation in your store which needs your immediate attention. One of our operatives has been trailing a suspect who has spent the last ninety-minutes in your store — and we believe he represents a threat."

Andre spoke in his most authoritative tone without pausing, to prevent Jepson from interrupting him. "This is not an immediate safety issue and you do not need to evacuate the store. The suspect is not believed to be armed — but is potentially a future risk to you. Am I being clear on this?"

“Yes,” responded Jepson hesitantly, being caught completely unaware by this call.

“Can you please repeat your name for me?”

“John Tooley. Central-region operations commander of the Metropolitan Police CTC and I need you to act immediately. This is an urgent situation.”

While making the call, Andre had followed Reece out of the photographic area and toward the customer service area. There was a narrow corridor leading into the customer service area itself. Andre realised he couldn’t follow Reece in there — but he didn’t need to.

“We are listening to a live-feed from our field operative. At this moment the subject is in your customer service area in the lower-ground floor. Our operative cannot reveal himself due to the nature of his cover. Check your CCTV coverage of that area and I’ll give you a description for confirmation. White male, approximately six-feet tall with dark, straight hair. The subject is wearing pale-grey trousers, a white, collarless shirt and a dark-blue jacket. The target is not carrying any items in his hands. Can you confirm to me that you have the target located on your CCTV-cameras?”

Jepson had moved over to the bank of monitors installed in his security control room. There were fifteen monitors in three-rows of five, with two extra-large monitors above the top row. Some of the smaller monitors were showing full-screen views of busy areas, including the main entrances, and the Oxford Street pavement outside the building. Others were split into four-separate screens, displaying four different views of the same area.

Jepson covered the mouthpiece of the phone and hissed, “lower-ground, customer services. Now!”

The woman on the control desk typed LG CS to access the area’s cameras and immediately, on one of the large monitors, four quarter-screens came up beneath the heading LOWER GROUND CUSTOMER SERVICES. One of the screens showed a man with his back to the camera, speaking with a store employee across a service-desk. Jepson pointed, and the woman moved her mouse-cursor over the screen, clicked, and the screen appeared full-size on the second large monitor, to the right of the first. Jepson recognised the appearance from the description given by the caller.

“We can see him on our screens. What do you want us to do?” he asked.

“Detain him until we get there. I repeat, he is not deemed to be an immediate threat, but please take action now, and hold him. I’m despatching a team who will be with you shortly. Are you sure you can handle this in the meantime?” demanded the fictional John Tooley.

“Yes, of course we can,” said Jepson, anticipating something interesting to break up an otherwise dull day. His team occasionally had to detain people for misdemeanours such as shoplifting. Occasionally, drunks and vagrants would enter the store and would need to be discreetly exited. He’d even had married couples having a domestic dispute in the store that got out-of-hand. But he’d never had to detain a potential terrorist. This was big-league compared to what he’d had to do in the past — and he wasn’t going to mess this up.

He also wanted to make sure that he personally got the credit for handling this operation. It would be good for his upcoming performance review with the store general-manager — especially after last-week’s unfortunate incident where they had mistakenly detained the wife of a Saudi prince for shoplifting.

“Get a four-man security team down there now, and tell them to wait for me,” he instructed the control panel operator. “And make sure they have restraining equipment with them,” he added.

“I’m moving my team there now. Is there anything else you want me to do,” asked Jepson.

“I suggest you check your CCTV footage for the past ninety-minutes as he’s been through your Chanel perfume counter, home appliances, books, and then he spent time with the photography sales assistant. Please check with them to see what he discussed — and don’t be fooled by any weak explanations of what he was doing. Get as much information for us as you can. Are you able to do this?” Andre was putting up a challenge to Jepson to see whether he would rise to it.

“I can do all that for you,” said Jepson, as he saw the scope of the operation escalating into the interrogation of a terrorist too.

Andre realised that Jepson had completely bought in to his deception, and had another idea to take it even deeper. “The suspect is using a stolen identity with the surname of Tassicker. That’s T-A-S-S-I-C-K-E-R. First name unknown. This is verified as a false identity, so don’t be fooled by it. I’m confirming to you that he is not an immediate threat to safety at this moment, but we need him detained. You are cleared to search and question him about his behaviour in the store — but please stay within your legal remit. Is that understood?”

“Yes Commander — you can depend on me,” responded Jepson, over-eagerly.

"I need to end this call and get our informant away quickly. Our assets need to be protected. Thank you for your assistance Jepson. I have every confidence in your ability to handle this matter appropriately. Our people will be with you shortly."

"You can be assured of my full support in this..." said Jepson. But the line had already gone dead.

Reece entered the customer service area to see a service counter with three smartly-attired assistants standing behind it. Two were busy serving customers, but the young man in the middle who was free, smiled broadly and asked, "How can I help you today, sir?"

"I'd like to buy a store gift-card please," said Reece in a slightly over-pronunciated tone. After his recent failure with mental communication, he wanted to be sure his verbal communication was absolutely clear.

"And what value would you like, sir?"

"Twenty-pounds please."

"Is this a gift for someone?"

"For my nephew."

"If you'd like, we can protect the gift-card against loss by registering its number. If it were to go-astray in the post, for instance, you can cancel it and get a replacement — as long as it hasn't been used of course."

"That sounds useful," said Reece, handing over twenty pounds in cash.

"If I can take an email address we'll send you a digital copy of your receipt which shows the gift-card's serial number, and how to cancel it and get a replacement if needed. Would that be useful for you?" suggested the assistant.

Reece provided his email address, and the assistant entered it into his computer system.

"You'll be receiving an email with all the information in, shortly," he promised him.

And naturally you'll be sending me an email to remind me about buying another gift-card a year from now, thought Reece. He sighed quietly. Every time you give somebody your personal information, it creates a digital-trail of footprints behind you.

Reece felt the pulse in his head as a momentary wave of detachment swept over him.

Digital trail of footprints. Digital trail of footprints.

There was a connection forming. He could sense this — but had no idea what it was about. He knew to keep his mind free. *Don't try to focus on second-guessing what was coming up*. His mind would be making its own new connection very shortly.

Digital trail of footprints.

No, not digital. Just a trail of footprints.

Footprints. Footprints.

Maybe not footprints either.

Fingerprints?

Yes, fingerprints, too.

A trail of fingerprints or a trail of footprints?

Why were both coming together in his mind at the same time?

A trail of fingerprints and a trail of footprints.

Yes!

Last night DD had made the comment that God had cocked it up by leaving his fingerprints all over the universe.

The Council offered their counsel.

What if it was deliberate?

What if it was a deliberate trail of fingerprints — or footprints?

Something that would act as a guide?

Something that was intended to be followed.

The anomalies formed a trail that was meant to be followed.

They weren't flukes of nature then?

No — the odds against them happening were too great.

You're saying they were deliberate?

Yes! The anomalies in life are there deliberately.

So you'll see them and follow them!

If you follow them from the past, all they'll do is get you to where you are today.

What's the benefit in that?

There doesn't seem to be one.

What if the footsteps don't stop?

You're saying they carry on going?

Yes. They head-off into the future.

Then they will lead you somewhere — won't they?

Maybe you just see the direction that they head off in?

That's a good start — having a direction into the future.

What will you do with this?

Maybe you will understand something?

But what will you understand in the future?

What will you understand in the future? This thought that had entered Reece's mind out of nowhere was a stunning question. One which he'd need to think deeply about later.

"Sir?"

"Sir!"

He must have been in a bit-of-a-daze while the thought came over him, as the sales assistant had raised her voice slightly to get his attention.

"Is there anything else I can help you with today, sir?" he asked.

"No. Thank you very much," said Reece.

He looked over the sales assistant's shoulder at the digital clock on the wall. It read 15h07.

The sales assistant was simultaneously looking over Reece's shoulder — at two, large, store security men. He thought they were standing closer to him than would be normal for a customer.

Chapter 50 Tuesday 15h07

Immediately the call with the Metropolitan Police's CTC commander ended, Jepson left the security control room and headed for the lower-ground customer service area as rapidly as he could without running. Nothing disturbed shoppers more than someone running inside a store, for this alarmed them and made them feel vulnerable, and when shoppers felt vulnerable — they stopped spending. It was his job to make sure the store was a safe, and secure environment in which people could do their shopping — and Selfridges strived to be the paragon of shopping experiences. And this was at risk due to a terrorist *in his store. On his watch!* Jepson knew this was a threat that he could neutralise.

His team of four security officers were waiting for him at the entrance to the customer service area. He left one man at the end of the corridor to prevent more customers from entering the area, and led the others towards the terrorist threat. As they turned the corner into the customer service area itself, he quietly instructed the female officer to stand against the back wall, from where she'd have a full view of the area — in case the suspect had an accomplice. He'd then told the remaining two men to stand close behind the suspect — and to be prepared for any offensive move. Jepson had then casually walked up to the counter and stood beside Reece.

"May I have a word with you sir?" he said discreetly. He tightened his grip on the fifteen-inch, three-million volt, stun baton that he'd been handed by one of his team. It was hanging in his right hand, hidden behind his leg.

Reece turned to his left to look at Jepson, which caused him to notice a rather-large man standing just over his left shoulder. As Reece turned around to put his back to the counter, he saw the second security man who would have been over his right shoulder.

"Is something wrong?" asked Reece.

"I'm not sure. That's what we'd like to verify with you Mister Tassicker."

"How do you know my name?" asked Reece.

"If you'd like to come with me sir, I'll explain everything." He showed Reece his ID card. "My name's Jepson. I'm the store head of security."

Jepson thought the suspect had been surprisingly compliant. He used his hands to guide the suspect into the store's service elevator, which was a subtle way to check for hidden weapons. They'd taken Reece to their secure room on the first-floor, where they explained that he'd been observed displaying some unusual behaviour that they needed to verify. The response the suspect had given them was a ludicrous story about trying to perform mind-control experiments on strangers — which Jepson and his team immediately recognised as a cover for something more sinister in nature.

Jepson had sent one of his team to speak with the sales assistants at the Chanel counter, and in the photographic area, and they'd reviewed the CCTV footage of Reece in the home appliance area too. Both sales assistants had given similar stories of how Reece had behaved peculiarly with them when they'd tried to serve him. In Jepson's mind, this clearly validated his actions in detaining the suspect.

It was now over two hours since they'd apprehended the suspect, and no-one from the Metropolitan Police had yet turned up. Jepson had tried to call Commander John Tooley to inform him they had the suspect detained — unfortunately, there was no record of a Commander John Tooley. Jepson considered that this name may be a coded alias, so he'd then asked to be put through to Counter Terrorism Command. When he'd explained who he was, the CTC had called Selfridges back to validate that Jepson actually was the head of store security. They then proceeded to confirm that there was no Commander John Tooley in CTC, and according to their records, no-one of that name in the entire Metropolitan Police force. It also wasn't a coded alias as that wasn't the way the Metropolitan Police operated.

Jepson was now concerned that he'd been tricked by somebody. He went back to his office and Googled the false name which the subject had given him. The search term *Reece Tassicker* produced several pages of links. When Jepson clicked on some of them, they seemed to validate the background the suspect had given him. Some pages also showed a photograph of Reece Tassicker — and it was clearly the same person as they had detained.

He headed back to the secure room where he'd left the suspect in the care of two of his staff. The suspect, who now appeared to genuinely-be Reece Tassicker, was clearly agitated by his prolonged detention, and Jepson decided it was prudent to take a different approach.

He suggested to Reece that someone may have been trying to cause problems for him, by informing the store security team that he, Reece Tassicker, was a potential terrorist. He decided to use the term *store security team,* rather than mentioning himself specifically as the solely-responsible person for this incident. He asked Reece if there was anyone he could call who would verify who he was — and that his reason for being in the store was for a mind-control exercise. Reece said to contact the Churchill hotel and to ask for Heather Macreedy, the conference director.

Jepson had called the hotel's switchboard himself to ensure he got the right location. He was then put through to Heather, who verified the identity of Reece Tassicker, and that he was genuinely involved in a mind-related exercise in Jepson's store — as were other people in various locations in the vicinity.

When she'd asked why he was calling, Jepson explained about the false call, supposedly from the Metropolitan Police, and that he'd detained the subject for questioning for the last few-hours, but that they'd release him immediately.

He also suggested that she *fuck-off from running any more of these stupid exercises in his store ever again.*

Chapter 51 Tuesday 16h30

Following his last discussion with Heather, Asif had requested an immediate-response support agent be sent out to interview Patrick Harris. These were support staff who responded to low-risk field tasks, such as gathering on-site information quickly, to assist the senior field agents. Within an hour of Asif's request, one of them had taken a Honda NSS300 Forza scooter from the motor pool, and ridden to the address supplied by Asif. The agent parked the scooter in the narrow gap between two cars, outside the specified address. This was one of the reasons the two-wheeled vehicles were the preferred mode of transport around London.

On either side of the street was a row of three-storey terraced houses, each with a basement room. Like many London streets, it looked tired and slightly shabby, but still expensive to buy — like all London property. The agent walked up the five red-brick steps and rang the doorbell twice. Appearing to be a rushed delivery-service, often got a better response than the polite single-ring approach.

The door opened to reveal a tall, lanky figure in a grey Hollister tee-shirt, floral board shorts, and bare feet. The agent took in these details quickly, before focussing on the man's face.

Confirmed.

This was the same person as in the passport photograph he'd been sent by Asif as part of the identification briefing-pack. It made his next question redundant — but he asked it anyway, out of courtesy.

"Are you Patrick Michael Harris?" asked the agent.

"Who wants to know?"

The agent opened his ID and thrust it in front of Patrick's face. Patrick Harris had never seen a MoD identity card. It certainly looked genuine to him. Genuine enough to make him nervous.

"Patrick Michael Harris?" repeated the agent, returning his credentials to his back-pocket.

"Yes," was the sheepish answer.

"We have some questions to ask you, sir. May I come in?"

"Who's the *we* that you're talking about?" asked Patrick suspiciously, looking around outside.

"You'll see shortly, sir," said the agent, in a tone clearly intended to close out that line of questions. Patrick let the man in.

"Is there a table we can use?" asked the agent.

Patrick led him through to a small dining room where a rectangular table and six chairs took up most of the space. The agent moved aside a large display of artificial flowers to clear one-half of the table.

"Please sit there while I set things up," said the agent, indicating a chair on the long-side of the table. He opened his backpack and removed two iPads from their protective sleeves, setting them up on frames, one facing Patrick, and the other facing the seat opposite, where the agent now sat. He plugged both iPads into a booster battery-pack, and then connected a small, white device, which was approximately the same size as a can of sardines. The screen on the device came to life, showing it was picking up the Vodafone 4G mobile network, with a five-bar signal strength. It also indicated that the local Wi-Fi network it created, had detected — and connected — the two iPad devices. The agent opened the Apple FaceTime program on each iPad, and waited for the link to be established. He'd deliberately remained silent while he connected the technology, which had made Patrick extremely nervous.

Finally the agent spoke. "Shortly, you will see the person who wants to ask you some questions. Please do as she asks."

The FaceTime link to Heather's iPad was made, and her face appeared on Patrick's iPad screen. The agent's saw a split-screen view of Heather and Patrick, while Heather saw a split-screen of the agent and Patrick. The agent's split screen allowed him to ensure that Patrick was correctly positioned for the interview.

The agent introduced himself to Heather, and confirmed the identity of Patrick and the address they were at. He also said the date and time aloud, and added an investigation code number, so the recorded interview could be filed appropriately.

The MoD had only recently started using this kind of questioning, but it was proving most effective and efficient on active-agent's time. To prevent the suspect from assuming they could lie to the talking-head on the iPad, the support-agent would sit behind the target's iPad, or sometimes even stand, holding it to their chest, so the suspect was aware that they were talking to two people, one of them obviously present in real-life. The support-agent had a writing pad and was making notes as the interview proceeded, and he kept a close watch on Patrick's body-language. When he felt that the suspect was not telling the truth, he made some notes on his pad. The entire situation was intended to make the subject feel nervous — which, in turn, would make it more obvious if he began to lie.

Heather had started the interview by telling Patrick they knew he was being paid regularly by the Peckham Institute, and that he was also claiming unemployment benefits. Asif had checked his bank account, and Heather listed the precise amounts he was receiving from both sources. She told him that if he didn't answer her questions truthfully, she would inform the Peckham Institute, who would stop paying him; he would have his benefit payments stopped; and as a final coup de grâce — he would be charged with benefits fraud. She told him that if he helped them with their investigation, then she might be willing to ignore whatever misdemeanours he was guilty of.

By doing this, Heather had made it clear to Patrick precisely how much they knew about him — and that there was a lot at risk if he didn't cooperate fully. She'd then opened the door-of-hope to allow him a glimpse of a happy future — but only if she was satisfied. *It was like training tigers in a circus* she imagined. The animals must have no-doubt who the master is — but that they will be rewarded nicely if they perform as requested. Heather then cracked the whip for the first time.

"How did you get involved with the Peckham Institute?"

"It was an advert on Facebook. Asking for people who could remember their dreams. It was being in some research and making extra money. I had to fill in a long online-questionnaire for them. They accepted me, and said I had to tell 'em what I dreamed about every day for seven days. They'd call me each morning — and I just said out my dreams. They paid me a hundred-quid for doing this, and if they liked what I told them — there might be more work with 'em. After the week were up they said I'd done really well, and that someone wanted to come and meet with me about doin' more work."

"What happened next?" prompted Heather firmly.

"A Welsh-guy came to see me. Gareth was his name. He went over the stuff I'd said in the questionnaire. He asked me more about what I was doing, and things like that. That's when he said he'd pay me seven-hundred quid a week. He did say that I had to stop claiming the dole-money. I guess I forgot to cancel it," he added with a clearly-insincere contriteness.

"I didn't know that the Ministry of Defence would be involved in checking dole-cheats," he added — beginning to sound more confident.

"We have a wide remit — especially when it comes to people like you," said Heather, cracking the whip for a second-time to put him back in his place. "What exactly do you have to do for this money?"

"I just report back on the dreams that I have each night. I know I'm a bit different to other people, 'cos I dream every night — and I remember them when I wake up. Most people can't do this."

"Were you given any special instructions on how to do this?"

"No, just to give as much information as I could. To separate my different dreams by giving them different numbers on the report. Not to make anything up, of course. And they said I was to write the last dream I had before I woke up, in the first position on my report-back."

"How do they contact you before you dream?"

"What do you mean?" asked Patrick, with a quizzical look on his face.

"Do they contact you daily, or weekly, to tell you what they want you to dream about?"

"They don't tell me what to dream about. They don't tell me nothin'. I just tell 'em what I dreamed about in the daily report."

"Do they get in touch with you at all?"

"Sometimes they send me an email telling me to send my dreams in on time. I over-sleep some days. Sometimes, they ask for more details about a dream, but not often."

"So you're saying they don't tell you what they want you to dream about?"

"No."

"Never?" asked Heather to get absolute confirmation on this point.

"No. They've never done that."

"How do you send them your reports?"

"By email. Which they want in by eight-thirty each morning."

"How many days a week?"

"Every day. Gareth said that's what they're paying me the money for. It takes about an hour each morning. Seven-hundred quid for seven-hours work. It's brilliant money. I'll answer any of your questions. Just don't tell 'em. Please."

"What's the email address you send your reports to?"

"I don't know off-hand, but it's on the computer."

"Give it to the agent before he leaves."

"Acknowledging that I will confirm an email-address," interjected the agent.

"What else do they get you to do?"

"Every week they tell me to delete all the emails I've sent, and to empty the deleted items folder."

"What day do they do that?"

"It's usually Wednesday."

"Agent, please forward all remaining emails onto Asif, now," said Heather, pointing her finger at the agent on her screen.

"Acknowledging I'll forward the emails to you," re-iterated the agent.

"Those are all the questions that I have — for now," said Heather. "If you don't tell the people at the Peckham Institute that we've spoken to you, I will ignore the fact you are breaking the law by claiming benefits. Is that understood?" Heather cracked the whip for the final time. *Get back in your cage*.

"Yes, thank-you," said Patrick, quietly, as Heather's head disappeared from the iPad's screen.

The first thing Patrick Harris was going to do tomorrow morning was to cancel his unemployment benefit.

Chapter 52 Tuesday 17h50

Heather was sat at her desk, confused by what the questioning of Patrick Harris had produced — or more precisely — what it *hadn't* produced. And that was the fact Patrick Harris, and presumably the other dreamers, *weren't being told what to dream about*. They simply reported-back whatever it was they dreamed of. If you had hundreds of people sending you their dreams every day, then you had a chance to detect some patterns — or commonality — *but not from just three people*. There was definitely something very unusual happening at the Peckham Institute.

"Heather, can you come over here. I think I might have something." Asif's voice broke into her thinking. She walked over to his panel of monitors.

"I looked at the most recent webpage postings and I've found a pattern. Look," he said, highlighting the last-four uploaded webpages.

Domain name: HTTP://WWW.PECKHAMINSTITUTE.ORG.UK/

WEBPAGE ADDRESS	**UPLOAD DATE / TIME**	
TGGEG-VCUUKEMGT-2	10-JUL-2014	03:14:15
SFFDF-UBTTJDLFS-1	11-JUL-2014	15:14:15
UHHFH-WDVVLFNHU-3	13-JUL-2014	03:14:15
VIIGI-XEWWMGOIV-4	14-JUL-2014	15:14:15

"Look at the first five-letters of each of the webpage addresses," he said, pointing to the four sets of letters on one of his monitors.

TGGEG SFFDF UHHFH VIIGI.

"There's a first-letter, a double second-letter, a third different-letter, followed by a single repeat of the second-letter. Can you see the pattern is the same for each one?"

"Okay," replied Heather.

"Now look at the second string of characters in each address," he said, bringing up a new display on the screen.

VCUUKEMGT UBTTJDLFS WDVVLFNHU XEWWMGOIV

"These also have identical character strings making them up. See how the third- and fourth-letters in each are the same?"

"Yes."

"Apart from the numeral in the last-place, I think that these addresses are all saying the same thing, except that they are coded differently."

"Go on."

"Now, let's put the webpage list in a different order. Not arranged by the upload date, but instead, ordered by the final-digit in the webpage address." He cut and pasted the lines of text into the revised order. "This is what we get."

Domain name: HTTP://WWW.PECKHAMINSTITUTE.ORG.UK/

WEBPAGE ADDRESS	**UPLOAD DATE / TIME**	
SFFDF-UBTTJDLFS-1	11-JUL-2014	15:14:15
TGGEG-VCUUKEMGT-2	10-JUL-2014	03:14:15
UHHFH-WDVVLFNHU-3	13-JUL-2014	03:14:15
VIIGI-XEWWMGOIV-4	14-JUL-2014	15:14:15

"Do you notice anything with the first-letter of each webpage address?" he asked Heather.

"S-T-U-V. It's in alphabetical order."

"Not just the first-letter — all the letters. The double second-letters go F-G-H-I and the fourth-letters go D-E-F-G. It's the same for all the other letters in the address."

"So what do they mean?"

"This was as far as I got when I called you over. I'd got stuck. But explaining it has given me a new insight."

"What's that?"

"If the number at the end of the address represents the place in a sequence, I wonder what position zero would be?"

"You mean, the one before the first address in the list shown here?" clarified Heather

"Yeah."

"Let's try it."

Asif copied the first address on the list to a different screen

S F F D F – U B T T J D L F S – 1

"Now, let's take the letter that comes *one-before* each of the letters here," said Asif.

Heather started to work them out. "The letter before S is R. The letter before F is E, so that's a double E."

Asif typed the characters on the screen as Heather spoke. Well before Heather had finished the task, they both recognised what was appearing on the screen:

REECE–TASSICKER–0

"Now, that's interesting," declared Heather.

"And I understand the code," said Asif. "The number at the end of the webpage-name indicates the number of characters that the alphabet has been shifted along."

"Why would they do that?" asked Heather.

"It's a very simple code to break, so it appears it's not designed to hide — it's probably more about confusion." Asif paused, sitting back in his chair, his hands behind his head. He stared at the list of webpage addresses on his screens. After a few moments he said, "I think it might be to confuse the search engines, so they don't reference and index the site. They just regard it as rubbish, as it doesn't match any known search terms."

"That could make sense," said Heather. "So what about the rest of the pages? What do they say?"

"Shall we work a few out now?" suggested Asif.

"Okay."

Asif's fingers rattled over the keyboard at speed as he copied some of the webpage details across to a different monitor. After a few minutes, he and Heather had converted the first eight addresses.

WEBPAGE ADDRESS	**REAL NAME**
EOIG-2	CMGE
PFTY-1	OESX
GEX-4	CAT
MQM-3	JNJ
QCZJ-1	PBYI
KW-4	GS
CXA-2	AVY
NDE-1	MCD

"What do these mean?" asked Heather.

"No idea," said Asif. "They look like random sets of letters."

“I somehow doubt that.”

“Me too. Let me finish decoding the full-list and we’ll look at it together.”

At that moment Heather’s phone rang. It was the call from Jepson at Selfridges. After a brief-dialogue, Heather ended the call.

“Who was that?” asked Asif, noticing the perplexed look on Heather’s face.

“That was Selfridges. They called to tell me to fuck off.”

“They are renowned for delivering great customer service you know.”

“I’m going to the lobby. It appears our Mister Tassicker will be returning imminently.”

“He missed his presentation,” pointed out Asif.

“I noticed.”

“Were you concerned?”

“Too busy with other things to be concerned — but don’t tell him that.” She took a moment to think. “I’ll bring him in here to show him what you’ve found.”

“His reaction to that should be interesting,” said Asif.

Chapter 53 Tuesday 18h09

Heather was standing in the hotel lobby, her arms folded, waiting for Reece to return. He came in at speed, leaving the revolving doors spinning wildly behind him.

"You missed your presentation," said Heather loudly, to get his attention.

"My presentation! Don't you want to know where I've been?"

"Apparently you were with Selfridges' security department. Fine gentlemen I'm sure. Especially as they work for a store that's renowned for delivering great customer service."

"Don't mention customer-fucking-service to me," said Reece, looking around as though he were searching for someone to punch.

"I see you also picked up some of their choice terminology while you were over there," she added.

"Doesn't this concern you?"

"A little," she lied. "Remember, I'm not your babysitter. Anyway, you're back now — and seemingly fine." She put her hand on his arm to calm him.

"This conference is my focus. Now, you haven't given your lecture, and you didn't announce the dream website launch. Maybe that's what this Selfridges security incident was about."

"You knew this was going to happen?"

"No. But we might have just worked it out."

"Worked what out?" said Reece, his agitation now mixed with curiosity.

"Calm down," said Heather, taking his arm and guiding him in the direction of her office. "We need your help to figure out what's going on."

"What do you mean?"

"Do you know the name Gareth Jones, or had any dealings with the Peckham Institute?"

"Never heard of either. Why?"

"You'll see."

Heather hadn't been the only person in the lobby waiting for Reece to return. After Andre had made the call to Jepson, and had seen the security team arrive at the customer service corridor, he'd gone back to the hotel. Andre was sure that when Reece was released by the Selfridges security people, he'd head straight back to the hotel, and he'd been in the lobby since then, waiting. He needed to be sure that Reece didn't return too-early, and was still able to deliver his presentation and announce the dream website.

Andre saw Reece barrel through the revolving door and talk with the conference director. He discretely repositioned himself behind a pillar, closer to them. This allowed him to overhear their discussion; particularly when Heather had asked Reece what he knew about Gareth Jones and the Peckham Institute. Andre watched them head back towards the conference area, before he quickly left the hotel. He realised they now had a severe problem.

But Andre was skilled in solving severe problems. He'd solved the problems with those two women a few weeks ago. *Permanently.*

Chapter 54 Tuesday 18h15

As Heather and Reece walked into her office, Asif called-out that he'd decoded the full-list of webpage addresses.

"You'll want to see this," said Heather, guiding Reece towards Asif's desk. "But first, I need to explain some things to you." She gave Reece an explanation of the Peckham Institute and their dreamers, Somnium Trading and its spectacular trading successes, the blank webpages on the Institute's website, and how they had been crudely coded.

"Now listen," said Heather, raising a finger to make sure Reece was looking at her. "You're going to see your name up there. Don't be alarmed." She then pointed him toward one of Asif's monitors.

"On the left is the webpage address as it was created on the website, and on the right is the decoded list."

Domain name: HTTP://WWW.PECKHAMINSTITUTE.ORG.UK/

WEBPAGE ADDRESS	**REAL NAME**
EOIG-2	CMGE
PFTY-1	OESX
GEX-4	CAT
MQM-3	JNJ
QCZJ-1	PBYI
KW-4	GS
CXA-2	AVY
NDE-1	MCD
VL-3	SI
TXJ-1	SWI
XWPE-4	TSLA
XPVX-2	VNTV
FHO-1	EGN
EEP-4	AAL
HWQ-3	ETN
FWID-1	EVHC
PBT-1	OAS
LVLV-3	ISIS
ZFMQ-1	YELP
SVGP-4	ORCL
JRRJ-3	GOOG
VYZ-2	TWX
FSRMXE-EYVIPME-QMPERS-4	BONITA AURELIA MILANO
CNGZCPFTC-LGUUKEC-HQTF-2	ALEXANDRA JESSICA FORD
PD-3	MA
EEO-3	BBL
TTE-2	RRC
YPN-1	XOM
XSV-3	UPS
TGGEG-VCUUKEMGT-2	REECE TASSICKER

SFFDF-UBTTJDLFS-1	REECE TASSICKER
UHHFH-WDVVLFNHU-3	REECE TASSICKER
VIIGI-XEWWMGOIV-4	REECE TASSICKER

Reece scanned the list and paused, staring at his name repeated four times at the bottom of the list. Before he could say anything, Heather spoke.

"Asif, those names in the middle. Those are the names of the two multiple-dreamers that died a few weeks ago. What dates were those two webpages uploaded?"

"I'm ahead of you with that. Those two pages were uploaded on the seventh and ninth of June — one day before each of the women died," said Asif.

"Can I just clarify something here," asked Reece. "This Peckham Institute creates a webpage called Bonita Aurelia Milano, and the next day she dies."

"Under suspicious circumstances," added Heather.

"And then soon after, they put up another new webpage called Alexandra Jessica Ford, and the following-day *she* also happens to die," said Reece, shifting uncomfortably on his feet.

"Under suspicious circumstances," added Heather yet again.

"And just below that my name appears four times!"

"Please stay calm," said Heather.

"Do you have a middle name?" asked Asif.

"No, why?"

"Just curious to see if they'd included your full name or not. Obviously they did," said Asif.

"Reece, you remember I told you we knew about the two other multiple-dreamers that you were conversing with online?" said Heather.

"Yes."

"Bonita Milano died on the eighth of June from a hit-and-run accident. Her online username was Bonita1974, Alex Ford died two-days later from an assault in her home, and her username was SweetDreamer. The Peckham Institute put up a new webpage on their website the day before each of them died, with nothing on it but their full-name in the webpage address."

"Then why is my name up there four times?" asked Reece, pointing to the screen.

"Because they put up a blank-page with your name on. Four times."

"Are you saying they've tried to kill me four times?" asked Reece.

"I doubt it," said Heather, "because you're still alive. Whoever is doing this seems very effective."

"So why am I a webpage-star four times over?"

"Strange things happened to you recently, didn't they?" she asked.

Reece nodded.

"Tell me precisely when they happened," said Heather. "Asif, see if these match-up with the webpage-upload dates."

"There was the first Post-it note in the copy of the Professor's book. I bought it on Friday at about six in the evening."

"Friday was the eleventh of July," said Heather. "Continue."

"Then I got the second copy of the book with a Post-it note in at about nine o'clock Sunday morning. Which was followed by the text at breakfast on Monday around eight, saying I'd receive a call just before I did."

"And then there was this afternoon's incident in Selfridges," added Heather.

"Yes," confirmed Reece.

Asif had been typing to capture Reece's activities. "Here's the summary I've created," he said, pointing to his middle monitor.

Domain name: HTTP://WWW.PECKHAMINSTITUTE.ORG.UK/

WEBPAGE ADDRESS	UPLOAD DATE/TIME		EVENT
REECE TASSICKER 2	10-JUL	03:14:15	Post-it #1 in book 18h00 11th July
REECE TASSICKER 1	11-JUL	15:14:15	Post-it #2 in book 09h00 13th July
REECE TASSICKER 3	13-JUL	03:14:15	Text message 08h00 14th July
REECE TASSICKER 4	14-JUL	15:14:15	Detained Selfridges 15h00 15th July

"They post four webpages with your name on, and shortly afterwards something peculiar happens to you. The first three were clear warnings to you about not going ahead with your dream website plans. And today's event obviously prevented you from giving your presentation — where you were going to announce it," summarised Asif.

"They killed those two women after one webpage was posted. So why haven't they killed you after four?" Heather wondered aloud.

Reece stared at her, unnerved by the matter-of-fact tone she used while pondering his seemingly inconsiderate lack-of-death.

“Asif, let’s look at the webpage-listings that you decoded. Delete the ones with people’s names on. We’ll focus on what’s left,” said Heather. Moments later, the revised list appeared on a monitor.

Domain name: HTTP://WWW.PECKHAMINSTITUTE.ORG.UK/

WEBPAGE ADDRESS	**REAL NAME**
EOIG-2	CMGE
PFTY-1	OESX
GEX-4	CAT
MQM-3	JNJ
QCZJ-1	PBYI
KW-4	GS
CXA-2	AVY
NDE-1	MCD
VL-3	SI
TXJ-1	SWI
XWPE-4	TSLA
XPVX-2	VNTV
FHO-1	EGN
EEP-4	AAL
HWQ-3	ETN
FWID-1	EVHC
PBT-1	OAS
LVLV-3	ISIS
ZFMQ-1	YELP
SVGP-4	ORCL
JRRJ-3	GOOG
VYZ-2	TWX
PD-3	MA
EEO-3	BBL
TTE-2	RRC
YPN-1	XOM
XSV-3	UPS

“Do these short codes mean anything to you?” asked Heather.

Reece quickly skimmed the list. “There’s UPS at the bottom which may mean United Parcel Service. You see their brown delivery vans everywhere. Higher up is YELP. That’s an online search engine that people use to find local services.”

He reached the top of the list and paused. *Nothing*. His eyes started down the list of codes again, as his mind searched for any connections. He was over halfway through — and nothing was obvious. Reece then switched his mind into an associative-mode, telling himself to say the first-word that the letters brought to mind. OAS and ISIS formed OASIS. But that was over two codes, so didn’t work. Then YELP. That was a word on its own. Then ORCL which formed the word ORACLE in his mind. Then GOOG, which instantly formed GOOGLE.

"I wonder if these are companies," he said aloud. "I think GOOG is the stock-market abbreviation code for Google. Why not Google these codes to see if there are more stock-market abbreviations in the list?"

Asif opened a browser-window, and entered the CMGE code into a Google search box. The first result showed it was the Nasdaq stock-code for China Mobile Games and Entertainment Group Limited. Asif then entered OESX, which turned out to be the Nasdaq code for Orion Energy Systems Incorporated. The next code, CAT, was the New York Stock Exchange code for Caterpillar Incorporated.

"I'll check the rest out, but I think Reece is right. These could all be stock-codes," said Asif.

Reece pointed at an earlier list of webpages that was still visible on one of Asif's lap-top screens.

"Can I see that detailed list of the webpage addresses?" asked Reece. Asif glanced at Heather, who surreptitiously nodded her approval.

Domain name: HTTP://WWW.PECKHAMINSTITUTE.ORG.UK/

WEBPAGE ADDRESS	**UPLOAD DATE / TIME**	
EOIG-2	07-JAN-2014	03:14:15
PFTY-1	14-JAN-2014	03:14:15
GEX-4	21-JAN-2014	03:14:15
MQM-3	28-JAN-2014	03:14:15
QCZJ-1	04-FEB-2014	03:14:15
KW-4	11-FEB-2014	03:14:15
CXA-2	18-FEB-2014	03:14:15
NDE-1	25-FEB-2014	03:14:15
VL-3	04-MAR-2014	03:14:15
TXJ-1	11-MAR-2014	03:14:15
XWPE-4	18-MAR-2014	03:14:15
XPVX-2	25-MAR-2014	03:14:15
FHO-1	01-APR-2014	03:14:15
EEP-4	08-APR-2014	03:14:15
HWQ-3	15-APR-2014	03:14:15
FWID-1	22-APR-2014	03:14:15
PBT-1	29-APR-2014	03:14:15
LVLV-3	06-MAY-2014	03:14:15
ZFMQ-1	13-MAY-2014	03:14:15
SVGP-4	20-MAY-2014	03:14:15
JRRJ-3	27-MAY-2014	03:14:15
VYZ-2	03-JUN-2014	03:14:15
FSRMXE-EYVIPME-QMPERS-4	07-JUN-2014	03:14:15
CNGZCPFTC-LGUUKEC-HQTF-2	09-JUN-2014	03:14:15
PD-3	10-JUN-2014	03:14:15
EEO-3	17-JUN-2014	03:14:15
TTE-2	24-JUN-2014	03:14:15
YPN-1	01-JUL-2014	03:14:15

XSV-3	08-JUL-2014	03:14:15
TGGEG-VCUUKEMGT-2	10-JUL-2014	03:14:15
SFFDF-UBTTJDLFS-1	11-JUL-2014	15:14:15
UHHFH-WDVVLFNHU-3	13-JUL-2014	03:14:15
VIIGI-XEWWMGOIV-4	14-JUL-2014	15:14:15

Reece studied it. "The shorter page addresses, which are likely to be stock-codes, seem to be put up exactly one-week apart. The other ones, which are the womens' and my name, don't follow the same pattern. Maybe the names are put up when something will happen."

"What do you mean?" asked Heather.

"Well, soon after these name pages are posted up, then a strange event happens. Maybe the pages are put up as a warning that something will happen to a person — with that name — the next day," replied Reece.

"Another view," said Heather, "is that these pages going up, actually causes something to happen to that person. If they posted a page called BONITA AURELIA MILANO because something was about to happen to her, wouldn't it make sense to try to help her? Either directly, or by reporting something to the authorities?"

"It shouldn't be hard. There can't be many people in the UK called Bonita Aurelia Milano," added Asif.

"My feeling is that the posting of a webpage address is malevolent, rather than benevolent, in nature," decided Heather.

"Why is the time for most of them in the early-hours of the morning? And why would someone be up posting a new webpage at that time?" asked Reece, trying a fresh thinking approach.

"It's probably pre-set," replied Asif. "The time is the exact-same to the second. If you tried to do that manually, you probably couldn't press the enter key at precisely the right moment. Then there are often system delays which would make the times differ by a few seconds. The webpage is probably created earlier, and simply scheduled to go-live around quarter-past-three in the morning."

"Even those scheduled for the afternoon, still go live at around quarter-past-three," added Reece.

"But why schedule them for *that specific time*, and not quarter-past-three on the dot?" asked Heather.

On the dot.

A single, giant-pulse surged through Reece's head. His personality seemed to temporarily exit his body, which gave him a peculiar detached feeling from reality. He knew a connection was about to be made.

On the dot. On the dot. On the dot.

He visualised a dot.

That's too small — make it bigger.

The dot instantly grew in size to be a giant, black circle.

The words *on-the-dot* circled around and around this giant dot.

Around and around in circles.

Circles. Circles. Circles.

What's the connection to a circle?

The word pi came into his mind from the lecture on varying constants.

"That time is pi!" he blurted out, not realising what he'd said.

"What?" asked Heather.

"The go-live time is 3:14:15 either in the morning or in the afternoon. The value of pi — the ratio of the diameter of a circle to its circumference — is 3.1415 to four decimal-places," he explained.

"What's a circle got to do with this?" she asked.

"Not sure. But maybe it's a special time for some reason."

"These webpage names are put up in code," said Asif slowly. He was clearly thinking through his logic as he spoke. "It's a simple code, with the key to deciphering it included in the webpage name."

"Go on," prompted Heather.

"We know there's no content on the pages, so the content has to be the name of the webpage. So what if the pages are always put up at a specific time to act as some kind of identifier to someone?"

"You mean that if someone were looking out for messages through the new-pages, they would only need to look twice-a-day. They wouldn't have to be continuously checking the website?" asked Reece.

"Yes," answered Asif.

"But who is the message for? We know it's not the dreamers," queried Heather.

Even while he had been talking with them, Asif's fingers had been rattling away on the laptop's keyboard.

"It turns out that all those short webpage names are American stock-codes," he said.

There was silence as they each thought of the implications of this information.

Reece broke the silence. "Can you check if anything unusual happened with those companies *after* the date their code appeared on the website," suggested Reece.

"Asif, get in touch with that business analyst at Cheltenham. The one who helped you understand the derivatives trading. Give him the list of these stock-codes, and get him to see if Somnium Trading made any trades in those stocks around the time of the webpage postings," directed Heather.

"And another thing," she added. "The Peckham Institute's dreamers say they are told to submit their dreams every morning without fail, right?"

"Yes."

"Get the inbound emails to Gareth Jones' email address for the mornings *after* a webpage has been posted." She paused. "And I also want the outbound emails from him for those mornings too." She paused again. "And get me any text messages he sent too."

"I'm on it," said Asif, as his fingers raced over the keyboard.

"Can you really do all that?" asked Reece with disbelief.

"Did you hear about operation Tempora in mid-2013? It was exposed by that whistle-blower Edward Snowden," replied Heather.

"That was where the Government was accused of snooping on people's phone-calls and emails wasn't it?"

"It isn't the Government doing it. It's us. Through our GCHQ facility. Asif, how long will it take you to get that information?"

"About thirty-minutes," replied Asif.

"Bloody hell!" said Reece.

"I'll bet you're glad that we do it now, aren't you?" said Heather, giving Reece a smug smile.

"I'll withhold judgement on that for now," he replied.

"That was really-useful — the way you think about things differently — so thanks. If anything else comes up, I'll let you know."

"I'll be in my room," said Reece, as he headed for the door.

It was barely thirty-minutes later that the phone rang in Reece's room. It was Heather.

"Asif has just received the feedback from GCHQ, and he says it'll be useful to share it with you too."

"What does it say?"

"Don't know. I've been in a meeting with the conference organisers and I'm heading back to my office now," said Heather.

"But keep a very open mind around what you might hear," she added.

Chapter 55 Tuesday 19h05

Asif had just finished his second read-through of the long email he'd received from GCHQ, when Heather and Reece walked into the room.

"Heather, I've got the feedback from the business analyst. And it contains a big surprise," he said.

"Good work. What's the surprise?"

"He looked for buying patterns for the stock-codes I sent through. For some of the shares, Somnium Trading bought a ninety-day option on the day after the page went live. That means the deal is settled out ninety-days later. Some of these were call-options — which means you believe the share is going to rise in value, while some were put-options, which you take if you expect the share is going to fall in value."

"And?"

"And when Somnium bought one of these call- or put-options, the share price moved either up-or-down significantly over the next ninety-day period. Every time they settled, they made a big profit."

"Every time?" asked Heather.

"Every time," replied Asif. "The analyst thought this unusual too. So he checked the performance of the other shares on the list — the ones that Somnium *didn't buy* — to see what happened to those over the next ninety-days."

"And?"

"They didn't change much in value. When you are trading call- and put-options you need big changes in the value of the share to make money."

"Peckham got it right every time?"

"Yeah. Somnium Trading only buys ninety-day options, so the ones bought within the last ninety-days — since mid-April — are still live. The analyst looked at those too. The ones they bought appear to be moving in the right direction for them."

"How much money has he made?" asked Reece.

"There are twenty-seven stock-codes listed in the webpages for this year. Fifteen are older than ninety-days. Of those fifteen share-codes, Somnium bought options on nine of them. Each of these nine paid out between seventeen and fifty-eight million pounds. The figures we found out earlier"

"How much in total?" asked Heather.

“Somnium made just over £317-million for this year to-date. There are another seven trades live at the moment, and as the analyst said, these are moving in the right direction for big profits too”.

“That’s impressive. Too impressive. Do the dreamers tell him what’s going to happen to the shares?” asked Heather.

“I looked at the emails from the dreamers, to Gareth Jones, on the morning after a stock-code webpage was put up. The emails the dreamers send-in are strange — but they are dreams after all. Sometimes it was about looking down over things from a high place, like on a mountain or from a church spire. One reported floating on a cloud high above the Swiss Alps and looking down into the valleys — like the start of the Sound of Music film. Another dream was about being scared at having to fix a broken weather vane on top of a church spire. Another of being a hawk and hovering for an exceptionally long-time, waiting for an animal to move — which turned out to be a battery-operated rabbit. But generally being high-up or going-up. After this kind of feedback is when Somnium buy a call-option betting that the share will rise in value.”

“Anything else?” prompted Heather.

“It’s similar for the dreams reported before Somnium buy a put-option — where they expect the share price to fall. The dreams then are of diving to the bottom of the ocean in some kind of strange submarine, being on a roller-coaster that starts going downhill and never stops, or being in an elevator that only has down-buttons and no up-buttons. The dream content is really peculiar, but I imagine if you read these dreams every day, and from the same people, you start to make sense of what’s in them. Especially if you’re only looking for an up-or-down indication.”

“What happens after the dreams have been received — and presumably analysed — by Jones?”

“There are no immediate outbound emails of relevance. However, he does send a text message from his phone with either the word UP or DOWN as the message content. He sends this to an unregistered phone, so we can’t trace ownership.”

“What about the dreams on the other days when there are no texts sent by Jones?”

“The dreams on those days seem to be a mix of random material. I think that Jones looks for a pattern in the dreams that indicates a rising or a falling. Based on that, he sends his up-down text. If he doesn’t see a pattern, he doesn’t send a text. On those days Somnium don’t make a trade.”

"Let's strip this back to basics," said Heather. "Once a week the Peckham Institute post a new, blank webpage at exactly pi time, with a specific US share coded into the address. The dreamers don't know about this. The next morning they feedback their dreams as usual. If the dreams give a clear picture of an upward or downward-movement, then Gareth Jones sends a message to an unknown mobile phone telling someone — presumably at Somnium Trading — to buy the appropriate up-or-down ninety-day option. The share price then moves significantly in the correct direction, and ninety-days later they end up making a huge profit."

"That's it," confirmed Asif. "Sounds like the perfect model for making big money."

"You're seriously suggesting that the dreamers are dreaming the future movement of a share price?" asked Reece incredulously.

"It looks that way," replied Heather. Reece was again jarred by the casual manner in which Heather could suggest such a thing — and not feel embarrassed by her seemingly outrageous comment.

"Somnium Trading don't have any registered employees and Paul Peckham is the sole owner of the company. I bet the text that Jones sends, goes to Paul Peckham. He then makes the trade through the company," continued Heather.

"After they've bought the option, do you think they actively manipulate the market to make the share move in the correct direction — or do they just sit-back and wait — because they know what's going to happen?"

"Good point, Asif." Heather thought for a moment. "Reece?"

"I imagine it's hard to influence the stock market to move a share's price significantly, just once, never mind doing it repeatedly. I think it more likely that they know what's going to happen — so they just buy the option and wait," said Reece.

"We're all missing a key point here," said Asif.

"What's that?"

"The dreamers aren't told what they are dreaming about. Only Jones knows their dreams are about the specific-share posted in their webpage the previous day."

"Mmmm. That's baffling isn't it?" agreed Heather.

"Should we bring Jones in for questioning?" asked Asif.

"For what reason? Is he doing anything illegal here? I don't think predicting the future is illegal — or else we'd have jails full of astrologers, gypsy fortune-tellers and investment advisors. It's beyond the realms of being normal — but that's not a crime."

"They seem to be involved in the deaths of those two women," pointed out Asif.

"Yes, but that's not our domain. Getting the police involved now may prevent us from understanding what's going on here. We'll inform them later. At the moment, this entire dreaming operation appears to be undertaken by Paul Peckham for self-gain."

"Do you have a remit to be getting involved here if someone has found a way to make money? It doesn't sound like it's illegal," pointed out Reece.

"True, but what if he — or others — start doing this for purposes that put national security at risk. That's the concern for us, and it's why we set up this conference — to try and drive some of these people into the open."

"It's certainly worked," said Asif. "What do we do next?"

"Where are Jones and his false-name colleague right now?"

Asif checked the Contactor system. "They are in their rooms, and it looks like they've been there for the past hour or so."

"If they still haven't moved in thirty-minutes, get the hotel to send housekeeping in to turn down their beds — to check on them. For now, we wait and watch."

"Reece, would you excuse us please? We've got things to do." Heather stood, and opened the door for him. "I hope you found that illuminating," she said as he left.

"Yes, thanks," said Reece. The incredulous story he'd just heard was spinning around his mind at such a rate, that he felt almost delirious.

As the door closed, Asif said "he seemed to handle that reasonably well."

"I'm not too sure," replied Heather.

"What do you want me to do now?" asked Asif.

"That's the reason I asked him to leave. I'd like you to review the dreamer's feedback emails for the times they posted webpage addresses with his name in," said Heather. "Those should be interesting dreams."

Chapter 56 Tuesday 19h45

After overhearing the conversation between Reece and Heather, Andre had immediately exited the hotel. He was already dialling Gareth's number as he walked through the revolving door. Dodging a black taxi-cab, he crossed the road and stood on the opposite pavement, where no-one could overhear his conversation.

"Gareth, we need to leave. Something's gone wrong."

"What?"

"They've linked what's happening with Tassicker to us. Get out of the hotel now. Take your computer, phone and any important documents. But don't take your suitcase, you'll look suspicious leaving without checking-out. Turn right outside the hotel, walk down to Oxford Street and meet me on the corner there. Act normally — and don't run at any time, otherwise you'll stand out, understand?"

"Yes, but..."

"I'll explain when I see you." Andre ended the call, went back inside the hotel and up to his room. He was registered under a false name, but he still needed to ensure nothing of importance was left behind. He unclipped the Contactor device from his belt, put it on the bedside-table, and left.

Four-minutes later, he and Gareth were in a black-cab heading south. Gareth had wanted to know what happened, but Andre motioned him to be silent. The microphone system within the cab that enabled the driver to communicate with the passengers, also allowed him to listen-in to what they were saying.

"Drop us off here," said Andre to the taxi-driver. He'd seen the red-and-white frontage of a Café Rouge, and decided that was a convenient place for them to make their plans.

Once they were seated, and had placed their drinks order, Andre spoke.

"I was watching the hotel foyer when Tassicker returned. He missed his lecture and so didn't announce the website. That part worked well."

"I know. They had another speaker in his place. So what's the problem?"

"As he came in, the conference director was waiting for him. She asked if he knew anything about you and the Institute."

"How did they make the connection between Tassicker and us?"

"Don't know. What concerns me is why a conference director would be asking a question like that," said Andre.

"That's strange. But he didn't announce the website, so the delaying tactic worked fi-ne," said Gareth.

"Given that someone's connected us to him, we may need to do more than just delay him," said Andre.

"What do you mean?"

"Termination," said Andre.

"But after those two women, I thought we decided against doing that again. It's too-much of an unknown risk for the future."

"I know. I'll have to ask the chief."

"What if we hurt him in some way? That might put him off his dream website for good."

"I'd considered that — but not after the way I heard that conference director talking to him. Something's not right there. We may need to take action against her as well. I'd better make the call."

Andre went outside, and walked a short distance away from the entrance to make his call.

"Paul, it's Andre. We appear to have a problem."

It was a brief call. Andre went back inside the restaurant and sat next to Gareth so he could speak quietly.

"The chief wants us to terminate Tassicker as a matter of urgency. I'll need a time and location for him tomorrow. We can't go back to the Churchill, so we'd better find a hotel around here."

"Once we're in a hotel, I'll set up the webpage," replied Gareth, patting his laptop. "The morning deadline is hours away — there's no hurry."

The tone of the conversation changed.

"We might as well get something to eat," said Gareth, waving his hand to attract the waiter's attention. They selected their meals from the chalkboard menu on the wall. The waiter took their order and left.

"What's happening with the latest cycle?" asked Andre.

"It was Eaton Corporation. The option closed out yesterday. It was well-up."

"Then let's have another drink to celebrate." Andre motioned the waiter over, and ordered two more beers.

Paul Peckham had put Gareth and Andre on a bonus-scheme to motivate them. Every time one of Somnium Trading's investments closed out *in the money*, they each received a £250,000 bonus paid into a Swiss bank account. With the dreamers' input, Somnium Trading's investments were doing staggeringly well.

The celebration drink was certainly justified. Gareth and Andre had each made £2,250,000 in bonuses so far this year — including this latest success.

Chapter 57 Tuesday 19h35

As Reece left Heather's office, and the door closed behind him, he realised his world had changed. Back inside the room, he, Heather and Asif had been discussing how a peculiar website page could make specific individuals have dreams that would predict the future.

And that had seemed like a normal topic of conversation.

Now, in the corridor — just the thickness of a door away — it all seemed so surreal and distant.

It was like walking out of a cinema part-way through a movie. Inside the darkened-auditorium, you were engulfed in the action, noise and visuals of the movie, but as the door closed behind you, and the soundtrack faded, you found yourself in a quiet corridor with a snack-vending area, where people waited for things to happen. In a cinema, you knew that through the doors behind you, it was just a movie showing, that could stretch reality in any-way that the director deemed most likely to win an Oscar.

The room that Reece had just left seemed like a science-fiction movie scene — but it was real. And inside were two people, trying to understand how that reality was happening. If this were a movie, Heather and Asif would be the stars. *A conference director and a technician are today's super-heroes* thought Reece, as he walked along the corridor.

He was mentally perplexed by the revelations of this new reality he'd just been exposed to. But at the more-basic level, he was also feeling hungry, thirsty and physically-drained by the exploits of today. He considered the restaurant as his next destination, but instead found himself heading for the elevators, and going back to his room.

He needed some dwell-time.

He'd ordered steak, frites, steamed vegies, a half-bottle of Merlot from the room-service menu — along with a green-peppercorn sauce for his steak. He wasn't going to spend the rest of his life mentally scarred by the vision of Professor Bartlett at lunch. In silence, he sat at the table in his room, eating his meal.

Time alone to reflect on things.

He listened closely to the sounds he could hear. The squeaky-scrape of his knife on the plate as he cut a small piece of the steak. The gentle tap of the fork as he speared the separated morsel. The juicy chewing-sounds of the food being crushed between his teeth, as the combined flavours of the steak and peppercorns were released into his mouth.

Bliss.

As he savoured the flavours, a strange thought went through his mind. Reece imagined his ancestral bloodline stretching back through time; through troubles and strife; warfare and disease; plagues and pestilence. Back through the middle-ages, dark-ages and bronze-age. Through the prehistoric times and the times of the distant ape-ancestors. And on, even before them — through the variety of weird-and-wonderful creatures that were his fore-fathers — all the way back to the era of the pond scum. Every one of those descendants had overcome tremendous odds, and survived countless, life-threatening situations to enable him, Reece Tassicker, to be where he was today — *sat in a hotel room eating steak with a green-peppercorn sauce.*

In the silence, he paid a mental tribute to their unyielding survival capabilities and their unrelenting desire to endure and procreate. It was a most-sobering thought to consider what those countless-generations had gone through, just so he could be the man he was. He emptied the remainder of the bottle of Merlot into his glass and raised it in a silent-toast to them.

If you were to believe the newspapers, then within a couple of generations we would either choke, poison, drown or starve ourselves to death due to the many, and imminent, catastrophe's we were bringing down upon ourselves. On the other hand, this might not happen — and life could continue for millions of years into the future.

Reece had no children. He wasn't in a relationship, so was unlikely to be having any in the near-future either. When he thought back over his line of almost-infinite descendants, he realised that if things changed for him from a family-perspective, he could easily be the springboard for twenty-thousand generations of his descendants. At some point in the distant future, would one of them ever look-back and consider the hardships he'd gone through in his life — so they could be doing whatever it was they would be doing — half-a-million years from now?

He thought about the Delicate Force, and how it had probably guided the very-existence of his descendants. It was here, now, *in this hotel room.* In whatever form it took. *Ready to assist mankind in our advancement into the future.*

The learnings of Monday had turned Reece's perspective on life-and-reality upside-down. What had transpired today made him feel that his head had turned inside-out as well. *People were having dreams about what he, Reece Tassicker, would be doing the next day.* It felt that the activities of his mind were no longer happening in the privacy of his own skull, but were visible to the outside world. The events of the last two-days had shocked his thinking so much — it felt like he was wearing his brain as a hat on an icy-cold day.

He took another mouthful of steak. He smiled to himself as he thought of DD's comment about God cocking it up by leaving his fingerprints all over the universe.

The anomalies are the fingerprints.

It's the irrefutably-hard evidence.

The Council wanted in on the thinking action. He let them take over for a while.

It's a deliberate trail of fingerprints.

Acting as a guide.

But taking you from-where and to-where?

From the past into the future.

Are we meant to follow the path?

Many will follow it.

Some might be involved in making the path.

Way-finders?

Could be.

But how will you know which is the right-way forward?

Maybe it doesn't matter.

What do you mean?

Possibly there are thousands or millions of ways forward.

It isn't about finding the right path.

Isn't it?

No. It's about forging your own path.

Yes!

Perhaps it's the fact that you are moving-forward that's important.

There will be many who will just stand still.

If you stand still, you can't stand out.

True.

So if you stand out, that's the proof you aren't standing still?

Yes.

By recognising that you stand out, that's the proof that you have moved forward.

Interesting thought.

How would we know we are moving forward?

People rarely change for the worse — it's usually for the better.

So any change is good change?

Yes. Just let the Delicate Force guide you.

Can we use it to help us to move forward?

That's what it's been doing for an eternity, isn't it?

True.

But we don't understand how it works.

Do we know how a television works?

No.

But we still watch it and enjoy the programmes.

Valid point.

Science will shoot it down.

What's that new-phrase we've heard recently that describes charity organisations?

Not-for-profit?

No, that's the old term.

Beyond profit?

That's right.

It's a good term.

And that's what the Delicate Force is.

I don't understand.

The Delicate Force is beyond science.

Not for the feint-hearted.

Only for the strong-of-mind.

A loud explosion startled Reece from his thinking.

He rushed to the window just in time to see a bloom of fireworks fading in the night-sky. He saw the trails as four new fireworks flew up into the air and exploded in huge-spheres of coloured pinpoints of light. They looked remarkably like four giant-brains expanding in the sky before fading into darkness.

A loud bang. A short delay. And a huge multi-coloured brain appeared in the sky, again fading into nothing.

Then another. Then four more.

The aerial-brains that materialised in the sky mesmerised Reece. The display continued for many-minutes, before a final crescendo of enormous-booms and staccato-crackles accompanied a myriad of explosive births of brains-within-brains.

Then silence.

Nothing.

In the quiet-emptiness, Reece felt a pulse in his mind, followed by a gentle-disconnectedness. He recognised an idea was forming. Reece stood perfectly-still, letting his mind explore this new connection.

The fireworks were like flares going off.

Distress-flares fired into the sky.

Hanging there, in the hope that someone would see them.

To get someone's attention.

Like a signal.

A signal?

This is what a signal is.

It's like a signal-flare standing out in the nothingness.

But a signal of what?

It doesn't matter. The signal is simply to get your attention.

Your attention of what, though?

You're missing the point.

There aren't different distress flares for different situations.

No! There are just distress flares.

You set one off to get someone's attention.

When others come to you, then they find out what the cause is.

But the signal is saying something.

What's it saying?

Pay attention to me!

Reece realised he didn't know why the fireworks were happening, where they were being launched from, or who was sponsoring them — if anybody. The fireworks didn't convey any content or meaning to him, they just got his rapt-attention. And the attention of many other people too.

It was the attention-getting that was important.

Was this what happened in nature and evolution too? Were the fingerprints on the universe there to be signals intended to get our attention?

He remained transfixed, staring out of the window. London is a city with relatively little high-rise development, compared to many other capitals. This allowed Reece a considerable view over the city from his window. On the far-horizon, the thin crescent of a new-moon hung low in the sky. Reece thought back to the presentation on coincidences in our universe, with the moon being of the precise size, distance and angle of inclination to cause eclipses of the sun. He imagined how that event would captivate our ancestors when it happened. But the daily-movement of the moon across the sky, and the way it waxed-and-waned over a four-week cycle must also have got their attention — even of the ape-men ancestors we had. Perhaps the changing moon was the first-signal that caught the attention of early-man. Even if it was to cause him, or her, to ask *Why does it change a little bit each night?* Was that moon-signal the trigger for curiosity?

On this morning's run, Sarah had said that the signals stick out like a thousand sore-thumbs. She'd also pointed out how they were always fuzzy, or vague, in a way that made them hard to prove. With the fireworks just now, he had no idea where they came from. He couldn't tell if the explosions in the sky were near — or far. He couldn't even estimate how big the balls of light were. He also had no proof that they'd actually happened. Sarah had also said that *Belief in the signals might be the evolutionary-hurdle that individuals need to clear, to open their minds for the future.*

Reece was now sure that the anomalies and disconnects were signals to encourage us to dig-deeper into the nature of nature. Not about analysing the past, but about moving forward into the future. Advancing. Evolving.

The steak, peppercorn sauce, frites, wine and fireworks were all finished. And so was Reece. He showered, cleaned his teeth and climbed into bed.

As he fell asleep he wondered how he could move himself forward into the future. He knew that Einstein had imagined himself riding on a beam of light, and that this image had helped him to develop the concept of relativity. His thoughts moved on to Einstein's miracle year. *The Einstein Switch* — now that was an interesting thought. What if we all had an Einstein Switch, *but didn't yet know how to turn it on?* Everyone has moments of brilliance they are proud of where, perhaps for a moment, the Einstein Switch flicked on — and then off.

But how would you keep it switched-on for a whole year like he did?

The Einstein Switch — as Reece referred to it — didn't stay on permanently. It clicked-in sporadically to help boost an individual's thinking. Reece didn't know it, but he'd flipped on his own Einstein switch while he was eating his steak in silence. The break-through thinking he'd had, came about because he'd started a chain-reaction of new neuron-connections with the questions he was posing to himself.

Reece didn't appreciate the fact at this moment in time, but flicking on the Einstein Switch in someone's mind wasn't about finding the answers. *It was thinking about great questions that was the essential trigger.*

Chapter 58 Wednesday 03h14

It was fourteen-minutes and fifteen-seconds past three, in the tired hours of a new morning. While everyone involved with the conference was fast asleep, a new webpage went live on the Peckham Institute's website.

HTTP://WWW.PECKHAMINSTITUTE.ORG.UK/WJJHJ-YFXXNHPJW-5

It wasn't long before the first of the computer programs colloquially known as *spiders* found the webpage. The spider recognised it as a new page and sent the information back to its host computer. The host computer analysed the page, didn't recognise any meaningful search terms in the page name, and saw that there was no content on the page.

Following the logic programmed into it, the page was tagged as zero-value to exclude it being indexed in the host computer's massive database of search terms. The host computer took what it found at face-value, and made no attempt to decode the webpage address.

If it had tried to break the simple code — it would have learned that the last part of the name translated to became REECE TASSICKER.

The dreamers' cycle was running again.

Chapter 59 Wednesday 05h00

The automated wake-up call instantly transitioned Reece from the end of a deep-sleep into the start of a new day. He lay still, giving the remnants of any dreams the opportunity to materialise — but surprisingly, there was nothing to capture this morning.

It was barely ten-seconds since the alarm-call had sounded, yet he felt unusually alive, alert and refreshed. He also felt both exhilarated and intrigued by the content of yesterday's talks, by what he'd learned from Heather and Asif, and also by his insight into the signals last night. His mind was revved up — but wasn't yet in gear.

Time to put it in gear he thought.

He put the hotel's complimentary robe on, opened the curtains and sat at the desk. He opened his notebook to capture whatever thoughts came through.

The Council were unexpectedly quiet. He gave them time by closing his eyes, and focusing on the slow in-and-out cycle of his breathing.

It's a beautiful July morning in London.

The sun is shining.

We're feeling good.

Paradise.

Orange-juice.

What?

That's the proof of paradise.

Explain.

It's a hot day, the sun baking down, and you're parched with thirst.

Someone offers you a tall-glass of freshly-squeezed orange juice.

The vivid orange-colour...

The tinkling of the ice-cubes floating on top...

The condensation that runs down the outside of the glass...

You raise the glass to your lips...

And taste the tart-sweetness of the orange nectar...

That feeling is the proof that we are in paradise.

Why else would such a taste-experience be a requirement of nature?

And do we think this orange-juice taste-sensation occurred as a natural development from the big-bang without any kind of beneficial assistance?

Unlikely.

Is it the result of the freaky-streak of luck?

One thing might be luck. But having so many other more-complex things in our world, surely goes beyond luck.

The evolution of our paradise isn't following a natural course of events then?

Agreed.

It's the orange juice proof.

There are other proofs too.

Such as?

The feeling of being in love. Is that a natural development?

Or finding a joke so funny that tears run down your face?

Or the exhilaration when your favourite sports team win a major trophy in the final minute of play.

Or watching a weepy-movie that brings out the emotional-side of you at the end.

They are all forms of proof in their own ways.

Why isn't there one conclusive-proof of the odds being stacked in our favour?

Aren't we the conclusive-proof?

In one way, yes.

But it's always good to have a conclusive sign of something.

By nature we are a sceptical race.

Are we sceptical of the existence of the Delicate Force?

More proof would be good.

Is circumstantial evidence good enough for you?

Try me.

Recall we made the red door on the sliding continuum — with God at one end and evolutionary-luck at the other.

Yes.

If everything were created by the click of two God-like fingers, that would certainly account for us seemingly taking all the optimum route-choices in our evolutionary journey.

True.

But would such a Divine involvement leave the end result of their work with a seeming desire for self-annihilation and subsequent destruction of their paradise home?

Good point. I think not.

The freaky-streak of luck at the other, pure-evolutionary end also seems ridiculously unlikely too.

Okay.

So what's left is something else which we called the Delicate Force. We haven't defined what it is — it's just some kind of pervasive force.

A Delicate Force seems like a contradiction in terms.

A huge-bulldozer can be used to build a child's tiny-sandcastle on a beach.

Tremendous power used in intricate ways.

A Delicate Force makes sense.

This Delicate Force has been responsible for the spectacular coincidences and amazing chains-of-events that have helped us to be where we are today.

So why can't we prove it exists and resolve the vagueness?

Perhaps we aren't meant to fully understand it.

Or to even know for absolute certainty that it exists.

You're saying that this mystery is part of the story?

What story?

The story you are going to write now.

My story?

Start writing it now!

It's about a woman.

She's called Melissa.

Start writing!

This had happened to Reece on previous occasions, where his mind told him to create a story to bring various streams of thought together. His laptop was on the desk beside him. He turned it on, and started typing the first things that came into his head. He didn't know where the story would go — but this was the point. His subconscious mind wove patterns with his thought-streams, throwing out story elements one after the other. He just typed as fast as he could to capture the picture his mind was weaving.

A woman called Melissa

Melissa is a fifty-four-year-old, quiet-spoken woman who lives in Hull. She has three grown-up children who have left home, and she works in a bank. She plays bridge at her local bridge club every Thursday evening. She likes to keep herself healthy through eat-

ing lots of vegetables, only drinking a few-glasses of wine in a week, and she likes to go walking along the nearby riverbank at the weekend for exercise.

Melissa also has extra-sensory perception, and for a bit of fun, she sometimes does mind-tricks for her close-friends where she guesses the next card to be turned over from a deck of playing-cards. One of her friends mentioned this skill to a colleague who worked at the local university; in the psychology research department, who might be interested in testing Melissa's skill.

And this is why at this moment in time; Melissa is sat at a table, facing a researcher, while a video-camera records the activity. The researcher takes the top card off the pile, and holds it so that only he can see it. He studies it closely. "Four of spades" says Melissa. He puts a tick in the column — and takes another card. This goes on until he finally picks up the last card. "Nine of diamonds. So how did I do?" asks Melissa. "You got them all correct" replies the researcher. "How do you do that?"

Melissa explains that when the researcher looks at a card, she sees the shape and colour of the suit, and a number in her mind, which she just says aloud.

"I'm just going to confer with my colleagues who were watching this on the video-feed," the researcher tells Melissa, and he leaves the room.

So what happens next to Melissa?

Reece paused in his story creation, for he can see two alternate endings coming up. Which one to choose? He decided to write up both — and choose later.

A woman called Melissa — Ending 1

Perhaps the research is published in a respected academic journal, which is seen by a main-stream journalist who writes about it for their newspaper. This article is read by a television producer, which results in Melissa appearing on breakfast-television the next morning. Her demonstration is so impressive, that she's offered her own television show by a quick-thinking executive. She goes on to become an international celebrity with all the subsequent fame and fortune associated with it.

A woman called Melissa — Ending 2

Or maybe the first part of the road to fame starts off the same, when the newspapers publish her story, but from then on things change. She is accused of reading people's minds in public — when they don't want to have their minds read. People report that the

PIN code to their bank-card has been stolen, and that security has been breached by Melissa.

TV interviewers realise that if they ask any question about her abusing her psychic powers, she may immediately read their minds and blurt out some of their personal secrets on live-television.

Her bank-employer recognise that their security has been compromised — as she can mind-read everybody's security-code if she wanted to — and so she is asked to resign with immediate effect.

Her friends start to become wary of her, and the local bridge-club ban her from playing, because she knows everybody's cards.

Melissa ends up spending more time alone in her apartment, rarely venturing out for fear of being victimised. She starts to drink excessively for comfort, living the life of a recluse. She loses all her friends.

Two-years later, one of the same newspapers that had initially made her famous, reports on the death of Melissa in her home. Foul play is not suspected, but police continue to investigate.

THE END

Reece re-read the story. He'd completed it so rapidly, from the thoughts that came into his head, that he didn't recall writing some of it. Whenever he used this brain-writing technique, he was always surprised how naturally it seemed to flow. The Council gave their opinions too.

Good story.

Some interesting twists too. Well done.

This is fiction, but if it weren't, which ending is most likely?

In the past, witches were frequently burnt at the stake.

Or drowned in ponds.

Perhaps the equivalent of that today is death by tabloid-newspaper.

In the story, Melissa scored fifty-two out of fifty-two when guessing the playing-cards.

So?

Would it have made any difference if she'd only got fifty out of fifty-two right?

Probably not.

Or what if she only got twenty-six correct out of fifty-two?

That's still a great achievement.

What if she only scored six out of fifty-two?

How would this compare to our score if we tried it right now?

If we tried it, we'd be lucky to get any right at all.

That fact is true.

If you had a great skill like this maybe you wouldn't make it widely known.

Perhaps in the past it was only the people with unusual-skills, and who also stayed quiet about it, that survived.

Maybe that gypsy-clairvoyant in the travelling-caravan, with the sign that says she comes from a long family-line of clairvoyants — is actually telling the truth.

They learned that's the way to make a modest-living, while sharing their gift with others — by always keeping a low-profile.

If Melissa had the skill of guessing whether a tossed-coin would land on heads or tails, it probably wouldn't help her to get it right one-hundred times out of one-hundred.

She'd end up like the second-ending in the story.

But what if she only got it right fifty-three times out of one-hundred — but consistently?

If we guessed the coin toss, then we should average fifty correct out of one-hundred.

True.

For someone to get fifty-three per cent right occasionally can be expected by the law of odds.

But to achieve this consistently is something beyond normal-expectations?

Of course.

So the Delicate Force is a helping nudge at the fifty-three per cent level?

Yes. It's not a one hundred per cent guaranteed winning driver for you.

Why did you choose fifty-three per cent as the number?

It's the same percentage that Daryl Bem achieved when he ran those tests and discovered future-leakage.

Interesting number.

Just slightly better than an even-chance.

Correct. It isn't meant to be so obvious and to be banked-on as guaranteed.

Possibly the Delicate Force touches you in a delicate way.

Like it isn't intended to be measured and observed?

But why shouldn't we be able to prove it?

Imagine being in a casino where the odds are fifty-three per cent in our favour.

Long-term success would be guaranteed.

Imagine if we knew there was a beneficial force helping or guiding us to a fifty-three per cent success rate.

There'd be no need for us to do anything about our future.

We can all just kick-back, because we know that everything will be hunky-dory for us.

That wouldn't be beneficial for mankind in advancing ourselves would it?

Not at all.

We've all seen the signals.

Even though we may not recognise them for what they are.

And people may have direct experience of some of the fuzzy aspects of life themselves.

Thinking back about anomalies, we've had a few happen to us haven't we?

Yes we have.

We've been brushing them off.

Assuming there must be some kind of logical or scientific answer.

But that's the whole point isn't it?

What?

There is no logical or scientific answer.

Correct. If we want to wait for some kind of scientific proof then we'll be waiting a long time — because it isn't coming.

If you asked any church-goer to prove the existence of God, I'll bet they couldn't.

Agreed, but so many people belief in Him.

They've transcended facts.

What?

Some people will only believe something when they've seen the facts and proof.

Others don't need proof.

They just have a sense of knowing.

That's called faith.

Yes.

Faith is a belief that transcends facts.

A magician can fool you into believing that he can do magic. But there are limitations to what a magician can do.

Perhaps people who have a faith are the enlightened ones.

They have a considered-ability to believe, adopt and embrace something without a need for facts.

Is it the same with the signals for the Delicate Force?

The proof is that you are seeing — and experiencing — the signals with your own eyes, ears and feelings. How much more proof do you need?

Maybe none.

Maybe it's not the time to be hesitating.

Why?

Because the opportunity for us to evolve is slipping away.

How do you mean?

Every single person is getting older day-by-day.

Every day is a day closer to death.

A day less to live.

And a day less to advance yourself.

In quantum mechanics, when you measure the waveform — you cause it to collapse.

What if trying to get close to the Delicate Force causes it to collapse too?

When researchers test people who do have an unusual mental capability, potentially it's the fifty-three per cent level that's being examined.

That ability to get just three-per-cent more things right than would be achieved by luck — but consistently.

It's the three-per-cent that's on trial.

And that's the waveform which may also collapse when subjected to measurement.

If there was a guaranteed proof of the fifty-three per cent level, then we would spend our lives visiting people like Melissa, trying to get some kind of guidance as to what choices we should make in our lives.

At the fifty-three per cent level, you can walk away from it easily if you wanted to — you wouldn't have to fight too-hard to overcome it.

So, if you believe in it, then it can have a beneficial effect on you.

If you doubt it then it's easy to ignore.

And if you believe in it, then it's easy to recognise that it's helping you.

There's no proof of the Delicate Force, and it may be centuries — if ever — before we do get any proof.

And when we do get the proof — it won't be needed.

Because we'll have moved on, and be evolving in other ways.

Your life and experiences are the only proof you are going to get.

Do you really need scientific-proof to tell you what you intuitively know already?

I shouldn't — should I?

No — you damn well shouldn't!

Reece thought to himself that it was time *he* was trusting his instincts more, and believing in some of the things he now felt were true. *But what sort of things could he be doing to advance himself and access the Delicate Force?*

At that moment the phone on the desk rang. It was Heather.

"We've got the dreamers' feedback on the dreams they had about you. Interested?"

Chapter 60 Wednesday 06h30

Reece knocked vigorously on the door of Heather's furniture-storeroom-cum-office. The door opened.

"Good morning! Good morning!" said Reece to Heather and Asif.

"You seem in high spirits," replied Heather, clearly unimpressed.

"It's a lovely morning and I've a feeling that great things will happen today," responded Reece, entering the windowless-space. "Doesn't this room depress you?"

"I've spent longer periods in much worse," she answered. Her mind recalled the hell-hole-of-a-cellar where she'd been imprisoned for ten-days in Pakistan, before being freed by the SAS. She quickly chased those nightmares from her mind.

"You've got something to show me?" said Reece.

"Asif, explain to Mister Happy what you've found out."

"I looked through the report-back emails the dreamers sent for the mornings *after* your name appeared in a coded-webpage address." Asif was looking at content on his monitors as he spoke.

"For the first-time your name was included, you found a Post-it note inside the professor's book. In the response from the dreamers, they refer to a shop where a little boy called William Henry Smith was selling books. The shop was on a station, and the trains would arrive at full-speed into the station, hit the buffer-blocks at the end, and bounce-back to where they came from. The buffer-blocks were made of rubber-bands, which could be used to catapult the departing trains up to full-speed quickly. Some of the trains consisted of freight-wagons carrying Cornish pasties and coal. The lumps of coal weren't black — for each piece was half-white and half-green. As the trains hit the rubber buffers, all the coal and the pasties flew out of the wagons, and straight into the mouth of a huge, red dragon which was sitting on the end of the station."

As Asif took a sip of his tea, Reece was grappling with how this psychedelic-weirdness could possibly relate to him. Asif continued.

"Then there are two-people on a children's roundabout, and the first-person puts a book in a bag, while the second-person gives them some money. Then the second-person takes the book out of the bag and gives it back to the first-person — who then gives them the money back. This keeps happening over-and-over, as the roundabout goes around. A crowd of people are looking at the departure board, which is showing a movie instead of train-departure times. This movie consists entirely of an opening title-frame which shows the words *Mind The Future* bouncing around like a screen-saver. A porter appears selling popcorn at £18.02 a box, and everyone buys some, so there's non left."

"This almost sounds hallucinogenic," said Reece, but as he thought back to some of his own dreams, he realised that they might sound equally-trippy to someone else. "Which part refers to me specifically?"

"It's all about you," said Asif. "Or more precisely, what you will be doing, where and when."

"I don't follow," said Reece.

"The Cornish pasties represent Cornwall. The green-and-white coal being eaten by the red-dragon represents Wales — the Welsh flag is green and white with a red dragon on — and there used to be many coalfields in South Wales. There's frequent reference to trains and a station, so we can assume a railway station is involved. The rubber buffer-blocks that make the trains bounce-back to where they came from, indicates the station is also a terminus and not a through station. Paddington station is the only terminus that has train services to Cornwall and Wales."

"Okay," said Reece, hesitantly.

"William Henry Smith is the person who started the WH Smith book-shop chain many years ago. You can google the term *Mind the Future* to see that it's a recently-published book. The popcorn-price of £18.02 actually refers to the time of 18h02. I re-checked the CCTV security-footage from WH Smith — and the time that you bought your book was 18h02," concluded Asif.

"So, they knew I'd buy a specific book, at an exact time, in a precise location?"

"That's the long-and-short of it."

"That's a little creepy," said Reece, wondering what else they'd dreamed about him.

"Gareth Jones receives these dream-feedbacks regularly, so it's probably quite-straightforward for him to decipher their meaning," added Heather.

"The other dreams about your second Post-it note were similar," said Asif.

"What about the text-message I received on Monday morning?" asked Reece.

"In that set of dream-responses, there's a plate of bacon and eggs, with a fried-egg at the top and bottom of the plate — and a piece of curved-bacon linking the two eggs — so that it looks like a telephone. The bacon-and-eggs-telephone starts to ring, and a man picks it up and speaks into it. There's a shop that sells websites in the form of cakes. The cakes are covered in small-berries that can talk. All they say is that their name is Brad. Outside the shop, people are lining up to describe their website and to have it made into a cake that the internet can connect to. The number on the shop's door is 812. The interpretation is that you will be called by this company at breakfast-time; 08h12 to be precise. According to your phone-records, you received the call at 08h12."

"How did you check my phone records?" asked Reece.

"You won't believe what information we have access to," said Heather. "What's the part about the fruit's name?"

"The friend of mine who's designing the dream-sharing website is called Bradley Berry. Brad for short," explained Reece.

"That's cute," laughed Heather.

"And the last dreams relate to you being at Selfridges at 15h07," said Asif.

"These dream-interpretations allowed the Peckham Institute to place Post-it notes in books you were going to buy, send you a text just before you received the call at breakfast, and also to set you up to be detained in Selfridges," summarised Heather.

"I don't understand what happened at Selfridges," said Reece.

"I got someone to call the head of security there. They used their MoD-status to carry a bit of weight. The guy was reluctant to talk, but eventually explained they'd received a very-convincing call from a fake commander in the Metropolitan Police CTC, who said there was a potential risk in the customer service area — which was you. That was why the store security people detained you," explained Heather.

"It still leaves a big question unanswered," said Reece. "What makes the dreamers have the dreams they do?"

"That's the million-dollar question we still need to answer," said Heather.

"At least we know what all the webpage addresses they posted were targeted towards," added Asif.

"That's true," replied Heather.

Except that it wasn't true. If Asif had refreshed the monitor-screen that listed all the uploaded website addresses, he'd have seen that a new one had been added last night.

Chapter 61 Wednesday 08h10

After leaving Heather, Reece went to the restaurant for breakfast. He was making his usual concoction of muesli, fruit, natural yoghurt and honey, when the Contactor device on his belt vibrated for the first time. He'd only entered a few names into it, and he saw that one of them was near him now — Annalie Killian. He looked at the photo displayed on the device to see it was the person who was helping herself to fruit juice.

She was an eclectically-dressed woman that he'd noticed numerous times during the conference, for she always wore strikingly-vivid clothes in African or Australian aboriginal patterns. Reece introduced himself, and asked if he could join her for breakfast. She was a South African living in Australia, and employed by a large investment company as a Catalyst for Magic. It was this intriguing job-title that had prompted Reece to enter her name on his Contactor list. He explained what he did — and then asked her about her role.

"I catalyse the magic of human beings as opposed to machines. It's my job to be the corporate maverick within our business, and to creatively disrupt what are considered the normal approaches. I have to stimulate innovation and fresh thinking across the business."

"A corporate maverick who's a catalyst for change — that must look amazing on a CV. Surely a large investment company must be inherently averse to risk and innovation — so how do you drive innovation in a business like that?" asked Reece.

"When you do it all the time, it tends to become absorbed into the business-as-usual work — and part of the fabric. To give an added-boost, I produce a week-long innovation-festival every other year that we call the Amplify Festival. I bring inspiring people to speak, and we invite companies to demonstrate innovative, new services. We transform our head-office in the centre of Sydney into a visual feast and learning campus, so there's no-excuse for staff not to attend" she said.

They talked all through breakfast. It wasn't often someone fascinated Reece with their enthusiasm for their work, but this woman in the striking leopard-print top was doing it today.

"Can I ask if you've discovered any peculiar snippets of information recently, that you thought to be fascinating in some way? asked Reece.

"An unusual question — let me think." She took a sip of her coffee.

"I was in Geneva last week at another conference, as I'm looking for speakers for our next Amplify Festival. Do you know what the Large Hadron Collider is?"

"It's some colossal-device to smash particles together at almost-the-speed-of-light isn't it?"

"Yes. It's built in a twenty-seven kilometre-long tunnel, close to Geneva, and I heard a fascinating story from someone who works for the organisation that runs it. While it was being built, two scientists were concerned that when it started up, it may create a microscopic black-hole that would start to consume the collider itself — and then consume the entire planet in a matter of hours."

"Seriously?" exclaimed Reece.

"Oh yes. These two scientists suggested an exercise whereby one-card was drawn at random from a deck of cards containing 100-million hearts — and only one spade. They said that rather than having an enormous deck of real playing-cards, this could be simulated using a computerised random-number generator. If time-travel were possible, then rather than needing to send a person with a message, the future-humans could simply influence the computer that was generating the random numbers. So that if the solitary-spade was selected from the 100-million hearts, then that would be a sign that the collider should not be switched on. I thought that was an amazing concept, especially as it came from two of the scientists involved with the project."

"That is fascinatingly-weird," commented Reece, who then paused to think. "But wait a minute. If the start-up *did* cause a black-hole to form, and which devoured the Earth, then surely there wouldn't be anyone in the future to send the message back saying not to start up the device?"

"That's the realm of the time-travel enigma isn't it?" she replied.

"Did they actually do this experiment?"

"Apparently not. However, it seems that the black-hole never materialised as the machine is working fine now."

"Unless this is what the inside of a black-hole feels like," said Reece seriously.

"Now that's what *I* call a fascinatingly-weird thought," she said laughing.

Chapter 62 Wednesday 09h00

Presentation #5

What do you believe?

By Dr Nanci Mahova
Department of Social Sciences
Bath University

I want to talk to you about some unusual beliefs that we hold to be true. The 'we' that I'm referring to, is all of us — personally as individuals — and not as a social society. A society is simply a collection of individuals, and can't hold any beliefs for itself. It's the individuals within society who can hold the same, or similar, beliefs.

The first part of my presentation is a little unusual because I'm not going to ask you what you believe — I'm going to tell you what you, as individuals, believe.

<u>OUR BELIEFS</u>

Our beliefs are the opinions that we hold to be true. Some of our beliefs are vast in nature, and unlikely to change much over time — such as a belief in a religion, and its particular view of God. Other views are of a lesser-nature, but may have been held for many years. You might believe that you have been driving the quickest route from your home to your workplace for the last four-years — until someone shows you a short-cut that avoids the congestion in the morning. You try it, and realise that you now have a *new* quickest route.

Beliefs like this, that have been held for many years, can be changed in an instant to a new belief. Not that there was anything badly wrong with the old belief — it has been updated based on new information.

Great civilisation like the Romans, Greeks and Incas thrived, even though some of their core beliefs weren't in line with today's knowledge and accepted behaviours. The gods they fervently-worshipped are no longer in vogue, and we now know that thunderstorms aren't signs that these gods are displeased with mankind.

Consider these examples of how our beliefs have changed over time, based on newly-discovered knowledge:

- 2,000-years ago people believed the earth was flat.
- 500-years ago we believed that the earth was at the centre of the universe.
- 200-years ago *bad-air* was assumed to be the cause of many diseases.

- 160-years ago we believed the Earth was only twenty-million years old and not 4.5 billion years old as we know today.
- 120-years ago blood-letting ceased to be an acceptable form of treatment for illnesses.
- 100-years ago we thought that time was fixed until a young Albert Einstein proposed his theory of relativity.
- 50-years ago we didn't believe something could be in two places at the same time until the double-slit experiment was first performed in 1961.
- 30-years ago we still thought homosexuality was a mental disease until the American Psychiatric Association declared it otherwise.
- 15-years ago we thought that living beings could only have one mother until Dolly the sheep was cloned from three mothers.
- 10-years ago we believed that a surgeon had to be present to perform a surgical operation until the capabilities of remote surgery (telesurgery) were developed.
- 5-years ago we believed that different blood-types would remain as an endless issue in transfusions, until Nature journal detailed research from the University of Copenhagen on a way to convert any kind of blood into Type O blood.

All these beliefs changed as a result of new knowledge being discovered, or developed, scientifically. These new-found facts made it easy for individuals to reposition their view on that issue.

Belief where there is no proof

Beliefs like these that have scientific backing behind them are one thing, however, there are many beliefs held by individuals that have no sound scientific-proof behind them at all. Does this mean that these beliefs are wrong? Does science have the right to say that when something can't be proved, then it can't be true? No, not at all. This is what faith is all about. Believing in something where there is no direct proof, but which *internally*, we feel to be right.

Let me show you some unusual things that people do believe in. These are drawn from a number of research exercises undertaken over recent years.

In 2009, to mark the 200th birthday of Charles Darwin, and also the 150th anniversary of Darwin's book *On the Origin of Species*, the religious think-tank Theos interviewed people in the UK on their views of evolution. The survey found that 50% of Britons do not believe in Darwin's theory of evolution, and that around 10% of people chose creationism (the belief that God created the world in the last 6,000 to 10,000 years) over evolution. Around 12% of respondents chose intelligent design (the view that evolution alone is not enough to explain how we got to where we are today) over evolution. Only 37% agreed that Darwin's theory of evolution is so well-established, it is beyond reasonable doubt; while almost one-in-five people (19%) believed it has little or no supporting evidence. Just over one-third of people (36%) stated that the theory is still waiting to be proved or disproved.

In 2008, Time magazine reported on a poll of 1,700 respondents undertaken by the Baylor University Institute for Studies of Religion in the US. This poll found that more than half of all Americans believe they have been helped by a guardian-angel in the course of their lives, when 55% of them answered affirmatively to the statement, '*I was protected from harm by a guardian-angel*'.

In 2010, online-research by the Bible Society and Christian Research into the views of 1,038 British people, showed 31% of them believe they have a guardian-angel watching over them; with another 17% saying they are not sure. One-in-twenty of the respondents believed they had seen, or heard, an angel.

A 2005 survey in the US by the Gallup organisation found that 41% of respondents believed in extra-sensory perception; 31% believed in telepathy; while 26% believed in clairvoyance. Additionally, 37% believed in haunted houses; 32% in ghosts; and 21% believed in communicating with the dead. These items were among those selected by people who agreed with the statement that humans have more than the *normal* five-senses.

A year later, Monash University in Australia conducted online-research with over 2,000 respondents from around the world, to determine what types of phenomena people claim to have experienced. They found that 70% of the respondents believed they had an unexplained paranormal event that changed their life, mostly in a positive way; while 80% reported having a premonition of some kind.

In a 2009 Nielsen poll, 49% of Australians said they believe in psychic powers, despite a distinct lack of any supporting evidence.

In 2006, two Oklahoma universities polled 439 of their students, and found that 23% of college freshmen stated a belief in paranormal ideas. This increased as students progressed through their studies with 31% of college seniors, and 34% of graduates believing in the paranormal.

In 2008, the Daily Telegraph newspaper reported a British poll of 3,000 people that found 54% of respondents believed in God, while 58% of them expressed a belief in the supernatural. Nearly one-in-four of those polled claimed a past-encounter with paranormal forces.

From these findings we can see that significant numbers of people have beliefs in areas which cannot be proved. While some of the items above may seem *extreme*, there are other aspects of life, in which huge numbers of people hold beliefs that can't definitively be proven. An internet search will deliver many so-called proofs that God *does* exist — while a different search will deliver an equal number of proofs that God *doesn't* exist. Either way, a large number of people *do* believe in God, and a large number *don't*. Similarly, it's difficult to prove that love exists, or to prove that you are actually in love. But it's a fact that many people do believe in the concept of love, and I'm sure that many people genuinely are in love.

Many people also believe in concepts that others are sceptical of. That's because these concepts either *feel right* to them, or they have personal experiences related to these concepts, which act as their own proof. If you believe in things which can't be scientifically proved, then that doesn't mean you are wrong in your beliefs, nor should you be embarrassed by them. *And neither are you alone in these beliefs.*

SPECIFIC AREAS OF BELIEF

Intuition

One feeling that many humans have is that of *intuition*, when you simply get a hunch or a gut-feeling about something. This unusual sensation is a feeling of sudden and strong judgment that we can't immediately justify, and may be interpreted as a kind of guide or warning. Even though this feeling may seem to *come from within*, it is actually initiated from a perception of something external to you, that you may not even be aware that you noticed.

Psychologists John Bargh of New York University and Tanya Chartrand of Ohio State University undertook studies with students, asking them their opinions on an image that was flashed in front of them for just two-tenths of a second. The participants were asked to respond instantly with their views. They found that everything is evaluated as good, or bad, within a quarter-of-a-second.

Subconsciously, our brain matches the inputs from all our senses, to the array of patterns it has learned through experience. The subconscious mind does this much faster than the conscious mind, and when it finds what it believes to be a matching pattern, it reports back its findings. In certain situations this reporting back may be in the form of a warning to be wary of something. All this happens to you before you are consciously aware of it — which is why it sometimes feels like an internal force acting upon you.

When we see a person, we may intuitively make a judgement about them based on what we see. However, there are occurrences where we may have no direct input of something — but still perform an intuitive action. Turning around because you feel that someone is standing behind you — for example.

We can also make an intuitive decision on our beliefs. We may not have hard-proof, but we can have a hunch, or a gut-feeling, about something that isn't a mainstream, accepted belief. Certain concepts *somehow feel right to us,* and worthy of our belief in them. This is your intuition in action.

Homeopathy

A homeopathic remedy is an alternative form of medical treatment that uses a very-dilute form of naturally occurring substances to cure ailments. These substances can be potentially harmful if taken in their normal state, which may seem counter-intuitive, but homeopathy is based on the principle that you *treat like with like*.

Many homeopathic products sold contain the code *30C* in their description, which denotes the level of dilution of the treatment. The letter C indicates that the dilution rate is 1:100, or one-litre of the homeopathic product has been mixed with 100-litres of water. For a 2C dilution, one-litre of this diluted-mixture would be mixed with another 100-litres of water, and then for a 3C dilution, one-litre of this 2C solution, would be mixed with another 100-litres of water — and so on.

A 13C dilution is equivalent to less than one-drop of the original substance being diluted into all the water on Earth. A 30C dilution would take this and dilute it by a further ratio of 1: 10,000,000,000,000,000,000,000,000,000,000,000. At this dilution, there aren't even enough molecules of the original concentrated substance for you to have any reasonable chance that there's a single molecule of the original concentrate in the treatment you have.

Homeopathy is deemed to work on the principle that between each dilution-stage, the mixture is shaken vigorously, to ensure that the *spirit* or *energy* of the original concentrate is spread to all the molecules of each successive level of dilution.

Most research investigations and testing into the effectiveness of homeopathic remedies have failed to prove consistent-and-positive benefits over the long-term. Despite this, the UK National Health Service continues to offer homeopathic treatments in clinics and hospitals.

Research carried out by market research company Mintel, estimated that retail sales of homeopathic and herbal remedies in the US were $6.4 billion in 2012. Additionally, an online poll of over 43,000 people by the UK's Guardian newspaper asking whether the National Health Service should provide homeopathic treatments showed that 41% of respondents said *yes*.

The placebo effect

When pharmaceutical companies are testing a new medicine, they provide one group of patients with the new drug, while they simultaneously have a *control group* of patients who *believe* they are getting the drug. This control group is actually receiving a sugar pill — or placebo — that has no medicinal benefits whatsoever. There is frequently a second control group who is given no treatment of any kind. The pharmaceutical company hopes to see a much-greater improvement among the patients who receive the new drug, than among those that don't, in the two control groups.

The interesting effect is that frequently, the patients in the first control group who receive the placebo, can show significantly better recoveries than those in the second control group who receive no treatment at all. This effect is known as the placebo effect, and is believed to come about because the patient is told that the medication should make them better, and so they believe this, and subsequently do improve their condition. There is discussion among researchers in this field as to whether the effect is from the pill they are given, or from the fact that they are seeing a doctor, a white coat, a doctor's room, or a combination of these.

The placebo effect can even go as far as sham-surgery or radiotherapy. In the sham-surgery, rather than perform an operation to treat a knee problem, the surgeon may just make a small incision in the side of the knee while the patient is under anaesthetic — and do no more. The patient goes on to make a similar recovery as though they had the full surgery performed on them.

These positive effects on health indicate that the mind can be a very effective tool in recovering from illness or injury to the body. The placebo effect is a fact, and it's another example of how we can use our minds for better purposes. *If we want to.*

Subconscious beliefs that affect our behaviour

Imagine an extreme case of the parents of newly-born twins naming one of their children Bright, and naming the other one Dull. Which one do you think would do better at school? Most likely the one called Bright. Instead, imagine the two children were named Alice and David. You might imagine they would then do equally-well at school.

A 2007 study by researchers from the University of California and Yale University, found that students with names starting with the letters A or B got higher grade-point averages than those whose names started with the letters C or D. They suggested that this could be related to the fact that throughout schooling, many exams and subjects are graded using the letters A through D, with students aspiring to achieve the higher gradings. This may happen to Alice and David through the subconscious beliefs they will develop about themselves through the course of their schooling.

This might cause you to question yourself. What's holding you back from embracing new beliefs in the power of your mind? And do you have some subconscious baggage that's preventing you from moving forward?

UNUSUAL THINGS PEOPLE BELIEVE IN

Psi capabilities

In 2002, the UK experienced the disappearance of two ten-year-old schoolgirls in the village of Soham in Cambridgeshire. Dennis McKenzie, a clairvoyant and psychic, assisted the parents of one of the missing girls to trace her activities using his psychic powers. Tragically, the girls had been murdered and their bodies were found two-weeks later. Kevin Wells, the father of one of the girls publically acknowledged the help Dennis McKenzie gave in the search for his daughter by saying that he possessed *'an extraordinary gift'*.

The sense of extra-sensory perception (ESP) is generally disregarded in academic fields, as testing of this sense has not revealed any conclusive capabilities or provable successes. Despite this, many believe in ESP and the abilities of people like Dennis McKenzie, as a part of life. Perhaps not as an everyday occurrence, but something that benefits them under certain circumstances.

There are other aspects of mental-capabilities that many people believe in, such as communicating with the dead; the transfer of thoughts and emotions through telepathy; the ability to locate objects and water through dowsing-techniques; having an out-of-body experience; healing by the use of different forms of energy; precognition of future events before they happen; and the perception of energy-fields in people, things and places. These capabilities are known by the generic term of *psi-skills*.

These are potentially deeper levels at which our minds can operate, that only very-few individuals have managed to activate. Perhaps there are relationships at the 53%-level between people who have certain capabilities, like clairvoyants who can see the future, and people who believe in clairvoyant skills, but can't perform them for themselves.

Some may regard this as a case of exploiters manipulating the gullible — and perhaps in some situations it is. However, the advice given by the person who has the ability, to their customer, is rarely specific and directional, as it occurs at the 53%-level, and is indicative only.

The two-people in this situation form an ecosystem, or a symbiotic relationship, where both depend on the other to keep the system live. And I'm not just referring to the fact that one is happy to pay the other money. It's a deeper-relationship at a cognitive level. A delicate relationship whereby an inexplicable level of cognitive-interaction occurs between the two individuals. Would such a delicate relationship stand up to being scrutinised by researchers in a laboratory experiment? I doubt it.

Voices in your head

In February 2009, a BBC study undertaken with parenting-skills expert Dr Pat Spungin, studied the lives of 1,446 young children in the UK. One of the findings was that one-in-five young children have an imaginary friend. Do we adults inadvertently chase away the imaginary friends of our children? What if they aren't imaginary at all, and are an integral part of a child's perceived reality?

Or what if this is how our minds evolve and develop? By definition, our offspring are one-generation further along the evolutionary-development time-line than ourselves, so who are we, as adults, to say definitively what is, and what isn't, a part of someone's reality. And potentially to someone whose mind is more developed than ours is?

New-age is old-age

New-age beliefs may conjure up images of long-haired, flower-power hippies from the 1960s and 70s. For others, it may be Gypsy Rose-Lee huddled over a crystal ball in an incense-and-candle filled room; a feng shui designer giving recommendations on the design of a building; or the use of acupuncture or Reiki to cure ailments. Whatever your perception, most of this is derived from practices and beliefs that have been around for centuries, and which are often based on the sources, and alignment, of energies inside and outside the body.

Ancient Buddhist and Hindu religious texts refer to the concepts of Chakras, which are energy-centres that exist within the body. Acupuncture is believed to have originated in ancient China, based on drawings which date from at least 1,600 BC. It's aligned to the Chinese concept of Chi, which is the life-force, or the flow of energy that exists in all living beings. This concept of Chi also extends into martial-arts, where one draws on this inner-energy for strength and technique.

There are religions such as Taoism (or Daoism) which were practiced for centuries before the birth of Christ, that are based solely on living life in harmony with the life-energy.

The ancient Romans and Greeks had a different view; that their numerous gods commanded the energies. They believed that through fervent worship, their gods would bestow the energies favourably upon them, as opposed to delivering them as punishment through terrible events like a storm at sea, or an earthquake.

Meditation is a technique used in different forms by many religions to gain inner-peace, and to access an inner-strength or energy. Meditation may be likened to yoga, or prayer, all of which require the use of a particular posture, designed to enhance the energy-experience. This concept of energies even extends into inanimate objects. Feng shui — the alignment of buildings to enhance the natural flow of energies — has been actively practiced since at least 4,000 BC.

The understanding and application of these energies through various religions, cultures and societies, has governed the lives of billions of people for thousands of years. Focussing on the energies kept them well, and when they became ill, the energies were stimulated through a range of practices designed to aid the recovery of the individual. This theme of energy prevails in most religions. Does it seem right that something that has formed, and still forms, an intricate part of life for billions of people for so long, doesn't have some element of truth to it?

In the past, the people who were able to lead and understand these energy-related activities would often have been priests — or the equivalent of an enlightened one. *Perhaps they were.* Perhaps they had insights that weren't crowded-out by the endless-tirade of mindless junk we encounter and consume today. Perhaps today, the people who can perceive, understand, and practice some of these unusual skills and capabilities, shouldn't be regarded as odd, but should again be considered to be *enlightened* in some way.

Believing in the power of something is the first step to gaining the benefit from it. Are the people who believe in the capabilities of the mind, the vanguards in the enlightenment of the future?

Observing and measuring abilities

Thoughts are created by the millions of electro-chemical reactions at the synapses in our brains, Even though these electrical discharges are microscopically-small, they can still be picked up by sensitive equipment. Early in 2011, researchers from the University of California, Berkeley, used sensitive equipment to pick up signals from people's brains — and were able to see what participants were thinking about.

The participants were shown a specific image, and specialised equipment analysed the blood-flow through various parts of the brain. This information was fed into a computer, which searched its database of video-clips to select the image which most-closely matched the data-stream from the participant. Currently, the converted images are quite blotchy, but when compared to the original image, they are remarkably similar. Once this technology is perfected, it may be possible for people to record their overnight dreams — and to watch them in full-colour the next day.

This technology by which we are able to pick up the micro-electrical signals that are generated by our thinking, has only been around for a few years, but our brains have been developing these electrical-signals for millions of years. Just as these newly-developed machines are capable of very-crudely picking up the brain-signals, what if other humans were capable of picking them up and understanding them? And potentially even communicating with them too.

Psychics are defined as people who have the ability to perceive information that isn't accessible using the normal senses. Extra-sensory perception and mind-reading are two examples of what psychics may claim to do. Others can foretell future-events, or are able to help people contact dead relatives.

Are the people who claim to have these unusual psychic-capabilities genuine — or not? Undoubtedly, there are some who are nothing more than highly-skilled entertainers or con-artists. But does this apply to them all? Academic institutions have done many tests on people with claimed psychic-capabilities, and none have proved conclusive in validating these powers.

James Randi is a former American stage-magician who is sceptical of psychic-capabilities. Through the James Randi Educational Foundation, he offers $1,000,000 to anyone who can pass a mutually-agreed, scientific test of their psychic-skills. He frequently challenges the leading public celebrities in the field to take his test. Many decline, and of those that have taken Randi's test, none have been successful. The one-million dollars remains unclaimed.

Despite the fact that there is remarkably-little hard evidence to support the diverse array of mental capabilities claimed by individuals, there are large numbers of individuals who still believe in all these different areas. They prove their belief by collectively spending large sums of money with the individuals who provide these services.

SUMMARY

We probably all have examples of weirdness that have happened to us at some stage in our lives, and which we don't fully understand.

When we are able to comprehend the true scale of the potential of the human mind, we may find that we all have a piece of the jigsaw. And when enough people put their pieces together, and start to form connections, only then will we see parts of the picture begin to reveal themselves to us. Only then will we realise the magnitude of the greater-system that we are part of. Even concepts like yoga and meditation, were once thought to be extreme, or weird — now they are readily accepted, and practiced by many.

There's nothing wrong with believing in new things that others tend not to understand. We have a history of killing new beliefs or belittling them. At one time, we even had an attitude of killing the people who had the new beliefs. Witches were regularly burnt at the stake, and organisations like the Spanish Inquisition ensured that many who had alternative views were tortured or killed because of them.

My three summary points are:

1. There are two bodies of knowledge — that which can be proven through formulas and experiment to show that it is a rigid, repeatable and scalable concept. And that which is more subjective in nature, and which a person can only know for themselves. The two are very different belief systems. Perhaps some scientists and academics who believe they are responsible for advancing our layers of knowledge, are actually the ones who are holding it back. Just because you can't prove it — doesn't mean that it doesn't exist. The fact that you can't prove love exists and you can't prove god exists, but you know with all your heart that you love god, shows that the power of belief is stronger than the power of proof. You have evolved this way. This belief is what helps you to move on, and live a better life for yourself and for others. Many people believe in something but also harbour doubts too. Being slightly sceptical can be useful, but to advance yourself mentally, you need to have a greater-belief in your beliefs.

2. Who can say that the old view of many gods is primitive? We have just as much hard-proof of the existence of our gods today, as the ancient Romans and Greeks had in their day. How can we conclusively say that today we are right, and two-thousand years ago, the people then were wrong? We should be willing to be flexible in our beliefs — and to be more accommodating of what others believe in — no matter how much it differs from our own current views.

3. As a member of a religious faith, if you begin to question your religion, then it can start to not make sense. Most religions have been struggling with this for centuries. It doesn't work to question things too-much, which is why some beliefs are often referred to as a faith. Could the same be true for mental-capabilities

and mind-powers? They are all operating at Daryl Bem's 53%-level, and so are subject to some doubt, and review. It has to be up to us as individuals to have our own faith in our own beliefs.

Tomorrow, what new thing will each of us believe in? We may not even know that we have a view on it, never mind a belief in it, until we begin to question ourselves. To move on, we have to believe in something different to what we believe today. And potentially, different to what others close to us, and society in general believe in. Sometimes these new beliefs may feel uncomfortable — but that's how your comfort-zone repositions itself.

So, enlighten yourself, and embrace a new belief today!

Chapter 63 Wednesday 09h05

Gareth Jones was deciphering the dreamers' reports from the last webpage-upload, and he recognised the location would again be Paddington station. Patrick had dreamed the trains were all in a race which started at exactly eleven-minutes past one. When all the trains departed at the same moment, they got jammed-together at the end of the station, because there wasn't enough space for them where the railway tracks converged. This gave Gareth the time as 13h11.

The next part confused Gareth. There was a teddy-bear carrying a suitcase, who wanted to board a train. Because all the trains had already departed, the bear sat down on his suitcase to wait for the next one. Since the trains were all wedged together at the end of the platforms, there would never be any more trains, and so the bear eventually turned to steel and sat there forever, not moving.

He'd seen references to bulls and bears in the dreamers' feedback before, but that related to how the shares were going to move. On the stock-market, a bull-market was one that was going to rise in value, while a bear-market was one that was going to fall. These metaphors existed in reality too, as on New York's Wall Street, there was a large, metal statue of a charging bull. But why a bear was being mentioned in this dream, he wasn't sure. *He hadn't posted a share-code in the webpage name last night.* He had the time and general location, but Paddington was a big station, so he needed more precision on the exact whereabouts of Reece Tassicker at 13h11.

Just as some people would enter three items of food into Google, to find recipes that matched the three food-ingredients they had available, Gareth sometimes did the same with the dream-content when he was stuck. He typed in the terms *suitcase*, *bear* and *Paddington station* and pressed the ENTER key. Google instantly returned a list of pages for him. Near the top of the results-page were some sample images for his search terms. Three of the four-images showed a metal-bear sat on a suitcase. He clicked one, and learned there was a metal statue on Paddington station of the fictional children's character, Paddington Bear. In the story, a lost-bear from Peru was found on Paddington station, and so earned the name of Paddington Bear. The statue was located in part of the station known — for some obscure reason — as The Lawn. It was an area completely devoid of grass, and which housed numerous restaurants and coffee shops to service the station's passengers.

Gareth dialled Andre's number on his mobile. "Reece Tassicker will be at the Paddington Bear statue on Paddington station at 13h11 today."

That was all Andre needed to know.

Gareth wondered what Reece Tassicker had planned on doing for the last four-hours of his life.

Chapter 64 Wednesday 10h50

Reece was listening to the closing-remarks of a presentation by a mobile-phone company executive on how the world was becoming more connected.

"Many of the developing nations like Brazil, India, Russia and China, have extended their mobile-phone network to cover vast areas that previously didn't have any coverage at all. Third-world countries too, are making great strides in providing network coverage to hundreds of millions of people. Simultaneously, the cost of a basic smartphone has dropped to such a level, that smartphone ownership will be the norm in many developing countries — just as it is now, in the developed world. Over the next few years, a billion more people will have access to mobile phone coverage, and to data connectivity on their phones."

The image being projected on the two giant screens behind the speaker changed to show images of people from diverse ethnic-groups using smartphones.

"These people are being connected to the internet — and to the vast bank of knowledge that is available there, via their phones — for the first time ever. What are they going to do with all this data? Hopefully it will enrich their lives in many ways. And what's really exciting is how they will start to add their own knowledge too. The beauty is that through the vast-array of free applications that are available, the developed world is making this knowledge accessible, and understandable, to everyone. Even the most-advanced concepts are being explained in everyday language that school children can understand — and in many different languages too. With ownership of a cheap smartphone and access to the internet, a billion new people will have the potential to speak to the world — *and to change the world.* Thank you"

As people left the auditorium and headed for the refreshment area, Reece felt the need to find a quiet space to consolidate his own thoughts. His presentation was scheduled for tomorrow, but given the way his views on so many things had changed over the last few days, he was feeling that he had a completely different message to get across.

He found what appeared to be an empty room and went inside. Rows of chairs were laid out, ready for a later presentation. He hadn't noticed an elderly woman, sat on one of the second-row chairs behind the door, until he was well inside the room. She was leaning forward with her head down. He'd noticed her previously in some of the sessions, as a person who tended to inhabit the back-row of the auditorium. He initially thought she was being ill, but then, with relief, saw she was observing something she held in her right hand. A shiny, silver ball was attached to a short thread, and was swinging side-to-side. The woman was deeply engaged in whatever she was doing, so Reece tried to quietly edge backwards out of the room.

"Can I help you?" she asked, without looking up.

"I'm sorry. I didn't mean to disturb you."

"I like to be disturbed, you know," she said in a clipped-and-precise English accent.

"May I ask what you were doing?"

"Of course you may. I'm using my pendulum to broadcast my daily remedies," she replied, not taking her eyes off the swinging pendulum. "You seem a bit nonplussed. Shall I tell you more?"

"That would be most interesting," said Reece who was truly curious about what she was doing.

"I'm Margaret, and I'm a people whisperer," she said, glancing up at Reece's face to see his response. She saw from his curious expression that he seemed genuinely interested in what she was doing.

"I'm trained in homeopathy, and I use my pendulum to understand what treatments people need from me. I used to work only with individuals, but now I can handle large groups, regardless of distancc. I was just sending my remedies out to the group I work with," she explained.

"How exactly do you do that?" Reece asked. Prior to this conference he'd have been sceptical of such things, but what he'd heard — and been involved in — recently, had made him more-accepting of the unusual.

"I write my group's initials on a piece of paper, and I ask if anyone is in need of a specific remedy. If they are, then as I broadcast my remedies, that person will pick it up."

"I thought homeopathy was about medication that consisted of very-dilute forms of the actual disease you are trying to cure. Treating like-with-like?" queried Reece.

"It is," she replied. "But homeopathy is simply about transference of energy. I've gone beyond using physical tablets — I transmit the energy directly. It's how I can treat people over long distances."

"That's impressive," said Reece, wanting to understand more about her unusual perspective.

"You do know that emotions are just energy, don't you?" she added, changing the direction of the conversation.

"No, I didn't."

"A person can switch from joy to sorrow quickly, without any physical change. That's an energy change — and I can pick up these energy changes in people. The different needs in the people I'm treating, display themselves as different energy-patterns."

"How does it work, exactly?"

"Exactly?" She gave a small laugh. "I can't describe how this works at all! I just know that it does. So I use it for the benefit of the people I'm treating."

"How are you able to use it if you don't understand how it works?" asked Reece.

"Do you know, young man, that in society today, we are extraordinarily-unaware of ourselves?"

"No I didn't," replied Reece.

"Surface-living is the order of today. We want to look good in the eyes of others, and so we are trying to escape from who we truly are. We have an inability for taking ourselves seriously. I try to remove the barriers that people are putting up around themselves, as we are blocking ourselves too much."

"Go on," prompted Reece.

"We need to return to harmony. Many people feel that they sometimes need to go away on holiday to get refreshed. But I have a different view. Instead of going away, we should make a list of the things we want to change in our lives and make *them* go away instead. Listing things you want to change, and then ticking them off your list, is invigorating and refreshing, often more so, and less stressful, than going on holiday. And that's what I do for people. I help them clear things in their mind and body that will allow them to be re-energised."

"That makes sense to me," answered Reece. He realised she was frequently referring to energy, and he got a sudden impulse to ask her a question.

"Margaret, what's your understanding of the purpose of dreams?"

She allowed her pendulum to swing between her fingers. Reece saw that it initially moved backwards and forwards before it started to rotate in a clockwise circle.

"The purpose of dreams is to make you aware of who you are. You must always keep aware of yourself, and your feelings."

"What about strange coincidences?" Reece wasn't sure how he'd asked that question, for it seemed as if his mouth and taken momentary-control of his head.

"Coincidences are part of your awareness. Coincidences are things falling together. Nothing happens by chance — as chance doesn't exist."

A voice floated in on their conversation.

"Reece, may I have a word please?" It was Heather.

Reece excused himself and thanked the woman for her time.

"How did you know where I was?"

"You're tagged, remember? We need your input on something."

"What?"

Heather led Reece out of the room. "Gareth Jones and his associate didn't sleep in the hotel last night. Housekeeping told us their beds were unused."

"So?"

"I'm concerned that given the capabilities of their dream operation, something might be about to happen."

"What if they'd heard all they wanted to, and simply went home?" suggested Reece.

"And left all their clothes and toiletries behind?"

"Mmmm. Their timing does seem coincidental," he admitted.

"In my experience, coincidences like this don't exist."

Reece felt a chill run down his spine. Heather had just paraphrased Margaret's precise words from a moment ago. *Coincidences are things falling together. Nothing happens by chance — as chance doesn't exist.*

Chapter 65 Wednesday 11h10

"I'm concerned about the disappearance of the two Peckham Institute people. Not for their sakes, but for ours. Let's think through what might be happening. Reece, we need you to help us out here," said Heather.

"There's one thing that's been nagging at my mind," said Reece. "Whether it's a person's name, or a company share, that they want the dreamers to dream about — why post it up as the name of a webpage, especially when there's no other information on the page?"

"And as the dreamers don't even know it's there," added Asif.

"Because somebody else has to be involved," said Heather.

"Right! Let's assume the webpage address is a message to them — and that's why it's always uploaded at a specific time — to make it noticeable. Someone else does what we did, and decodes the address to see the message."

"But why not send them a message directly?" asked Asif.

"Maybe Gareth Jones doesn't know who the person is," suggested Heather.

"Do you think Peckham has set up a segmented-operation for security reasons?" said Asif.

"What's that?" asked Reece.

"Where the two different parties don't know of each other, and so can't communicate directly," explained Asif.

"The reader of the webpage knows it's being created by someone at the Peckham Institute because it's on their website. That means that the receiver could contact the webpage creator if they wanted to," pointed out Reece.

"But how does the person who decodes the webpage address, influence what the dreamers dream about?" said Asif.

"Wait! Always focus on one thing at a time," suggested Reece. "First, let's consider the issue of who could be receiving the coded-message *before* we move on to what they do with it."

He paused to slow things down before continuing.

"There are many more-efficient ways to give someone a message than putting it in the most public of all places — on the internet. Potentially anyone can see it — just as we did. And they seem to leave it up there permanently."

“Why aren’t they removing the page as soon as they receive the dreamers’ feedback?” mused Asif aloud. “If webpages keep being added, and not taken down, then as time goes on, there’ll be a long list of them, which seems risky. They’ll be leaving a complete trail of what they’ve done over time.”

Reece felt the pulse in his head. He paused, perfectly still; staring at the same arbitrary-point on the wall that he had been when the pulse occurred. He experienced the familiar disconnect from his surroundings.

Trail.

Time.

Trail. Time. Trail. Time. Trail. Time

Why were these words going through his head?

“Are you okay, Reece?” asked Heather, concern in her voice.

He held up his hand to stop her. He just needed a few-seconds undisturbed for the full connection to be made.

Time. Time. Time.

Trail. Trail. Trail.

Time. Time. Breakfast time.

Annalie Killian and her story about the two-scientists with their massive deck of cards.

Yes!

Now what about trail?

Trail. Trail. Trail.

Walking trail

Footprints. Leaving footprints.

Digital footprints.

Yes!

Two connections at once!

That’s good, thought Reece.

“What if the mystery person isn’t somewhere — *but sometime*?” he said, breaking the short-silence.

“What?”

“What if the webpage addresses, with their hidden codes, are created for someone to see in the future?” Reece paused. “If Peckham Institute create a new webpage, it could be up there for years couldn’t it?”

"Yes," said Asif. "It would be their choice when to remove it."

"Asif, you showed us that all of my strange-occurrences happened to me *after* I'd interacted with someone."

"Keep going," said Heather.

"When I bought the two-copies of the book that had the Post-it notes in, I was dealing with the WH Smith cashier. The text message I received was just before I got a call from my website designer. The security at Selfridges picked me up just as I was buying a gift-card from the sales assistant. There was a digital-transaction taking place each time."

"So?"

"When you pay for something — like my two books — you get a receipt. Have you ever looked at the amount of detail on a receipt? It has the date and time of purchase, details of the item you bought, the location of the store, how you paid for it, and even the cashier's name and the till number that you paid at. For the call I received at breakfast, my mobile network company would have full details of me receiving my call, who it was from, and probably my cell-location when I got the call too."

"And what about Selfridges?" asked Heather.

"When Selfridges security got hold of me, the sales-assistant said he'd just sent me an email confirming the details of my gift-card purchase, in case it got lost. That email would be date-and-time stamped, so someone would know the time when I bought the gift-card — even though I paid for it with cash. Our digital-activity leaves a detailed digital-footprint behind us of what we've done."

"I can see that," said Heather, "but how can the dreamers know that information?"

"What if someone in the future sees that a webpage address — with my name in — has been created up there at the special time of pi? They can then look back through the records to see what my digital-footprint was on the next day *after* the webpage went live. For example they might have seen I was booked on a specific flight to Johannesburg, or that I bought a train ticket for the Heathrow Express, or that I made numerous calls," said Reece, getting quite animated as his thinking developed.

"Someone would need deep resources to be able to find information like that," said Asif. "I'm not sure that even GCHQ have the power to access all that information immediately."

"What if the person who reads the coded webpage address is ten- or twenty-years in the future? All this information about my personal activities would be archived. It would potentially be low-risk information because it's so old, and therefore more easily accessed," suggested Reece.

"That seems to fit together — except for two things," said Heather. "Who is doing this in the future, and how do they send things back through time?"

"The *who* could be anybody I suppose. The three of us have a good chance of still being alive fifty-years from now don't we?" Reece started to speak more rapidly as the ideas formed in his head.

"What if we believed, that at some time in the future, we'd be able to communicate with ourselves in the past? To make it easier, we leave markers, or breadcrumb-trails, to show where we should come back to."

"That's far-fetched," said Heather.

"Have you listened to any of the presentations that have been given over the last two-days? Some of those involve us not being in the present time, and being able to see the future — just a few seconds ahead. But the fact is — *we can see the future*. The principles involved with humans being able to see ten-seconds into the future are probably the same as those involved in being able to see ten-years into the future. And if you can see into the future then why can't you see into the past?" Reece felt like he was on a roll with this line of thinking.

"Are you talking about time-travel here?" asked Asif.

"No, not really." And Reece related the story of the two scientists with their 100-million playing-card deck.

"When you think of time-travel, you imagine a person going back in time to do something personally. We've all seen films on that — and the effects it can have. The equipment needed to send a human being back through time would be incredible. But what if you were able to send energy from the future, back into the past, and that energy was able to influence someone's dreams, for example."

"But how can you influence the past when it has already gone and happened?" asked Asif.

"Take this discussion we're having. It's definitely real and it's definitely happening right now for us, isn't it?" posed Reece.

"It is," confirmed Heather.

"But imagine if a totally-unexpected message appeared on one of your monitors that said *Hello from Heather, Asif and Reece in the future* — and it was dated 16 July 2034? For the three of us sat here now, this has miraculously-appeared from the future. Yet the three of us, twenty-years from now, would be saying *but the past is already gone and happened — how can we change the past?* But the point is we did do it."

Heather and Asif stared at him blankly.

"Let me give you another example," said Reece. "Let's say that from today onwards, I'm going to prepare myself for when I can be influenced from the future — as I believe that one day I'll somehow be able to do this. I decide that every Sunday at midday, I will be on my computer and using a website that creates a random-number whenever I click the CREATE button. When I'm doing this, I'll be ready for a sign from the future.

At some point in the future, on a Sunday at midday, I press the button on the website to create a six-digit random-number — and a number appears. Then I click the button to create another random-number, but it's the same as the first-one. Finally, I click again to create yet another random-number — and that's also the same number as the first-one. In a random-number generator, the chances of this happening should be impossibly-small. But as it had just happened to me, then I can conclusively say that this was the signal that my future-self has just sent me from the future. Three consecutive, identical, supposedly-random numbers. That was the proof I was waiting for to show me that I can influence things through time."

"How could that be achieved?" asked Asif.

"I don't know. But intuitively, it feels that it would be an awful-lot easier to manipulate some microscopically-small amount of electrical-energy, to influence the output of a computer programme, than to send a person through time."

"Fair enough," acknowledged Asif.

"Incidentally, did you know that energy can never be created or destroyed? It can only be transferred from one form to another. There's a finite amount of energy in the whole universe, and today's energy will be used again in the future — many times over — and potentially in many different forms. So the same energy that was present in the past, is here, right now, and will be there in the future. Maybe we shouldn't think too much about the mechanics of how it works, but just the effects of what it can do."

"It seems far-fetched," said Heather. "However, this could be how Somnium Trading are able to be totally-correct when they pick their ninety-day share options. They've been told from the future what the movement would be over the coming ninety-day period."

"Maybe they've found a way to extend the ten-second future-horizon time-leakage mentioned by the speakers, to ninety-days," suggested Reece.

"Okay," said Heather, "I'm not going to enjoy writing this up in my final-report — but let's ignore that for now. Let's also assume they can see what we're doing when we leave a digital trail. From now on, if it's important, then avoid doing it digitally. We need to get Gareth Jones and his accomplice isolated from their technology, because if that's how they see the future — we don't want them posting any more requests for information. Especially about us."

"The way they left the hotel leaving all their stuff behind makes me think they've been spooked for some reason," said Asif.

"I agree," replied Heather. "Let's shape up a plan to detain them. Reece, we'll need you to be the bait to attract them."

"What a wonderful idea," said Reece, sarcastically.

Chapter 66 Wednesday 11h25

Heather's plan seemed quite straightforward to Reece. Arrange to meet — and then nab them for questioning. The first part required Reece to make a call to Gareth Jones.

"Gareth Jones," answered the voice on the other end of the phone.

"Gareth, hello. My name's Reece Tassicker. We've never met, but we're both attending the conference in the Churchill hotel. Now, this may sound strange to you, but last-night I had a dream that you and I need to talk about something. It was the most-unusual dream. I'm sorry if this sounds peculiar — but I knew when I woke-up that I absolutely had to talk with you."

"That is most peculiar," said the voice suspiciously. "Where did you get my number from?"

"I had to practically beg the conference director to give it to me. As the dream was so real, I lied to her about an emergency — and she gave it to me."

Reece heard a muffled conversation on the other end of the line. The voice said, "I'll call you back shortly. I can see your number on my phone."

And the call ended, abruptly.

Several minutes later, Reece's phone rang.

"Reece, it's Gareth Jones. Sorry for needing to call you back, but some very-strange things have been happening to me at this conference. I actually got really worried and left yesterday — in a rush. Look, I'm going to be quick as I'm feeling a little scared by this. I'll meet you on a train. I'm going to Oxford this afternoon and I'm catching either the 13h27 or the 13h57 departures from Paddington. It will be good to meet and talk about your strange dream too. Is that okay with you?"

"Certainly," said Reece.

The call again, ended abruptly.

At one-end of the call, Andre told Gareth he did well, but that he needed to take the battery out of his phone — so it couldn't be traced.

At the other-end of the call, it was Asif who spoke.

"My system shows those two trains are stopping trains from Paddington to Oxford. If he was serious about going to Oxford, there are express trains leaving at different times that would get there quicker. I think he may not get on the train at Paddington — but might be joining at one of the suburban stops on the way."

"There's no chance to get our people covering all the stations," said Heather. "Let me see what I can do to have some people on the train as back-up. Reece, you and I will leave here in an hour. It's a fifteen-minute walk to Paddington, so we'll have enough time at the station to get tickets and prepare."

Heather then excused herself saying she had things to organise.

Chapter 67 Wednesday 12h40

Heather and Reece had left the hotel, walking to Paddington station. They were waiting to cross the busy Edgware Road, when Reece heard the wail of police-sirens in the distance. He could see a large number of flashing-lights approaching rapidly, which impelled drivers to move over to let them through. Some out of courtesy, and probably some out of fear, given the number and noise of the sirens. Two police cars passed Reece line-abreast, with a large CASH TRANSIT sign mounted to the roof of one of them. Following the first two-cars was an armoured security-van, trailed by two more police-cars in-line, followed by a second armoured security-van. Four more police-cars in a two-by-two formation brought up the rear; one having another huge CASH TRANSIT sign mounted on top. The eight police-cars kept their sirens wailing continuously, which produced a painful cacophony of oscillating shrillness, until the convoy started to recede from them.

Reece thought this to be an innovative change from the times when valuable-item transits were done secretly. It made more sense to make the convoy into an unavoidable attraction. If any criminals tried to hijack it, there'd be a large number of the general public aware of the event. The police were doing the opposite of normal expectations.

As they stood on the pavement waiting to cross the road, Reece noticed that Heather had changed out of the shift-dress she'd been wearing earlier, and now wore a deep-blue, round-neck sweater with a charcoal-grey pants and jacket combination. He wondered why she'd bothered changing.

They'd arrived at Paddington station with ample time to spare. Heather went to buy two return-tickets to Oxford, and used cash to pay — just in case they were tracking *her* digital activity too. As she returned, Reece heard a tone from his phone, indicating a text message had been received. It was from a number that wasn't in his contacts — so no name came up. The message was clear though.

HAVE BEEN DELAYED. TAKE THE 14H06 TRAIN. GARETH JONES

He showed his phone to Heather. "What do we do?" he asked.

"We wait here. No point going back to the hotel." She reached around to her lower back, and from beneath her jacket pulled out a small radio, which had been clipped to the top of her trousers.

"Sierra-one to Zulu-one, Zulu-two. The target train is now the fourteen-hours-zero-six to Oxford. Stand-down in the meantime — but remain on the station. Acknowledge please."

Two double-taps of static noise emanated from the radio. She re-clipped the radio to the top of her trouser band. Reece looked at Heather enquiringly.

"We have two-people supporting us on the station. They'll be with us on the train too."

Heather glanced down at her watch. It was seven-minutes-past-one.

"Stop looking around," she said firmly. "It's their job to watch us — not our job to look for them."

"Sorry," he said sheepishly. "So what do we do?"

"We sit quietly and wait. We don't make phone calls, and we certainly don't buy anything with our credit cards. Do we?" She said this with a strong emphasis on the word *we*.

"Let's sit over there," she said, pointing to a waiting area which identified itself as *The Lawn*. "There are coffee shops so we can get a drink."

Reece could see the WH Smith shop where he'd bought the two books, just a few-days ago. *That's where all this started,* he thought.

He had another thought. *If he bought a third copy of the book, would that also contain a Post-it note with a message to him?* He was sorely tempted to look, but then thought better of it.

The Lawn was a large, open-plan area which housed an array of fast-food outlets and convenience shops. Everything the traveller — who wasn't actually travelling at that moment — could want. They looked for a place to sit, but the lunchtime trade were taking up every available seat.

Reece grabbed Heather's arm, and guided her over to one corner.

"As we've got plenty of time, I need you to take a photograph of me — with this." He'd taken her over to a large bronze statue of Paddington Bear. The bear was sat on a suitcase and wore a duffel coat, an oversize hat, and a lost expression.

"My nephew will love this picture," he said, handing her his phone.

Heather thought twice about doing this, but in the end, she relented.

"You mustn't send any emails from your phone, as you know they can be tracked," she warned him.

"No problems. I'll send the photo to him next week," he replied.

Reece sat on the plinth, next to the statue, and put his arm around the bear's shoulders. He looked at the camera. Then he looked at Heather's face, just beyond the camera. He studied it a little-more closely than he'd done previously. She had an attractive, heart-shaped face with brown eyes, which seemed a little larger than they should. Her face was lightly tanned, and the only make-up she wore appeared to be a muted-red lipstick. Black, wavy, shoulder-length hair symmetrically-framed her face. He hadn't acknowledged this before, but he thought that she had a most-attractive face. *Beautiful, actually.*

But the look on that beautiful face currently seemed to be a mix of mild-exasperation and extreme-indignation.

Heather framed the bear and Reece in the centre of the screen — and touched the camera-icon to take the photo.

Over the next few milliseconds, the computer chip embedded on the circuit board inside the phone, did exactly what it was programmed to do. The chip had no idea what the actual photograph was — it simply converted the electronic signals from the camera's lens into a huge map of binary code. It then converted this binary code into a digital file format, which it saved immediately onto the memory card located adjacent to it on the circuit board. It allocated the file a name which incorporated an image sequence number.

It also added some information to the file known as meta-data. This meta-data included the size of the picture in pixels and megabytes, the shutter speed, aperture setting, zoom focal length of the camera, and a host of other data items.

It also included the date and precise time the photograph was taken.

Reece frequently used his phone to take photographs of interesting things that stimulated his creative thinking — and also things that his clients would be interested in seeing. To safeguard these photos if he ever lost his phone, he'd set up a cloud based, data back-up service for his mobile phone.

Within seconds of the photograph being taken, his phone used the station's Wi-Fi network to access his data back-up service. It automatically uploaded the digital file into his back-up account, together with all the associated meta-data. Included in the meta-data were the following two items:

Date: 16/07/2014

Time: 13h11

Heather handed the phone back to Reece, who slipped it into his jacket pocket.

A man wearing a Danny's Doughnuts green and white vertically-striped apron, complete with a matching cap, walked up to them. He held a number of small, paper carrier-bags, filled with doughnuts. The bags were branded with the same green and white stripes as his uniform, and each had a Danny's Doughnuts logo printed boldly on the side.

He held out two of the bags, offering one to each of Reece's hands.

"Complimentary doughnuts for you, sir?" he said in a jovial Welsh accent.

Reece, taken by surprise, took the proffered bags. They were brimming with doughnuts, but still seemed surprisingly heavy considering what the contents were. The deceptive weight made the thin-string handles press firmly into the flesh of Reece's fingers.

"And also for you, madam?" said the Danny's Doughnuts man, thrusting his last two carrier-bags at Heather.

"No thanks," she replied curtly. Heather lifted her gaze from the two bags, intending to give the Danny's Doughnuts-man her *I'm-not-interested* look.

She ended up giving him her *I'm-shocked-at-what-I-see* look.

The smiling face framed between the stripy-green apron and Danny's Doughnuts cap — was that of Gareth Jones.

Barely had the shock registered on her face, when a hard jab in the side of her ribs made her wince. She looked round to see a well-built man holding a coat over his right arm, which looked unusually long, and which pointed towards her ribs.

"That pain you just felt was the barrel of a silenced gun," whispered Andre, drawing back the coat just enough for Heather to see the menacing, dull-black cylinder of a silencer poking out.

"And that," he said, pointing to a small, grey plastic box that Gareth was discretely showing them in the palm of his hand, "is a micro-explosive device." It was the size of a box of matches, with rounded corners and a bright-red dot on the side facing them. Reece stood motionless, in shock at what was happening, the two complimentary bags of doughnuts still held in each hand. Gareth slipped the device into Reece's trouser pocket, and Reece immediately felt its weight press against his inner thigh.

"That red-dot shows which side faces inwards — towards the victim. And it's controlled by this," he said, waving a key-fob sized remote control in his hand.

"If I press this, you'll hear a muted crack as the device explodes, sending shards of metal into his groin. It will sever his femoral artery, shatter his pelvis and cause severe internal damage to his stomach and abdomen. He'll bleed to death in less than a minute.

If I need to detonate the device for any reason, then you — conference director — will also be shot. Or, if I have to shoot you for any reason, then I also detonate the device."

He again jammed the gun into Heather's ribs. "Take the bags of doughnuts. I want to see both of you carrying them — one in each hand."

Gareth held out the two bags. Heather reluctantly took them. She briefly scanned the area, looking for her two support-agents, but to no avail.

"Follow him. *Move!* And don't either of you say a word to anyone," hissed Andre.

Gareth led them out of The Lawn area. Reece and Heather followed, walking side-by-side, with Andre just a pace behind them. Gareth led them on a route across the station concourse that avoided the busiest areas. He headed towards a large brick-building that formed the back wall to platform one. They went through an entrance-way in the wall, which led into a small passage that didn't appear to lead anywhere. Near the end was a metal door set into the right-side of the wall. It had a square, glass window in, at eye-level, and a small sign, identifying it as the Danny's Doughnuts storeroom.

Gareth entered a five-digit code into the push-button security panel on the wall. There was a solid *click* as the electrical lock released, and the door swung slightly ajar. Gareth walked in first, holding the door open to allow Heather and Reece to enter.

The room formed a long, thin rectangle, with the door at the end of one of the long, white-painted walls. It was the storeroom for all the ingredients and equipment that Danny's Doughnuts needed to keep the travelling public supplied with coffee, milk-shakes and doughnuts — the essentials for any long-distance rail journey. Andre lifted the coat off the gun, and waved the barrel to motion Reece and Heather down to the end of the room, farthest from the door. Gareth pushed the door closed, and the lock clicked firmly into place.

A long metal table was against one wall, and took up much of the space in the room. Shelving around most of the remaining wall-space held bottles, boxes and packets of assorted Danny's Doughnuts ingredients. Against the back wall of the room, were six grey lockers and two plastic chairs, which the staff used to change into their work uniforms. Reece took all this in as he scanned the room, and gasped as his eyes went to the final corner, which he hadn't yet seen. The body of a young man lay wedged between the end locker and a shelf containing coffee beans. A pool of blood puddled around his head, and the eyes were wide-open. Reece immediately knew he was looking at a corpse.

"Both of you, lean over the table as far as you can. Keep your arms stretched-out in front of you, and don't let go of those bags," said Andre, with the same calm-menace in his voice that an approaching thunderstorm has.

"If you have any doubts that I'm being serious, you can speak to the gentleman on the floor. His name is — or was — Richard. He didn't want to lend me his uniform." He motioned Gareth towards him.

"Take the gun," said Andre, passing it to Gareth, "while I search them."

"Put your chins on the table and look straight ahead at the wall," Andre commanded.

"We weren't expecting two people. Only you," he said, pointing at Reece.

"Why a conference director would be here, when her conference is still going-on, is unusual," said Andre. He ran his hands over Heathers arms and shoulders and then down her rib-cage and back, moving his hands expertly from side-to-side. His hands reached her waist-line and stopped. He'd felt a bulge on her side. He flipped-open the left vent of her jacket and removed the radio, clipped to the waist-band of her trousers.

"Interesting," he said. "What does a conference director need with a secure-band, high-specification radio like this?"

Heather thought about trying to explain how it was for speaking with her team at the conference. But she realised Andre obviously knew about security communications, and so wouldn't have been fooled by that. Anyway, in another moment, any conference-related story she tried to concoct would be exposed as a lie.

Andre dropped the radio to the floor, and stamped on it with his heel. There were numerous differently-pitched cracking-sounds as the radio shattered. He stamped three-more times, and the radio became a useless array of broken parts. He put his hand back on Heather's lower-back and moved it across to her right hip. Another bulge, and he flipped this side of her jacket open.

"Even more interesting," he said, removing the pistol from the soft-leather holster clipped to the band of Heather's trousers.

"Why would a conference director need a Glock 7.62-millimetre pistol?" he said, slipping it into his coat pocket. He finished searching Heather by removing her phone and wallet from her pockets. He then searched Reece, finding only his phone to be of interest.

In rapid succession, Heather's and Reece's phones found themselves sharing the same fate as the radio — at the heel of Andre's shoe. Andre opened Heather's wallet and pulled out her identity card.

"Heather Macreedy. Field Operative with the Ministry of Defence. That's also very interesting. We simply planned to explode the device on you from a distance Mister Tassicker. Then all our problems would be solved. But when we saw you with the conference director at the Paddington Bear statue, we knew something was up."

"I thought we were supposed to get the Oxford train just after two o'clock? A text came through on my phone," said Reece.

"That was just a ruse to distract you. We were never going to be on any train," said Andre. "Sit on those chairs. Now!"

The two chairs by the lockers were facing at right-angles to each other. Heather sat on the left-one and Reece on the right. Gareth used the sights to aim the gun, first at one of them, and then at the other, in a manner meant to indicate malice and alertness.

It worked on Reece — but not Heather. She started to realise that Gareth wasn't used to handling a gun. *No-one experienced with weapons would need to use the gun-sights at such close range.*

"You, conference director, remove your jacket," said Andre.

Heather removed it and put it on her lap. She needed to prepare a defensive response, and any item may prove useful — including her jacket.

"Put it on floor behind you," said Andre.

She lifted it over her shoulder and dropped it on the floor behind her.

"Now lift the front of your sweater up, and over your head."

"What?" exclaimed Heather.

"You were armed — and I don't trust you. Do it now!"

Gareth pointed the gun at her, to reinforce Andre's demand.

Heather raised the front of her sweater to reveal a flat, well-toned stomach below a black, well-filled bra. She lifted the sweater over her head and started to remove an arm.

"Stop there," said Andre. "Now drop your trousers."

"My trousers?" exclaimed Heather, involuntarily.

"You heard me."

Gareth made an exaggerated wiggling-motion with the gun.

Heather stood. The sweater was tight around the back of her neck, which made it difficult to get her arms down to the buttons on the side of her trousers.

"Can I take my sweater off? It's difficult to move my arms like this?" she said.

"That's the point of keeping it on. I think there's more to you than meets the eye," said Andre. "Now — the trousers."

With great-difficulty, Heather undid the buttons and the zip, which allowed her trousers to fall-down to her ankles. Her well-toned stomach was separated from a pair of shapely thighs by a pair of black bikini-briefs.

She looks good in that matching bra-and-bikini-brief combination — and with a very-trim body too thought Reece.

NOT THE TIME! responded the Council.

Heather started to step out of her trousers.

"Stop," said Andre. "Leave them there, around your ankles. Now sit down."

"We need to find out precisely what these two know. Especially the MoD one," Andre said to Gareth, and he paused for a moment.

"I'll need to get some packaging tape to secure them. And something else that I can use to make them talk."

"What will you use for that?" asked Gareth.

"I'll find something to improvise with. There are many ways to create sufficient pain to make people talk. Gareth, you stay here, and keep them covered at all times."

He pointed to the gun. *"You know how to use this."*

Gareth nodded, and Andre walked out of the storeroom. As the door made its solid locking click, there was another metallic-rattling sound from the door — and then silence.

Gareth stood there, pointing the gun first at Heather, and then at Reece.

"Sit still and don't move," he said.

Heather knew from her training that one of the essentials to survival, was never to lose your mobility and freedom. She realised that she'd lost some of her mobility in the way her sweater and trousers were around her neck and ankles. She estimated they had barely five minutes before Andre returned with his restraining material — and whatever other *worrisome* items he could find. The dead body on the floor — and most-likely the two dead women — were proof that Gareth, and particularly Andre, were serious in what they planned to do.

She knew they had to act now, before Andre returned. Heather chewed briefly on her lower lip. A plan was starting to take shape in her mind.

Chapter 68 Wednesday 13h25

Heather sensed there was a grain-of-sand in her mind, waiting to become a pearl. It was based on something that Andre had said to Gareth. Something that had sounded peculiar when it was said.

Just before he left, Andre had said to Gareth *You know how to use this*. A higher-pitched emphasis had been put on the word *this*, which Heather picked up from her psychology training. She'd initially assumed that Andre was saying it as a statement — when in actual fact, the raised emphasis at the end, showed he was positioning it as a question! *Andre had been checking that Gareth* was *competent with a firearm.* Another indication he wasn't very experienced in their use.

Gareth had also just told them to *sit still and don't move,* which was a double-reference to the same action. From what she knew of Gareth based on the background information Asif had found, he was well-educated, so a sentence-structure of that nature showed he was nervous — and stressed.

He was also standing so close to them, that he had to train the gun first on one of them, and then on the other. If he'd stood further back, then he'd be more removed from the danger-zone of an attack on him, and he'd be able to cover them both with just a minor movement of the gun.

That was a quick analysis of the aggressor. *Now to consider the weapon,* she thought.

Because Gareth was standing so close, Heather could see the gun was a Browning nine-millimetre, with an extended safety-catch. People with large-hands, like Andre, often fitted an extended safety-catch to ensure they could quickly release it when needed. Being a crack shot wasn't much use if the safety was still on when you pulled the trigger.

She could also see Gareth was not comfortable with a gun — as the safety-catch was still on. If she were in his position, the safety would most-definitely be *off.* That was another part of her training. If you were pointing a gun at someone, you were a trigger-pull away from shooting them, and the safety should always be off. If you had the safety on — then why were you pointing a gun at someone?

Heather looked closely at the way Gareth was holding the gun. *He was making a fundamental mistake.* The safety-catch was on the left-side of the gun and designed to be operated by the thumb of the right-hand. In a two-handed grip, the left-hand would overlay the right. This kept the right-thumb free to operate the safety-catch. She could see that due to Gareth's inexperience, he was using the two-handed grip *the wrong way round.*

His left-hand would most likely block the safety-catch when he took it off. It would only cause a fractional delay until he fumbled the safety-catch down — but that would buy her a little more time when she most needed it.

This comprehensive analysis of aggressor and weapon had taken her mind barely twenty seconds. She was under pressure; their survival was at stake; so her brain was operating at maximum speed.

She now knew what her plan was. Time was short. She had to put it into action immediately.

"No. Not now. The time's wrong," she said, in a barely-audible tone.

Gareth and Reece looked in her direction.

"My dream can't be wrong. No." She said, in a louder voice, rocking the upper-part of her body backwards and forwards.

Both men stared at her. She leaned forward, putting her face down on her knees.

"No. Not now. I told them no." She started to sob-quietly to herself.

"I'm just a conference organiser. I don't want to die. They made me do it," she cried. "The fake ID card. I'll tell you everything. They made me do it!"

Reece was surprised by her outburst. He thought there'd be more to her than breaking-down this way.

"They paid money to the people with the dreams. But not for my dreams," she said, rocking backward and forward with fake convulsions. The backward motion caused her feet to rise off the ground, which allowed her to gradually shake her trousers from around her ankles. Her feet were now free of their restraint.

"I'll tell you everything about their dreamers' programme. They made me do it," she cried. "I'll prove it to you. Just ask me *anything!*"

ASK A QUESTION! she mind-shouted at Gareth.

"What dreamers programme? Who made you do what? What are you talking about?" said Gareth.

HOLD THE GUN TIGHTLY! she mind-shouted again.

"They told me about the dreams the MoD people were having."

SQUEEZE THE GUN TIGHTLY!

She was sending out mind-shouts between her revelations.

"What dreams? Which people?" Gareth asked, desperate to know more.

"The people who took the special drugs that made them dream."

Gareth felt he was getting some information out of the woman. Just to make sure it wasn't a trick, he held the gun tightly, and pointed it at her head.

"What drugs? What are they dreaming of?" he yelled.

TIGHT. TIGHT. SQUEEZE THE GUN TIGHT.

"The pharmaceutical drugs to see the future."

Reece hadn't been initially sure what was happening with Heather. He thought she was breaking down, but he now realised she was concocting a deliberately-false story.

She was planning something.

And he had to be ready to help!

He slowly moved his feet into the best position for a sudden lunge forward. He lowered his hands onto the sides of the seat — ready to push with his arms too. He needed to be the proverbial coiled-spring, leaping to save her.

Heather had been waiting for Reece to get himself ready. *Finally he'd understood.*

She gave a last mind-shout to Gareth.

HOLD THE GUN VERY TIGHT!

Reece was so prepared, and ready to make his *coiled-spring* move, that when Heather used a mind-shout on him to *GRAB THE GUN NOW!* all three of them were startled at the speed with which Reece flew forward off his chair.

Gareth had been focussing on Heather and what she'd been saying, when, from the corner of his eye, he was aware of Reece careering towards him. He tried to push the safety-catch down, but his thumb was in the wrong position. He looked down at the gun, taking his eyes off Heather. As he again tried to slip the safety off, his hands were grabbed by both of Reece's.

There were now four inexperienced hands tightly gripping onto one gun.

The momentum of Reece's lunge had forced Gareth's arms around so that the gun was pointing towards the wall. Reece's head now momentarily-blocked Gareth's view of Heather.

With her trousers free from her ankles, she quickly stood, turned slightly to her left, bent her right knee, and leaned side-ways on her left-leg. She straightened her right-knee with as much force as she could muster, which caused her right-foot to strike-out horizontally.

She'd timed the kick perfectly. Her heel struck Gareth half-way up his now-exposed rib-cage, fracturing two of them in unison.

The pain caused Gareth to lose focus on the gun, which allowed Reece to fumble it out of his hands. Heather quickly pulled her right-arm free of her sweater, yanked it over her head and free of her left arm, then turned to face Gareth. She landed an open-palmed punch to the underside of Gareth Jones' jaw. Reece heard the sharp, snappy-sounds of shattering teeth, as Gareth flew backwards, landing hard on the table with his legs hanging over the side.

Heather quickly grabbed Gareth's semi-conscious head in her hands. Reece was surprised at the speed with which she wanted to show care and compassion to the injured man.

His view quickly changed as he watched her smash Gareth's skull down hard on the steel-table, changing the semi-conscious Gareth into an unconscious one.

Reece stood holding the weapon, not sure what to do with it. Heather reached out and took the gun from his hands. She ejected the magazine; checked to see how many rounds were in it; slid the magazine back into the handle with a firm slap of her left-palm; drew-back the slide until she could see into the firing-chamber; verified there was a round in the chamber; let the slide go back into position; and then she put the safety-catch on.

Watching the efficient-swiftness with which she checked the gun, Reece realised he had completely underestimated Heather. She was no longer a conference director in his mind. She was a life-saving goddess of martial arts and weaponry.

"He'll be back any moment. Open the door and check the corridor," she told him.

He looked through the small window in the door, but couldn't see down the corridor. He slid back the catch which over-rode the electrical lock, and gingerly pulled on the door. It didn't open. He used more force on both the lock-catch and the door, but it still wouldn't move.

"Door won't open. I think it's been locked from the outside."

Heather had gone through Gareth's pockets and found his mobile phone – which for some reason wouldn't turn on. She didn't know there was no battery in it.

She did know there wasn't time to waste trying to sort out the problem, and she threw the phone in the corner in frustration. She looked around and rapidly considered her next course of action.

"Don't you want to get dressed?" asked Reece.

"Modesty isn't the issue here. Staying alive is. Give me that explosive device."

"What explosive device?"

"The one in your pocket."

In all the commotion, Reece had forgotten about the device Gareth had slipped into his pocket. He reached deep into his trouser pocket and gingerly passed it to her. She looked around. All the metal lockers were padlocked closed. There was no obvious place to put the device that would prevent the shards from flying around the confines of the small room if Andre set it off.

Two large tubs of strawberry milkshake syrup were stacked on the metal table. She lifted the top one, put the device on the lid of the bottom tub, then placed the tub that she held, on top of the device. The table would protect them if they were underneath it, and the liquid in the containers would help contain the effects of a small explosion.

Heather scanned the room.

"I need you to make a distraction that will give me a few seconds delay when Andre returns. And do something with him," she added, pointing at Gareth. "If he sees him lying there like that, he'll know something is wrong."

"What should I do?"

"You're the creative one — just do something. We're trapped in here like rats in a barrel, so I need to prepare a shooting position."

What to do? thought Reece. *Why didn't she just call the police on that phone?*

Police. Police. Police.

A connection formed. He'd use the same approach he'd seen the police convoy using on their walk to the station. Rather than hide Gareth — he'd make him more obvious.

He slid Gareth's unconscious body across the table, and sat him up against the back wall, facing the door. On the shelves next to the table, were five-litre containers of doughnut glazes of assorted flavours and colours, and packets of different doughnut toppings. He took down the blueberry-flavoured glaze which, for some reason, was a vivid-blue in colour, and a large packet of lime-green coloured sprinkles. He also took four large packets of coffee beans, ripped them open, and poured them on the floor by the door. Reece then set to work with the doughnut glaze and the topping to create a new look for Gareth Jones.

Heather had found a roll of plastic safety tape, which was used when they wanted to prevent people entering an area while they were cleaning. She wrapped it around the handle of the door, and fed both ends to the back of the room.

There was a metallic noise at the door.

Heather hissed at Reece to kneel-down beside her, under the table. She passed him the ends of the safety tape.

“When he opens the door, he’ll be able to see down here through that small window. When I tell you, pull hard on this tape to open the door wide. That’ll give me a clear shooting line to him. Understood?”

Reece nodded.

Heather had the gun in her outstretched hands; her shoulder nestled against one of the table legs for stability. She’d have a good line-of-sight to his lower body when Andre came through the door.

Three rounds in his legs should bring him down, then another to the upper torso should be sufficient — to start with she thought.

And the gun’s safety catch was most-definitely *off*.

Chapter 69 Wednesday 13h28

Andre removed the padlock he'd put on the outside of the door as he left. He didn't want any off-duty employees of Danny's Doughnuts walking in while he was away.

Earlier he'd been in the corridor waiting by the security door for when an employee came to get fresh supplies. He'd pretended to be on his phone, making a call. He apologised for being there and said he had a personal call to make that he didn't want anyone to overhear. The young man had smiled, nodded and entered the code on the keypad to access the storeroom. Andre had made a mental-note of the code, before pushing him in the room as soon as the door had opened. Removing the silenced gun from under his coat, he told the young man to take off his Danny's Doughnuts cap, apron, and name-badge — which he'd done without hesitation.

Andre then shot him in the head.

Andre entered the same five-digit code to re-open the door. The electric lock clicked and the door opened slightly. As Andre pushed the door open, he was able to look through the square window in the door, to see down the length of the storeroom.

He was expecting to see Gareth's back, as he stood guard over the two seated people. However, his mind was busy thinking about what he'd do next to get them answering his questions quickly. They weren't going to have much time in the storeroom before other employees wanted to use it.

His hand was still on the door handle, as he pushed the door open, and stepped into the room.

Things had changed since he left.

Sitting on the table with its back against the wall, was an indistinguishable figure, with a lime-green head and a deep-blue torso, who appeared to be asleep.

This scene was so far-removed from what he was expecting, that his brain took a fraction-of-a-second longer than usual to process this abnormal scenario.

Andre's leg was in mid-stride, and as it landed on the ground, it slipped, as the coffee beans Reece had spread there, rolled, underneath his shoe. Andre heard the word *Now!* shouted from inside the room.

Reece had been taking in the slack of the safety-tape as the door opened.

On Heather's call, he yanked the tape as hard as he could. This pulled on the inside handle of the door, causing it to open a little-more, before hitting the restraining stop fitted to the floor. This was all Heather needed. She already had the gun aimed on the target zone. She moved the gun slightly, aimed, and fired into Andre's visible left leg. The silencer reducing the noise to a muted *phut*.

The bullet passed through his fleshy calf-muscle, before embedding itself in the brick wall behind. Andre's nervous system transmitted the new signals instantly from his injured left calf, which registered in his brain as intense pain. This additional stream of information was immediately included in the mass of assessments his brain was performing to understand the current situation — and to react with what should be his next course of action.

They were armed; they had shot him; they were in a good defensive position; he had Heather's gun; it wasn't silenced; it would make a lot of noise if he used it; that would attract attention; it would be hard to shoot at them around the door without exposing himself to more harm; the blue man with the green head had to be Gareth; he hadn't flinched — he must be dead or unconscious.

All of the knowledge, training, experience and predictive skills that Andre possessed, combined to tell him that his best option was to escape the area immediately.

He limped down the corridor as quickly as he could, and out onto the main concourse. He couldn't run here — it would make him stand-out. Anyway, he was injured, which slowed him down.

The station was busy with tourists. He could use the crowds for cover as he made his way to an exit. Immediately in front of him was one of the main departure boards with many people standing around. He walked into the centre of this crowd and kneeled, as if tying his shoe-lace. He needed a moment while he worked out his options for escape.

He also needed to slow the conference director and Tassicker down — just in case they were following him. He reached into his pocket for the remote control and pressed the button.

When she saw Andre move back out of the room, Heather cautiously followed, gun at the ready. She peered through the small, glass window into the corridor. *Nothing*. Using the steel door as protection for her body, she quickly glanced down the corridor.

Empty.

Heather was no longer being pursued. She was the pursuer. The roles had reversed, so the tactics had to change.

She headed down the corridor to where it joined the main concourse, unscrewing the silencer as she ran. It made a dull, metallic ring as it dropped onto the floor. When she used the gun now, she needed it to make maximum noise.

She knew Andre wouldn't be far away, but from the corridor she couldn't spot him. The concourse was busy with people — groups standing everywhere. One large group was standing immediately in front of her, watching the departure boards for their train to be announced. A few of them were staring at her. She realised she was only wearing her underwear.

She recognised this was the key for success at this moment.

Get attention. Create a scene.

Heather ran out onto the concourse, where an oversize, purple Louis Vuitton suitcase caught her attention. She raised her gun and fired three shots into it. For a brief moment Paddington station went silent — except for the three loud reports echoing under the vast over-arching roof. Everyone stopped moving, heads instinctively turning towards the source of the noises. All except for one nearby figure who stood out by continuing to move.

That was her target.

Then panic set-in amongst the passengers on the station. They started to run away from the crazed, gun-wielding woman dressed only in black underwear. They cleared a path in front of her, as she ran directly towards Andre — who had now doubled back towards the storeroom corridor.

"Stop!" she yelled.

There was no clear shot due to the panicking-passengers. She needed assistance.

Where were her back-up?

She fired twice, this time at a hideous, tartan suitcase, to attract more attention. Six-bullets used, five-remaining. Her training made her automatically count every shot she took.

Andre realised he wasn't going to outrun Heather, so he stopped and turned, slipping his right hand into his jacket pocket. Removing the gun, he raised it towards her. He would do whatever was needed to ensure his escape from this situation.

Heather had focussed her attention on Andre's hands, just as she'd learned in her weapons training. Knowing what your target's hands were doing was essential to not being out-manoeuvred when in close proximity. She saw the black shape appear out of Andre's pocket and immediately recognised it as her own Glock that he'd taken from her earlier. Heather realised that what had been a pursuit was now about to turn into a shooting match.

And Andre wouldn't be as concerned about not shooting innocents as she was. She knew she needed to up her game. It was time to take the man-shot.

In combat simulations Heather had always attained excellent ratings. She knew it was her ability to remain totally calm when under fire. She never quite understood why, or how, but in moments of extreme conflict, everything appeared to slow-down around her, seemingly allowing her ample time to assess her actions and to line up the shot on her target. She knew how to bring this state on, and she knew that she needed it now.

She drew a single large breath, stopped running and dropped to one knee. Her arms forming a rigid triangle from her shoulders to the Browning pistol held in her hands. She was in a rock-steady firing position. As she slowly breathed out through her pursed lips, everything seemed to slow down around her.

Andre's turning towards her and his removal of the gun from his pocket seemed caught in a time trap. Almost as if every movement was being performed in intricate slow-motion. He hadn't managed to point the gun at her yet for it was still aimed at the ground, some distance in front of her.

But it wouldn't stay that way for long.

She considered shouting a warning to him, but she knew she wouldn't be able to form the words fast enough. Her aim was perfectly in the centre of his torso. Even as he rotated his body in the turn, her shot would still be a traumatic-stopper.

Despite Heather's intense focus along the sights of the gun, her peripheral vision was still active. She noticed the outline of a person wearing a bright red top and blue jeans about to run across her sightline from the right. An unfortunate station passenger running in the wrong direction at the wrong place at the wrong time. The passenger's motion was much quicker in this time-lapse scenario than that of the relatively stationary relationship between Heather and Andre.

If she waited any longer, the person would block her vision of Andre, and once the innocent had passed, Andre would have a clear shot at Heather — if he bothered to wait that long.

The only sound she could hear was the slow hissing of her breath as she forced it out between her lips. It helped her to focus on the instant at hand. The innocent passenger was now incrementally crossing in front of Andre's body. Heather shifted her aim marginally to the left and firmly squeezed the trigger. She saw the barrel of the gun rise in her shot's recoil, yet the only sound she could hear was the slow continued exhale of her single breath. Then the figure of the passenger blocked her view of Andre.

She forced the front sight of the gun down, back to the same aim-point as her first shot. Ready for a second — if she had time.

The passenger continued moving to the left, slowly beginning to reveal Andre. Initially she could see his left arm, but that hadn't held the gun. As his right hand came into view she saw the gun pointing way over to the left — away from her. She watched as his hand seemed to open slowly, and release its grip on the weapon, allowing it to fall freely – but slowly — towards the ground.

Heather's mind had again used its ability to act as a time machine for her – but now it needed to switch back into real-time mode. She took a deep breath in and the moment was over. As reality returned to normal, the sounds of the station returned to Heather's ears. People were reacting with an enthused level of chaos brought on by the sound of her last shot.

The bullet had slammed into the humerus bone of Andre's upper arm, causing it to splinter badly. The impact knocked him backwards, onto the ground, the gun dropping from his now-useless right hand.

Heather ran over to where he lay, clutching his bleeding, and shattered arm. She dragged the gun away from him with her foot and stood over him, pointing her gun at his chest. She was extremely nervous about what would happen next, and quickly looked around.

There were armed Metropolitan Police running towards her. They might think *she* was a deranged killer — and potentially shoot her. She had no ID card on her; she was in her underwear; she had discharged a weapon numerous times in a public place; she'd shot Andre; and she was still pointing a weapon at him in a threatening manner.

This definitely has the potential to go badly wrong, she thought.

It was about to get weirder, too.

Chapter 70 Wednesday 13h31

Reece had seen Heather leave the storeroom, and wasn't sure what he should do. He realised that he'd better help her and had just stood up from behind the table when Andre had detonated the explosive device. The shock-wave had blown Reece backwards, hard against the wall. He slumped to the floor, briefly disorientated.

And with his head and body covered in bright-pink strawberry milkshake syrup.

The explosion had the opposite effect on Gareth Jones, who was just coming out of his own unconscious state. A large box of paper drinking cups lay on the table, and had protected him from the spraying strawberry syrup. However, the concussion wave acted like a dose of smelling-salts to him, jolting him back into the real world.

And it was a real-world filled with pain.

He had a searing pain from two broken ribs, which made him cry-out as he moved. His mouth was filled with blood, mucus and overly-sharp objects, which he realised were the remnants of some of his shattered teeth. This made him cry out again. As he opened his eyes, he saw that his hands, arms and upper body were covered in a blue, sticky substance. And there was a god-awful smell and taste of some sickly-sweet fruit all around him. Gareth had no idea what had happened to him, but he knew he needed help. And a lot of it.

And now!

He staggered off the table, moaning loudly and made his way out of the room.

In his own blurry stupor, Reece saw Gareth leave the room. He stood-up awkwardly, trying to regain full-control over his arms and legs. He knew that he had to help Heather.

He forced himself to walk. He wobbled badly — regained his senses — then he too, set off through the door.

Two armed members of the Metropolitan Police force pointed their Heckler & Koch MP5 machine-pistols at Heather, and shouted at her to put her gun down. She immediately complied and kicked it along the ground towards them — but more importantly — away from Andre. They then shouted at her to put her hands on her head — which she duly did.

Surely they can see I have no concealed weapons, she thought.

She knew it would be pointless trying to explain anything on her own — given the circumstances. At least not until her back-up arrived.

For Heather, the second-worst thing, other than being shot, would have been to have the Metropolitan Police handcuff her, and make her lie on the floor, in the middle of Paddington station, at lunchtime — wearing only her underwear.

Perhaps that's the worst-case scenario. Being shot might be significantly better, she thought.

The policemen kept their guns trained on her and told her to kneel down and keep her hands behind her head — which she did.

Andre was making up some story that he was just an innocent bystander who had been shot by a deranged woman. The police seemed to be believing him, more than anything she could say.

At that point, two men walked deliberately towards the policemen, trying to discretely get their attention. It was Zulu-one and Zulu-two — her back-up. She realised that they had a dilemma. Ideally, they should have walked up with their ID cards clearly open in front of them — to allow the police to immediately verify their identity. However, as they were undercover operatives, this could destroy their specifically-developed anonymity for any future operations. One of the policemen trained his gun on the two men and instructed them to stay away.

It was at this precise moment that Gareth Jones exited the corridor and onto the station concourse at a run. He'd seen the two policemen standing over Heather. All he knew was that he needed someone in a uniform to help take his pain away.

"What's happened to me? What's happened to me?" cried Gareth with an anguished howl, and through a set of shattered teeth. Heather turned her head to see the figure of Gareth Jones, with a vivid-blue upper-body and a lime-green head running towards them waving his arms.

Right behind Gareth was another figure. A man with an upper-body and head entirely-covered in a bright-pink liquid. This bright-pink man also started to run towards the policemen, following the blue-green man.

As the two armed policemen, Heather, Andre, Zulu-one and Zulu-two — and a large number of enthralled passengers watched, bright-pink man chased, and caught up with, blue-green man — just a few meters shy of where Heather was kneeling. Bright-pink man executed a perfect rugby tackle around the legs of blue-green man, bringing him crashing to the ground. This made the blue-green man howl loudly, and beg the policeman to help him.

Zulu-one, Zulu-two, Reece, Andre and Gareth were all trying to get the attention of the two policemen, to explain their part in this situation. Everyone was giving advice on what needed to be done next. One policeman was shouting into his radio that they needed urgent back-up, while the other was calling for immediate medical-support to treat the injured.

The policemen were also trying to get the public to stay where they were, as they'd need witnesses for this situation — while the station-tannoy was simultaneously broadcasting a pre-programmed emergency message in six-different languages, telling people to evacuate the station.

The only calm person was Heather. She was kneeling on the ground, hands behind her head, with two machine-pistols pointed at her, knowing there was nothing she could do — except to remain calm and still. *And I have to be the one wearing only my underwear.*

Barely four-minutes had passed from the time Andre had returned to the storeroom, until this moment of complete pandemonium.

The large number of the general public who were on the concourse when this occurred, seemed to be doing one of three things. Some were still running away from the disturbance; others were crouching on the ground to avoid any more shooting that may occur; while a number of hardy individuals were standing, oblivious to any danger, and recording the entire event on their mobile phones. For many, this was going to be the best part of their holiday.

Eventually the pandemonium was resolved.

But it took a long while.

Chapter 71 Wednesday 17h50

Heather sat on a broken swivel-chair at a damaged-desk in a windowless-corner of the large, open-plan Criminal Investigations area at Paddington Green police station.

She was sipping from a bottle of San Pellegrino water, while slowly swinging the broken-chair from side-to-side. It made an infuriating, high-pitched squeak on each little clockwise movement, which was why it found itself in the broken-furniture area of the office.

At this moment, both the sipping and the squeaking were helping Heather to think. She was trying to focus on what to do next in the questioning of Andre and Gareth. Unfortunately, she kept being distracted by thinking of what she might see of herself tomorrow, on YouTube. In fact, a group of male detectives over in the far corner seemed to be looking at her a bit strangely, as though they knew something that she didn't.

Jesus Christ! Don't tell me it's up there already.

She forced her mind back to her big issue — Gareth and Andre. Both had received medical treatment for different wounds. Gareth had a heavily-bandaged chest for his broken ribs, and would eventually need significant dental work if he ever wanted to eat spaghetti again. He was currently in a cell in the basement. Andre had a shattered right arm and a gun-shot wound to his left leg. He was being kept overnight in a secure room at the nearby St Mary's Hospital. An inch more to the right, and her shot would have shattered the bastard's shin-bone. Then she wouldn't have had to leave the doughnut storeroom. *I need more practice on the shooting range*, she told herself.

She'd complimented Reece on him making such a bold move to grab the gun. She told him how she'd reacted instinctively to what he did. He'd explained to her that he wasn't sure what made him do it — but that it seemed to be the right thing to do in the moment.

She'd not told him the truth for two reasons. Primarily, because she wasn't going to tell anyone of her ability to mentally-nudge people when she needed to. The second reason was that she could see the pride oozing out of him at his actions — so she decided not to spoil his moment of glory. She'd suggested that he go back to the hotel to clean up, as she needed to organise the next actions with the police.

He also stank to high-heaven of artificial strawberries.

Her rhythmic sipping, swaying and squeaking continued. Heather had a conundrum to solve. If the questioning of Gareth and Andre became protracted, then someone, somewhere, might start uploading webpage addresses — and decoding the dreamers' outputs to interfere with her work. And once that started, she could never be sure what was going to happen next.

Time was their friend, and her enemy.

There was also Paul Peckham. A man with deep pockets who would soon be aware that something had gone wrong. And who knew what he might do when vast sums of money were at stake — and also when money was no object. She needed Gareth and Andre to confess the whole story rapidly.

But how?

As she listened to the repetitive-squeaking of the chair, a plan started to form in her mind. A way to get everything she needed to know — and potentially more — from Gareth and Andre.

She used one of the office landlines to call Asif, and told him to put Anthony Thorpe in a taxi, and send him over to St Mary's Hospital.

While he was on his way, she'd start with Gareth. He was an intellectual type — not the kind of person disposed to spending time in prison. *Especially if it was going to be a long time!* As she walked the staircase down to the basement, her approach firmed itself up in her mind.

Some rooms in buildings are decorated to create a sense of joy, and to inspire a positive, happy and uplifting feeling. But not the interrogation rooms in the basement of Paddington Green police station.

Perfect thought Heather.

Gareth Jones was an absolute mess. The hospital had tried to clean him up so they could check him thoroughly for injuries. They had thrown away his blueberry, doughnut-glaze encrusted shirt after they had bandaged his broken ribs, and he now wore a green pullover that looked like something even the most down-market of charity shops would reject. There were still a good number of lime-green sprinkles in his hair — along with an overpowering smell of blueberries. They'd obviously given him some painkillers as he seemed slightly doped-up.

She realised that all this would work to assist her in her task.

Heather started by lying to Gareth. She gave him a completely-fabricated explanation of how the MoD had been tracking the Peckham Institute's activities for several months. While they had no issues with them making money from their ninety-day options, they had big issues when they started killing people. She said that the whole conference had been set up — at great expense — solely to attract the attention of the Peckham Institute. And that Reece Tassicker had assisted them by volunteering to be the bait.

Gareth was staring at her, eyes-wide in stunned disbelief. So she continued with her plan.

"You and Andre were involved in the murder of three people. A serious crime in itself, which my colleagues in the police will no-doubt want to discuss with you. But we at the MoD are involved because you compromised the security of the United Kingdom."

She paused to let this sink in.

"Andre holds an Eastern European passport, but you are a British citizen. That fact escalates your involvement in this into an act of treason."

She'd been watching out for — and observed — a distinct reaction from Gareth as she made this statement. At that precise moment she sent out a mental nudge.

TREASON IS A TERRIBLE CRIME!

"While the police will likely charge you as an accomplice to three murders, there will be a separate charge of conspiring against the state. We have ample proof of what you've been doing, so the trial will be a formality."

YOU WILL DEFINITELY BE FOUND GUILTY!

"Because what you've done has the potential to compromise the security of the country, we couldn't have you locked up in a normal prison for all that time."

A LONG TIME IN PRISON!

"You might start blabbing to the other lifers. The murderers, rapists and child-molesters."

A LIFE-TIME LOCKED UP WITH VILE SCUM!

"So you'd be removed from society to spend the next thirty-years in a military prison."

THIRTY YEARS IN PRISON!

"You and Andre ran the whole operation. So the blame, or should I say guilt, lies entirely with you two. We know you didn't kill the people yourself. That was Andre. He's cooperating fully with us to get a reduced sentence. But he's different to you, isn't he? He's got the character to handle time in prison."

BUT YOU COULDN'T HANDLE IT!

"He's telling us the full story. About him. About Paul Peckham. And about you."

WHAT'S HE SAYING ABOUT YOU?

“Paul Peckham will be here shortly. People like him enjoy the rich life. He won’t want to spend time in a prison hell-hole, so he’ll be telling us everything too. I imagine he’ll do all he can to distance himself from your dirty work. He’s already told us that he was doing it solely for the money — and he’s shocked at what you’ve done by killing people. He asked if he could bring his lawyer, and we said that’s fine. After all, making money isn’t a crime is it?”

“No,” said Gareth weakly. It was the first thing he’d said.

“Unlike what you did.”

IT’S A HOPELESS SITUATION FOR YOU!

“What do you think we’re going to do with your dreamers programme?”

“I don’t know,” answered Gareth.

“We aren’t going to close it down. It’s an amazing set-up that you’ve created. We’re going to take it over and develop it. We can do that, you know. We can do almost anything with the budget and resources we have.”

She paused.

“But we need someone who can make it work effectively for us. Someone with experience at doing this kind of thing. I believe there might be a role for you as part of an MoD-run programme.”

HOPE!

“We’ve some great plans. It’s really advanced stuff. It would fascinate you.”

YOU WANT THIS!

“I think you want to tell me everything, don’t you?”

TELL HER EVERYTHING!

And he did.

It didn’t take long for Heather to understand the full background to their operation. Once Gareth started talking, it seemed that he couldn’t unload the information fast enough. Perhaps he felt that he was in a race to tell her everything before Andre could tell his story. She sensed his desperation to answer any question Heather put to him. He’d even told her how much he and Andre had in their Swiss bank accounts.

A lot of it she knew already, and Gareth had filled in the gaps. *Except for one*. Apparently, even he didn’t know the answer to that specific question.

She realised that while Gareth had an academic interest in the field of dreaming, Andre was the dirty-work man, and probably only motivated by money. A lot of money too.

They'd found out Andre had formal military training, along with some background in quasi-mercenary activities in Eastern Europe. That was going to make her job of convincing him to talk a lot harder.

Unless Anthony Thorpe could make it easier.

Chapter 72 Wednesday 19h10

Heather walked the short distance from Paddington Green police station to St Mary's Hospital, and found Anthony Thorpe waiting for her in the large reception area. She took him up to the first-floor, and on the way, explained her plan to him.

"This man caused the deaths of three innocent people. And maybe more." she said, squeezing Anthony's arm in a comforting manner. Heather used a gentle nudge on him.

Anthony Thorpe felt the name *Gail* come into his mind at that moment.

"I think this man has never been scared of anything in his life. If you could make him scared — to experience what it feels like to be alone and helpless — that would be useful. Can you do alone and helpless?" asked Heather.

"Leave it to me," he said. His tone sent a chill down Heather's spine.

Anthony Thorpe knew exactly what it was like to feel alone and helpless.

They arrived at the secure room and found a plain-clothes police officer sat on a chair outside. He'd been expecting them. Heather showed her ID and he allowed them entry. They walked into a small ante-room, which was barely large-enough to hold the four chairs that were in it. There was straight-through access to a second door, that had a large, glass panel set into it. This ante-room was where additional security people would be if the nature of the detained suspect demanded it. Today, the room was empty.

"Make yourself comfortable here, Anthony. You can see him through the door," said Heather. "I'll just prime him beforehand."

She walked into the room to see that Andre had his right-arm in a cast that was strapped to his chest, and that his left-calf was bandaged and raised up. His uninjured left-wrist was handcuffed to the side of the bed. Heather had told the police to keep him handcuffed to make him feel helpless.

Heather closed the door behind her, and stood in silence, with her arms folded. Their eyes held each-other's stare. It didn't take long before Andre turned his head to look away, not saying a word.

"Gareth just told us everything." She paused and waited in silence.

He didn't respond.

"A pity that you'll never get to spend that two and a quarter million pounds in your Swiss bank account isn't it?"

"What do you mean?" he asked.

“As I said, Gareth told us everything.”

She walked out of the room letting the door swing closed behind her. She nodded to Anthony Thorpe, who now sat on one of the chairs, where he had a clear view of Andre through the window in the door. As Heather left the ante-room, Anthony Thorpe started his work.

Fifteen minutes after she’d left, Heather got a message that the patient in the secure room wanted to talk to her. *Urgently.*

Heather was standing at the end of Andre’s bed, watching him sobbing — and begging her to help him. From the smell in the room, he’d clearly soiled himself, and his left calf — where Heather had shot him — was bleeding through the heavy bandage. She’d asked Anthony Thorpe to wait outside in the corridor so he couldn’t hear anything that Andre said.

Heather explained that she could help him, but only if he told her what she needed to know. He said he’d tell her everything, as long as she didn’t leave him alone again. She was surprised by what seemed his genuine fear of being left alone.

Gareth had told her so much, that there weren’t many areas to fill in. Andre admitted to killing the two women, telling her exactly how he’d done it. There were a few things with the dreamers that still didn’t make sense. Andre told her that Paul Peckham kept a lot of distance between himself and the Institute, and rarely came to see them.

Based on his knowledge of economics and the stock-market, Paul would send Gareth an email with a share-code in the subject line. He selected shares that he believed would exhibit the greatest price volatility over the coming ninety-days.

When Gareth analysed the feedback from the dreamers, he would send Paul a text message saying up or down, based on whether the dreamers had a firm view on the direction of movement. Other than that, all Paul did was to fund the running expenses of the Institute — and pay their bonuses into their Swiss bank accounts. The one thing that Andre couldn’t explain was the same thing that Gareth couldn’t explain. *What made the dreamers dream of what they did?*

When he’d answered all her questions, Heather said she’d get him a nurse to fix his dressing and to clean him up — for the room stank badly of shit. She got up to leave and was shocked at the way he cried-out for her not to leave him. She took a step backwards, away from him, and he tried reaching out to her with the arm that was strapped to his chest. This caused so much pain that it made him shriek. She took another step backwards, and with tears streaming down his face, he begged her to stay.

Whatever Anthony Thorpe had done had been unbelievably effective she thought.

She walked out of the room, oblivious to Andre's screams.

Anthony was waiting for her in the corridor. Heather noticed that Andre's screams couldn't be heard there, for the ante-room acted as a very effective sound insulator. On the door was a plastic-frame with a slider, that allowed one of two indications to be displayed. It currently showed SECURE ROOM — PRIVATE. Heather moved the slider across to see what the alternate-display was. It showed DO NOT ENTER. MEDICAL EXAMINATION IN PROGRESS.

She left the sign in this position.

Part of Heather's debriefing plan for Gareth and Andre had deliberately-included getting Anthony Thorpe involved. She wanted to gauge how useful his skills could be.

Very useful indeed she thought to herself.

As they left the hospital, and climbed into a taxi back to the hotel, Heather realised she'd forgotten to tell the nurse that Andre needed to be cleaned-up.

Never mind.

Chapter 73 Wednesday 20h15

Back at the hotel, in a quiet corner of the coffee lounge, Heather had asked Anthony what he'd done to Andre.

"Most people believe there are only five senses that humans can experience. Those of smell, touch, taste, sight and sound. However, we have so many more."

"Really?" This was news to Heather.

"Of course. We can sense pain, itch, heat and cold on our skin. Pain can also be sensed in the bones or in the organs. We have the senses of thirst and hunger, and the corresponding feelings of a full-bladder or full-bowel. There's your sense of balance which is in your ears, and there's the sense of location, motion and acceleration in all your limbs."

"Wait — what's that about your limbs?" queried Heather.

"We're able to sense where our limbs are at any moment and what they are doing. If you close your eyes and put your hands out and wave them around, you can sense exactly where they are — can't you?"

"Yes."

"That's also a sense we have. It's called proprioception."

"And are there any others?"

"There's also the sense we have of time-passing, but I've not been able to master that one yet." He said this in an almost self-deprecating manner.

"And you can influence all these senses?" she asked.

"To differing degrees of success, yes."

"So what did you do to Andre?"

"I started with his sense of balance. Even when you are lying down you can lose your sense of balance — like the feeling that the room is spinning. I gave him that — and then added a little nausea."

"Interesting," said Heather.

"I saw that one arm was bandaged to his chest and the other hand-cuffed to the bed. So I gave him an itch in his foot, but interfered with his proprioception. It must have been extremely-irritating, and disturbing, as he kept banging his itchy foot on his injured leg. This seemed to cause him an extraordinary amount of pain. So I let that continue for a while."

“Okay,” said Heather, getting slightly concerned about how far Anthony Thorpe would let things go. She recalled that Andre’s leg-wound had been bleeding through his bandages when she’d spoken with him.

“The pain caused him to cry out, so I inhibited his swallow reflex, which caused him to start to choke. I closed down his sense of hearing so that all he could hear were the internal sounds his body was making. I had to stop the choking quite quickly. There’s always the risk that the person may drown on their own saliva.”

“Yes, of course,” said Heather, trying to keep her voice as calm as possible. Anthony Thorpe was reeling off the list of his capabilities as though he were dictating his shopping list before going to the supermarket.

“Each time he tried to call-out I just invoked the choking reflex. I encouraged him to empty his bladder, and evacuate his bowels, to enhance the sensation of being helpless. Naturally he tried to call out again at that point for assistance, so I let him choke for a while. I think it must have been quite disconcerting for him, with the room spinning and him not having any sense of where his limbs were.”

Anthony Thorpe went silent for a while. Heather was too nervous to speak, as she was sure her voice would fail her — whatever she tried to say.

“So, how was that for alone and helpless?” asked Anthony Thorpe in a quiet, factual-tone.

“That was quite appropriate, thank you,” said Heather, deliberately down-playing his achievement. She wasn’t sure whether she should feel impressed or terrified at what he’d told her he could do.

“You know I’ve been developing my skills over many years, but I’ve never been able to test myself properly — to see how far I could go. It was nice to see what I can actually do on someone who deserved it,” he said, staring resolutely at Heather.

Heather felt the chill of an Arctic gale blow down the full length of her spine. She wasn’t certain, but she may have just experienced a sense of extreme fear. *Had Anthony Thorpe just done that as a warning to her?*

Whatever, Professor Bartlett got off easily thought Heather, imagining what this man could potentially have done if he’d been so inclined. Then she recalled the fact that the discrediting of Anthony and Gail Thorpe — which had subsequently led to Gail’s death — had been funded by her department.

That was a really disturbing thought for Heather Macreedy.

As she walked back to her office, Heather realised that Paul Peckham was clearly well-removed from the operation of the dreamers. With Gareth and Andre detained, she probably had a window-of-time when they'd *not* be at risk from the dreamers.

She'd need to consider how they wanted to move forward before speaking with Peckham himself.

Chapter 74 Thursday 08h50

"In many ways you were right about the dreamers, Reece." Heather was in her office, explaining the Peckham Institute's operation to Reece and Asif.

"They advertised for people who were vivid-dreamers and who could accurately recall their dreams afterwards. They were typically younger, poorly-paid people that were recruited, and they paid them well — so they didn't need to work. They also took DNA samples from each of them, and genetically-tested them to see if they had a long life-expectancy. Apparently they wanted people they could use for many years — decades in fact — and for a very good reason. The information the dreamers receive is coming from the future."

"Seriously?" said Reece.

"Peckham himself explained all this to Gareth and Andre when they did their first successful-trade. When he was younger, Peckham had a strange dream that he could send a tiny thing back through time. This tiny thing was so amazingly-useful that you could do absolutely anything with it. This thing was so small, however, that no-one could ever see it. Because they couldn't see it, they never knew that they'd received it — and so they didn't use it."

She continued. "These dreams developed bit-by-bit over time, and eventually in one dream, he found out that this small thing was so small and light that it couldn't be weighed. It had no mass. He had this dream repeatedly, and eventually spoke to a physicist he knew. He asked him what was very small, weighed nothing — but could do everything. The physicist thought it a strange question, but said it sounded like energy. Energy has no mass — but can be used to do anything."

Heather took a sip of her coffee and continued with the explanation.

"Peckham knew that the mind was housed in the brain, and that the brain used electrical- and chemical-energy to do its thinking — and its dreaming. That's when he experienced an epiphany that even he thought crazy at the time. What if he were able to send dreams to people from the future? *Dreams in the form of energy.* He realised he could make a fortune if he could send back information on how the stock-market was going to perform — from the future. At first he thought it impossible, and that it would remain, literally, just a dream. But it was actually a dream that he had, that he could do this. He had the insight that *this was itself a dream being sent to him from the future.*"

She took another sip of coffee.

“Peckham imagined himself twenty, thirty or forty-years from now, having found a way to send information back in time — as a form of energy that could be picked up by people in their dreams. He asked himself *What would he do with this knowledge?* The first thing he would do would be to send the information back to himself — not to anyone else, of course. He’d always been an active-dreamer in his youth, so his older-self sent a dream back to his younger-self, that when he was much-older, he’d be able to send dreams back in time. That was the recurring dream he’d had, that had developed over time. The future-self kept sending it to him to make sure he believed it.”

Reece and Asif sat enthralled, like children listening to a fairy-tale.

“And he did believe it — eventually. That’s when he sold his stock-broking business — for a lot of money — to fund the setting up of the Peckham Institute. They found dreamers who would be the recipients of the energy-from-the-future, and set up the dreaming mechanism which is now working — as we’ve seen. Peckham selects a share that he thinks will be volatile in the stock-market over the next ninety-days and Jones creates a webpage-address with this coded-in. This webpage stays up forever, and at some point in the future Peckham sees this new webpage address, decodes it, and looks back over the historical-performance of the share around the time the page first went live. It’s similar for whatever digital-transactions a person made too — if that was the focus of the webpage. They send this information back through time in the form of energy, that makes the dreamers dream of the relevant information.”

“Why did they only post a share webpage address weekly?” asked Asif.

“Apparently it gets too confusing to decode if there are too-many relevant dreams coming through. By only posting once a week — and at the pi time — Jones knew to place particular emphasis on the last dream they had on those particular nights.”

“Why did they kill those two women and not me?” asked Reece.

“Those women were discussing their concurrent dreams, and Gareth and Andre didn’t want anyone discovering anything that might jeopardise their operation. After killing them, they got some kind of feedback about disturbances and follow-on future effects. They concluded that killing people somehow influenced the future too-much, when compared to the limited effects of making money on the stock market. Apparently this is the reason they didn’t want to kill you Reece — they just wanted to dissuade you from creating your dream website. It was only when Andre overheard our conversation in the lobby, on your return from Selfridges, that they decided to kill you — as you knew too much. And me too,” she added.

"So, when in the future is Peckham supposed to be doing all this?" asked Reece.

"None of them know. When they first started using the dreamers to get the correct movement of the shares, they knew that it worked. And that was all that mattered."

"Why do they only trade shares in the US?"

"The split was to help minimise suspicion. To prevent links between the dreamers in the UK and Somnium Trading's gains from the US stock-market."

"Why don't they see all the webpage addresses in the future at one-time?" asked Asif.

"They tried numerous things when they initially tested the process out. Putting up detailed questions, or doing multiple-pages in one day, didn't get meaningful feedback. They found that simple codes, or names, worked best. Even they aren't sure how it works in the future. When they post a new webpage, they plan to leave it up there forever, so Peckham will eventually see it in the future. They don't know why he doesn't see all the webpages in one-go. Gareth said the process works — so they just use it the way it is. He thinks that because the input from one page, or action, might influence the next, someone in the future watching a full-list of pages, may find they subtly change as the actions are executed. But this is just his guesswork."

"So even Paul Peckham doesn't know how he can send energy as dreams back in time," said Reece.

"No. And that's the question neither of them could answer. But he knew he would be able to do it sometime in the future. And that we know for sure. Reece, it seems that your example of being ready for a message from the future with your midday Sunday random-number generator, was absolutely right. If no-one is ready and waiting for a message — then they're never going to receive one. Paul Peckham had the open-mindedness to acknowledge this possibility — and then to set up a mechanism to be ready for it. You have to give him credit. That was a highly-insightful and ballsy move on his part."

The phone on Heather's desk rang.

"Heather Macreedy," she answered.

"What the bloody-hell is going on now Heather?" shouted the voice on the other end of the call. Heather held the phone away from her ear, again.

"First there's the Professor Bartlett sneezing and vomiting videos. Then I have some kind of security-issue at Selfridges that I hear about. Then I've got the Metropolitan Police onto me about a shooting disturbance at Paddington station."

"What happened was..." But Heather wasn't able to finish her sentence as the tirade on the phone continued.

“The report that you submit at the end of this exercise better be a bloody good one. In fact, rather than me reading your confidential report written under the Official Secrets Act, I might as well watch the whole bloody thing on YouTube. Or read it in the papers. This was supposed to be a discreet undercover operation. You do know what the term *undercover operation* actually means don’t you? Tomorrow when that conference ends, I want to see you in my office to explain all this.”

The phone went dead in Heather’s hand.

“I lost my dignity on Paddington station yesterday — now it sounds like tomorrow I might also lose my job.”

“Well, I’m sure you’ll be getting lots of offers to be an underwear model,” suggested Reece.

“Don’t you bloody-well start!” said Heather.

“And what are you sniggering at?” she yelled at Asif.

“What will you do about Paul Peckham?” asked Reece, trying to deflect Heather’s ire.

“It’ll be difficult to charge him with a crime, because I don’t think he’s done anything illegal. Given the money he has, and the quality of lawyers he can hire, we’d have a big problem getting a case against him for receiving information from the future. All he’d do is threaten to go public with it, and we’d be up to our eyes in time-travel nonsense.”

Images of her boss reading her report on the conference, with a final conclusion stating *It was all done by time travel* filled her head. And they weren’t good images.

“We’ve got ways to put him on a leash though. We give him a choice of keeping his wealth, but being monitored continuously with regular lie-detection tests — or he risks losing everything. We have special mobile phones that give an exceptionally-clear signal. We use them to monitor the voice-patterns of the person we call while we ask them questions. If they don’t answer a question truthfully, they are immediately detained. They never know when we are going to call them, or what we might ask. It’s a simple and effective deterrent that would work well with Peckham.”

“And the dreamers network?” asked Reece.

“We’ll just shut it down. The dreamers don’t know anything except the fact that they dream — and they’ve always done that. They aren’t any risk to us. They’ll just have to get a job, or go back onto social security.”

“That’s unfortunate for them.”

“That’s the way it goes,” replied Heather.

"Well, that's one way it could go," countered Reece, thoughtfully. "Instead, why don't you do the exact opposite of that?"

"What do you mean?"

"What if you let the whole dream operation continue? Keep Peckham on your leash, and tell him he can use the system for occasional-gains for himself, as long as he finances the running of the whole thing."

"But why?" she asked. "Just so Peckham can make money, but not as much as he did before?"

"No. So you can use the system yourselves — from an intelligence perspective."

Heather was silent. Stunned that he could suggest such a thing.

In just a few seconds, the neurons in her brain made tens of millions of new connections, and the possibilities of what Reece had suggested exploded into a realm of beneficial opportunities.

"Very interesting idea," she replied, her mind elsewhere.

"And for the break you're giving him, maybe some of his money should be used to explore new lines of research in this area too. Under very-secure circumstances, of course."

"Of course," smiled Heather, liking Reece's idea a lot.

"By the way, haven't you got your presentation today?"

"Right after lunch."

"I'll see you then," she said.

Reece went straight back to his room. Based on what he'd heard, seen and experienced over the last few days, he knew that he had a very-different message he wanted to put across in his presentation.

Chapter 75 Thursday 14h35

Presentation #6

The Delicate Force

By Reece Tassicker

Partner

Ingenious Growth Ltd

At the end of my presentation I'll be giving you a set of techniques to help you be more creative in your thinking — and which will also enable you to get a head-start when it comes to your future evolution. Before that, I'll be showing you how the most amazing period in the history of mankind — is right now. And before that, I'll demonstrate where your ideas come from. But, I'd like to start with...

THE STRANGENESS OF REALITY

99-Donk: The theory of exceptions

99-Donk is a joke about a caterpillar with a wooden leg. What stands out aren't the ninety-nine times when the normal thing happens, it's when the exceptional and unexpected thing occurs. It's about the anomalies in life.

When it comes to who we are as a species, there are gaps in our knowledge which leave some of our most-fundamental questions unanswered. How life started; where intelligence came from; how we developed from asexual-reproduction to sexual-reproduction; how DNA divides, rebuilds and repairs itself without any form of intelligence. Evolution should be able to account for the answers to these questions, but it can't. Evolution is a theory in tatters. It adequately covers the *99s*, but absolutely fails to explain the *Donks* — these huge-gaps in our development.

We've also heard about anomalies at the cosmic, human and atomic-scales that can't be explained. Things that we've conveniently brushed under the carpet to be forgotten about, because they don't comply with the scientific laws we've developed over time.

It's these *Donks* — the anomalies and discontinuities that we can't account for, that have done most for our evolution. A decisive-alteration to a new and better direction, is of greater advantage than continued development in any single direction. It's the Donks that matter rather than the predictable 99s. We must acknowledge that something caused the Donks to mysteriously occur.

99-Donk is a paradoxical-theory of exceptions. We need to passionately-embrace *the existence of the Donks* — and then ignore them, to avoid becoming obsessed by them.

Signals everywhere

The anomalies and discontinuities act as signals for us, and these signals exist on three distinct levels; Enduring signals, Capability signals and Instance signals:

Enduring signals are those which have existed for a considerable period of time, ranging from millions to billions of years. They are astonishing in some way, given the expected course of natural events, or in the surprising things that living-species have been able to achieve. From the disturbing and mystifying attributes of quantum mechanics, where two different-states can exist at the same time; to where particles appear to be communicating over vast distances at many times faster than the speed of light; to how a scientific constant that should never change, actually has changed over time; and to the mysteries of how life and intelligence came about.

Capability signals are attributes possessed by humans that may defy common sense and reasoning. Some people may refer to these as gifts, because these individuals have the ability to do something extraordinary, that few-others can achieve. Examples of Capability signals include an ability to see into the future, and phenomenal memory-recall skills.

Instance signals are events that occur to individuals in relatively-short time frames, and which are completely unexpected. They may be internal in nature, such as our intuition, or flashes of genius-inspiration. Or they can be external in nature when somebody, or something, interacts with us in an unforeseen-way. An example of this is *synchronicity*; meaningful-coincidences that occur to an individual which are totally unexpected.

The Enduring signals have been instrumental in getting us to our evolutionary-state today, while the Capability and Instance signals form an active part of our own, individual current-lives.

It can sometimes be difficult to classify exactly what is, and what isn't, a signal, as they are self-interpretive in nature. In 1964 in the US, Justice Potter Stewart was involved in a case regarding whether a particular film was obscene or not. In his concurring opinion, and describing what obscene actually meant, he stated that "*I know it when I see it*". The same exists for the Capability and Instance signals in our lives. Different things happen to different people, but when something that is anomalous occurs, it could be a signal. *You'll know it when you see it*.

If you look back at strange occurrences in your life, you're likely to find an anomaly that either doesn't make sense, or that seems too coincidental. People or places; events or times; when you had an amazing thought pop into your head from nowhere; times when you had a dream; or a sudden sense of intuition that extraordinarily-appeared to be correct. Think back to what caused those things to happen to you, *and to happen at that particular moment*. There's likely *not to be* any logical reason as to why they occurred when they did — and why they should have occurred to you, and nobody else. These are Instance signals happening to you.

Whispers in your thunderstorm

Whatever form signals take when they occur to you, they will most-likely be at the threshold of your awareness. They will be *tenuous*, *ephemeral*, *ethereal* and *peripheral* in nature. But what do I mean by these terms?

Tenuous: lacking in clarity, vague, thin in consistency:

When an idea comes to you, it usually isn't fully fleshed-out or detailed. It may often be just a word — or a short-sentence, that shouts itself into your mind without any sense of arrival. It's suddenly there — as a concept to be taken further.

Ephemeral: lasting a very short time, transitory, short-lived:

When a new idea pops into your head, it's often fleeting in nature — such that if you don't pay attention to it, then it evaporates and maybe lost forever. This is a similar situation with psychic abilities too. They aren't hard and unyielding, they are temporary in nature.

Ethereal: extremely delicate, refined, light, airy, exquisite:

When an idea appears in your mind it is conceptual in form, such that it often gives you latitude and scope to develop it in a number of different ways. It isn't hard and defined — it offers flexibility and opportunity. It is open to interpretation.

Peripheral: near the surface, outside of, situated at the edge of:

Anomalous experiences are happening to us regularly; however, you only notice them when they happen above your threshold-of-awareness. This threshold changes depending on a number of factors including how busy you are, or how tired and inattentive you are.

We all live hectic, tumultuous, thunderstorm lives. However, when a signal occurs, it won't be in the form of a thunderbolt that hits you. It will be something much more delicate — something that you will need to pay attention to. It will be more-akin to a *whisper* in your thunderstorm.

Be aware. Pay attention. And always react.

FINGERPRINTS ON THE UNIVERSE

Freaky luck or the hand of God?

We've seen the phenomenal odds that were stacked against our being here today. Either everything in nature that we see around us, occurred by the longest, most-incredible run of good luck, or we've had a helping-hand in some way.

Was it the hand of God? I'm going to keep this exceptionally brief so I can move on. To say there was the hand of a deity behind everything, would be an easy explanation. The Intelligent Design perspective is that there has to have been some kind of intelligence involved in our development to account for the gaps in the evolutionary model. Their view is that this is God. However, I don't believe that an all-powerful deity behind our existence would let innocent people (and especially children) suffer, in the most terrible-of-ways, as occurs in various parts of our planet on a daily-basis.

If it isn't the hand of God that's been involved, and we haven't won the universal-jackpot — then what is it that's helped us to get to where we are, on so many different levels over time? There must have been some kind of force (or energy) helping and guiding our overall evolution. This wasn't a divine, or perfect, force — but an *all-pervasive, delicate force,* that gave us an evolutionary-edge at key stages on our journey over the last 13.8 billion years since the big bang.

This *Delicate Force* is an all-enveloping force, but which is also extremely-subtle in nature. Like a hurricane, made up of an infinite number of tiny breaths, each of which can individually move just a single leaf, or they can combine to blow down an entire forest. If this Delicate Force was of a divine origin, it would likely be perfect in its actions. But it isn't a perfect force. And as it performed its purpose of moving us beneficially-forward along our evolutionary path, it has left its fingerprints on the universe. These fingerprints are the signals, showing us the evidence of where it has exerted its influence along the way.

You don't interrogate a pineapple

What is this *Delicate Force*? Who put it there? What powers it? Where does it reside? When does it act on us? Why does it not make itself known to us? How big is it? How does it influence specific areas?

I don't know. But I do know that you don't interrogate a pineapple.

If you are thirsty on a hot day, and someone offers you an ice-cold, peeled-pineapple on a stick, you'd gladly take it — and satisfy your thirst by eating it. You wouldn't ask what its country of origin was, what its molecular structure was, or how old the plant was that bore it. You'd just eat it and enjoy the experience as it quenched your thirst.

We have the capabilities to build towering structures, perform corrective surgery on unborn babies, and to send spacecraft to distant planets. But if we try to create a single human cell without using another cell, we have zero-ability. The universe creates a human brain out of nothing, to become the most amazing intelligent-thought generation and memory-storage machine ever. But when we try to understand how it does this using our supposed intelligence, we fail completely. Why did nature make something that is way beyond our ability to comprehend? Maybe we aren't meant to look in there. Maybe the skill comes in just using it in smart and creative ways to design and develop beautiful things and sensational futures.

The Delicate Force itself can't be observed or measured, or its effects predicted, and neither can it be captured, bottled and reused later. It's a delicate and ephemeral force that is giving us a slight, but beneficial, advantage over the laws of probability.

We don't interrogate a pineapple before we eat it, so why do we feel the need to interrogate the force that has so successfully delivered us to be who and what we are, over the course of our evolution from lifeless chemical elements to be today's human being. This Delicate Force has conclusively proved itself over time — so why don't we trust it to continue exerting its influence without needing to know why and how?

Measuring the Delicate Force

I don't believe it will be possible to conclusively prove a psychic-capability in our lifetime, because we aren't mature enough as a species to handle this. This doesn't mean psychics aren't real though — and that some people don't have these abilities right now. This begs the question of *why can't we measure their capabilities, and the Delicate Force?*

The double-slit experiment, performed at the quantum physics level, has proven repeatedly, that just by observing and measuring something, you cause it to break down and change into another form. The atomic-level foundation of everything that exists in our universe, isn't built of solid-models and substance, but instead consists of vague, fuzzy and changeable concepts. As Stephen Hawking postulates, nothing is real unless — and until — it has been observed.

Potentially for us to be real, there must be some external body observing our universe. So if the fact that things at the smallest atomic-scale, and grandest cosmic-scale can change, dependent upon whether that thing is being observed or not — then surely it is valid to assume that at the intermediate human-scale, the same effect applies.

Perhaps this is why we can't measure the Delicate Force, and the way it influences our lives and capabilities. The Delicate Force gives us a glimpse of what's behind the fabric of reality, but if we try to remove this veil to undertake definitive-testing, the nature of nature is to let the veil fall firmly closed after a first glimpse.

Letting us peek behind the veil, is how nature teases us, and leads us on to future development.

In Daryl Bem's experiments, he found his results of time-leakage existed at the 53% level. This is way beyond the realm of usual-expectation in an experiment where you'd expect a 50% normal-split, but not enough to provide uncontroversial-proof of the existence of this ability within humans.

In Bem's experiment, he had 3,600 test-instances where the participant had a fifty-fifty chance of selecting the correct curtain to reveal the image. He achieved a 53.1% correct-answer rate. This is equivalent to tossing a coin 3,600 times and expecting to observe 1,912 heads and 1,688 tails. With coin-tossing, the chance of this happening is just 1 in 80,150 — which are remote odds indeed. If Bem had achieved a 70% success-rate, then that would have been dramatic, and attention-getting. If the experiments had been repeated by others, who also consistently achieved results at the 53% level, then this too would have gained attention. But these experiments have been repeated and strangely, the results can't be verified by others.

Daryl Bem is a highly-respected academic, and he must have had some doubts about his results before publishing his work. If there had been flaws in the testing of the participants, or if the analysis of the results had been done wrongly, then his reputation would have suffered considerably. I'm sure he's a very-smart man, and that he and his team checked this thoroughly before deciding to take the bold move of publishing the findings.

Perhaps this was the Delicate Force allowing him a glimpse of the fact that time-leakage is possible, and that it exists behind the fabric of reality. But that's all that we, as a species, are mature enough to handle from an evolutionary perspective. The veil on this particular subject has been allowed to fall very-firmly closed. *For now.*

The abilities of people who claim to have psychic powers are never absolute — there is always a significant degree of inaccuracy or interpretation needed. Very few people have these skills, and for those that do, their skills are probably on the edge of our capabilities as humans. Submitting these skills to definitive-testing when they are still in the early-stages of development is potentially an undesirable practice — for it may curtail the future-development of the capability in the individual. Would we ever give an eight-year-old child, who is learning the basics of mathematics, a test under conditions potentially-conducive to failure — and then deride them publically when they fail? *No, never!* The same applies to these still-developing skills of psychic powers too.

Maybe we never will be able to conclusively prove that these capabilities exist. For if someone could demonstrate a capability such as mindreading, with complete-accuracy, and total-repeatability, then for many this may be perceived as a huge threat. Would you want people like this walking the streets, reading your thoughts — especially as you wouldn't even know it was happening? There could be a significant societal-backlash against someone who could demonstrate this ability. On the other hand if everyone could do it, and we could all share our thoughts, then it would be a normal part of life for us. But not now.

It's worth bearing in mind that the people who are able to perform the amazing mental-mathematic challenges, like multiplying large numbers together in their head, or people who can remember 100,000 digits of pi, would likely have been burned at the stake, or drowned, only a few-hundred years ago.

If ever there was a mass-development of this type of psychic-skill in the population, it would likely start in very-few people, and develop steadily over ensuing generations. So, for many years, there would be just a small percentage of the population able to do this. How would the rest of society feel about these privileged few? We might likely see them as a threat — and not as an opportunity to show the rest of us how to achieve this. From a mental evolutionary-perspective, we are too-immature to accommodate people with this capability in normal life. And this is why we will never be able to conclusively prove these capabilities in our generation.

Imagine if Bem's results at the 53% level could be repeated consistently, like the double-slit experiment — and with the same guaranteed results. The media would become obsessed with time-travel, and one of the early-considerations for a number of individuals, and organisations, would be how to get-rich-quick. Not the response that an emotionally-mature species should have.

However, if this occurs ten-generations from now, when we are more mentally-mature, we might start to explore how we can use it — not for personal gains — but for the benefit of society and mankind. We may then have the evolutionary-maturity to handle this — at which point the 53% experiments may become consistently repeatable.

Churches don't have a God demonstration-tool that proves the existence of God, for if they did, they'd have much larger congregations than they do now. But who can say conclusively that it *wasn't* the Delicate Force that caused the virgin-birth of a baby some 2,000 years ago? Was this the ultimate capability signal?

For now, all we have are the vanguards. The people who have identified to themselves that they have special-capabilities to some degree. These are the people who are many-generations ahead of the rest of us in the evolution of their mental-capabilities.

Believe in you — the living proof

Against absolutely-phenomenal odds, the Delicate Force persevered in every aspect of our physical and biological Universe since time began. We are the living-proof of this. It did it without any need for recognition, and it is still at work today — *right now*. It's not God telling us to believe in him. It's the force of evolution telling us to believe in ourselves. We may not understand what causes it — in many ways it's similar to gravity — we should just accept it, and use it. We may not have all the proof we'd like, but why must we be overly-concerned about questioning something that is clearly of benefit? Would you bother taking your TV apart during a great programme, because you suddenly realised that you don't know how a television set works?

The Delicate Force is a concept that science will want to prove to validate it. With our current-level of understanding, it may well be elusive against the force of a strong investigation, but it will rapidly fill its own vacuum when supported by the power of belief. The evidence is clear, but proving it exists will be a tough nut to crack.

In the past, the discovery and scientific development of new-fields has preceded the explanatory-theories — often by decades — and even centuries. Sir Isaac Newton developed his theory of gravity in 1687, and today, we still don't know what causes the gravitational effect. But it will become like the search for the fundamental particles in atomic physics, the inside of a black hole, and the reason why the ancients built Stonehenge. Once found, it will only lead to further layers of the unknown, and new questions to ask that require deeper levels of exploration. What is important is that we don't need to know how the Delicate Force works to use it — just like many other natural aspects in our universe.

Some of the things we believe today to be facts about what the human mind can or can't do, will undoubtedly be proven wrong in the future. Which ones we can't say. Many people believe in things that others are sceptical of. That's because they just want to believe in them, or they have personal experience of them, or they can do them themselves. If you believe in things which can't be scientifically proven, then that doesn't mean you are wrong in your beliefs. Neither are you alone in them. It possibly means the others aren't as enlightened, or as fortunate as you, to have had the experiences which you've had.

As we evolve, the new philosophies of understanding will be passions, beliefs, and capabilities, regardless of scientific proof — but based entirely on empirical demonstrations. *And potentially, non-consistent delivery.* This is about accepting anomalies and disconnects — the peculiarities and deviations in the norm. This will not sit well with many members of the scientific community, as so much of science rests on the laws and relationships that can be proven to be unequivocally-consistent through the application of equations and formulae.

Science may have to embrace uncertainty, and cross the barrier that separates the rational of the physical and objective world — into the irrational and subjective world of the consciousness and para-psychology.

I'm six-feet tall. When I stand against a wall and stretch one hand up, I can reach to seven-feet six-inches. Six-inches above that — at 8 feet and ½ inch — is the world-record for the high jump, achieved by Javier Sotomayo of Cuba. I find it unbelievable that anyone can jump that high. To watch these athletes do this, they need to know in their minds it is possible, and commit to achieving it in reality. You need to believe in things to make them happen. The high-jumper has to believe that he can clear the bar — and to have absolutely no doubts whatsoever. This doesn't mean that positive thinking alone will help you clear the bar. Mental evolution is about believing that you can do something — then attempting it, and committing to practice that belief.

The mind will be the driver of modern evolution. Perhaps acknowledging the existence of the Delicate Force — even though it can't be proven — is the first stage of enlightened thinking.

The second stage is when you decide to use it, and you commit to moving on. This is the real sign that your mind is ready to evolve.

The Delicate Force and your reality

The Enduring, Capability and Instance signals are the indicators that the Delicate Force has been, and still is, guiding and aiding the development of mankind. Anomalies exist in the patterns of our lives, as we've all experienced things we can't account for in some way. These anomalies are the things that we should build on. If anomalies occur in our lives in a small way in one area, then why shouldn't they occur in other areas of our lives, and potentially in bigger-ways too?

We heard how the true reality exists in your mind, and that it can be heavily-influenced by the range of filters that you apply, including your frame of mind and your belief set. You are completely in control of your reality. It you are a joyous-person you will see hope and opportunity, and if you are a fearful-person you will see threats and insecurities. Similarly, if you are a person observant and expectant of signals and the Delicate Force, you will readily see them.

You need to be especially aware of the Instance signals. Pay attention to them when they occur, and always react to them. Instance signals usually aren't of relevance to anybody but the recipient, as the occurrence, and nature of the moment would be meaningless to others. They are intended solely for the individual to whom they occur. They leave no proof of their existence, except in the mind of the person who experiences the unexpected moment. Perhaps when you get a glimmer of a new idea, or a dim perception of a signal, you are getting a reveal behind the fabric of nature. The electrical-connections that link your mind to the outside world are being interrupted and enhanced by the Delicate Force.

<u>THE TIME IS NOW</u>

Taking responsibility for our own evolution

Every single one of us went through the process of being stardust at the beginning of creation. Progressing from floating pond-scum to living in trees as apes, to eventually being able to sit-down and press a TV remote-control to watch a live sporting-event on the far-side of the planet. Is this the peak of our evolution, and of our unearthing of new knowledge? Have we discovered most of what can be discovered?

As a race we are inclined toward vanity, and are proud of our achievements, so we probably like to think so. However, we are completely wrong. We have come a long way in our evolutionary process, and we have created vast amounts of knowledge. But we are always only at the beginning of the future.

Stretching out ahead of us is an immeasurable amount of unknown knowledge, and infinite-ways for us, as a species, to evolve. When we look back at where we've come from and what we've achieved, we probably have a right to be impressed. But when we deem to look forward, at where we have the opportunity to go, we should be amazed at the potential we have in the future.

Historically, evolution may have favoured the tall, the strong and the fast, but perhaps not any more. When it came to speed on land, the cheetah won with a top speed of over seventy miles an hour. However, a smart man (or woman) on a bicycle, can go faster than a cheetah. The next phase of our evolution will favour the smarts in people, over the physicals. Not in our ability to perform mind-tricks like calculations and memory-recall, but in our ability to do other amazing things with our minds, such as accessing the future and other psychic capabilities.

Examples of evolution are all around us in the form of the Enduring signals, and some of the Capability signals, that have existed for many years. But it's also possible for the brain to evolve *instantly, and on-demand,* as a new neural-connection is made. This happens whenever you get a new idea or an *Aha-moment*. Perhaps too, that gut feeling you have about something, is also the force of evolution at work. The Delicate Force won't drive you like an automaton, but it can help you through light-touch guidance and inspiration. It also helps us through the stimulation of new thoughts and fresh thinking.

The last fifty-years have seen remarkable advances in many fields including science, technology, medicine, and the thinking associated with these fields. For the previous 13.8 billion years the Delicate Force has been assisting our evolution, but in the last five decades we've taken on the momentum of growth and evolution for ourselves. We are potentially capable of achieving far more, and in much-shorter timeframes, than the Delicate Force could ever achieve. The Delicate Force will still be involved in certain aspects of our development — but we are now primed as a race, and able to drive our own evolution much faster.

Incremental evolution

It doesn't matter how small the force, or how vast the universe is, a force will always make a change. A child's crayon-drawing makes the universe a tiny-bit richer from what that child created. That child's action changed the entire cosmos for the better — in just a few minutes.

Small forces acting on a gigantic mass, produce miniscule changes. The Delicate Force exerting its gentle influence on everything in the universe, produces small — but continual — benefits. This has been happening since the big bang, and so we've had some 13.8 billion years of continuous, small changes. The Delicate Force has been helping us to work against the tide of a universe descending into disorder and chaos, and has somehow been consistently tipping the odds in our favour, by guiding our evolutionary-development since time began.

Evolution happens on an individual level. We can't change our biological make-up, but we can change many aspects of our lives that will positively influence our offspring — and those of the people around us — in a multitude of ways. The Delicate Force has got us to the amazing place we are today, and it is still around us exerting its delicate influence. So what are we going to do with it — and how will we now accelerate ourselves as a species?

We are living in the nexus

Let's review some key-aspects in our development in the past.

One-billion years ago we were pond-scum.

2,500,000 years ago we were ape-men.

700,000 years ago we started using fire and basic tools.

300,000 years ago our modern species of homo sapiens developed.

50,000 years ago we started communicating in language, rather than grunts.

5,000 years ago we started writing things down.

500 years ago we were able to print books.

100 years ago we started listening to radio broadcasts.

60 years ago television became widely available.

20 years ago the internet started to gain widespread usage.

In 2007 the first smart phone was released.

The arrival of the twenty-first century was a watershed in the accessibility to public knowledge. Not only was it easy for anyone with an internet-connection to access information anywhere around the world, but vast amounts of new information was being added daily. From academic research papers, to news feeds, to online encyclopaedias, to the myriad of independent-sites where individuals have compiled their own research and view-points on a mind-boggling array of subjects. From the best recipe for a vegetable lasagne to how to spot a zombie. It's there in the form of articles, videos, images, newsletters and discussion groups — and all just a few keyboard-clicks away.

The internet was initially developed by the US military as a network designed to withstand a nuclear-attack. If part of the network were destroyed, the remaining parts could still operate due to the many links between all the different parts of the network. This is remarkably similar to the structure of the brain, where each neuron is linked to a large number of other neurons.

The internet can be considered as a massive-extension of your brain, allowing you to access the aggregated collection of global knowledge, and with the ability to discuss topics with others, and to create new perspectives. Because the internet doesn't belong to any one person, it's effectively a shared-brain for anyone connected to it.

Until the internet gained mass-usage, the only way we had for effective two-way immediate-communication between groups of people was in meetings or on telephone conferences. The internet changed that, and allowed people to start online discussion-groups, forums, chat rooms, blogs with comments — and so much more. As internet connectivity spread, and the cost of computers went down, more people were able to engage in these discussions.

And then came the miracle of mobile.

Smart mobile-phones enabled people in less-developed countries, and in areas where homes had no electricity to power computers, to communicate and access the internet. These devices have developed to such an extent, that over the next few-years, another billion previously-unconnected people will have access to instant communication, and the internet, using cheaper versions of smart-phones.

Shouldn't this seem like a miracle of technology to us? *Because it is.* Yet we have accepted it as part of our everyday lives. The last fifteen years — and the next ten years — will be looked back on as the time when the planet's population gained instant access to the knowledge of the world — in the palm of their hand.

Just as the Cambrian era was an Enduring signal that spawned all sorts of new life-forms on Earth, this twenty-five year period will (in the future) be recognised as a signal in itself, that advanced the collective knowledge of mankind. And more importantly, allowed our minds to connect with that knowledge, to develop new and more powerful thinking. This generation will be recognised as a nexus — the point in our evolution when the human race were all connected together.

The enlightened one cometh

To these extra billion people, the ability to communicate with anyone, anywhere in the world and to use the internet to access a vast amount of knowledge from their own homes — will seem like a miracle. Freely-available applications will help them translate materials to-and-from their own language, and to aid the co-creation and sharing of new knowledge and insights.

There are over 150-million public blogs on the internet today. The beauty of these blogs is that whether their aim is to be authoritative on a particular issue, or to express personal-opinions on a topic of interest, there is effort and passion going in to the creation of them. Any thirteen-year-old with access to the internet can create a blog, provide a new viewpoint on life, and find considerable evidence to support their opinions.

These thirteen-year-olds are the Socrates, Platos and Aristotles of tomorrow. Someone with a new and enlightened opinion is out there somewhere — and when you discover it, you'll recognise it as something that aligns with your own beliefs, and you will add to this voice in some way.

The internet, and access to it via a cheap smart-phone, means that the next messiah could be a child-philosopher from a developing country. Someone who is putting two and two together for the very first time — and coming up with a totally new answer that changes our lives significantly.

Many people believe in things that they think are particular only to them — and that this makes them peculiar in some way. The internet allows one solitary voice to call out, and to attract others who believe in the same thing, to rally around the call — from anywhere in the world. To start a new area of belief.

We are fortunate to be part of this connectivity-era in our evolution. This could only ever happen once in the history of mankind — and we are living and creating this special-time, right now. What will you do to make the most of it?

USING THE DELICATE FORCE

My work requires me to find ingenious, new answers to old, business questions. From this conference, I have a fresh understanding of where new ideas come from. I realise that I've been allowing the Delicate Force to influence my thinking in different ways, and I'd like to share some of these techniques with you to help you with your creative thinking — and also to help you interact with the Delicate Force.

Know you are a movie star

The human race is seven-billion people strong. We might think that we have evolved from pond-scum as a species — but this is wrong. We are seven-billion humans who have evolved, and are still evolving, *individually.*

We are all different in so many ways. We are destined to be different. Otherwise, why would nature have gone to the effort of giving everyone different fingerprints and DNA — for just two examples? Stop thinking of us as 7,000,000,000 people, and start thinking of the world as you, and 6,999,999,999 others.

We are born as individuals; we die as individuals; and in between we act out the theatre of our lives. Our performance continues twenty-four hours a day, seven-days a week, 365-days a year, until after many years, we have to take our final curtain-call on our closing-night. There is no audience, just (one-short of) seven-billion other actors, each performing the lead-role in their own plays. The world, quite literally, is our stage.

We know that our reality is created in our minds in the form of a multi-sensory, 3D-movie, which is our interpretation of the physical world around us. Other people have their own realities too. In the movie of your life, you are the star, and everybody else has a supporting-role to you. But they are simultaneously starring in their own life-movie, where you are playing a supporting-role to them. Sometimes you may just play a brief, walk-on role in somebody else's film — or you may be the co-star. Your film is a separate production to theirs, but the movies interact with each other. Just like your realities.

When you have a part in someone else's movie — make the moment count. Put on an Oscar-winning performance that will benefit both of you. Do what you realistically can to make their movie a great success. Share something with them that you feel will be of value. Help them in some way. Have a meaningful discussion about something. Even if the opportunity for a meaningful discussion doesn't occur, note what interesting things you can glean from that interaction that will be of value to you. Something that will give you a different perspective to start a new stream of thought.

As far as you are concerned, all the other actors in your movie are subordinate to you, the star. In your mind, consider that everything is being done for you alone, and that they are there to provide you with input and signals. *Be the star that you are in your movie.*

Put your mind to good use

Do you believe that you can evolve yourself mentally? If you believe you can, then you're absolutely right. If you believe you can't, then you're also absolutely right. The choice you make is entirely up to you.

Great thinking only needs one resource — and that's time. Convenient, uninterrupted-chunks of *your time*. Anywhere from ten-minutes to an hour. It doesn't matter if it's while you are walking, exercising, relaxing, driving or travelling on public transport.

Resist reading rubbish on the train. Forsake fiddling with Facebook on the bus. Instead, spend this time doing some quality thinking. It's fun, exhilarating, stimulating and incredibly rewarding. And it also helps your mind to evolve.

You can never recover time that you waste, and it's proven that people with a history of stimulating their minds are able to keep their mental-faculties for longer in old-age. So, for both your time and your mind, it's a classic case of *use it or lose it*.

Thinking is the great equaliser

Everybody can think about something. Anyone can think about anything. All you need to do is to choose a thinking-topic that interests you. With a new and stimulating focus, your brain can make millions of new connections each second when you start to develop your thinking. You just need the desire, interest and a good question.

And you don't have to be a genius to think differently. Ten-year old Clara Lazen of Missouri, was using a ball-and-stick kit in a school chemistry lesson to understand how molecules form, when she showed her teacher a model she had made, and asked him if it was a real molecule. The teacher sent a photograph of it to a chemistry-professor friend, who validated that it was truly, a new, theoretical-compound called Tetranitratoxycarbon. When the professor published a paper on the molecule in the Computational and Theoretical Chemistry journal, Clara was given co-author status.

In 1969, Tanzanian student Erasto Mpemba was making ice-cream in a school cooking-class, and couldn't understand why a warm-mixture of ice-cream would freeze quicker than a cold-mixture. This effect has become known as the Mpemba effect. It's actually due to slightly-different bonds between the oxygen and hydrogen atoms in warm-water compared to cold-water. But a simple observation — and query — by another school-child allowed their name to live on in a newly-discovered effect.

Whether your thinking is purely in the mind, or whether it is tinkering-thinking, where some kind of physical item is the focus of your attention, it's still the same principle being applied. A sense of exploration or experimentation, and a desire to come to a conclusion of some kind.

Many of our ancestors probably didn't have much time for thinking beyond how they were going to care for their family. They may not have had much opportunity to interact with appropriate people to share and develop their views. In the past, thinking was the domain of the privileged few. Today it's very different. We have a desperate need for new approaches to existing issues. Fresh thinking is highly-valued. Where individuals look at the same things as others — *but see something different*.

Looking for information or opinions on something? There are 150-million blogs on the internet, spanning every topic imaginable. The beauty of these blogs is the effort and passion that frequently goes into the creation of these information sources. You may have to filter it, as there's a lot of superfluous material, and you have to shape your own beliefs on it too. But the fact is that it exists — and it's there for you to use in whatever way you desire.

Many people have experiences they think are peculiar only to them, and that this makes them *different* in some way. The internet enables a solitary-voice to call out, so that others who believe in the same thing, can rally around the call — from anywhere in the world. One website, or forum, where people start to discuss a topic — and to realise there are others who have had the same experience, is the genesis of a new area of belief, and growth.

Thinking is a miracle. We know what parts of the brain do, but we have no idea what the mind is, how memories are stored for up to a century, or how thinking actually takes place. The beauty of creative-thinking is that it's a miracle that anyone can do. Sometimes you may feel a little uncomfortable about this. It's like sitting in a roller coaster just before it starts moving. That nervousness is the excitement of what's about to happen. *Go for it! Use the miracle.*

Go solo

You're the star of your movie, so you have the right to act as a prima donna in your thinking. Your thinking is best done on your terms. You decide what's going to be considered and how you're going to go about it.

When Michelangelo painted the Sistine Chapel, he had assistants — but they worked directly under his control. They mixed paint, applied the plaster that he painted onto, and supported all his needs while he did the painting. Some of the minor figures, and parts of sky, were done by others, but under his instructions. He knew what he wanted to achieve — and he had no intention of letting others tell him what to do.

When it comes to your thinking — be absolutely in control. You decide what to do, and what to trial. There will be no recriminations under any circumstances, so feel free to take risks. Be an artist, and deliver something beautiful and awe-inspiring. The output will be your masterpiece that you'll take the credit for.

Own it. Lead it. Create it.

Be a serial creative

People who are creative in their work understand that you can't be permanently-creative. You have to prepare, lead in, and build up to the moments of creativity, and creative-thinking is no different. Be aware of the points where maximum benefit can be achieved, and focus your thinking-efforts on these key-points. Make a list of aspects of your life where you'd like to make a significant impact — and work through these systematically.

It's best to focus on just one topic at a time to encourage new connections to form in a non-confusing manner. So, create a list of things you'd like to eventually cover. You've got the rest of your life for this.

Pose a killer question

Before you start any thinking on a subject, make sure you have a killer-question clearly identified at the start. Pose yourself a question that's so strong and amazing, that even if you only got the answer *partly right*, you'll still be impressed with yourself. If you ask a boring question, it doesn't matter how well you answer it — the output won't be something that advances you as an individual. If you start by asking a question that has never been asked before (at least by you), but potentially by nobody, then this is the zone where the Delicate Force can do the most for you.

If you feel your killer question is too big, then break it down into component-questions, and address those individually. It's important to have a focus for your thinking, as a blank-canvas is a disaster waiting to happen. Frame your question by writing it down, and re-working it until you have it perfectly formed. Never start exploring for opportunities until you are completely satisfied that you have your killer question.

Then let your mind start to loiter with intent, so you begin to answer it quickly.

Put yourself at the tipping-point

Being fixated on a perspective and seeing if the Delicate Force will influence you to change your view won't work. You need to put yourself at a tipping-point in your mind where the Delicate Force can guide you at the fifty-three per cent level, by giving you signals and triggers.

For example, ask yourself an open-question and wait for ideas or thoughts as to what the solution may be. You may even consider a number of possible answers to a question where all are similarly desirable, and then you can wait for influence on the best-one to choose. You will find that the more you are willing to trust your intuition, the more the Delicate Force exerts its influence on you.

The Chattering Mind

If I were to give you a simple exercise to think of an empty chessboard for thirty-seconds — and nothing else — could you do it? Or would your mind start to wander, and think of things that are related to a chessboard? Would voices in your head start shouting-out words that your mind began to visualise? Things that weren't about an empty chessboard? That's the chattering mind at work. A variation of this exercise is to try and think of nothing — and invariably you will think of something. Probably many things. The mind never seems to be able to stop and focus, it's always chattering-away on some seemingly-random subject. *It never wants to shut up.*

However, this constant chattering is the key to forming new connections in our thinking. It may seem more logical, that if we are supposed to be the most intelligent species on the planet, we should be able to focus on things without being distracted by random thoughts. The chattering mind is a Capability signal and is one of the greatest assets we have. It is the source of much of our fresh thinking. All we need to do is to learn to master it, and to use it to our advantage.

At any moment, your chattering mind is busy on a number of issues in parallel — whatever concerns are at the fore-front of your mind at any given-moment. To start to use it on your focus-issue, you have to push the lesser-items out of your mind, to allow the desired topic — your killer question — to become the sole-focus of the chatter.

Rich triggers

Staring blankly into space won't help you to answer your killer-question. You need to find some stimulus that gives you fresh thinking and new ideas, by feeding rich triggers into your mind.

Rich triggers come from rich sources. For example, read (or skim) literature that is different to what you'd normally read. Use the internet to research interesting areas, or listen to a talk by someone on an interesting subject. Other good examples are items from artists, directors or designers, which have many hours, days or years of considered, creative input, which is new and meaningful to you. Use these rich triggers to identify new and inspiring elements that help you advance your thinking on your killer question.

Explore-for-four

Become smart in just four-minutes. With the internet anyone can improve their knowledge on any subject in a matter of minutes. You don't have to become an expert in a subject, but just smart enough to enable you to make new connections with that content that spawn useful new perspectives and ideas. *Skim it and move on!* This is all you frequently need to build-up and advance your thinking.

Speak to people about the thinking topics that interest you, and start conversations with them. Commit yourself to learning something from every interaction you have.

Breaking patterns

Do you remember learning to drive when you were younger? Having to press the accelerator slightly to get the revs up, and then letting the clutch out slowly. A seemingly simple operation, which at the time may have been completely beyond your abilities. The car would either stall, or leap down the road like an epileptic kangaroo. Now things are different, for on a long-journey you may change gear several-hundred times, and not consciously think-once about the sequence of hand-and-feet manoeuvres needed to complete a gear change. This is because your brain has learned the necessary pattern, and whenever you need to change gear, the brain calls up the process subconsciously.

Patterns are the brain's way of making our life easier, and so allowing us to focus on other things. Imagine if you had to re-learn how to tie your shoelaces every time, or to remember that your underwear goes on the *inside* of your clothes and not the *outside*. There are so many aspects of your life where you have learnt patterns to make things easier or quicker. And each time you use a pattern, it helps to reinforce it in your mind. This is a powerful capability of the mind — the ability for self-learning and adaptation — *except when you want to do something different.*

When driving in deep mud, or snow, you may find that the wheels are in a rut made by other cars driving the same route, and that when you turn the steering wheel, nothing happens. The car keeps travelling along the rut. A similar thing happens in your brain where some of the neural pathways are so well-used by your thinking, that they have formed mental ruts. In our lives, we are surrounded and trapped by our routine beliefs and regular activities. Patterns that you can't break.

Every new idea you get is due to the formation of a new neural-pathway being opened up in your brain. You are literally rewiring your brain when you think interesting thoughts. So you have to help your mind by doing things that break the patterns, and deliberately force it to do something different — to make new connections.

To change your patterns start by recognising where you have them. Make a list of where you do the same things repetitively — and then make a plan of how you can change these to gain different perspectives. The changes can be significant — or slight — just make sure that when you are doing the new thing, you are being observant for new sources of inspiration and stimulating triggers.

Mind-blowing

Start to value your mind and your time. They are both precious resources. We often allow too much mindless junk to occupy our time and our mind-space. The problem is that this stuff ends up being tattooed on your brain, and starts to prevent the useful and meaningful material from being absorbed. Mind-blowing is a way to clean out your mind, by reducing the volume of rubbish that you put in there.

Stop wasting your time — and start using it. Wherever you have a chunk of quality time, decide whether you want to use it to progress your thinking exercise — or whether you are going to waste it on mindless nonsense.

The choice is always yours.

Know your hot zone

Work out when your best time for powerful thinking is. Where is a practical and convenient place to do it? Do you think best when drinking a cup of coffee, or while out walking the dog? Test things — because often knowing what doesn't work is as valuable as knowing what does.

Create your own special places, times and rituals for amazing thinking and be on-or-off *only*. Don't try to do it all the time — know when you want to do it — and then stop when you need to stop. Don't expect it to happen all the time. Einstein had his miracle year — so you will get your miracle time, too. Just know when you want to turn your Einstein Switch on.

And don't dilly-dally on the way

The nature of nature is to move forward in one, or a number of directions. *But always to move forward.* Unfortunately, we've developed the ability to sit in the middle-ground and become bogged-down by analysis — trying to decide which is the best way forward.

Analysis isn't a part of our natural way of life. It's not about a selection from options — it's about the degree of better — and anything better, is more-advantageous than not moving at all. When you position your mind at a tipping-point, you don't stay there for long. As soon as you get an insight, or a signal, then you move on in that direction. If it's wrong for you, then stop and try something different, but at least you've tried and learned something. We aren't meant to dilly-dally in the middle.

Get some voices inside your head

The BBC did some research which showed that around twenty per cent of young children have an imaginary friend. If we are looking for guidance in some way, then of course we can ask another real person. But when we don't want our thoughts to be known by someone else, or when we need an answer right now, and there's no-one else around, we need to create an internal-dialogue in our minds.

This dialogue can help us with many issues, as the people that we create inside our minds will always have our best-interests at heart. So why not create your own council to counsel you?

Design them to give you different perspectives to the ones you are likely to develop as a normal-part of your thinking. Give them names and faces to help them become personal and permanent. Let them assist in the interpretation and perspectives of your reality. Give them a voice and listen to them. They can become your wise-counsel.

IN SUMMARY

Cardinal John Henry Newman, a significant religious-figure in the UK in the 1800s, once said *"Growth is the only evidence of life"*.

The conference presentations we've heard have helped me to understand the scale of the anomalies and discontinuities in our lives, and to appreciate that it isn't important to worry about looking backwards. What's important is to help discover what we don't know as we move forward and evolve. We've seen that we can all be actively involved in this as individuals — and I think this is a most exciting opportunity for us all to embrace.

Is the Delicate Force nudging us forward by inspiring us to achieve greater things with our minds?

I believe so.

People who have this realisation are the ones who are the vanguards of the next-phase of our evolution. From now on, I intend to be one of those vanguards.

Every time a new thought pops into your head; or if you get a hunch about something; or you have an intuitive feeling about a person; or if an unusual coincidence happens to you; these sensations are all signals for you. You are the one meant to receive them. If you've ever sensed any of these things, then the small-flame of the Delicate Force is burning inside you. Let me help you to throw some petrol on it!

Become a vanguard too!

Thank you.

Chapter 76 Thursday 15h45

His presentation turned out to be the last one of the conference. After the chairman had summarised the day's events, and formally ended the conference, the auditorium emptied quickly as the remaining attendees headed home. A significant number had left immediately after lunch, so Reece had a much-reduced audience listening to his presentation.

Heather walked up to congratulate him.

"You mean you actually stayed in a session and heard my presentation?" said Reece, surprised.

"It looked like you needed some additional support. I'm sorry there were so few people listening. I did notice that you didn't announce your dream-sharing website."

"That can wait for another time."

"You know that's what triggered all of this, don't you?"

"Yes, it did," he laughed.

"Hey man, great talk. Fascinating stuff — not what I was expecting from you though," said DD. "My life's going to be a lot different when I re-cap on all you brought together just now," he added.

"DD, I want to say thanks for the insights you've given me over the last five-days. I'm sure you recognised some of our conversations in there."

"My pleasure, man."

"You're obviously leaving," said Reece, pointing to the suitcase DD had in tow.

"Yeah, got to dash." He shook hands with both of them.

"I'm on the overnight flight back to Johannesburg, and heading off to Paddington now for the train to Heathrow. Hey, did you know there was some weird-action yesterday afternoon at Paddington station?"

"Really?" said Reece, hoping he sounded surprised.

"Apparently there was a real-hottie in sexy black-underwear shooting suitcases while two guys covered in blue and pink syrup were fighting on the ground. Sounds like the start of the ultimate porn-movie doesn't it?"

"And where did you hear about that?" asked Reece, innocently.

"The news was on the big-screen TV in the lobby just now. They showed some YouTube clips of it. Got to dash. Bye."

They watched DD leave.

"Feel like a drink at the bar?" asked Reece.

"I so desperately need one," said Heather.

In the bar Heather explained some more developments to Reece.

"Your suggestion on the dreamers being useful to us, was a good one. I'm putting a plan together on how that could work. It'll be a bold move and will need some creative thinking to make it work. You like to be involved?"

"That sounds very interesting. We should talk more on that," he replied.

"What's next for you? Will the infamous dream-sharing website ever go live?"

"You know, I'm not sure it will," said Reece. "Possibly we all get to have a dream about a thing we're meant to remember. And maybe it's not about matching your dream to someone else's — it's about knowing you have this special thing, and it's what you do with it that matters."

"You've been exposed to some amazing events these last four-days. The way you handled it, and think about things, is actually a special-gift. Do you know that?" she said.

"It's odd that this all started with a dream," he said, changing the subject.

"It was a number wasn't it?" enquired Heather.

"Yes," he said. "What I find interesting is that you've never asked me what the number is."

"What is it?"

He wrote the number 31415031 down on a napkin.

"What does it mean?" she asked.

"Not sure. But the first bit, the 31415 is the first part of pi, 3.1415 isn't it? That number is more meaningful now. And the time of almost-quarter-past-three will never be the same for me in the future."

"Show me that number again," she said.

He slid the napkin over to her.

"That's curious. The last five-digits of my mobile-phone number are 50314," said Heather.

"I wonder if that means that you and I are supposed to be together then?" suggested Reece.

Heather ignored his comment.

"I mean, you do look good in your underwear. Especially in a public place like a railway station," said Reece.

“Focus on the number, Reece. Maybe it’s the start of a sequence, and that the next digit is four — from my phone number. Perhaps as you go through life, you’ll keep finding the next-digit at meaningful moments,” suggested Heather.

“That’s an interesting thought,” said Reece.

They sat in silence for a while.

“What’s your full mobile number?” he asked.

She wrote it down on the napkin.

“If I were to call this number and ask you out to dinner tonight, would you come?”

“No,” she replied.

“Oh,” said Reece, disappointed. “You can’t mix business with pleasure, I suppose.”

“The answer is *no* because my phone was smashed yesterday, so I’d never get the call.”

“Okay,” said Reece. “In the absence of both our phones, I’m asking you now. Would you like to have dinner with me this evening?”

“Yes,” she replied, “anywhere but in this hotel.”

“And somewhere they don’t have crayfish tails meunière on the menu,” he added.

THE END

(BUT THE STORY BEGINS ON THE NEXT PAGE)

Chapter 77: The extraordinary event that started this book

It's dark, it's cold, it's raining, I'm fourteen and I'm delivering milk early one morning on a council housing estate in Bury.

Bury is a small industrial town in Lancashire, and this particular council housing estate is decidedly down-market. And this particular road on this particular housing estate, backs on to a large pond on the edge of some open fields. As it's been raining for the best part of a week now, this means frogs. Lots of frogs. The continued rain and the fact that most of the gardens are badly overgrown, provide the perfect conditions for frogs to venture far from their pond.

Many of the street lamps aren't working either, so I'm using peripheral vision to see where I'm going. (You know, you don't look directly at where you want to go as you see nothing, but instead look slightly to the side). I'm looking slightly to the side now, anticipating some glint of light off the empty milk bottles near the door. I hear the soft *crunch* before I actually feel it under my boot. I stagger forward, quickly trying to lift my foot, but the damage is already done. One flat frog.

There's the reflection off the empty bottles — that's my target zone — so I slide the two full bottles down the side of the empties. I feel a *clunk* as they touch the ground, so I release my grip on them, and slip my fingers into the necks of the empties.

Squish.

The rain also brings out the slugs, which like to congregate around the neck of the bottles. And I've got a big one splendidly-smeared between my first and index fingers. This is the only street on my round that has the frogs, but the slugs are everywhere.

I drop the empty bottles into the plastic carrier and stoop to wipe my fingers on a small patch of grass that I'm sure has ambitions of being called a lawn at some point in its future. Two bottles of silver-top delivered and two creatures killed. I feel guilty about this as I don't like to see animals suffer — well, I'm not overly concerned about the slug.

I enjoy this job too much to let these things worry me; that's why I've been doing it for the last couple of years. It's also great pocket-money, as it pays a lot more than my friends earn doing a paper round — and they have to work the evenings too.

Five years later...

Farnworth, Bolton and Bury, three former cotton-spinning towns North of Manchester that shaped the first two-decades of my life. They were at the heart of the cotton industry in the nineteenth- and early-twentieth centuries, and as cotton needs a damp climate for spinning, that probably indicates how much it rains in this part of the world.

In the distance, on the top of Holcombe Hill is a Victorian folly. A strange-looking tower that was built for no other purpose than to be a strange-looking tower on top of a hill. There's a local saying in Bury that when you can see the tower, it's going to rain, and when you can't see the tower, then it's raining.

The cotton's all gone and so have most of the old cotton mills, however, the rain's still here. But not right now, thankfully. It's just after four o'clock one August-morning, and I'm delivering milk again. It's my summer vacation from university, having just completed the first-year of an engineering degree, and I'm back on the milkround earning some holiday money. As I've got my driving licence and can drive the milk-float myself, I'm now the main milkman, and not the helper.

I still love this work. We start at three o'clock each morning, aiming to deliver all the milk before people go to work. I enjoy the solitude for the first few hours until my assistant arrives at six. That's the job I did for several years, and so I have a soft-spot for the young kid who will be here later to help me out.

The most efficient way to deliver milk is in a series of loops. You drive the milk-float about fifty-metres up the road, fill a plastic carrier with the required types of milk, and then deliver to the houses in a loop, centred on the float. When the loop is finished, you drive another fifty-metres up the road and repeat the process.

Ordinarily, it would be getting light by now, but as rain is forecast for later this morning, the cloud cover is making it quite dull. I'm halfway along Garstang Drive, delivering milk to some detached, middle-class houses on an open-plan housing estate in Bury. Behind the houses to my left are the open fields of a farm, and I can hear the cows there, lowing. There's a main road just ahead, and even at this time of the morning, I can hear traffic on it.

I drive the float up the road, fill the carrier, and start walking the delivery loop. The final house is a bungalow where I'll leave the last two silver-tops that remain in my carrier. I remove the two full bottles, lean forward, and place them on the right-hand side of the step next to the door. Slipping my thumb and first-two fingers into the necks of the three empty milk bottles, I hear glassy-clinks as the bottles touch each other. I squeeze a little tighter to get a firm grip on the glass before I lift them up.

And in a single breath, my life changes.

As I lift the empty bottles, an ice-cold bolt of lightning seems to shoot down my spine. The back of my neck feels like a thousand pairs of tweezers have each yanked on a single hair. Intuition kicks in hard. Something bad is about to happen.

I stand up, and spin around. Anticipating that somebody, or something, will be right in front of me — but there's nothing there. I'm in a corner where the garage joins onto the house, adjacent to the front-door. And as I've just turned round, I know there can't be anything behind me.

I scan the immediate vicinity. Everything seems exactly as it should be. I look in the distance — but all seems in order there, too. Houses, gardens, pavement, road, my peculiarly-shaped milk-float. Nothing out of place. So why do I have this instinctive feeling that something is badly wrong?

For five years as a kid, I'd delivered the milk each day before I went to school, and when you'd spent as much time as I had working in the dark, and hearing things moving in the undergrowth, you weren't easily scared. Things startled me of course, like frogs jumping against my hand, or a sleeping-dog in a doorway that growls in the dark and then runs off. But you get used to them, and just acknowledge them for what they are — *frogs and dogs in the dark.*

But none of these incidents had ever left me with a sense of foreboding like I'm feeling now. I'm just beginning to think that perhaps something had startled me, when the situation suddenly intensifies to a whole new level.

When you are at a beach, playing in the surf, with the waves crashing in, it's fun attempting to face up to a big wave. That feeling you get as a wall of water impacts your whole body, just before it knocks you off your feet — that's the body-slam feeling. This is what happens to me, except that it's not water I feel. I get body-slammed by terror.

A moment ago, I was feeling that something bad was about to happen. Now I'm instantly-engulfed by a feeling of absolute, and all-encompassing, terror. Something is horribly, horribly wrong.

And I have no idea what it is.

There, across the small garden of this house, on the other side of the road, is my milk-float with its dim, yellowing light on the back.

Right now, that's not a milk-float. It's a beacon of hope in a nightmare of fear.

I sprint over the lawn, through two flower-beds, and across the road as fast as I can. I reach the float. There's no point getting inside as there aren't any doors on it. This pathetic-looking, little vehicle is the only place of sanctuary from whatever is causing my terror.

I stand there, my back hard-against the side, looking all around. Desperately seeking the cause of all this. But there's nothing I can see that is out of place. And there are no unusual sounds I can hear either. In fact there is no noise at all. Absolutely nothing. No traffic noise. No cows lowing. No insects buzzing. Nothing. It feels like the whole world is holding its breath in anticipation of a cataclysm.

I realise that for the first time in my life, I'm experiencing pure silence. How can the world suddenly be so quiet? How can everything be so motionless? Absolutely nothing is moving. In the still, mugginess of that August morning, another fear grips my mind.

If I scream will any sound come out of my mouth?

Then, with an unparalleled sense of instantaneous clarity, I know exactly why I'm so terrified.

I'm experiencing the most massive, and complete, sense of isolation imaginable.

I don't hear a voice in my head telling me this, and neither do I experience a sequence of thoughts that lead me to this conclusion. It's a sudden-knowing of absolute certainty, that *I am the only living thing in the entire universe.*

This is the cause of my terror. The moment this knowledge fills my head, my feeling of terror disappears, just as quickly as it came.

The distant traffic noise returns, as do the sound of the cows, and the buzzing of the insects. From start to finish this whole event has probably taken around thirty seconds. I stand motionless in a kind of shock, wondering if the whole thing actually happened — or whether I'd just imagined it.

Then all my doubts vanish, as dogs right across the housing estate begin to howl.

I've heard much-lesser examples of this in my time as a milkman when, for some reason, a dog in one house would start howling and a couple of dogs in neighbouring houses would respond. But I'd never heard *so many* dogs doing it. Every dog on the estate has joined in, and it continues for around a minute, which is way, way longer than any previous occurrences.

This mass howling is really creepy, but it's nothing compared to what's just gone on. One thing I do know for sure. This howling is a validation that whatever I just experienced, actually did happen. *I haven't imagined it.*

Once the howling ceases, everything is back to normal — except for me. I wait where I am for a while, and then busy myself, needlessly re-arranging the milk crates on the back of the float. I don't know if something else is going to happen or not. Once the float is sorted, it's time to move on. I feel okay now, but I really need to know what just happened.

A little later, I pass a milkman from another dairy, who gives me a wave and a cheery *Morning* — just as he usually does.

When I finish my round, I catch-up with the other milkmen back at the depot. None of them mention anything unusual — so I stay silent on the matter. Later that day I check the radio and television news for anything peculiar, but nothing is reported. The local and national newspapers don't mention any unusual events either. It appears that I was the only person to experience this phenomenon — along with scores of dogs, of course. I didn't talk to anyone about this because, well — it may have seemed tantamount to being afraid of the dark — which I certainly wasn't.

I later tried to understand what it was that I'd been a part of. As a teenager at that time, it was fashionable to be an atheist, and to almost disdain religion. So did I have a religious experience to put me back on the right track? Had God spoken to me and sent me some kind of invisible visitation? I didn't think so. If I were to receive a message from God, it probably wouldn't be in the form of the terror of a universe devoid of life. And the howling dogs didn't really seem in keeping with one of His doings either.

Was it some kind of alien encounter? There were no strange spacecraft, no lights in the sky, no unnatural humming sounds, no scorch-mark patterns in nearby fields, no dead and mutilated cows with key organs missing. Nothing. Or had I just been abducted by aliens? Doubtful — unless the alien world consisted of housing estates that look just like Garstang Drive in Bury. So I could quite confidently dismiss a close encounter of any kind.

Did some kind of nocturnal, supernatural activity take place? I didn't see or hear anything of a supernatural nature, and when you'd spent as much time as I had working in the dark, you took a distinctly pragmatic approach. It's dark because there isn't any light, and if there was light, you'd be able to see that there wasn't anything to be scared of. And that's, that.

So, at the time, I had no idea what my experience was all about — but a number of things were very clear to me. The entire event seemed to have been centred on me, as I was the only person who was out-and-about that early in the morning, in that particular place.

The incident had a clearly defined start and finish, without any build-up or fade-out. I was aware of something being wrong in an instant, even though I didn't know what it was. When it stopped, and the sounds of the traffic, cows and insects returned, they didn't build up — they simply came back — and everything seemed like a normal day again. Well, for a second or so until all the dogs started howling.

I'd never experienced the emotion of extreme-terror before, but it ensured my total attention was focused on what was happening around me. In hindsight, the feeling could have been something positive in nature — but what kind of positive feeling would make a person pay so much attention to something? Terror grabs your attention a lot more effectively than euphoria.

The howling of the exceptionally-large number of dogs acted as a validation that the event really did happen. If the dogs hadn't howled, I may have dismissed it as something in my imagination. There could have been any number of other validations, such as a tyre on my milk-float going flat, or the float refusing to start — but I believe the whole incident was intended *not to leave any physical imprint on the world.*

Another form of validation could have been for this to occur to more than just one person, and to have involved my assistant — but then again, perhaps that's not how these events work. Anyway, I'm glad that a young kid like him didn't have to go through that sense of terror.

Finally, the message I experienced was in the form of a definitive truth; that I was, without any doubt whatsoever, the only living thing in the entire universe. It wasn't a fear of anything evil, or that I was being threatened, or that my life was in danger in any way, just the dread of being absolutely, and totally, alone in the universe.

If I'd received the thought that I was the only living thing in Bury, or in the UK, or even on Earth — it would still have been a mind-blowing revelation for me. *But why in the entire universe?* I'd been interested in space and astronomy ever since I saw my first science-fiction show on television, and for as long as I can remember, I'd held the belief that we weren't alone in the universe. It's so massive that there must be other planets out there with some kind of life on them. So, even if I was all alone on Earth, these other life-forms would still exist on their planets. The *alone in the entire universe* part didn't seem to make any sense.

I knew it was impossible for me to be the only living thing in the universe, so the next time an experience like this occurred, I'd be more prepared and rational, and would try to understand what was happening. That summer passed, as did many more. Unfortunately,

I never had another experience as momentous as the event of that August morning. However, I've had many lesser, but still significant, occurrences that I discovered are linked to that first one.

I didn't know it at the time, but this sense of universal-isolation wasn't referring to me being the only living entity, while the rest of the universe was biologically dead. It was showing me how it feels to be *disconnected* from the universe. The terror of being totally unconnected to anything else. We don't have this feeling as a normal part of our lives — most fortunately — because in some way we are connected to everything else. *But how, and by what?*

The experience I had as a milkman doesn't fit any of the laws of nature or the way life is meant to be. It broke the rules of normal-expectations. It was an anomaly in my life — a chink in my reality that revealed something that I hadn't noticed before. It was an Instance signal for me. A powerful and personal wake-up call. And since that event, I discovered that life and reality only had the *appearance of normality*.

When you look closely at your own reality, you too, can observe some chinks in it. If you focus on these chinks, you will begin to see that there is something behind our reality, that we all take for granted in the lives we lead. If you want to look through these chinks, and to understand what you see, then you must be prepared for some surprises. Things that will shake your perspectives and change your view of the universe and your world.

There's a scene in the film The Matrix, where Morpheus offers Neo a choice of taking the blue pill, where he can continue his life of blissful ignorance as a human battery, or he can take the red pill and find out the truth about his reality. When you started reading this book, you'd already selected the red pill.

The co-stars I owe a special thanks to…

When I started writing this book on my experiences, findings and understandings, I couldn't get it to flow properly. I stopped, and re-started it with a different approach after Reece Tassicker appeared. He helped to define the new structure and the storyline that you've just read.

So thank-you Reece!

You'll have read how you've all been co-stars in the movie of my life. And conversely, I've been a support-character in your life-movie — where you are the star. I hope I've added as much for your movie, as you have to mine.

Being the star of your own movie, with everyone else playing a supporting role to you, isn't meant to be about vanity, self-importance, arrogance or elitism. Nobody ever won a best actor/actress Oscar for a film that only had one cast-member.

You need other people in your movie to help you shine. And they need you. So play your role in helping them to the best of your abilities. *Step up. Lean in.* Whatever two-word aphorism encourages you to support others in their roles, the way they support you in yours — then get started. *Do it!*

To you, the people I've worked or socialised with, I've known some of you for many years, and our continued interactions have nudged me in so many positive ways. Whether you have been senior to me — or junior to me — was irrelevant. It's what we achieved together, the things you said, your style and way of doing things, or a trait you implicitly or explicitly showed me, that enabled me to learn something from you. Thank-you for being a valued guide and teacher.

Looking back at my terrifying experience as a milkman; in a perverse way I'm fortunate that it happened to me. It made me understand how being completely disconnected is the farthest-end of the negative scale. This in turn helped me to think about what could be at the farthest-end of the positive scale. This is impossible to define. For as we develop and evolve as a race, whatever end-point we identify, can always be pushed-out a little more.

This was part of the understanding for me. That it's about striving to go as far as we can as individuals in the positive direction. And we achieve this more readily when we understand how much we can learn and gain from others.

You have helped me to move forward in so many ways. And I want to thank you for this. You may not have been aware, but I was constantly admiring you. Whether it was around a camp-fire, coffee-table or boardroom-table; whether you were colleague, class-mate, client or close-friend, I've been observing things that I could learn from you — and hopefully sharing things with you too.

Sometimes they were big things, and sometimes small things. But the mere fact there are elements of our interactions that have stayed in my mind, are indeed proof that you have influenced me. And that these memories are likely to continue to do so in the future.

Let me show you some examples, of how you've helped me over time

Many of you have shared a fact, a small piece of knowledge, or an opinion that I found particularly meaningful. Especially when it went beyond the immediate relevance of the moment of discussion, and it's become something that stays in my mind for some reason.

Others of you have used unsolicited (and complimentary) adjectives to me about traits I was demonstrating that I was totally unaware of. As a result, I changed to try to demonstrate more of those elements in my personality.

One of you was in a meeting for the final wrap-up of a project. Someone asked a question, and you didn't say a word. You simply made a gesture with your head towards me. That gesture is what triggered me to write the 145,000 words that became this book.

And with deepest respect, another of you, in Sydney, met with me for the first time.

We had a thirty-minute meeting scheduled.

It was in your office, for you were a director of a large company.

We started talking and we seemed to form a connection.

We weren't talking business — we were talking about things that mattered to us.

You told your secretary to cancel your next meetings to give us more time.

You told me that you'd pass my details on to someone else who'd like to meet me.

When we finished, I said I'd give you feedback after I'd met with this person.

When I got home that evening, you'd already sent my details onto this other person.

I recall sending you an email to thank you for your time.

It took several weeks to set up the meeting with this person.

But it happened in the end.

Six-weeks after we first met, I called you to tell you how the meeting went.

The receptionist sounded a little confused.

She put me through to the managing director of your company.

He asked me how I knew you.

I told him we'd only met once.

He explained to me how three-weeks ago, you'd complained of a headache.

You'd been admitted to hospital.

And that you'd died two-days later of meningitis.

Apparently, you were in your early-forties.

You were well-liked and highly-respected in your business.

You left a wife and young family.

You were a part of my life for only two-hours.

And yet this book is dedicated to you.

You are the un-sung hero of my life.

You represent all the un-sung heroes in everybody's life.

And specifically, I'd like to thank the following people. I remember things about our interactions. I remember you. That means I learned from you — and I'll continue to apply those learnings.

The team involved with establishing Ingenious Growth: *Keith; Malcolm; Naomi; Phil; Rich; Richard; Stephanie and Wouter.*

The amazing Seren team who I had the privilege to learn from: *Lauren A; Ian B; Matthew B; Joris B; Chris B; Luke B; Maria B; Sean B; Catriona C; Matthew C; Ronin C; Iain C; John D; Ben D; Louise D; Almero DuP; Gerry D; John D; Jade E; Ben F; Keely F; Charlie F; Darren F; Matt G; Mariana G; Paul H; Elizabeth H; Fiona H; Adam H; Niharika H; Clare H; Terry H; Jonathan H; Philip H; Lavelle H; Stephanie I; Ellen J; Sian J; Hannah K; Sven K; Ben L; Catherine L; Clare L; Kwong L; Ollie M; Chris M; Anthony M; Noemi M; Kate M; Vikas M; Hara M; Tobias M; Nuala M; Tiina M; Michiko N; Esteban O; Oznur O; Emma P; James P; Rob P; Simon P; Chit R; Jonathan R; Kathryn R; Mark R; D'Arcy R; Chris S; Richard S; Russell S; Rachel S; Justin S; Li Szu T; Richard T; Natalie T; Rose T; Tina U; Dominic V; Richard W; Karen W; Bill W; Amy W and James W.*

All the great folk at O2 Telefonica who I spent so much time working with: *Karen A; Yvonne B; Ian B; Mike B; Ricardo B; Margarita B; Caroline B; Rob B; Anita B; Sarah B; Sarah-Jane B; Richard B; Chris B; Alex B; Jonathan C; Tony C; Sheryn C; James C; Paula C; Tom C; Lynne C; Catherine D; James D; Pete D; Nichola E; Sam E; Tanya F; Ian F; Andy F; Robert F; Mark F; Leanne G; Rob G; Lucio G; Rob G; Hugh G; Simon G; Kim G; Kirsty H; Leandro H; Laurence H; Markus H; Phil H; Tom H; Zahir H; Lilly H; Emily J; Marina H; Pinaki J; Alistair J; Martin J; James K; Nicolette K; Rob K; Will K-C; Claire K; Ian L; Jon L; Louisa C; Natasha M; Mark M; Gordon M; Paul M; Jag M; James M; Ricky M; Nick M; Gary N-B; Trevor N; Ed P; Mark P; Sharon P; Dave P; Sandy R; Keith S; Dav S; Mark S; Pilar S; Iain S; Akash S; Jonny S; Charles S; Simon S; Allison S; Tony S; Nicola S; Dave S; Jac S; Sam S; David S; Mark S; Ryan S; Tom S; Justin T; Deirdre T; Bec T; Claire V; Ariane vdV; Graham W; Oli W; Tiff W; Steve W and Raúl Z.*

The brilliant and award-winning PDD design team: *Stu B; Fay B; Simon B; Jamie B; Fanny C; Shayal C; States C; Sarah C; Tim C; Diane C; Alex C; John C; Karsten F; Diane F-H; Rob G; Helen G; Gillian H-M; Lara H; Miles H; Ian H; David H; Julie J-B; Abby K; Graham L; Barry L; Liza M; David M; Ben M; Angela M; Fiona M; Steven M; Heather M; Eva M; Emily M; Graham M; Mehmet O; James O; Paul P; Matt P; Gillian R; Steve S; Paul S; Philip S; James S; Julian S; Dominic T; Gemma W and Alun W.*

Fantastic clients who it's been my privilege to work with at Seren and PDD: *Jan B; Lee C; Mike C; Amy G; Gail G; Andrew H; Maxine H; Sharon H; Lisa J; Lucy K; Susan M; Philip M; Andrew M; Paul P; John S; Brian S; Bettina vS; Claire W; Agnes W; Jennifer L; Erin C; Kristoffer A; Tarik A; Marko A; Tim A; Rachel A; Satoshi A; Marc A; Nav B; Louise B; Nikki B; Alan B; Richard B; Andrew B; David B; Willem B; Gavin B; Remy B; Aapo B; Nick B; James B; David C; Stephen C; Harry C; Bertrand C; Steve C; Jason C; Lee C; Giles C; Pedro C; Neena D-P; Olly D; Mark D; Iain E; Craig E-W; Cecile E; Mark F; Stewart F-M; Simon F; Thierry G; Roger G; Chris G; Massimo G; Jonathan G; Fiona G; Stephen G; Graeme H; Guy H; Simon H; Claire H; Stephanie H; Ian J; Patty J; Graham J; Garrett J; Paul J; Sara J; Jarkko J; Tracey K; Louise K; Katie K; Janina K; Toni K; Tero L; Michael L; Florence L; Silvia L; Jose L; Hema M; Eric M; Frank M; Georgina M; Austin M; John M; Ailsa M; Katherine M; Jean M; Ran M; Ann M; Zhangjing. M; Nick M; Gabriella N; Piers N-S; Asif N; Nick N; Diego N; James O;*

Phil O; Harbir P; Marco P; Justin P; Sameer P; Tomi P; Marek P; Mark P; Richard P-J; Sami P; Tom P; John P; Jo R; Alexandra R; Arturo R; Jonathan S; Susanne S; Ben S; Lars S; Amanda S; Doug S; Julie S; Richard S; Clare S; Beverly T; Isheta T; Trevor T; Lauren T; Jessica T; Jeremy T; Julian T; Ollie T; Mark T; Clint T; David T; Olivier vC; Alessandro V; Richard W; Daniel W; Sophie W; Tim W; John W; Sharon W; Chad W; Alan W; Tim W; Carl Y; Farrukh Y and Johnathan Z.

The UCT MBA class of 1991 who made it an incredible year: *Garth, Cherin, Alex, Richard, Graham, Jacqui, Carol, Marco, Alex, Andrew, Norbert, Keith, Stuart, Patrick, Ian, Collin, Jochen, Anthony, Nick, Linda, Paul, Cedric, Richard, Monica, Alan, Judy, Richard, BJ, Rob, Hazel, Peter, Robin, Mike, Jules, Sharmila, Jean, Neil, Robert, Ross, Chris, Dhesan, John, Nick, Andreas, Simon, Ronnie, Gary, Rod, Gareth, Kel, Rowan, John, Colin, Nick, Eugene, Ken, Chris, Michael, Jay, Anton, Pete, Jay, Pete, Japie, Eric and Mario.*

And old friends and colleagues from around the world: Corey B; Charles C; Brian C; Lynda C; Nathalie D; Steve D; Sonya F; Grant F; Nanci G; Katharine S; Gavin K; Patricia K; Libby P; Adrian P; Emma T; Natasa M; Mark M; Dilip M; Ed B; Jason S; Gareth R; Oded R; Richard M; Michael M; Mike M; Caroline J; Tim J; Alan I; Don Y; Gilli C; Steve W; Caroline S; Jane & Philip W; Ruth W; Maki L; Lorraine & Martin H, Audrey H and Jonathan H.

And the myriad of people whom I've lost touch with: *I still remember many things about many of you.*

There's also my infinite ancestral trail:

My parents; Sheila and Geoff who've given so much to me.

The grandparents I was able to meet when I was young; Mary, Harry and Edith

Then there's the remainder of my ancestral-line that I never had the privilege of meeting. I've traced you back through thirteen-generations of our family-tree. As far as Flarswort Thomason, who was born in 1500 and died on Christmas Day 1542 in Croston, Lancashire.

This though, is just the tip of my ancestral iceberg.

Back through time, and with total-certainty, there are ancestors who were never given names, and those that only spoke in grunts. Before them were the ape-like creatures who were preceded many generations earlier by egg-laying mammals. Before them, my family were fish — some of whom learned to adapt to dry-land living. And even before that, my ancestors were basic creatures that floated in the sea, and who developed from single-celled microbes. Before that we were chemical molecules.

We've certainly come a long way. But where are we going to? That's the important question.

To all of you I've met, one way or another, I hope I've helped you be an even greater lead-star in your life-movie in some way. If we haven't connected with each other (yet), then hopefully this book will give you a few ideas to help you move forward a little.

Then I've done what I can — *for now*.

But I promise not to stop trying.

Want to know more?

Visit the Ingenious Growth website at www.IngeniousGrowth.com

Find us on Facebook at www.Facebook.com/TheDelicateForce

Contact Chris Thomason at TheDelFor@gmail.com

Search terms to help you discover more for yourself.

Here's a list of search terms that are related to the content in various chapters that you can use to explore, and gain a deeper understanding. I haven't given specific website addresses, as this approach allows you to develop your own interpretation of the available information, to form your own opinion and beliefs.

Chapter 12: Hyatt Churchill hotel London; Conference Navigator Guides.

Chapter 13: How stretching can be bad for you; running breathing patterns.

Chapter 16: Counter terrorism science and technology centre.

Chapter 24: Dark energy; dark matter; things that don't make sense about gravity; the mystery of gravity; are the constants constant; variation in the fine structure constant; John Webb and Julian King; Oklo uranium mine and the fine structure constant; DNA dividing; junk DNA; less than 10% of human DNA is functional; naturally occurring chemical elements; abiogenesis; origins of life; memory; the mystery of dreams; introduction to quantum mechanics; wave–particle duality; double-slit experiment; Copenhagen Interpretation; probability wave quantum physics; quantum entanglement experiment; spooky action at a distance experiment; consciousness and quantum mechanics; no fruit fly evolution even after 600 generations; Evolution: A Theory in Crisis; Darwin lack of transitional fossils; the Cambrian explosion; monarch butterfly mystery; Future of Humanity Matrix-type simulation.

Chapter 26: Human body composition; formation of the universe; Hawking rate of expansion of the universe; fine-tuned universe; Goldilocks zone; fine-tuned earth; conditions for life on earth; cell division process; second law of thermodynamics; order and disorder in the universe; asexual to sexual-reproduction.

Chapter 28: Intelligent design.

Chapter 29: Geoffroy Berthelot official world-records; Giuseppe Lippi world-records; 2009 ISF ban high-performance swimsuits; hour record for bicycles; UK sports sporting giants; Alfie Clamp; Brooke Greenberg; Gabby Gingras; Natalie Adler; Harry Raymond Eastlack; German super-boy born in 2000; John Perry lipodystrophy; Wim Hof Iceman; gtum-mo; Jill Price hyperthymesia; Stephen Wiltshire; Leslie Lemke; Derek Paravicini; Daniel Tammet; Allan Snyder Centre for the Mind; child prodigy; Kim Ung-Yong; Mohammed Hussain Tabatabai; Arran Fernandez; Sufiah Yusof; man with tiny brain; Albert Einstein Miracle Year papers; Kwabena Boahen brain power; K-supercomputer maps how the mind works; Solomon Shereshevsky; mnemonics; Akira Haraguchi; Ramón Campayo.

Chapter 31: Mihaly Csikszentmihalyi; flow.

Chapter 32: Mindwerx; Jennifer Goddard; World Memory Championships; Mental Calculation World Cup.

Chapter 42: Benjamin Libet experiments; unconscious decisions in the brain Max Planck Institute; Daryl Bem experiments; Feeling the Future; energy cannot be destroyed or created; Kodjo Yenga.

Chapter 61: Annalie Killian; Amplify Festival; LHC startup Holger Nielsen and Masao Ninomiya.

Chapter 62: Theos evolution research; 2008 Baylor University Institute research study on religion; 2010, online-research by the Bible Society and Christian Research; 2005 Gallup poll on extra-sensory perception; research on belief in phenomena; 2009 Nielsen poll on psychic powers; Oklahoma universities poll on belief in paranormal; Daily Telegraph British-poll on belief in the supernatural; homeopathic remedy dilution; the placebo-effect; 2007 study by University of California and Yale University on names; psi abilities; Dennis McKenzie medium; 2009 Pat Spungin study of young children; chakras; chi energy; feng shui; 2011 research University of California, Berkeley signals from people's brains; James Randi million dollar challenge.

Chapter 75: Clara Lazen; tetranitratoxycarbon; Mpemba effect.

And a special thanks to…

Annalie Killian, Jennifer Goddard, and Margaret Harris for their willingness to appear as cameos in the book. Each of you has your own amazing story to tell.

Ed Bernacki for allowing reference to the Conference Navigator Guides.

Stephanie Baillache and Justin Stach for kindly helping with the manuscript review.

Ralf Laue for assisting with the content on the Mental Calculation World Cup.

Book club discussion questions

The storyline:

1. *What did you find more interesting, the story or the presentations? Which were more enjoyable for you?*
2. *What passage resonated most with you in a positive way? Why? And in a negative way?*
3. *What surprised you the most about the book?*
4. *Has any similar occurrence to those in the book ever happened to you? How did you react when you read that part of the book? How did you re-act when it happened in real life?*
5. *What scene was the most pivotal for the book? Why?*
6. *Were there any particular quotes that stood out for you? Which ones?*
7. *If you could have changed the ending, what would you want to happen? Why?*
8. *Has this book changed any of your views or beliefs about life?*
9. *What do you think will happen now for the main characters?*

The characters:

10. *Which characters do you like the most / least? And why?*
11. *Did any of the characters remind you of someone you know? In what ways?*
12. *Are there any characters that you can identify with personally?*
13. *How did the secondary characters of Heather, DD, and Samuel come across to you?*
14. *How do you feel about the style of writing for Samuel's internal mono-logue?*
15. *What were the dynamics between Reece and Heather? How did this change through the story/*
16. *Who do you think the characters might look like?*
17. *Which characters didn't feel comfortable for you?*
18. *If you could have one of the characters having a greater or a lesser role — what would it be? And why?*

The book:

19. *Did having the factual presentations interspersed in a fictional story work for you?*
20. *How else could the book have been structured?*
21. *How appropriate was the book's title? Would you have titled it differently? If so, what would your title be?*
22. *Did you enjoy the structure and style of the writing? What would have made it better for you?*
23. *Which other books would you compare this to? How does The Delicate Force stand up to them?*
24. *What's the most important thing that you feel you can take away after reading this book?*
25. *Have you understood any life-changing revelation from reading this book?*
26. *At what stage did you decide that you liked / dis-liked it? What were the key factors that led you to this decision?*
27. *Overall, what's your favourite thing about the book? Your least favourite thing?*

About the author

Chris Thomason is an engineer who started his career in the UK automotive industry. He emigrated to South Africa to work in the gold and platinum mining industry, and was fortunate to experience the transition to democracy first hand. He also spent time running a gold mine in Mozambique at the height of the civil war there. In 1999 he moved to Australia to live on Sydney's Upper North Shore where he worked in the area of business innovation. He returned to the UK with his family in 2006, and is the managing director of Ingenious Growth, a company that delivers ingenious business growth opportunities for their clients in a broad range of industries.

A registered European Engineer, a Chartered Engineer, and a Fellow of the Institution of Mechanical Engineers, Chris lives in Reigate, in the Surrey Hills with his wife and son.

The Delicate Force is his first book, but it won't be his last.

7893658R00245

Printed in Great Britain
by Amazon.co.uk, Ltd.,
Marston Gate.